# *The* DETROIT ELECTRIC SCHEME

## D. E. Johnson

Minotaur Books 🙠 New York

THE DETROIT ELECTRIC SCHEME. Copyright © 2010 by D. E. Johnson. All rights reserved. Printed in the United States of America. For information, address St. Martin's Press, 175 Fifth Avenue, New York, N.Y. 10010.

www.minotaurbooks.com

Library of Congress Cataloging-in-Publication Data

Johnson, D. E. (Dan E.)
   The Detroit electric scheme / D. E. Johnson. — 1st ed.
       p. cm.
   ISBN 978-0-312-64456-7
   1. Electric automobiles—Fiction.   2. Automobile industry and trade—
Fiction.   3. Murder—Investigation—Fiction.   4. Detroit (Mich.)—
Fiction.   I. Title.
   PS3610.O328D47 2010
   813'.6—dc22

                                                                2010021849

First Edition: September 2010

10   9   8   7   6   5   4   3   2   1

For Shelly, you saved my life.

*The*
# DETROIT ELECTRIC SCHEME

# CHAPTER ONE

*November 1910*

The first part of the body I saw was half of the left arm. It hung off the side of the hydraulic roof press, hazy in the dim yellow light of the gas lamps. I walked farther into the machining room, cutting through shadows of pulleys and concrete pillars. Odd flecks of matter on other machines sparkled as I moved. The factory was silent other than a slow drip, like a leaking faucet.

Closer now—a black coat sleeve dangled from the steel plates of the press, pinched just below the elbow. A bright crimson cuff encircled a red wrist. A red hand sagged, palm out, five dark droplets stretching from the ends of red fingers, then letting go one after another and plunging into the pool two feet below. The room smelled of a butcher shop—viscera and blood.

I crept past the drilling machines and looked down the aisle. The lower half of a large man hung from the front of the press, trousers shiny black above dark-stained stockings and garters. His black button-top shoes, heels pressed against the machine, leaked still more droplets into the dark pool only a few inches below them. The body was upright and complete to the waist. It ended there, where the upper and lower plates of the press met, as if the rest of the man had simply disappeared.

My first thought was of a terrible accident, but the Anderson Carriage

Company's machine operators didn't wear suits, and no one would have walked away from this at six o'clock. I covered my nose with my handkerchief, crept nearer the puddle, and looked inside the trousers. The torso was huge, easily fifty percent larger than mine. The tops of the hipbones were sheared off, the rest a mess of blood and tissue.

Acid burned the back of my throat. I tasted bile and bourbon, and spun away from the body just in time to spray vomit across a stack of sheet aluminum. Hands on knees, I retched until my stomach was empty. When I could look again, I wiped my mouth and edged to the other side of the machine. The right arm hung in the same position as the left, but a gold ring encircled the beefy fourth finger of this hand. I reached out for the dripping ring finger and faltered, but steeled myself, took hold of the slippery wrist, and raised the arm. It was heavy but moved freely, like the arm of a huge marionette.

I held the hand up near my face and ran my thumb over the ring. UNIVERSITY OF MICHIGAN glinted out between thin crimson lines, with FOOTBALL and 1908 engraved on the sides. Now I saw a black monogram on the sleeve, almost obscured by blood—J.A.C.

John Anthony Cooper.

I let go of the wrist and jumped back. The arm thumped against the side of the press, and blood sloshed around my shoes. I backed away, reaching behind me for obstacles, not able to take my eyes off the ring. My heel and then my back hit the wall of the old battery room. I stopped, perhaps twenty feet away from the press, absently wiping my hands on my trousers. The factory was still.

This was insane. Cooper had called me at eleven, demanding I meet him in the machining room at the factory. I told him to leave me alone. We hadn't spoken in months, and I had no intention of beginning now. I was afraid Elizabeth had finally told him what I'd done, what she'd done. But he said she was in trouble and needed my help. Against my better judgment, I came.

From outside the room, a scuffle of boots on the concrete floor broke the silence. I whirled around, looking at the open pair of four-foot-wide doors that connected the machining room to the rest of the factory. Yellow light bounced up and down in a manic dance on the stack of pallets outside the room. The footsteps got louder, echoing like an advancing army.

I panicked. I ran to the back of the room and jumped onto one of the workbenches, threw open the window, and dove headfirst onto the macadam below.

A shrill whistle cut through the air, and a shout rang out behind me. "Stop! Police!"

I hit the ground hard, but scrambled to my feet and hurtled across the test track to the field behind. With only threads of moonlight to guide my way, I crashed into the tall grass and immediately came down on a rock. I tumbled to the ground. Bolts of pain shot up from my ankle.

Behind me, shoes hit pavement with a percussive scrape followed by a thump and a curse. I jumped up again and ran, as best I could. Whistles screeched, men shouted, and the light of lanterns bobbed off the trees and grass. Surging adrenaline masked the pain in my ankle. I raced alongside the tracks past the Detroit Foundry Company and over Grand Boulevard, instinctively heading south toward my apartment, passing row houses, factories, and warehouses. The sound of the whistles faded, and the lights gradually dimmed until I could see them no longer.

I dropped to the ground at every sound, every passing streetcar and wagon. When I reached East Ferry Street, I crouched behind a tree. Clouds of steam huffed from my mouth as I peeked out, looking and listening for pursuers. I reached for the bill of my cap to pull it down farther onto my forehead, but it wasn't there. Now I saw that my hand was stained with dark splotches. I squatted and ran both hands through the frost-covered grass, the palms and the backs, over and over, erasing John Cooper's blood. My hands finally clean, I stood again and leaned against the tree, trying to think.

The machining room's concrete floor was covered with my bloody footprints. My touring cap was missing. The car I had signed out from the Detroit Electric garage less than an hour ago sat—by itself—at the curb next to my father's automobile factory, where the man who was going to marry the woman I loved lay crushed between two blocks of steel.

———

I straightened my clothing and limped the last six blocks to Woodward, trying to appear at home in front of the mansions lining East Ferry. From there I took a streetcar the last mile to the corner near the pretentious apartment building on Peterboro where I had lived for the last year and a half. The building loomed like a toy castle, gray granite with towers and turrets, but only three stories high. I crept up to the front door, digging into my pockets for the key.

I cursed. In my haste to meet Cooper, I'd forgotten to bring it with me. I hurried around to the back door, gripped the knob, and jerked up on it while giving a hard twist to the right. The door popped open. I silently thanked my landlord for his laziness and let myself in, treading softly on the stairs, hoping to reach my apartment unnoticed.

No sooner had I stepped into the upper hallway than the door to my right burst open. Wesley McRae leaned out, wearing black trousers with suspenders, an undershirt, and a derby. His long blond hair stuck out in tufts. "Not like you to just be toddling in at one in the morning, Will. On a Wednesday night yet." He arched his eyebrows. "Care for a nightcap?"

"No." He'd asked before. I'd always declined—politely. But now I couldn't stop shivering, and the bourbon in my kitchen was calling me.

"Just one?" He held up a half-full bottle of Usher's Scotch whiskey. "It'll warm you up."

I opened my apartment door. Without turning around, I said, "No. Thanks." I flipped on the lights and swung the door closed, then hobbled to the kitchen and grabbed one of the bottles of Old Tub from behind the flour and sugar in an upper cabinet. I took a long drink, and another.

It wasn't fair. I slammed my fist onto the kitchen countertop. A sob escaped my throat. I tried to choke down the next one, but the thought of Elizabeth grieving John Cooper opened the way for the events of this night to catch up to me. I fell to the kitchen floor with my head in my hands, crying for Cooper, crying for Elizabeth, but mostly, I'm ashamed to admit, crying for myself.

Some time later, I stood and leaned against the icebox, lighting a cigarette with shaking hands. I picked up the bottle again but hesitated.
My mind wasn't functioning very well as it was, and I needed to think.
When I set down the bottle, I noticed a dark smudge on the white lino-
leum floor. I bent down and ran my finger over it, coming up with a
crimson smear. Shocked, I looked at my black oxfords. The shiny finish
was dulled and streaked. Dark spatters blemished the cuffs of my brown
tweed trousers. My mind again filled with images of Cooper's torso and
legs, his hands, his ring, his blood.

I pried off my shoes with my toes and dropped them in the garbage
pail. My trousers, stockings, and garters followed them. I threw on some
clean clothes, hiding my features with the flipped-up lapels of my tan
duster and a black derby pulled down around my eyes, then grabbed
the trash bin and hurried to the door. There I stopped and listened for a
moment. It was quiet.

I began to open the door but stopped short, remembering that the
key to the Victoria was still in the pocket of my trousers. I fished them
out of the trash, pulled out the key, and dropped it in my pocket before
opening the door and peeking into the hall. Seeing no one, I crept down
the stairs with the trash bin and slipped outside to the muddy alley behind the house next door. Almost no light shone here. I could just make
out the vague rounded shapes of the metal garbage cans lining the alley,
but I had no trouble finding my way. It was a late-night trip I'd made
many times before, though this was the first time I was carrying anything
other than empty bourbon bottles.

I pushed aside some of the contents in the first can and emptied my
trash bin into it. A small animal bolted away, startling me. My arms
jerked back, and the metal bin hit the side of the can with a clang. I
stood motionless for a moment, listening for a response. When I was as
sure as I could be that no one had heard, I covered my clothing with the
other trash and retraced my steps to my apartment. Along the way I
examined the carpet on the landing and hallway, and the finish of the
maple stairs. There were no stains I could see.

I slipped back into my apartment and scrubbed the bloodstain off
the kitchen floor. My mind raced. I couldn't go after the Victoria or my

cap even though they were certain to lead to me. Being seen near the factory was too big a risk.

If the cap was in the machining room I could say I'd left it there earlier. But the Victoria would seal my fate. The garage's record book would show I had picked up the automobile at 11:30 P.M., thirty minutes before the police found it next to the building that contained John Cooper's freshly crushed body.

I could report the automobile stolen, but with it sitting next to the factory no one would believe me. I couldn't very well say anyone else had left it there. No one but me had driven the Victoria for months. I had to change the record book, to make it feasible I had left the automobile there earlier. To do that, I would need the cooperation of Ben Carr, the night supervisor. It was my only chance.

I again donned the hat and coat, and limped back to the Woodward Line streetcar stop. After what seemed an interminable wait, the southbound car came in. I dropped a nickel into the fare box and sat on the scarred wooden bench seat in the back row. Scattered about were eight other people, most of them asleep. The car started up with a jerk and began to rattle down the track. I shivered and snugged the duster around me. Twice, the conductor walked down the aisle, giving a gentle kick to the feet of his regulars, waking them at their stops. My head felt heavy and dull. Raucous curses and laughter poured from a few saloons on the way, but most of the city was quiet, a huge mausoleum in the cold night.

When I disembarked in the business district, I hurried to the Detroit Electric garage, leaning into the frigid Canadian wind whistling in from across the river. I passed our tiny showroom with a few automobiles lurking in the dark, and skirted the brick pillar that supported the right side of the red iron archway overhanging the main entrance and garage doors.

I took a deep breath and rapped on the window in the door. A few moments later, Ben Carr peeked through the glass. He was a small man of about fifty, with elfin features and a sharp chin, dressed in the chargers' gray-striped coveralls.

He opened the door and stood back. "Mr. Anderson, sir." He touched the brim of his cap, and a worried look crossed his face. "You're out mighty late. You didn't have a problem with the Victoria, did you?"

I stepped inside, wincing as I came down on my injured ankle, and closed the door behind me. "No, but I wanted to talk to you about that." The garage buzzed with the sound of stored electricity and smelled of ozone, like the fresh-air scent of an approaching rainstorm.

He glanced down at my feet with a little frown. "You okay, Mr. Anderson?"

I looked around the shop. Dozens of shiny blue, green, and maroon Detroit Electrics lined the room, mostly the coachlike coupés and broughams, with a few open-bodied runabouts and Victorias sprinkled in. No one else was in sight. I put a hand on his shoulder. "I'm fine, Ben. I just need a favor." My voice trembled.

"Sure, anything, Mr. Anderson."

"Come on, Ben, I'm Will."

"Okay, uh, Will." The name that had come so easily from his mouth when I was a child now stuck in the back of his throat.

I pulled him into a charging bay between a pair of coupés. "Who else knows I took the Vicky out tonight?"

He squinted while he thought. "Charlie was washing cars up here, but," Ben tapped the side of his head, "he don't notice nothing. The other two were charging in the back. So, probably nobody."

"Okay, good. See, the reason I took it out was that I couldn't sleep. I've been worried about the mileage test."

Ben shrugged and nodded.

"Here's the thing. I drove down to the factory, figuring I'd take it out on the test track and then perhaps I'd be able to sleep. But I had just gotten there when a police car came barreling in. I left the Vicky and went home before they saw me." I toed the scuffed wooden floor and bowed my head. "See, I haven't exactly been doing a bang-up job at work, and I thought if I got mixed up in this my father would have finally had enough. I'm afraid if he finds out I was there, he'll fire me." I glanced up at him. "You can cover for me, can't you?"

"What do you want me to do?"

"No one from the day shift was in early yesterday, were they?"

He shook his head.

"Then all I need you to do is change the pickup time from 11:30 P.M. to 5:30 A.M. It'll just look like I took out the car in the morning. Nobody will know the difference, right?"

He rubbed the back of his neck. "I guess."

"So you'll do it?"

He hesitated a moment before nodding his head.

"Thanks, Ben." I clapped him on the back. "I won't forget this."

When I limped out the door, he was looking down at the floor, his forehead creased in thought.

I finally got home around three o'clock. Leaving the lights off, I grabbed one of the bottles of bourbon from the kitchen and hobbled to the sofa in the parlor. I sat sideways with my feet up and took a long drink. The bottle shook against my lips. My ankle was swollen and throbbing, and I knew I should ice it, but it seemed just too much effort to chip off the ice.

I lit a cigarette and lay back, trying to still the tremors in my hands. In the dark, all I could see was half of John Cooper's body dangling from the maw of the gargantuan press, one swallow away from disappearing altogether.

# CHAPTER TWO

I was startled upright by a loud pounding on my front door. The bottle of bourbon fell onto the wood floor with a thunk and rolled away, glug-glug-glugging as it emptied. The room was dark, and it took me a moment to orient myself. My ankle throbbed. The horror of the night flooded back. I swung my legs off the sofa, closed my eyes, and leaned forward, cradling my head in my hands.

The pounding continued, a rhythmic thump that got louder and louder. I pushed myself up from the sofa and limped to the door, each step accompanied by a grunt at the pain in my ankle. I bent and looked into the peephole.

My father's secretary, R. W. Wilkinson, in a gray homburg and winter coat, was beating on my door with his fist, his mouth in a tight grimace, his full beard and mustaches shuddering with the effort. It was frightening behavior from the neat, compact, and nearly unflappable man who had worked for my father since we moved to Detroit in 1895.

The fifteen years that had passed since then seemed to flow away. Again, I was that skinny seven-year-old boy, needing my father, or more often Mr. Wilkinson, to make it better.

I swung open the door, squinting against the electric lights in the hallway.

"Thank God you're home!" He pushed past me into the foyer. "John Cooper has been killed."

"Cooper? Killed?" My voice sounded phony, even to me.

"Yes. At the factory. In the machining room. Your machining room."

I switched on the light and pulled out my watch. The hands pointed to 3:53.

Wilkinson took hold of my arm. "Your father wants to know if you need his help."

I rubbed my eyes, stalling. "His help?"

"Do you need his help?"

"What do you mean?"

"The Victoria is parked beside the factory, and what appears to be your cap is on the bench near the window from which the police say the killer escaped." He looked me in the eyes. "And there's not much question about motive, is there?"

"I had nothing to do with it." I struggled to remember my alibi. "I forgot . . . I forgot to bring the automobile back to the garage after work. And I must have left my cap there yesterday."

His head tilted to the side, and he squinted a little, appraising me. "Your touring cap?"

I shrugged, trying to look casual. "I wear it at work sometimes."

"And you say you left the Victoria parked at the factory?"

I broke eye contact. "Yes. I drove it in the morning before work and didn't have time to return it without being late. I was going to bring it back after work, but it slipped my mind. I came in the side door and left through the front door. I didn't see it. I forgot."

"That was foolish."

"I know, but I always take the streetcar. It's just habit."

"You're lucky it wasn't carted away in pieces. Or perhaps not, under the circumstances." Wilkinson frowned and glanced at the doorway. "Your father told the police the car belonged to the company and he didn't recognize the cap. You do the same."

I nodded once.

"Now get dressed. We're going to the factory."

"Why?"

"The police want you to confirm the identity of the body."

"Me? Why me?"

"You know . . . er, knew him better than anyone else in the company. Your father mentioned to the detective you were college friends before he realized . . ." He trailed off.

"Realized what?"

Wilkinson set his jaw. "That you may be in trouble. Get dressed." He pushed me toward my bedroom.

I limped through the parlor. It smelled like a saloon.

He called out from behind me. "I telephoned you twice. Where were you?"

"I was asleep. I'd had a few drinks." I hoped the smell and the Old Tub bottle on the floor helped confirm my answer.

My hands shook as I dressed in a plaited white shirt, a wing collar, a black sack suit with matching waistcoat, and a striped gray and ivory tie. It took me three attempts to manage a reasonable-looking Windsor knot. I grabbed a new pair of calfskin boots I had been planning to return. Even though they were marked as tens, they were much too large for my feet. This morning I could barely get the right one over my ankle. I hoped if it came up, the boots would also leave a larger footprint than my other shoes.

I grabbed the duster and black derby from the coatrack by the door, and followed Wilkinson outside. The wind had whipped up from downtown, and a cold drizzle slapped me across the face. At least now I had an explanation for my shivering.

My father's 1908 brewster-green Model L roadster was parked next to the curb. Even in this kind of weather, my father, a robust man, insisted on driving the open-bodied roadster rather than my mother's enclosed coupé. The Model L was Detroit Electric's first automobile. Even though it was less than three years old, its appearance owed more to a sleigh or the ancient Curved Dash Olds than an automobile of modern design.

We climbed on, and I sat back, trying to stay dry. Wilkinson started the car and pulled away from the curb, the electric motor silent against the rain pattering on the leather top of the roadster. He turned up Woodward to Grand, where he cut over to Russell.

I tried to prepare myself for seeing the body. It was critical I act like this was the first time. I'd been shocked, surprised, horrified. It didn't seem a stretch that I would be again.

It finally occurred to me that I had never thought of the most basic question here—who killed John Cooper? And he'd wanted to talk to me about Elizabeth. Was she mixed up in the same thing he was, and if so, was she also in danger?

Wilkinson turned onto Clay and pulled up to the curb in front of the main factory building. Three black 1910 Chalmers Torpedo runabouts from the Detroit Police Department—one shy of half the celebrated fleet of patrol cars belonging to the "Flying Squadron"—were pulled onto the curb a few feet away from the main factory entrance, aimed at the door like three converging sharks. The Victoria was out of sight, parked around the side of the building.

A policeman, in a dark uniform and tall bobby hat, stood in the doorway with his arms crossed, silhouetted by the factory lights behind him. He must have recognized Wilkinson, because he didn't say anything, just stood aside and waved us by.

Once we were past the policeman's range of hearing, Wilkinson said, "What did you do to your leg?"

"Fell off a curb and twisted my ankle. I wasn't paying attention."

He glanced at me, frowning, before continuing on toward the back of the factory. "You seem to not be paying attention to a number of things."

The shadows cast by the gas lamps brought back the grisly image of Cooper's body. My heart pounded. The echoes of our footsteps surrounded us as we passed through the paint department, then the large body shop and its huge woodworking machines. Unfinished automobile bodies, like stripped wooden carcasses, littered the floor. Next came electrical, then the trim department and its stacks of untreated cow and goat hides, their rotten flesh stench making me breathe through my mouth. Finally, about two-thirds of the way back, my department— machining. Other than the motors, which were made at our plant in Cleveland, all our automobile parts were finished here, including the seamless aluminum roofs stamped out by one of the largest hydraulic presses in Detroit.

A policeman slouched outside the wide doors to the machining room. The brass buttons on his double-breasted navy blue coat glinted dully in the factory's dim light. My father was just inside, sagging against a drill press, next to the general manager of the plant, William P. McFarlane.

I had never seen my father so shaken. His remaining hair was white, and he was no taller than the average man, but his deep-chested frame normally conveyed the impression of someone larger and younger. This morning he just looked small and old.

As I walked in I tried to smooth my gait, but it was impossible. I limped to my father, who reached out for my arm and turned me away from the roof press. Searching my eyes, he whispered, "Are you all right?"

I nodded, not trusting my voice.

He looked over my shoulder. "Did Wilkinson explain?"

I nodded again.

The lines on his face were like the deep grain in an oak barrel, more prominent than I remembered. "And you're all right?"

"Yes."

His eyes held mine. "It's not pretty."

I looked at Mr. McFarlane, who nodded solemnly. He looked no better than my father. McFarlane was a bony Scotsman, and his long drooping mustaches, with flecks of gray now showing in his natural red, seemed to reflect his state of mind.

I took a deep breath. "Let's get it over with."

Two more Detroit policemen were leaning against the side of a welding machine, engaged in a quiet conversation. Another was scraping something from the stack of sheet aluminum into a tin. It was vomit. My vomit.

A short man in a black suit and derby peered into a camera set up in front of the roof press.

The press was open.

We walked to the end of the aisle. Cooper's body lay there, on the concrete floor. Flecks of matter on the shiny coat and scarlet shirt were the only evidence of his upper torso. Of his head, it was difficult to say what remained.

My knees buckled, and I fell to the floor. It was no act.

One of the policemen behind me guffawed. After a moment, my father helped me to my feet. Now I saw another man squatting just outside the perimeter of blood with a lantern in front of him. To his side was a shiny wallet, the contents next to it, lined up in a tidy row.

Wiping his hands with a handkerchief, he stood and began walking toward me. He was a big man, not so big as Cooper, but six feet tall and two hundred solid pounds. A ragged purple scar cut from his left ear to his mouth, completely ruining his small, almost pretty features. I put him in his late thirties.

He extended his hand. "I'm Detective Riordan. You're William C. Anderson, Jr.?" His voice, high for a man his size, lilted with just a trace of an Irish brogue. His eyes, shadowed by a black fedora, were ice blue and piercing.

I shook his hand and nodded.

He pulled a cigar from his waistcoat. "What'd you do?" His face was expressionless.

"W—What do you mean?"

His eyes bored into mine. "How'd you hurt yourself?"

"Oh." I stuttered out a laugh. "I fell off a curb. I'd been drinking."

He lit the cigar and blew the smoke over my head. "You don't say."

I couldn't tell if he was being sarcastic.

My father cleared his throat. "Detective, we don't . . . that is, smoking is not allowed in . . ."

Riordan glared at my father for a moment, then stuck the cigar in the corner of his mouth and turned back to me. He puffed on the cigar and pointed at the mangled corpse. "Do you recognize this . . ." He searched for the word. "This man?"

I shrugged, feeling my face go red.

"I need you to look at something." He took me by the elbow and brought me past the photographer to the other side of the machine. "Watch the blood." The pool had expanded another couple of inches. I was thankful for the cigar. It helped mask the smell of the body.

Detective Riordan bent down and pointed to Cooper's right hand. "Have you ever seen that ring?" The hand and ring were stained red, the ends of the fingers smudged with black ink. On the other side of the aisle, a card lay on the floor, five black fingerprints stark against the white background.

"I . . . I don't know." My voice shook. "What kind is it?"

"Look carefully."

I glanced down at the floor, making sure to keep my shoes out of the blood. Leaning in, I pretended to study the ring. "University of Michigan?"

He nodded.

"1908? Football?"

He nodded again.

I turned away from the body and mumbled, "Cooper . . . John Cooper."

Riordan touched my arm. "Not just the ring. Does the rest of him look like Cooper?"

I nodded, not looking back. A white light flashed with a *whump*. I jumped, startled.

Riordan walked around me and looked down into my face. "And the clothes? They're his?"

I half turned and glanced at the suit and shoes. "The monogram—" *Shit*. I couldn't see it from here. "Are the shirt cuffs monogrammed?"

He ran a hand over his jaw and then nodded.

"J.A.C.?"

He nodded again.

"John Anthony Cooper."

"How about this?" He raised my cap off the deck of a radial saw.

I shrugged. "Could be his. Doesn't just about everyone have one of those?"

He spoke around the cigar clenched in his teeth. "No."

"Most automobile enthusiasts, then."

He glanced at the policemen standing by the welding machine before looking at me again. "Do you recognize this particular hat?"

"No, I don't think so."

"What do you suppose Mr. Cooper was doing here so late at night?"

I shrugged. "He was here a lot, but he worked for the Employers Association of Detroit. Someone there might know. I don't."

"Your father said Cooper ran the labor bureau's security division for the EAD. I'd guess he made a lot of enemies."

"I don't know. Probably."

"Do you know if Mr. Cooper had any relatives nearby?"

"I don't believe he did. Last I knew his parents lived in Columbus, Ohio."

A bemused expression played across his face. "A Michigan man from Columbus, eh?" He looked past me to the body. "Interesting guy." Keeping his eyes on Cooper, he said, "And the automobile out by the curb?"

"It's the company's."

"Who drives it?"

I glanced at my father and couldn't read his expression. "I do."

"Really." Riordan raised his eyebrows and turned to look at my father. "Interesting your father didn't mention that." He looked down at me again. "Why is it here?"

"I forgot it and took a streetcar home. I had it out early yesterday morning for practice."

"Practice?"

"Yes, I drive it for the company. Endurance runs, mileage tests, that sort of thing."

"Sounds like a pretty important automobile."

I shrugged.

"It's surprising you'd forget it. Wouldn't you say so?"

"It's the company's test car. I drove it yesterday morning and forgot it when I left. I never drive to work."

"But you did yesterday."

I nodded, hoping I wouldn't have to say anything more.

He smiled, and the scar spread a grotesque grin all the way to his left ear. "That's all for now. Thank you."

I limped down the aisle and cut between two drilling machines, avoiding the blood in front of the press. Detective Riordan squatted down again and inspected a footprint. I hobbled back to my father. He tilted his head toward the door, and I followed him away from the press.

I had just reached the door when Riordan called out again. "Oh, Mr. Anderson? Junior?"

I stopped.

"You were out awfully late last night, weren't you?"

"What?"

"Where were you?"

"I had a few drinks with some friends."

"When did you get home?"

"Oh, ten thirty, eleven."

He pulled a notepad from the inside pocket of his coat and glanced at it. "I asked Mr. Wilkinson to telephone you at one forty-five and two thirty. He let the phone ring for a good five minutes each time."

"Like I said, I'd been drinking. I was asleep."

Detective Riordan returned the notepad to his pocket and smiled at me. "Deep sleeper."

# CHAPTER THREE

My father slammed his office door shut and hissed, "What did you do?"

From a burgundy club chair facing his desk, I looked out the window. There was still no sign of dawn. I was numb. "I didn't do anything."

He came around to the front of the chair and leaned over me, his face red, a vein standing out on his forehead. "Did you kill John Cooper?" He enunciated each word with precision.

"No. I can't believe you'd even ask me that." If he thought I'd killed Cooper, what chance would I have with a jury?

His pale blue eyes, shot with red, blazed at me. "The Victoria was not here when I left yesterday."

"I didn't kill him," I said, looking defiantly into his eyes.

"Do you swear?"

"Father, I swear I didn't kill John Cooper. I had nothing to do with it."

He straightened and shuffled around the desk like an old man. "Then how did the Victoria and your cap get here?"

"I guess I left my cap on the bench yesterday, and you must have missed the Vicky. It was there."

He sat in his big leather chair, leaned forward, and put his elbows on the desk, looking no more convinced. "They're going to look at you for this. You know that, don't you?"

"Yes. But I'm innocent."

His face reflected his disappointment in me. It was an expression I'd come to know only during the past year and a half, having been the golden child for the previous twenty-one.

I was his only son, born eight years after his second daughter, and I was his hope for keeping the company in the family. At one time we'd both been confident that would happen. After prep school, I graduated from the University of Michigan with a degree in engineering and then began my employment with the Anderson Carriage Company. My father had planned on immersing me in our automobile company—Detroit Electric. I was to spend six months in each of the auto factory's departments, in order to fully understand their workings. I started as the assistant manager of machining. A year and a half later, I was still the assistant manager of machining, and only hanging on to that job by a thread.

He stared at me frankly from across the desk and shook his head. "You know, when I look at you, I see your mother."

Though he and my mother got on well, I don't think he meant it as a compliment. She and I were similar in many ways—wavy dark brown hair and slightly recessed brown eyes, prominent cheekbones, thin nose, reedy build, and a melancholy personality. My sisters favored my father more than I did.

He pursed his wide lips. "Take the Victoria back to the garage and go home. Stay home."

"What about John?"

"They'll be moving him shortly. Mr. McFarlane and I will get everyone together at the beginning of the day to tell them what happened. Quash the rumors before they start." He sighed. "Poor Elizabeth. The police giving her this news . . ."

"I'll tell her," I said.

He met my eyes again. "Are you sure?"

I nodded. Maybe this would begin to repay my debt.

"Did Cooper have many friends here?"

"I don't really know." Elizabeth had broken off our engagement in August of the previous year. John began courting her around Christmas. Since then, I had avoided him as much as possible. "Probably the security men."

After graduating from Michigan in 1908, Cooper went to work for the Employers Association of Detroit, the company that helped manage security for area manufacturers. Their primary job was to keep the peace, which meant keeping the unions out. John made sure they stayed out. He was a natural for the job—big and tough, yet friendly and gregarious. He inspired loyalty in his people and was more than willing to wade into a fight when necessary.

I helped him get the job. I also introduced him to Elizabeth.

"All right," my father said. "Go. I'll tell everyone you're putting the Victoria through its paces in preparation for tomorrow."

I had walked to the door before I realized what he said. "We're still doing the mileage test?"

"If the weather's right. Everyone's ready. Mr. Crane has those Edisons cooking." His eyes narrowed. "And Baker's advertising their world record on the cover of this week's *Automobile* magazine. We need to put an end to that."

Now I saw the man who had built this company from nothing.

I wiped the rain off the maroon leather seat of the Victoria, climbed on, and headed toward Elizabeth's parents' house on East Jefferson. The first hint of daylight struggled to break through the heavy cloud cover, and the wind still whipped a cold rain into my face. Like my father's roadster, the Victoria had an open cabin and wasn't pleasant to drive in this weather, although the fixed roof offered a little protection from the rain.

It wasn't yet eight, and that meant there was a chance Elizabeth's father would still be home. I didn't want a confrontation with Judge Hume this morning, so on the way I stopped at Schenck's Automat to grab some coffee and kill some time. Even though the restaurant was crowded, the cashier quickly exchanged my quarter for five nickels, two of which I popped into slots in the glassed wall in front of me—one for a slice of coffee cake, the other for a coffee cup, which I filled from the nearby spigot. I took my breakfast to one of the long white lacquered tables in back, occupied only by a pair of businessmen hunched toward each other, involved in some earnest discussion, straining to hear over the clanks of plates and a hundred competing voices. I sat as far away from them as I could and took a sip of coffee.

Elizabeth would be brokenhearted, distraught, possibly hysterical. Because her fiancé had been murdered. *Her fiancé.*

I slipped my brown calfskin wallet from my jacket pocket and opened it. Behind my library card sat an ivory-colored piece of paper, the creases beginning to tear from my incessant folding and unfolding. Leaving the note inside, I returned the wallet to my pocket. I didn't need to read it. I knew it by heart.

> *Dearest Will*, it said in Elizabeth's flowing hand,
> *I've decided on six—boys, girls, I don't care, though I do so want you to have William III to carry on the family business. I know you will be a wonderful father to our beautiful children. We are going to be the happiest family ever!*
> *Love and Affection Always,*
> *Lizzie*

When I began working at Anderson Carriage, she sent notes to my office, at least one or two a week, some silly, some serious. All of them, though I didn't realize it at the time, showed how much she loved me. I'd thrown them away. This note I found on the floor behind my desk drawers a couple of months after she broke off our engagement.

I took a gulp of coffee and sat back in the chair. The last time I had been to Elizabeth's house was in March, when I'd made a drunken attempt at getting her to take me back. I shook my head at the memory, such as it was, filtered through the haze of a massive quantity of bourbon. I'd staggered to the Humes' and found Frank Van Dam's red Oldsmobile Palace touring car at the curb. That meant John was there. Frank was John's best friend and one of his employees at the EAD. I marched up the steps to the porch and used my fist to hammer away at the door.

A few seconds later, John threw it open. Frank stood behind him, another hulk, nearly as big as Cooper. I demanded they remove themselves. They refused. I shouted over them, proclaiming my undying love for Elizabeth, then took a swing at Cooper. My next memory is of him dragging me like a rag doll down the sidewalk and dumping me out the gate. I'd cursed John and all his progenitors at the top of my lungs.

My next thought roiled my guts. I had threatened him.

I'd said I was going to kill him.

Elizabeth and her parents might have heard. Frank Van Dam had definitely heard. But surely they would know it was the empty threat of a drunk.

I was an idiot to go back there. Elizabeth hated me and had every reason to do so. But I'd promised my father I would tell her about John, and it was possible she'd know who wanted him dead. I had to go.

At nine o'clock, I limped the remaining three blocks in the rain and climbed the wide stairway to the front porch of the Humes' spacious yellow and white Queen Anne. Alberts, an older man who served as the Humes' butler and chauffeur, answered my knock on the paneled wood door. His gaunt face was a blank canvas, betraying no reaction to seeing me after so long. He took my coat and hat, and in a formal voice asked me to wait in the parlor.

I warmed myself at the large stone fireplace while I waited, breathing in the aroma of wood smoke mixed with furniture polish and disinfectant. It hurt just to be within the cheerful green-papered walls of this room. Elizabeth and I had spent many happy hours here during the nearly four years we courted, most times under the watchful eye of her mother. The other times, when her parents were gone, had been even happier, until the last. I shook my head to clear it. I had to think about Elizabeth.

"Will?" Elizabeth's normally clear alto was husky. "What are you doing here?"

I spun around and stood for a moment in shock. Elizabeth was thin to the point of emaciation, with haunted green eyes peering out above hollow cheeks. Her long blue skirt bunched underneath her belt, and the white plaited shirtwaist hung about her like a windless sail. Her curly auburn hair, normally swirled into a glorious chignon, hung dull and lifeless over her shoulders. She looked more like an impoverished immigrant than the daughter of a wealthy jurist.

And it was my fault.

I took a deep breath and gathered my wits. "Elizabeth, please, sit."

She stepped lightly as if the soles of her feet were injured, and perched on the edge of the straight-backed white sofa. I reached out to take her hand, but she pulled it away.

"What do you want?" Her voice was lazy, words drawn out like she'd just awakened. Her china-white face was a frozen mask. She was still beautiful, to be sure, a Gibson Girl with delicate features contrasted by sensuous lips, but the look was gone. Her eyes, which had always spoken of a hidden knowledge she alone possessed—a confident look, arrogant even—now stared back at me blankly, half open.

"I'm sorry to have to give you this news." I stopped, still searching for the words, the phrases that might cushion the blow. Finally, I just said, "John is dead. He was killed at my father's factory last night."

Her eyes widened, and she slumped against the back of the sofa. "Dead? But . . ."

"He was crushed in a hydraulic press. It doesn't appear to have been an accident."

"He was murdered?"

"Yes."

Her head slowly tilted toward me. "Did you do it?"

"What? No. Why would you—"

"Then who did?" She closed her eyes and nestled into the sofa.

"I don't know. Whoever it was seems to have gotten away. . . . I wondered . . . Do you have any idea who could have done this?"

"No." Her mouth opened and closed, like she was rehearsing a response. "Why would anyone want to kill John?" She sat up and looked at me again. "Thank you, Will. I appreciate you telling me."

Though she was acting strangely, I was encouraged by her lack of enmity. I reached out again to take her hand. This time she let me. "I'm so sorry, Elizabeth. For John, for everything. But there's something else. He called me last night. He said you were in trouble."

With no inflection, she said, "Trouble?"

"Why would he say that?"

"I don't know."

It was obvious she was lying. "Please. Let me help you."

She pulled her hand from my grasp and stood. "You should go."

"But, Elizabeth—"

"Will, go."

"I think you may be in danger. Please."

She turned and began to walk from the room, each step slow and careful.

"I'll go." I stood. "But please, let me help. God knows I owe you."

She stopped at the doorway and looked back at me. The faintest trace of a smile crossed her lips. "I know. But I don't need your help. Just go."


I drove the Victoria to the Detroit Electric garage. A canary yellow extension brougham pulled out from the overhead door in front of me, a white-gloved "chaser" at the helm. That would be Mrs. Capewell's automobile, the first stretch Detroit Electric sold and certainly the only time canary yellow had ever been special-ordered. When the brougham passed, I pulled into the garage and drove back to the elevator, exchanging greetings with the chasers. This was everyday life and a welcome respite. The events of the past ten hours faded from scarlet to black-and-white.

Mr. Billings, the day manager, shouted over the commotion, "Ford! Mrs. Ford!"

The first "Ford!" made me jump. I glanced around, but no one seemed to have noticed.

A chaser grabbed the keys off the board and ran to Mrs. Ford's green Model C coupé, an elegant automobile that to all appearances was an opera coach without the horses. He removed the charging cables, started it up, and pulled out of the garage.

It had been one of my father's first big successes in the automobile industry to sell Henry Ford an electric for his wife. She had many reasons to drive a gasoline car, not the least of which was Mr. Ford's temperament, but it was humorous to think of Clara Ford starting a Model T, or any gasoline automobile for that matter—engaging the hand brake, setting the spark and throttle, hand-cranking the engine until it started, hoping it wouldn't kick back and break a wrist (or, in a twist of irony, cause "Ford elbow"), then racing back into the auto to reset the spark and fuel before the engine stalled. Few women would even consider performing such unladylike activities.

I eased the Victoria onto the elevator, rode with it to the second level, and pulled off to the side. The garage was loud—metal banging on metal, shouted conversations, the grinding hum of the air compressor. Detroit Electrics in various states of repair filled most of this floor, and mechanics were at work on a number of them. I nodded at one of the men while turning the corner into the rotten-egg stink of the battery room, the realm of Elwood Crane, Anderson Carriage Company's battery expert. Never was a man so aptly named. He was nearly six feet tall and perhaps 120 pounds, nothing but two arms, two legs, and a grin.

Elwood, wearing a welder's mask and thick rubber gloves, was leaning over the acid tank against the back wall and didn't see me come in. I waited for him to finish pouring a bottle of sulfuric acid into the tank. "Elwood, I've got the Vicky for you."

He pulled off his mask. "Does your head hurt as much as mine does?"

I nodded. He had no idea.

"Joe called in sick today. I thought he had a stronger constitution than that." Elwood laughed and began peeling off his gloves. "Oh, I meant to ask you last night. Did you hear Ford's putting a magnetized rear axle on the new Tin Lizzies?"

"What?"

"Yeah, so you don't lose all the parts that fall off." He cackled and waved me to the opposite corner of the room. "Feast your eyes on these." He pointed at two stacks of Edison batteries on his special charging bench. "Best I've tested yet."

I had to smile seeing the Edison nickel-steel batteries—a row of narrow steel boxes—tucked into wool blankets atop the bench, their battery connectors hooked to a pair of red and black cables hanging down from the charging board.

Elwood and his crew built Detroit Electric's lead-acid batteries, so it was in his best interest to dislike Thomas Edison's latest invention, but he was probably more excited than anyone else. To most people these boxes would have been ugly or utilitarian at best, but Elwood gazed at them through the shimmering mist of love. "These beauties will put us in high gear," he said.

"And it's about time."

"You ain't just a-whistling 'Dixie' there," Elwood said. "What's it been, ten years since Edison started promising he'd have them ready any day?"

"Hopefully it'll be worth the wait."

"It will. An electric that'll go a hundred-plus miles between charges? They'll sell themselves." Elwood put a hand on my shoulder. Even though he was only a few years older than me and I was the son of the company's founder, he was the authority, with a breezy self-confidence that was contagious. "Two hundred and two miles tomorrow—minimum. And be here at five, no later. As soon as Dr. Miller arrives, we'll get you on the road."

A large white bandage was taped across the bottom of his forearm. I took hold of his wrist and raised his arm so I could see it. "What'd you do?"

He hooked a thumb over his shoulder at the acid tank. "Going too fast, you know me. Got me a splash of sulfuric."

"Maybe that'll get you to start paying attention."

He grinned and gave me a playful shove toward the door. "Get outta here. But don't be late tomorrow."

"Yeah, yeah. I'll be here. You have the Edisons nice and toasty for me." I limped down the stairway and out of the garage, heading toward Gratiot and the J.L. Hudson Department Store. My ankle was loosening up, and the rain had stopped, but I was exhausted. Even the sun peeking out above Windsor's skyline failed to warm my spirits.

Hudson's had a huge selection of hats and caps, and also had the advantage of being an extremely busy store, so I thought it unlikely my purchase would be remembered. I bought a brown herringbone touring cap in the same style as the one I lost at the factory, just a shade or two darker. I couldn't explain away the loss of the cap I wore most often, and hoped this would be a passable substitute.

With my new cap tucked away in a bag, I hopped a streetcar back up Woodward. The trolley was packed, like it was every weekday morning. I had to fight for a spot hanging precariously off the back steps, which was as good as it usually got anyway.

I got off at the stop near Peterboro and was heading up the walk to my building when Wesley McRae bounded out the door. He was turned out perfectly, as he always seemed to be, in a pair of striped blue trousers and a blue jacket with an ivory silk cravat and matching porkpie hat. A folder bursting with sheet music was tucked under his arm. Energy seemed to radiate from him. Though we were around the same age, I didn't have one-tenth his vigor.

"Good morning, William," he called out.

"Morning," I muttered.

He put out a hand and stopped me. "Are you all right?"

"I'm fine."

He bit his lip and looked at me with narrowed eyes. "All right . . . If you say so. Well, I'm off. Crowley Milner noon till four, the Comet motion picture house until eight, and then it's off to the Palace Gardens Ballroom until the wee hours." He swept past me.

I unlocked the door and climbed the stairs to my apartment, my mind on nothing but sleep. With a little sleep I would be able to help Elizabeth and puzzle my own way out of this mess. I opened the door to my apartment and stopped in my tracks. A white envelope lay on the floor just inside. Typewritten on the front was WILLIAM C. ANDERSON, JR.—OPEN IMMEDIATELY! I brought it into my study, sat at the desk, and slit the top with my letter opener. A single piece of paper was inside. I flipped it open, and as I read, my heart began to thump faster.

*Mr. Anderson,*

*I know you killed John Cooper. I saw you leave the factory and throw away your clothing. You will not be pleased to know that your shoes, trousers, stockings, and garters, covered with John Cooper's blood, are now in my possession, and that I would be an unimpeachable witness should you happen to be arrested.*

*I'll be in touch.*

# CHAPTER FOUR

With shaking hands, I dropped the note on my desk. I was going to spend the rest of my life in prison. In a daze I wandered to the kitchen, poured myself a large bourbon, and sat at the table. A chill of fear started at the base of my spine and shot up my back as an image filled my mind.

The Michigan State Prison in Jackson: fourteen-foot stone walls, cold dank cells barely seven feet long by three feet wide, hard labor, and worst of all, the most notorious and depraved reprobates in the Michigan penal system. For the first time I wished Michigan had the death penalty. The electric chair would be preferable.

I had to focus. Who could have written this note? He had been at the factory and followed me home. I tried to remember faces from the streetcar, but they were all a blur. My head buzzed, and it was getting difficult to keep my eyes open. Just an hour or two of sleep, and I'd be able to think. My mind was sluggish, but one thing was clear—I had to talk with Frank Van Dam. If anyone other than Elizabeth would know what John was up to, it was Frank. I'd telephone him and see if I could figure out who had written the note. Then I'd go to Elizabeth's, try to talk some sense into her. I stripped off my suit and climbed into bed.

———

John Cooper stood over me, flattened, two-dimensional. He jerked a gun from his belt, stuck it in my face, and thumbed back the hammer. His eyes narrowed, and he said, *It's time for you to pay, Willie-boy.*

I sat bolt upright in bed, sweat pouring down my face. The moon, just a tick past full, beamed through the window, lighting my bedroom to ghostly grays.

A dream. It was a dream. I jumped out of bed, switched on the lights, and glanced at the clock. Two thirty in the morning. Some fourteen hours of sleep. Fear is exhausting.

I had slept through yesterday's opportunity to telephone Frank or do anything for Elizabeth, and the cloudless sky outside pretty well ensured I'd be tied up with the mileage test until late at night. I had to keep up the pretense of normalcy. Anyway, I couldn't skip the test and have any hope of remaining employed. Other than the endurance runs I'd made with the Victoria, my job performance was pitiful at best. My father had told my supervisor, Mr. Cavendish, that I was to be treated like any other employee. Had that been the case, however, I'd have been fired long ago, given that every morning I was either hungover or still drunk. But Cavendish seemed near the breaking point.

Frank and Elizabeth were going to have to wait. I hoped Elizabeth could.

Like every day, the first thing I did was make my bed. It was a point of pride that my apartment was neat, particularly since I'd let my maid go shortly after Elizabeth broke off our engagement. The empty liquor bottles were simply too embarrassing.

I made a cold beef sandwich and a pot of coffee, and sat at the kitchen table trying to force my mind into gear. The sandwich and two cups of coffee later, the haze started to lift. I tried to puzzle out the identity of the presumed blackmailer. (Even though he hadn't asked for anything yet, it seemed inevitable.) It could be a policeman, but that seemed unlikely. Though "Detroit policeman" and "blackmailer" were by no means mutually exclusive professions, I was sure I had lost them at the factory.

The only people who knew I was out that late were Ben Carr and Wesley McRae. Ben could have followed me from the garage, but I couldn't imagine why. And Wesley could have seen me dump the clothing, but he was home when I got back. I couldn't think of any way he would have even heard about the murder. It seemed possible the killer had written the note. He had been at the factory and could certainly have followed me home. But it would make more sense for him to just give the clothing to the police. No one else would have a stronger reason to see an innocent man convicted of the murder.

The idea that *any* man would be able to overpower John Cooper seemed ludicrous. Even armed to the teeth, the murderer couldn't have persuaded him to climb onto that press, and if John was unconscious, few men could have lifted him high enough. A gang, perhaps? According to the newspapers, there were enough of them around, though mostly groups of teenage hoodlums. This didn't seem like the work of boys.

The roof press wasn't complicated to run, but it seemed likely the killer had been familiar with it beforehand. A union man made sense. The unions would do anything to get a foothold in an automobile company. Once they got their claws into the first one, they would have the leverage they needed to break others. What better way to make a statement than killing the man causing you the most trouble, and framing me, the son of the owner of an open shop, for it? They get two for one.

It was probably one of the unions in the American Federation of Labor. They'd been making runs at my father's company for more than a decade. John and his predecessors' planted men had identified many union organizers over the years. They were fired without comment.

The Industrial Workers of the World were another possibility but seemed less likely. The Wobblies were relatively new, particularly in Detroit, and were concentrating on unskilled workers, the ones the AFL disdained. In the automotive industry, that was a tiny percentage of the workforce. I doubted John had run afoul of them.

I wondered if I should call the police and explain the whole situation, but quickly decided against it. What would I tell them? That I was being blackmailed for the return of my blood-soaked clothing? I could just as easily drive myself to prison. But I would make sure Riordan looked at the AFL.

Until I could get Frank's take on this, I didn't see any alternative to waiting for the blackmailer to make his next move. In the meantime I had to help Elizabeth, to make whatever amends I could. Something was seriously wrong with her, that much was certain. Her behavior was so peculiar. How could she have so little reaction to the news of her fiancé's death? Could her behavior be explained by drugs? By some sort of brain-damaging poison? Or could she have changed so much in a single year?

John didn't say she was in danger, he said she was "in trouble." Pregnant? Given her appearance, it didn't seem possible. "Trouble" could mean danger. It could mean almost anything. I had to find out. If her trouble proved to be related to John's murder, I might be able to piece something together that would also help me. But there wasn't much room for hope.

As soon as I was able, I would go back to Elizabeth's house. If she refused to talk to me, I would speak with her mother. If that failed, I would try to get her father to listen to me. One way or another, I was going to help her.

At four o'clock I dressed in my motor toggery: a loose-fitting dark gray sack suit, calf-length leather boots, gloves, goggles, my new cap, and my tan cotton duster. I roughed up the cap in the dirt of the backyard before catching a streetcar to the garage. My ankle was nearly back to normal, but still I shuffled the last hundred feet. I wasn't eager to see Ben Carr again.

He wasn't in sight when I entered the garage. I whispered a prayer of thanks and hurried up the steps to the second floor. The Victoria sat on the automobile elevator. Elwood and Joe Curtiss, Detroit Electric's head mechanic, both in gray coveralls, were bent over the front battery compartment. The empty battery lift hung over them. Other than their murmured conversation and the hum of electricity, the shop was quiet.

I joined them at the automobile. "Morning, Elwood, Joe."

They both straightened and greeted me. Joe was an older and shorter version of Elwood—light brown hair, brown eyes, and a gangly build— but a little more filled out from his two decades as a mechanic. Joe and

Elwood were my best friends at the company. I suppose, given that I'd lost touch with just about everyone else, they were really my only friends.

Elwood grimaced. "Tough about John Cooper, huh?"

I nodded. "Yeah, it's horrible." I could hear my voice tremble. The news had likely spread across the city by now.

"Cops figure anything out yet?" Joe said.

"Not that I know of."

He leaned back against the Victoria. "Did you know Cooper?"

"I did. We went to college together."

They both offered their condolences. Joe said, "He was the football player, right? The huge, good-looking guy?"

I grunted out a laugh. Huge? Good-looking? John was Michelangelo's *David*, except six-five and thickly muscled. "I suppose you could say that."

"How did you know him?"

"We boarded at the same place in Ann Arbor." The memory of our first meeting put a smile on my face. I hadn't thought of it in years. "The first time we met we were freshmen. I recognized him from the football games but was sure he didn't know me from Adam. One of the sophomore football players cornered me with a pair of sheep shears and was about to give me the 'freshman haircut.'"

Joe frowned. "The what?"

"Oh, it's a wonderful tradition. You corner the kids who are already scared to death of the older men, and you whack off their hair so they look like they've just escaped from a mental institution."

Elwood shook his head. "It's a good thing college is for you intellectual giants. I don't think I'm smart enough to figure out stuff like that."

"Real funny. Anyway, John recognized me from the boardinghouse and gave the other guy a thump on the head. That was the last time anybody tried it. Come to think of it, it was the last time anybody at the U of M physically challenged me in any way."

"You figure the murder was personal," Joe said, "or something to do with the Employers Association?"

Elwood nudged Joe, who turned and looked at him with knit eyebrows. "What?"

With a quick shake of his head, Elwood ducked back into the battery compartment.

My stomach suddenly hurt. I turned back to Joe. "John was engaged to Elizabeth Hume, my old girlfriend."

"Oh. You never said." Joe was quiet for a moment. "What'd he do at the EAD?"

"He ran security for the labor bureau."

Joe looked at me blankly.

"He called it 'hiring strikebreakers and whopping troublemakers,'" I said. "He took care of both of them."

"Shit." Joe shook his head. "Cooper hired scabs *and* broke heads. The AFL would want to crucify him."

Elwood finished connecting the wires to the battery. I forced a smile and said, "Are we ready?"

"The batteries are fully charged and all warmed up." Elwood grinned and gestured toward Joe. "But I can't speak for the rest of it with this grease monkey running the show."

I turned to Joe. "Everything good?"

"Yessiree. Outside of the batteries, which Mr. Screw-loose here has undoubtedly bungled, everything on this sweetheart has been cleaned, tightened, oiled, or greased. It's perfect."

"Sounds good," I said. "But let's go through the list to be sure."

Joe nodded, and we ran through the various lubrications and adjustments he had performed. He was thorough. The Victoria was ready.

Dr. Miller, our official observer, arrived a few minutes later, dressed in tall boots and a gray three-piece suit with a matching cap and oilcloth duster. A kind man with a full beard and keen eyes behind pince-nez glasses, the doctor was well known for his sterling character and would be an impeccable witness. On the surface he was the ideal observer. He was my doctor, a friend of my father, and the owner of a 1910 Detroit Electric coupé. My father had suggested him for the role. I wanted to tell him no but couldn't do that without telling him why. To my parents, I'd explained the broken engagement as a loss of love between Elizabeth and me, a widening of our differences as we grew older.

I would never tell them the truth.

Dr. Miller rushed up to us, grinning with delight like a small child. "Are we going to set a world record today?" He pushed his goggles up onto his forehead.

"No question about it," I said.

A few months before, Baker Electric had established a record of 201.6 miles on a single charge. We were aiming to beat them. I had to concentrate.

Dr. Miller shook my hand vigorously. "That's what I like to hear. Chip off the old block."

He apparently had memory problems.

Joe showed Dr. Miller the certification for the new odometer, and he and Elwood gave us their blessings. I was relieved my father had not come down to send us off. The less I had to think about the Cooper mess, the better the day would be.

Unfortunately, we had no more than buttoned our dusters and pulled our goggles over our eyes when Dr. Miller said, "I heard about the murder at your father's factory. Did you know the man who was killed?"

I nodded and climbed into the Victoria.

Dr. Miller hopped in, and we began the descent to the first floor. "Did you know him well?"

I nodded again and looked away.

He patted me on the knee. "Don't want to talk about it? I understand."

"Thanks." I knew if I told him about John and me, and especially about John and Elizabeth, I wouldn't be able to get off the subject all day.

The elevator clunked to a stop. Joe and Elwood had taken the stairs and were already sitting in the blue Model T that would serve to confirm our odometer reading.

I twisted the key in the end of the controller stick to start the auto, and ticked the amp and volt meters with a finger to be sure the charge was full. Everything was perfect. I pulled the steering lever down in front of me and pushed the controller to first speed. We crawled through the garage, Joe and Elwood following behind. I turned left up Woodward. It wasn't yet five thirty and still quite cold, in the thirties. A streetcar approached, rattling down the tracks toward the ferry docks. When it passed, the street was nearly silent. I could feel, more than hear, the hum from the Victoria's electric motor. I took a deep breath, determined to enjoy this day. It might be the last attempt I'd ever make for a world record, or, for all I knew, the last time I'd ever drive a car.

Dr. Miller tapped my shoulder. "Isn't it awfully cold to be doing this? Won't the batteries suffer?"

I shook my head. "It doesn't really matter how cold it is outside, so long as the batteries are warm. Mr. Crane got them nice and toasty, and when they're working they stay warm. We'll be fine."

He nodded.

I took advantage of the nearly empty downtown streets, driving with the lights off to preserve the batteries. The electric street lamps lit the way well enough. Even in the dark, the majesty of this city, "the Paris of the West," was clear. We passed skyscraper after skyscraper—the Penobscot, Majestic, and Hammond Buildings, the Ford, and the Dime—brick and stone edifices disappearing into silhouettes lit by the bright glow of moon and stars. The empty lots that had peppered the area when we moved here were gone. Buildings of all descriptions—offices, homes, stores, factories, warehouses, showrooms—had sprung up everywhere.

We looped through the downtown area, alternating between the two most efficient speeds—second, which ran at eight miles per hour, and fourth, which pushed us up to seventeen. Even though the city speed limit was ten, it was worth the risk to try to get the record in a single day. And a speeding violation seemed much less significant than it would have a few days ago.

I could hear snatches of conversation between Joe and Elwood over the *putt-putt-putt* of the Model T behind us, but Dr. Miller and I were quiet. I was lost in my thoughts, and he seemed satisfied to just enjoy the ride. It was a relief he hadn't yet brought up Elizabeth. I hoped it stayed that way.

Thinking I'd run past Bennett Park, the home of the Tigers and my favorite summer locale, I turned down Trumbull and headed back toward the river. Trumbull was one of the few streets that still had the old

Edison light towers, 125-foot-tall monstrosities that had been in most of the downtown area when we moved here in 1895.

"Don't you live around here somewhere?" Dr. Miller said.

"Five or six blocks that way." I waved vaguely toward my left. "On Peterboro."

I left the lights off, though the Edison towers were widely spaced and did a better job of lighting the sky than they did the street. With the headlights of the Model T trailing us, I thought I could still see well enough.

"Funny, that," Dr. Miller said, pointing across me to a fallow cornfield that took up a city block, the only remaining vestige of the rural roots of the area.

"Farmer named Parker," I said. "Land speculators have been trying to buy him out for years. Stubborn old cuss."

The doctor nodded and shoved his hands in his pockets.

Just before the intersection at Temple, I pushed the controller to fourth speed for the long straightaway.

Suddenly a two-foot-high barrier loomed in front of us.

# CHAPTER FIVE

Cursing, I jammed on the brake pedal, shoved the steering lever away from me, and yanked back on the controller stick. The brakes squealed. The car jerked hard to the left and tipped right, the tires on my side a foot off the ground before the Victoria crashed back down to the cobblestones. Dr. Miller bounced off the leather interior of the automobile and slammed into me. I grabbed hold of him and helped him sit up. "Are you all right?"

He pushed his goggles onto his forehead and blinked a few times. "Yes, I think so." He stretched his arms and legs. "No harm done."

We both looked over the passenger side of the Victoria. A brown horse lay in the middle of the street.

"Damned horses," Dr. Miller said. "They're nothing but a nuisance."

A dead horse in the street wasn't an unusual sight, what with the thousands of them working in the city every day, but this one had scared the hell out of me. I took a deep breath and looked at the odometer. Our run had almost ended at nineteen miles.

Joe and Elwood appeared simultaneously on either side of the Victoria. After making sure we weren't hurt, they quickly inspected the automobile and waved us on.

I pushed the controller stick forward again. The Vicky seemed fine, but I kept it in second speed with a close eye on the road until the sky began to brighten. When I could see well enough, I pushed the controller up through third to fourth.

Dr. Miller pointed at a steaming pile of horse manure in the middle of an intersection. "I thought the automobile was supposed to solve *this* part of the pollution problem."

I shrugged. "Maybe someday." Even now, deep into the "horseless age," there were still easily fifty horses in the city for every motorcar.

"Well, I can't wait for that day," he said. "Oh, for a clean breath of air."

I nodded my agreement. Depending on the time of year, we breathed either coal smoke or horseshit. In the winter, the air was hazy with smoke, and snow turned gray within a day. During the summer the pungent odor of fresh manure filled the city. Worst of all, when the wind was up during a hot stretch, horseshit fine as dust blew in through the windows and coated the insides of every home and business.

More people now were heading to work. Soon the intersections would clot with horses, wagons, bicycles, pedestrians, and automobiles competing for the right of way, so I headed up Woodward out of town. We passed the "Crystal Palace," Ford's new plant in Highland Park. I'm sure the esteemed Dr. Freud would have a few things to say about Mr. Ford, or Albert Kahn, the architect. Five massive smokestacks towered a hundred feet over the factory in a gigantic phallic display, billowing great gray plumes into the blue November sky.

At Six Mile Road, the pavement changed from red brick to concrete—the first mile of concrete road in the country, not surprisingly located directly in front of the exclusive emerald links of the Detroit Golf Club. I turned right on Seven Mile and then headed back into town through Hamtramck.

"My Lord," Dr. Miller said. "Look at this place. Last I was here, there was nothing but farms."

Buildings had been thrown up everywhere, filled with shops and businesses, most with signs scrawled out in some Eastern European language. Men, women, and children filled the wooden boardwalks, chattering and shouting, none in English. They were bustling about everywhere—to shops, to schools, but most of all to the four-story concrete and glass Dodge Main Assembly Plant that had recently risen in a matter of only a few months. Practically overnight, Hamtramck had gone from a sleepy farming community to an immigrant Mecca.

I nudged the doctor. "You know the Dodge brothers give their workers free beer?"

He snorted. "Those louts. I'm surprised they don't drink it all themselves. It's a wonder they can even run a business."

"They may be drunks, but they're serious about their business. Everyone else was running away from Mr. Ford after his other companies failed. They saw something no one else did, and it's worked out pretty well for them."

Dr. Miller gave a grudging nod. John and Horace Dodge were infamous for their boorish behavior, and a man like the doctor had a hard time getting past that to see their genius. He looked up at the building as we drove past, chasing the glittering sun sparking across the wall of windows. "What do they make for Ford?"

I laughed. "Almost everything. Ford's men don't do much with the T except slap them together."

He shook his head. In his world, successful men were, for the most part, gentlemen. In the new world of automobile manufacturing, the tycoons—Ford, the Dodges, Leland, Durant—were mechanics.

At noon the odometer read 86.3 miles, and according to the meters the batteries still had better than sixty percent of their capacity remaining. There was a long way to go, but we had a good chance. In need of a break, I drove down to Preemo's saloon. Over a couple of beers and the free buffet lunch, Elwood, Joe, Dr. Miller, and I discussed the state of the electric automobile business (growing), the gasoline automobile business (growing exponentially), and the steam automobile business (fading fast).

For the first time since I found the body, I could focus on something other than the image of John Cooper crushed in a press.

After lunch Joe filled the gasoline tank of the Model T, and we drove out through the stately neighborhoods of Grosse Pointe and then back again to Jefferson and East Grand. As I drove across the bridge to Belle Isle, I felt a deep pang of regret. Elizabeth and I had spent many nights leaning on the railing of this bridge, looking over the river at the sky-scrapers of Detroit on the right and the village of Windsor, Ontario, on the left. We talked about our future—marriage, children, someday grandchildren.

Shit.

We spent the rest of the afternoon on Belle Isle. The road encircling the island was pristine and nearly deserted this time of year—at least until evening, when the casino's business began to pick up. On a fine sunny day such as this, even the repetitive drive was enjoyable. The temperature was hovering near sixty degrees, and we stripped off our dusters and enjoyed both the view and the fresh air coming off the water.

Dr. Miller tilted his face up toward the sun. "Ever been to Central Park in New York?"

"No, sir."

"Ah, you should see it. Magnificent. Many parallels here, of course. Designed by the same man, Olmstead, you know."

Leaves fluttered down from majestic maples and oaks as we drove past picnic grounds, walking paths, baseball diamonds, and buffalo grazing in a grassy pasture. The Model T had fallen back a hundred yards or so, and its engine's irksome farting had faded into the background. Water lapped against the shores with a gentle *shhh, shhh, shhh*, interrupted by the occasional laughter of children on a playground and hum of conversation from couples on a bench here, in a canoe there.

The entire island was lovely—the bathhouse, zoo, aquarium, and boat club, the Spanish-style casino with vaulted towers and covered verandas, and the conservatory, its copper dome gleaming in the sun.

Dr. Miller cleared his throat. "Say, Will, we've never really talked about Elizabeth's . . . problem. The damage had been done long before I got to the house. There was nothing I could do."

"I know." I didn't want to discuss it.

He was quiet for perhaps half a minute. I felt his eyes boring into the side of my head. "Did you know," he said, "she was going to abort the child?"

My head felt like a lead weight. "I didn't even know she was pregnant."

"What I don't understand is why you didn't just move up the wedding date. That sort of thing happens all the time."

I barked out a harsh laugh. "Because she hated me. She refused to even see me by then."

Dr. Miller made a noise like he'd been punched in the stomach. He reached over and patted my knee. "You're a good boy, Will, a good man. I'm sure Elizabeth has come to terms with it by now. You need to let yourself get on with your life. She did it, not you."

He was quiet on our next few circuits of the island, for which I was very grateful. How could I have responded to that? Get on with my life? If only he knew.

Just after four we passed the bridge for the seventh time. My father was waiting for us atop Comet, his chestnut quarter horse. I was surprised to see him here, and hoped his presence didn't announce some other development in the Cooper case. He dismounted and exchanged greetings with Dr. Miller, then looked up at me. "How far have you gotten?"

I looked at the odometer and made a quick calculation. "One hundred thirty-four point one."

"You've got what, sixty-seven and a half miles to go? Are you going to make it?"

I glanced at the meters. "It'll be tight. We've got somewhere between thirty and thirty-five percent capacity left."

"No time to talk then." He slapped the side of the auto. "Daylight's a-wasting, gentlemen. Get back to it."

I pushed the controller forward. When we reached the bridge again, my father was gone, probably back to the factory. It wasn't like him to spend any time on a weekday away from his business.

By six we had made five more circuits and were at 165.3 miles—less than thirty-six away from the record. It was beginning to get dark now, so I drove back down the Belle Isle Bridge to Jefferson. On the corner was Electric Park, home of the best roller coasters in Detroit as well as the Palace Gardens Ballroom, where Wesley McRae said he was singing. Screams echoed down from the Ride through the Clouds coaster, while dozens of people exited the park into the street. The corner, always busy, was at a standstill, and we wasted precious electricity in the fifteen minutes it took to negotiate a left onto Jefferson.

Joe and Elwood shadowed us downtown. There was enough daylight left to see the advertisements that had thankfully been invisible this morning—Uneeda Biscuits, Coca-Cola, Vicks Magic Croup Salve, Vitagraph Pictures, on and on and on, pasted onto every surface and soaring above the buildings in ostentatious displays.

I kept the car in second, and we circled the city at eight miles per hour. At this speed we didn't need our goggles, and my eyes kept darting from the odometer to the voltmeter and back to the street. At 9:28 P.M. with the odometer at 199.5 miles, the voltmeter bottomed out. I flicked the glass in front of it, but the needle stayed where it was.

Dr. Miller held out both hands, fingers crossed. "Don't panic. I've driven my coupé for quite a while after the meter showed it was empty."

There was nothing to do except keep driving. At 9:45 P.M., we hit 201.6 miles. My eyes stayed on the odometer. The last number clicked over, and Dr. Miller shouted, "Huzzah! You've done it!"

Two hundred one and seven tenths miles—a new world record. I stopped the Vicky, and the doctor wrapped his arms around me in an enthusiastic embrace. The Model T pulled up next to us, and the two men jumped out and ran over to our car.

Elwood pushed me to the side so he could see the odometer. "Yes!" He jumped in the air, shouting, "Take that, Walt Baker, you old so-and-so!" He and Joe shook hands with both Dr. Miller and me before Elwood gestured for us to continue. "Let's put some distance between us and them."

They climbed back in the Model T. I pushed the controller up to first and then second. As each additional mile rolled up on the odometer, Dr. Miller and I shouted and laughed, until finally, an hour later, at 211.3 miles, the Victoria slowed and stopped about a quarter mile from the garage.

We climbed out and shook hands. While Joe waited with the Victoria, Dr. Miller and I piled into the Model T for the short drive to the garage, where my father was waiting. When Joe returned aboard the tow wagon, we popped the cork on a bottle of champagne and toasted the new world record. I expected my father to pull me aside at some point, but he acted normally, as if I wasn't suspected of killing someone in his automobile factory. He even gave me some good-natured ribbing when Dr. Miller explained in excruciating detail how I'd almost driven straight into a dead horse.

Joe, Elwood, and I stopped at Louie Schneider's as we often did, and knocked back a couple of whiskeys before I caught the streetcar home about midnight. I couldn't keep the grin off my face. The other riders edged away from me, likely assuming they were riding with a lunatic. But I didn't care. I had set a world record!

I was whistling as I strolled up the walk to my apartment building, feeling tired but satiated. Sleep sounded just right. I unlocked the door and stepped inside.

Rough hands spun me around and shoved me against the wall. My hands were jerked behind me. Cold metal rings snapped around my wrists.

"Wh—What are you doing?" I sputtered.

A hand grabbed my shoulder and spun me away from the wall. A young Detroit policeman with two chins and a bottlebrush mustache poked a stubby finger into my sternum. "Riordan wants to talk to you." He jabbed me again. "And he don't like waiting."

Detective Riordan sat down at the table across from me and folded his arms over his chest. In the harsh light of the interrogation room the scar on his face, shadowed by a black fedora, was a jagged burgundy slash. The whites of his eyes blended into pale blue irises. His pupils seemed to literally stand out, boring into mine. "Mr. Anderson. You can be a very difficult man to locate."

I stared back at him. I was just drunk enough to be brave. "And you work very late hours."

"Not normally." His eyes narrowed. "Mrs. Riordan gets irritated when I miss dinner with the kiddies. But when someone I need to talk to doesn't show up at work or at home all day, I have to make exceptions."

I had been sitting in a hard wooden chair in this windowless eight-by-eight room for at least an hour, though I couldn't be sure of the time as my hands were still cuffed behind my back. The room smelled sour, a funk of sweat and fear. It was very warm, and I still wore my duster over my suit.

"How about you take these things off," I shook my hands, and the cuffs clattered together, "and I'll tell you what I've been doing?"

"He cuffed you?"

I just stared at him.

Riordan came around behind me and unlocked the handcuffs, apologizing for the "rookie." I couldn't tell if he was serious or just playing with me.

He sat again. "Where have you been?"

I hung my duster on the back of the chair and told him about the mileage test. He asked questions and seemed impressed when I told him how far we had gone.

"Maybe the police department could use a few of those electrics," he mused. "Most of the driving is around town."

He seemed to be trying to make me comfortable. I was wary, waiting for a trick question. The courage the whiskey had given me was splintering.

"So, Will. May I call you Will? That's what everyone at the factory calls you."

I nodded.

He said, "The cap," and sat back.

A bead of sweat slid down the side of my face. I knew I should tell him I was at the factory that night. Between the Victoria and the blackmailer, it would only be a matter of time until he knew. But I couldn't. I was too scared. So I stared at the table. My watch ticked in the pocket of my waistcoat. Finally I said, "What about the cap?"

"Everybody seems to think it was yours, Will. Your motoring cap."

"It wasn't mine." I took off my hat and flung it onto the table, harder than I'd intended. "As you can see, this one is mine."

He picked it up and examined it. "Very nice. Looks pretty new."

I shrugged.

He set the cap down. "Tell me about your relationship with John Cooper."

"We were friends."

"How did you meet?"

"We lived at the same boardinghouse while we were at the University of Michigan."

"Were you still friends?"

I hesitated a beat too long. "Yes. Sure."

He studied me. "Close friends?"

"Not so much anymore." I wiped sweat from my forehead.

"Interesting. Why do you suppose that is?"

I shrugged again, trying to act nonchalant. "Well, I didn't see him that often. His work kept him busy."

"But he was at Anderson Carriage all the time."

"Right, well, we were both busy."

Riordan sat back and cocked an eye at me. "So he spent a lot of time at the factory, but you didn't see him often. Why is that?"

"People drift apart. It happens."

"Any particular reason you drifted, Will?"

I didn't know what Riordan had found out, but I wasn't going to volunteer anything. "No."

He stared at me for a long moment. "Seems people liked John."

"He was very charming."

"Was John still close with anyone else from college?"

"The football team always got together for homecoming in Ann Arbor. But I don't think he was particularly close to any of them."

"At Mr. Cooper's apartment," Riordan said, "we found four sets of fingerprints—two men and two women. The women proved to be Cooper's maid and Elizabeth Hume. Cooper, of course, was one of the men. The other also had big hands. Any idea who that might be?"

I thought for a moment. "Well, John spent a lot of time with Frank Van Dam. He's almost as big as Cooper, probably six-three, two forty."

"How might we get ahold of Mr. Van Dam?"

"He works for John at the Employers Association. Well . . . worked for John, I guess."

"Tell me about him."

"What do you mean?"

"What kind of man is he?"

"I don't really know him. He mostly hangs—hung—around with John."

"What did he do for Cooper?"

"He was John's right-hand man. You know, kept the peace, knocked some union guys around, that kind of thing."

Riordan wrote something on his notepad, then shifted in his chair. "What do you like to drink, Will?"

"Oh, I don't know. The usual, I guess—beer, whiskey, that sort of thing."

"Bourbon?"

I shrugged. "Sometimes."

"Hmm. And what size shoes do you wear?"

*Shit.* "Eleven. Or ten. Depends on the shoe."

He nodded and pursed his lips. His scar puckered near his mouth. "Ten? That's interesting, Will." He didn't say anything else.

I tried to keep the fear out of my voice. "Is there a point to this or can I go home?"

He crossed his arms and looked up, deep in thought, his eyes searching the ceiling. "Ten," he said again.

"Look, I didn't kill Cooper. It had to be the AFL."

"Why do you say that?"

I explained to him about Cooper's job, about how the unions would want him gone, about how doing it at our factory would serve their purposes.

He just sat slumped in his seat, staring at me from under the brim of his fedora. When I finished, he said, "Huh," and went back to staring at me.

I couldn't take any more. "I had nothing to do with it. Let me out of here."

"Sure, Will, sure," he said in a soothing voice, holding his hands out in front of him. "Settle down. I wouldn't want to make you angry. You might run to your daddy, get me in trouble."

"Why don't you—" I stopped myself and took a deep breath. Exhaling, I stood, grabbed my cap and duster, and stalked to the door. I threw it open and turned back to Riordan, who still sat at the table. "Leave me alone. John was my friend. I'm innocent."

He gave me a wry smile. "Oh, no, Will. Everyone's guilty of something. Even a rich boy like you. I've just got to figure out what you're guilty of."

# CHAPTER SIX

After calming my nerves with a few drinks, I climbed into bed. It seemed my head had just hit the pillow when pounding on my front door awakened me. It was still dark outside. I rubbed my eyes, threw on a robe, and stumbled to the door.

Ben Carr stood outside. "Mr. Anderson! I gotta talk to you."

"What is it?" I asked, a quaver in my voice.

He kneaded his old gray cap with both hands and looked around. "Could I come inside for a minute?"

*Oh, God.* "Sure." I held the door open.

He hurried in and turned back to me. "It's the police, sir. They was at the garage asking about the Vicky. I had to show them the logbook."

"The logbook? You changed the time, didn't you?"

"Yes, sir, but it's out of order."

"What do you mean?"

His face was slick with sweat. "It's twenty-seven lines out of order. In the book before you checked out the Victoria, there's twenty-seven pickups after five thirty in the morning."

"Damn."

"I've got a family," he said. "I can't go to jail."

"You don't think I had something to do with John Cooper's death, do you?" Suddenly it mattered a great deal what Ben thought of me.

"Whether you did or not ain't my place to say. But I lied." He hung his head and continued in a murmur. "I lied to the police. And I don't think they believed me."

Stomach acid burned the back of my throat. My little house of cards was fluttering down all around me. "I understand, Ben. I'll make sure they know I changed the time. That you had nothing to do with it."

His brow furrowed. He looked down at the floor and then met my eyes. "Okay. But I ain't going to jail."

Going back to sleep was impossible. I tossed in bed for half an hour, my mind racing. Disgusted, I threw off the covers and stomped into the kitchen. Frank Van Dam *had* to be able to help me. While I waited to phone him, I drank a pot of coffee and slurped down a bowl of Toasted Corn Flakes.

I wasn't certain if Frank worked Saturdays, though I had to assume so. It didn't seem likely that the Employers Association would give its men the entire weekend off when everyone else was working. I'd phone him early at home, try to catch him before he headed off for a day of breaking heads. At seven I went into the den, sat at my desk, and, once I'd retrieved Frank's telephone number from a list of EAD emergency contacts, I picked up the telephone's receiver. A few seconds later the operator came on the line, and I asked her to connect me.

His mother, whom I'd never met, answered the phone.

"Hello, Mrs. Van Dam," I said. "Is Frank home?"

"Who is this?"

"Will Anderson."

"Why are you calling Frank?" she said, her voice filled with suspicion. "What do you want from him?"

"Nothing, Mrs. Van Dam. I just need to talk to him."

"Well, he's not here."

"Do you know where he is?"

"That's none of your business."

"Do you know how I might get in touch with him?"

"No."

"It's very important. Please."

"Leave Frank alone." She hung up.

I shook my head as I fumbled the receiver back onto the telephone. As far as I knew, she didn't even know who I was, yet she was suspicious and afraid. There had to be a reason for that. Frank must know what John had been doing. At lunchtime I'd try him at the Employers Association.

After dressing, I walked to the streetcar stop. It was cold, and the sky was clear, a brilliant cornflower blue. A newsboy was hawking the *Free Press*, and I picked one up while I waited for the trolley. I didn't even need to open it. The front-page-center headline read: GRUESOME MURDER AT ANDERSON CARRIAGE.

I quickly scanned the article. As I expected, the first half was a grisly description of John's body. Blood sold newspapers. One of the police quotes was that the crime scene "was one of the more gruesome in the history of the city." One of the *more* gruesome? I didn't want to try to imagine anything worse.

The Employers Association was offering a thousand-dollar reward for information leading to the conviction of the murderer. The article went on to a short biography of John, highlighting his football career at Michigan, including the 1905 season during which they outscored their opponents 495–2. Most important, the article said the police had no suspects at this time. That was encouraging.

A streetcar was coming, so I pitched the paper in a garbage bin and waited for the car to stop. As always, the trolley was crammed to overflowing, men and women hanging off the sides with the barest of footholds. The motorman looked straight ahead, not slowing at all, and passed by at full speed. The crowd at the stop cursed him and questioned his parentage until the car was out of sight. I joined in. We had to get to work. Even though it was illegal, every day during rush hour, trolleys passed by their stops.

I hopped from foot to foot, not able to stand still. The next car stopped, and I wedged a toe onto the front step. I jumped off just down the block from our factory and walked through the main entrance in a stream of Anderson employees. It was a madhouse in the morning, everyone scattering in different directions, more to the carriage building than the automobile factory. Our car and truck business was growing, but it would be a while before we surpassed the revenue of Anderson carriages and wagons.

I walked to the factory office, which was something out of a Dickens serial: cramped and grim, with two rows of small desks for the managers and assistant managers of each department. Our desks all faced Mr. McFarlane's office—a real office with large interior windows that allowed him to keep an eye on us.

I opened the door and slipped inside, hoping to remain unnoticed.

A cry went up. "Will! Congratulations!"

Mr. McFarlane burst out of his office, raced over to me, and shook my hand. "Will, my lad. Well done, well done." He clapped me on the back. "That'll give those Baker boys something to stew on, now, won't it?"

I had completely forgotten about the record. I nodded and smiled, accepting congratulations from everyone except Mr. Cavendish, who merely glanced up from his desk, then consulted his watch with a small shake of the head. When the rest of the managers arrived, Mr. McFarlane stood at the front of the office and announced a world-record celebration that evening at six, cake and punch to be served. The news of the celebration got a rousing "Hurrah!" from the group; the cake and punch a disappointed groan. My father wasn't a teetotaler, but he felt it his moral obligation to set a good example for his men.

For me, this was not good news. I had to talk to Frank. I had to help Elizabeth. I had too much to do to stay late, party or no party. But I had to stay. Normalcy. Act as if nothing's wrong.

My desk was piled high with papers, so I hurried through my first duty—a circuit through the machining department to check that the men were working on the proper parts. They were stationed at the machines, grinding, drilling, sawing, and stamping, no conversation other than a shouted "Coming through!" or its German equivalent. The cacophony made talking impossible: high-pitched squeals from drills boring into metal, the angry sound of electric saws, the scream of a grinder shaping a piece of steel, but most of all, the *SLAM! SLAM! SLAM!* of the presses as the top plates crashed into sheet metal.

Two men were trying to maneuver a cart loaded with iron rods down the aisle next to me and kept running into the outside wall of the old battery room, which jutted out into the department like a tumor. I gave them a hand, pulling the front away to free it.

A few years ago, Elwood's battery department moved from here to the Detroit Electric garage on Woodward, but the equipment stayed—the charging board with its red and black cables dangling down like the legs of an insect, the lifts and tables, a small casting furnace, a welding machine, and four coffin-sized lead-lined tanks set up on sturdy iron feet. The engineers didn't want to have to run down to the garage every time they needed to recharge or test a battery, and had successfully lobbied to keep the equipment here.

The room took up valuable space and was nothing but a hazard for us. The engineers never used the welder or furnace, but kept the tanks filled, which was why one of my responsibilities was to ensure every morning that the chains locking down their sliding metal covers were in place. It was a little silly, given that the keys to the padlocks hung on a nail by the door. Still, more than once I had found an open tank, which was hazardous in the extreme, especially the acid tank. The sulfuric acid used to make the electrolyte for the batteries was one of the most caustic chemicals known. Small quantities could burn through skin or blind a man.

I looked through the windows, which ran the length of the wall on either side of the pair of wide doors. The tanks looked secure, but I went in anyway and pulled on the chains before heading back toward the office. When I walked past the roof press I tried not to think about John, though I couldn't help but look for traces of blood. The sharp odor of bleach overpowered the normal smells of metal and grease, but other than that there was no evidence of a man being killed on this machine only two nights ago.

I couldn't get out of there fast enough. I returned to my desk and began the tedious process of completing the daily paperwork—filling out dozens of parts requests for the foundry, ordering raw materials, calculating the department's payroll, approving dozens more parts requests from other departments, and filling out the appropriate work orders. I caught myself in mistake after mistake. God knows how many

I missed. I'd have to read a form six or seven times for it to even register, while my mind jumped to John's body, Riordan, the killer, the blackmailer, Elizabeth.

I would go see her after work, force my way in if necessary. She *would* listen to me.

It didn't seem possible the killer could be anyone I knew, but I worked the idea just the same. I still had no theories other than the American Federation of Labor. The problem was, I'd never heard of an AFL union going to this kind of extreme. Not that they were opposed to violence, but usually it was the bosses, or in our case, the Employers Association, who upped the ante like this. I had to consider other possibilities.

As far as I knew, no one hated John, nor was I aware of anything he had done that would make someone angry enough to kill him. But he was no angel. John wasn't always the kindest person. People his size often don't learn to couch their comments in ways that would make them more palatable, simply because they don't have to. John didn't seem to notice when something he said cut a person deeply, but it was invariably someone he thought to be stupid and bothersome.

Until a year ago, it had never been me.

Revenge seemed a possibility. In 1906, police had questioned him about the death of a University of Chicago player in a football game. Maybe someone in that boy's family had it out for John. It seemed a remote chance. Not only would his family have no reason to frame me, the death happened four years ago, was ruled accidental, and was certainly nothing out of the ordinary—dozens of boys were killed that year in football games. John had anchored Michigan's flying wedge and was responsible for multiple broken bones, punctured lungs, concussions, and untold numbers of bruises and contusions. The players knew the risk.

A little after ten o'clock, one of the secretaries from the main office stuck his head into the room. "The IWW is picketing outside. Keep all the men in their departments."

The managers and their assistants rushed out of the office and spread throughout the factory. I cut over to the administration building and ran up to my father's office, joining Mr. Wilkinson at the window. He was peering between slats in the blinds at the mob forming in front of the factory. Fifty or so dodgy-looking men milled about in the street, many of them carrying placards with messages such as CAPITALISM IS MURDER! WORKERS UNITE, and IWW AT ANDERSON NOW! More men were arriving all the time.

My father hurried out of his office, mopping his forehead with his handkerchief. "Wilkinson, where are they?"

Wilkinson dropped the blinds with a snap and turned back to my father. "They said it was going to take some time to round up enough men, but not to worry. They'll take care of it."

One of the men in the mob threw a rock toward our building. I put my nose against the glass and looked down the side of the factory, trying to see what he was aiming at. Two blue-suited Anderson security men stood at the door, holding nightsticks. A rock hit one of them in the midsection. He doubled over for a second and then ran into the mob, his associate right behind him. They waded in, swinging their truncheons.

The other union men closed ranks around them and in seconds had both security guards on the cobbles, kicking and punching them.

Before I knew what I was doing, I was out the front door. My father shouted, "Will! No!"

I waded into the mob, throwing wild punches, only now realizing I had no business here. Fortunately, more Anderson employees streamed out of the building behind me, shouting and joining in the fight. A fist glanced off my forehead as I worked my way toward the security guards, who were lying on the ground absorbing kick after kick. I threw myself at the union men, getting in a couple of good licks before a right hook knocked me over backward. A boot connected with my ribs, and then another. I curled up, trying to protect myself.

A roar sounded over the shouting mob. The men stopped kicking me and began to run away. I looked toward the source of the noise. A line of cars had stopped in front of the factory. Perhaps thirty men in dark suits and hats rushed into the fight and began pummeling the IWW men with heavy clubs and blackjacks. Half a dozen blue-suited Detroit policemen followed them, wielding truncheons. The EAD had arrived.

I looked for Frank Van Dam, but he was nowhere in sight. Had he been there, I would have seen him. With Cooper dead, Van Dam would have easily been the largest man in the crowd. It was odd. He'd never missed a mix-up before. I had assumed Frank would be taking over the labor bureau's security, but it appeared not.

I looked through the rest of them, trying to find a familiar face. Though I had a nodding acquaintance with most of the Employers Association's men, I didn't recognize any of these. Rough looking, with stubbly chins and cheap suits, they seemed to be enjoying themselves as they waded into the fray, smashing their bludgeons into heads, midsections, and knees with a brutality I had seldom seen.

It was over in seconds. Eight or nine Wobblies were laid out on the cobblestones. The rest had scattered to the winds.

I pushed myself to my feet. A cop I'd seen before dragged an unconscious man past me. "Hey, Anderson. Gimme a hand."

I took hold of the man's other arm and helped the policeman drag him to the paddy wagon. A pair of horses stood placidly at the front.

"Where's Frank Van Dam?" I said to the cop.

He shrugged. "Don't know. Thought I'd see Frankie here, too."

My father came out and chastised me, though I heard a hint of pride behind his words. I returned to the managers' office and got back to work on the stack of paper, though I spent more time tapping my pencil on the desk, thinking, than I did working.

Did the Wobblies coming here today make them more or less likely to have been involved? I wasn't sure, though I thought it less likely, as it made more sense to distance themselves from the murder if they'd been responsible. On the other hand, I'd never heard the Industrial Workers of the World described as "sensible."

The next time I looked at my watch it was two o'clock. I'd missed my lunch break by an hour and a half. That told me all I needed to know about my state of mind. I asked Cavendish if I could take a break to use the telephone. He glared at me for a moment, smirked, and shook his head.

It was clear from the phone call this morning that Frank's mother would never let me speak with him. My only chance was to catch him at work. Phoning Frank would have to wait until Monday.

# CHAPTER SEVEN

The cake, chocolate with chocolate frosting, stood three feet high, in the shape of an automobile, though the elongated front end made it look more like a gasoline car than an electric. Inscribed on top in white frosting was DETROIT ELECTRIC WORLD RECORD—211.3 MILES ON A SINGLE CHARGE! It was quickly cut into pieces by two of our female typewriters and handed out to the men along with a tangy red punch.

My father stood on a wooden box and raised his arms over his head. "May I have your attention, please?"

The four hundred or so men who had been milling around and chatting while they ate turned toward him and listened. I was fidgeting, anxious to leave, though no more than many of the other men, who were late for their after-work smoke. Anderson Carriage employees were occasionally caught smoking at work, but most, knowing it was worth their job, managed to hold off until their lunch break or after six, and then smoke only off of the company's property. They had good reason. My father paid higher than average wages (more than five dollars a day for skilled craftsmen), limited the workweek to fifty-four hours, hired no one under sixteen years of age, and was known as a fair man, often keeping on employees who were unable to do their jobs because of age or injury.

My father cleared his throat and projected out over the floor. "I'll make this quick because I'm sure you are not interested in hearing anyone, even someone as entertaining as I, go on all night." He smiled, and the men laughed politely.

"There are forty-six companies building electric automobiles in this country today. Well, actually, that was yesterday. Who knows how many more sprang up today?"

The men laughed again.

"Of those forty-six companies, only one made history yesterday—Detroit Electric. A Model A Victoria, powered by Edison batteries, driven by Will Anderson, and witnessed by Dr. J. O. Miller, went two hundred eleven and three-tenths miles on a single charge, breaking the Baker Electric record by almost ten miles!"

The men cheered.

"We will be running advertisements in *Horseless Age* and *The Automobile,* not coincidentally the same magazines in which Baker ran the advertisements for their record."

The men laughed and gave a hurrah. They seemed to truly like my father, in spite of what some might feel was a bit of priggishness, and the general tendency of many men to resent their superiors.

"This gives us real momentum. The quality of Detroit Electric automobiles is second to no brand, be they electric, gasoline, or steam." His voice had been steadily rising, and now he shouted, "This year we will overtake Baker as the number-one supplier of electric automobiles in the country!"

Applause and whistles echoed through the plant.

He held out his arms, quieting the men. "But our job has only begun. Remember, our competition is not just electrics but all automobiles."

"Even Ford?" one man called out from the back.

The rest of the men erupted in laughter.

"All right, all right," my father said with a chuckle. "I'll concede it may be a stretch to say all motorcar companies are direct competitors. But we can't forget about Pierce-Arrow, Lozier, and Packard, even Cadillac. They all compete with us for the same affluent customer. Remember, in Detroit alone there are more than thirty companies that will produce over two hundred thousand automobiles this year. Our production is a small fraction of that.

"But . . ." He paused for dramatic effect. "The Edison battery gives us the opportunity to compete with gasoline motorcars in touring. This has been the only real obstacle in our battle against the manufacturers of internal combustion engines. But to continue to rise above the other makers of electrics, we will need to work together, striving hand in hand, to improve our quality even further, to build the best automobiles ever produced."

He smiled again, warmly, and held out his hands as if to hug the entire group. "And the only reason this is possible is that you men are the best autoworkers in the country. Now go on, get home before your wives start searching the saloons."

A cry went up. "Three cheers for Mr. Anderson!" As the men hurrahed, my father's face lit up, and his blue eyes sparkled. He loved his work. He loved his men.

After the party, my father asked me to join him in his office. We sat facing each other across his desk. He was no longer grinning. "I talked to Mayor Breitmeyer and the police commissioner. They both agreed to do what they could to keep you out of the investigation into Cooper's death. The commissioner said he would relay that message to Detective Riordan."

"Thank you, Father."

He shook his head. "But we can't have this kind of distraction at the factory. You're going on vacation. Starting tomorrow."

I took a deep breath and nodded. "All right." It would give me time to work this out. "For how long?"

He shrugged. "Until I tell you to come back."

"But I've only got a week coming."

"You've got money saved, don't you?"

"Yes, some."

He stood, signaling the meeting was over. I followed suit.

"I won't let you starve." He came around to my side of the desk, put his arm around me, and steered me toward the door. "Will, I don't believe you capable of murder, and I'll do everything I can to help you. I just don't think it's a good idea to have you around here right now."

I nodded. "I understand. Thank you for your support, sir." We shook hands, and I left his office.

I took a streetcar to Elizabeth's house. No lights were on, but I knocked anyway. I asked the neighbors on both sides if they knew where the Humes had gone. They had no answers. I waited on the porch for almost two hours, but no one appeared.

The streetcar ride home seemed to take only a few seconds. I was thinking about my predicament. Suspected of murder, banished from work, and unable to help Elizabeth. They say trouble comes in threes. I hoped it was true.

I put on my winter coat and sat out on the fire escape with a bottle of bourbon, smoking and thinking. I thought about John and Elizabeth, about Riordan and my father, about how I had been spiraling into the abyss ever since I ruined Elizabeth's life. At one in the morning, dispirited and staggering drunk, I went to bed.

I finally woke the next morning after ten with a bone-dry mouth and native drums pounding in my head. I made a pot of coffee and sat at the kitchen table, trying to figure out how I could best help Elizabeth. Nothing of value occurred to me. When I walked out of the kitchen, I froze. A white envelope lay on the carpeting in front of my door. I picked it up cautiously, as if it might contain explosives. Just like the previous one, WILLIAM C. ANDERSON, JR.—OPEN IMMEDIATELY! was typewritten on the front. Had it been there when I first walked into the kitchen? I couldn't remember, but as bad as I felt, that wasn't remarkable.

I opened the door and stuck my head out into the hall. No one was there. I closed the door, ripped open the envelope, and unfolded the letter with trembling hands.

*Dear Will,*
    *I have decided to sell your clothing back to you. Bring $1,000 in an envelope to the clock tower at the downtown Michigan Central Depot at 5:00 P.M. tomorrow night.*
    *Come alone and unarmed.*

*If you bring in the police or deviate in any other way from these instructions, the clothing will immediately be delivered to Detective Riordan. This is our little secret, Will.*

*See you tomorrow.*

I didn't have a thousand dollars. The money I had on hand and in the bank totaled just over six hundred, a tidy savings for a twenty-two-year-old with an expensive drinking habit. But where would I get another four hundred dollars?

It was unthinkable to ask my father. He would force me to tell him what was going on. My mother wouldn't be able to get it. My sisters wouldn't give it to me. Elwood and Joe were the only people I could think of. They weren't wealthy by any stretch, but maybe one of them would surprise me.

I sat at the kitchen table and reread the note. In the first letter the blackmailer addressed me as Mr. Anderson. This time he called me Will. That seemed to indicate he knew me. I knew no one in the AFL or the IWW. I came back to Ben Carr and Wesley McRae. Ben was the only person who knew I had taken out the Victoria. He would have been able to follow me to the factory and then gone to my building. He could have seen me come out with the clothing. I couldn't imagine he had anything to do with John's death, but if the killer and blackmailer were two different people it might be possible. He didn't have much money. A thousand dollars would be a year's pay for him.

No. I was being paranoid. I had known Ben most of my life. He was a nice guy, an honest guy. Besides, he could never have written the notes. The grammar and vocabulary suggested a highly educated person, which he certainly was not. I doubted Ben even had access to a typewriter. I decided to forget those suspicions. It wasn't Ben.

Could it be Wesley? He was educated and articulate, and he knew I was out that night. His friendliness could be a ruse, an attempt to throw off suspicion. To get the letter up to my apartment, the blackmailer had to have access to the building. He either lived here or knew the trick to opening the back door.

But that wasn't exactly a secret. Anyway, Wesley had been friendly since I'd moved into my apartment. No one would wait a year and a half to spring a blackmail scheme. And a thousand dollars would be insignificant to him. He had plenty of money, that was certain. Just the settee and chairs I'd seen through his doorway were worth as much as my parents' entire houseful of furniture.

My mind reeled as I tried to think who else it might be. I had so little to go on. For a split second, I considered bringing the notes to Riordan, but that seemed like the worst thing I could do. Once he got my clothes, I was on my way to prison.

I would have to pay the blackmailer. If I got the clothing back, it might be possible to worm my way out of this. If not . . .


That afternoon, I crammed on board a streetcar, trying to ignore the irritating Wrigley's Spearmint Gum advertisements pasted everywhere. You couldn't turn around without seeing some sort of advertising for this gum. Wrigley was wasting an incredible amount of money trying to promote a flavor no one wanted.

A few minutes later, I hopped off and jumped another trolley that took me up Michigan Avenue. I figured I'd try Joe first, given that he was the elder of the two. Hopefully, he'd been able to put away some money. I walked the last two blocks, down Twenty-second Street to his house, a narrow white clapboard two-story with an enclosed brick porch on the front.

A metallic pounding on the other side of the house caught my attention. I walked up the drive, where I could see Joe's legs sticking out from underneath an old delivery wagon propped up on jacks.

"Joe?"

He slid out from underneath the wagon, a quizzical expression on his face. "Will. Hi."

"Have you got a minute?"

He pushed himself to his feet and wiped grease off his hands with a rag hanging on the side of the wagon. "Sure. What can I do you for?"

I leaned in close to him. "If you've got it, I need to borrow some money. Quite a lot of it."

"Sure. What do you need?" He pulled his wallet from the back pocket of his trousers.

I hesitated. This was stupid. But I'd come all the way down here. "Four hundred."

"Dollars?" He was incredulous. "What do I look like? J. P. Morgan?"

It was as I thought. Still, my heart sank. "Yeah, sorry. Never mind."

"I could maybe come up with twenty bucks. But that's about it."

"No, that's all right. Don't worry about it."

With fear beginning to fog my mind, I took a streetcar to Elwood's house—same result. I was out of ideas. I returned home and paced the floor, much too nervous to sit. My father was my only hope. But he'd never give me the money unless I told him where it was going. No plausible lie occurred to me, and I couldn't tell him the truth. He'd involve the police, force me to tell them what I'd seen that night. Riordan would never believe it. I'd be going to jail for the rest of my life.

The blackmailer wasn't my only concern. I called the Humes' house, and Alberts answered. When I asked for Elizabeth, he said she wasn't home and declared in a frosty voice that he would inform her I had called. Should she be interested in speaking with me, she would call back.

I hung up and grabbed a bourbon bottle.

I drank and I thought. Eventually I just drank. By that evening, my apartment had begun to feel like a cell, so I climbed out the window and sat on the fire escape with my bottle, looking out over the back lawn, huddling down inside my greatcoat to stay warm. Three or four blocks away, a small fire flickered through the darkness. The faint odor of burning leaves carried over the wind.

The first time I saw Elizabeth, her face was lit by the dancing flames of a bonfire. We were seventeen. I'd come to a Halloween party with some school friends. Perhaps two dozen people stood around the fire, but I saw only one.

I couldn't breathe. I'd heard men say that a woman's beauty took their breath away, but I'd always considered the idea to be a mawkish exaggeration. Yet I couldn't catch my breath. Her auburn hair hung in soft curls around her finely cut face—a perfect face with large eyes, high cheekbones, soft lips—a face at once aristocratic and kind.

One of my friends nudged me. "Will?"

"Wha—huh?"

"She said hello."

I realized my mouth was hanging open. "Uh, hello," I said.

She wore a long woolen coat that fit her form, a form that promised the same perfection as her face.

I took a step forward and nodded. "Will Anderson. Pleased to meet you."

She beamed at me. I found myself breathless again. Her smile was open and warm, not at all the usual coquettish look of a seventeen-year-old girl. She held out a delicate hand, encased in a dove gray glove of kid leather. "Elizabeth Hume." She cocked her head to the side. "You're a handsome boy, Will Anderson."

"Lizzie!" the girl next to her exclaimed.

Elizabeth let go of my hand and glanced at her friend with a naughty smile. "Well, he is."

I didn't leave her side the rest of the night. The next evening I met her parents.

She had been mine for almost four years.

I pulled out Elizabeth's note and held it up in front of the window, reading it again and again by the lamplight.

A man's voice called up to me. "Hey, Will." In the dark, I could just make out Wesley McRae standing below me, his head tilted back.

I stuffed the note into my coat pocket.

"Mind if I come up for a snort?" he said.

The liquor had dulled my mind to the extent that no excuse occurred to me. "Sure, why not?" I stood, wobbling a little, and began walking down the steps to drop the last length of stairs. "Give me a minute."

"Stay there," Wesley said, pulling his porkpie hat down farther on his head. He jumped into the air, grabbed hold of the metal edge of the landing, and swung himself onto the fire escape like a monkey.

The landing had to have been four feet over his head. "Son of a bitch. How'd you do that?"

He laughed as he climbed the steps. "Gymnastics training. When you're an entertainer, you've got to be ready for any opportunity that comes along." He stopped in front of me, and the light pouring through my window illuminated his feminine features—full lips, large brown eyes, no hint of a beard. His long blond hair curled behind his ears.

I was suddenly uncomfortable, remembering the times I'd seen an older man leaving his apartment early in the morning.

He held out his hand for the bottle. There wasn't anything I could do about it now, so I gave it to him. I hoped he didn't have any diseases I could catch.

Taking a seat in the corner opposite me, he tipped back his head, took a swig, and wiped his mouth with the back of his hand. "Whew! Old Tub, huh? I'm a Scotch man myself, but that's good bourbon." He held out the bottle. "Thanks."

Nodding, I took it from him and surreptitiously turned the top of the bottle against my trousers. He brought out a cigarette case from his jacket pocket and offered me one. I accepted it, though not without some trepidation. He lit mine and then one for himself.

"So." He turned his head and looked out over Second Street. "Nice view up here. I can see why you come out." His breath swirled from his mouth in clouds.

I took a big swallow and handed the bottle back to him.

"Much obliged." He took another drink. "So, Will. What were you reading?"

"Huh?"

"When I was down there." He hooked his thumb toward the lawn. "You were reading something."

"Oh. Nothing."

An uncomfortable silence hovered over us for a few moments before Wesley said, "I couldn't help but notice you've been suffering from a bout of melancholy for, oh, more or less since you moved in. But lately it's been worse, hasn't it?"

I took a deep drag off the cigarette and nodded, keeping my eyes pointed away from him.

"Want to talk about it?"

I grunted out a laugh. "No, but thanks."

He nudged my knee with the bottle. I took it back from him. "Listen," he said. "I've been in plenty of tough situations. Talking always helps. When you talk about it, you think better. And who knows? Maybe I can help."

I cocked my head at him. He was rich. Maybe he *could* help. "Well, I need some money."

"How much?"

"Four hundred dollars."

He was blowing smoke out the side of his mouth and stopped mid-exhale. "Four hundred?" He blew out the remaining smoke and shrugged. "Sure, no problem. But I'll have to get to the bank. Tomorrow soon enough?"

I nodded but couldn't say anything, dumbfounded that he'd agreed without a second thought.

"Why don't you stop by Crowley Milner tomorrow? I'll be there from noon until four. Or I could just bring it back tomorrow night, but I won't be home until late. I'm singing at the Palace Gardens Ballroom."

"I'll come by Crowley Milner. Thanks, Wesley. I'll pay you back as soon as I can."

He waved me off. "Whenever you've got the money to spare. God knows, I've got more than I know what to do with."

Whatever suspicions I'd had regarding Wesley blackmailing me disappeared. My blackmailer certainly wouldn't be lending me money.

We sat up there for quite a while, talking some but mostly drinking. I told him about my father's company and a little about Elizabeth, but I skirted the subject of my current problems. He didn't press the point. When he said he needed to get to bed and started back down the steps, I stopped him and asked him inside for one more drink.

He turned, clearly surprised. "Sure. That'd be nice."

We climbed in the window to the parlor. Seeing it as I imagined it would look from Wesley's eyes, the room was less than impressive. The wallpaper was dull blue. An aged green chenille sofa faced two white upholstered chairs across a small cherrywood coffee table. Flanking the sofa were a pair of scratched end tables. The only other furniture in the room was an old oak bar where I kept my "show liquor"—the single bottles of Scotch, bourbon, rye, Tennessee whiskey, and brandy that were only used when I had guests. My real drinking whiskey stayed in the kitchen cupboard.

Wesley looked around the room. "Nice place."

"Thanks." I asked him to sit, then poured him a splash of Scotch and myself a shot of bourbon. We talked a few minutes longer before he finished his drink and announced it really was time for him to leave.

I led him out of the parlor into the foyer and opened the door for him. The hall was empty, which was more of a relief than I'd care to admit.

# CHAPTER EIGHT

The next morning I woke at five thirty with a hangover. I was already so keyed up I couldn't think. Assuming Wesley really was going to lend me the money, in less than twelve hours I would be paying a blackmailer, possibly the man who'd killed John Cooper. This was insane. My mind whirled. *Pay him. Go to the police. Leave town. Buy a gun and kill him. Pay him.* . . . I had to pay him. It was my only chance of getting out of this and still having the hope of a normal life afterward.

I called Elizabeth again. Alberts said he'd given her the message and refused to answer my questions. With a curt "Good day," he hung up on me.

At eleven I headed to the streetcar stop to go to Crowley Milner, the newest department store in downtown Detroit, hoping to catch Wesley before he started work. The first two trolleys were crammed so full I wouldn't have been able to squeeze on with a shoehorn, so by the time I got there it was nearly noon.

I walked in through a brass-trimmed door onto a floor of polished rose-colored marble, the air fresh and clear with just a hint of perfume. European imports filled the mahogany cabinets, and salesmen and -women, their manners as impeccable as their dress, waited around every corner. I asked where I might find Wesley and was directed to the middle of the first floor, declining three offers of assistance before I saw him. He was sitting at a glossy white grand piano, arranging his music, a small crowd fanned out in chairs to his right. An easel next to the piano held a sign that read, THE GUS EDWARDS MUSIC COMPANY IS PROUD TO PRESENT . . . WESLEY MCRAE, THE SCOTTISH SONGSTER!

"Hi, Wesley."

He looked up and smiled. "Hello, Will." He lowered his voice. "I've got the money for you. I'll just have to get my coat." He stood, but paused and pulled his watch from the pocket of his waistcoat. Glancing at it, he said, "Can you possibly wait forty-five minutes? These slave drivers will dock me if I don't start on time."

Given my state of mind, I didn't want to wait forty-five seconds, but with no other choice, I agreed.

I lit a cigarette and took a seat in the back, near the wide bins of sheet music arrayed behind the chairs. A few men and children were in the audience, although most of the white wooden seats were filled with women—a few younger ones in shirtwaists and skirts of muted colors, more of them dowagers in colorful day dresses of cotton or crepe. I had to duck to see Wesley under the sea of elaborate chapeaus adorned with feathers, baubles, and other assorted gimcracks, some of the hats' brims a yard wide.

Wesley looked out at me and smiled before projecting his voice to the small crowd that had assembled. "Good afternoon. My name is Wesley McRae, and I'll be playing selections from Detroit's own Gus Edwards Music Company for you today. Why don't we start with an old favorite—with a little twist? Here's one of Gus's classics." He played the intro to "In My Merry Oldsmobile" and began to sing. His fingers caressed the keyboard, and his strong tenor filled the store. He replaced every "Oldsmobile" with "Detroit Electric," which sounded ridiculous and threw off the rhymes ("Come away with me, Lucille, in my merry Detroit Electric"). Still, I had to appreciate the effort.

Next, he played a collection of Edwards tunes from the new Ziegfeld Follies show: "The Waltzing Lieutenant," "Mr. Earth and His Comet Love," "Look Me Over Carefully," and more. Ziegfeld was big in Detroit, a city that strove for both the sophistication and the gaiety of New York.

While he played, dozens of people purchased music, most of it from the Gus Edwards bins. Wesley was a good plugger, well worth whatever Edwards was paying him.

After a flourish on the piano and a bow, Wesley stuffed his music into the bench, held up a forefinger, asking me to wait, and hurried to the back of the store. A moment later he returned wearing a gray overcoat, fitting his ivory porkpie onto his head. With a nod, he led me toward the entrance.

I stayed a couple of feet away from his side. He didn't seem to notice.

"Gus Edwards is selling like hotcakes. They can't get enough of Wesley McRae." In an operatic voice, he sang, "The Scottish Songster," and broke out into a laugh. "And I found out this morning Gus is buying another one of *my* songs. 'The Honeysuckle Rag.'"

"That's great, Wesley. Congratulations." I tried to be enthusiastic, but I could hear the indifference in my voice.

"Christ, Will, call me Wes. Wesley's what my mother calls me."

We walked out to bright sunshine. I hadn't noticed it on the way here. The sidewalk was packed with people out enjoying what could be the last of the year's nice weather. I offered Wesley a smoke and took one for myself. We walked against the stream, dodging women's hats, until we reached a little alley next to the store.

He took a quick look around, pulled an envelope from his pocket, and handed it to me.

I slipped it into my pocket. "Thanks, Wesley, er, Wes. I can't tell you how much I appreciate this."

"Don't mention it." He leaned against the brick wall and blew a smoke ring toward the sky. "These new Ziegfeld tunes are the worst. I can hardly bring myself to bang them out on the piano."

"They sounded good."

Giving me a sideways glance, he said with mock seriousness, "To Philistines like you, perhaps." He laughed. "They'll never get a million-seller out of that dreck."

Next to the alley's entrance, the driver of a green Model T laid on his horn. *Ah-ooh-gah! Ah-ooh-gah!* It had to be a Klaxon, the loudest, most obnoxious horn on the market. A People's Ice Company wagon was double-parked in front of him, the driver nowhere to be seen. The man in the Ford, around thirty years old with long side-whiskers and a petulant expression, pounded again on the horn. *Ah-ooh-gah! Ah-ooh-gah!*

I saw red. "How'd you like to eat that horn?" I shouted.

The driver looked at me, startled, and began to say something before thinking the better of it. I realized now I was standing in the street, cigarette crammed in the corner of my mouth, my hands balled up into fists.

Wesley grabbed me by the shoulder and tried to pull me back to the alley. "Will, calm down. Come on back here."

After a long look at the driver, whose eyes didn't leave the back of the ice wagon, I followed Wesley.

He nodded toward the Model T. "He looks like a guy who'd go straight to the cops if you patted him on the back. You've got to make them hit you first—in front of witnesses."

"Sounds like you've had experience."

"Well, let's just say I've had a difficult time getting the Detroit Police Department to see my point of view. They like to exercise their frustrations on people like me."

Taking a long drag on the cigarette, I nodded. *People like him.*

"Will, it's obvious your problem is about a lot more than money. Tell me about it."

I flicked the butt onto the street. "Trust me. You don't want to know."

He pushed himself off the wall and turned toward me. "Listen, Will. You may not understand what being friends is all about. I want to help you."

Friends? For a year and a half, I had treated him like dirt. I stop only to let him loan me four hundred dollars he probably doesn't expect to get back, and he's willing to call me a friend? I searched his eyes and saw only sincerity.

He shrugged. "You just said I should trust you. Well, *you've* got to trust somebody sometime."

"I just . . . all right." I leaned in close to him so I could speak quietly. The words tumbled from my mouth in a torrent, like a Catholic's final confession. I told him about Cooper's phone call, finding the body, running from the police, leaving the cap and Victoria at the factory, and, finally, the blackmail notes.

The creases in Wesley's forehead got deeper and deeper. When I finished, he shook his head and blew out a deep breath. "Do you have the notes?" I pulled them from the inside pocket of my coat. He looked over the pages and laughed out loud. "Unimpeachable, is he? Nobody with a vocabulary like that could be too dangerous."

I grabbed his arm. "The person who wrote this may have put John Cooper on top of that press and crushed the life out of him. He could be very dangerous."

Wesley bit his lip. "Do you think he'll leave you alone after this?"

I thought about it. "The police are already suspicious of me, and they don't even know about Elizabeth yet. If they get the clothing, the trial will take about five minutes. But I might have a chance if the evidence is destroyed." I sighed. "What choice do I have?"

"You're right. But you'll figure something out." He looked at his pocket watch and began to walk back toward the store's entrance, then stopped and clapped his hands. "I'll help. It'll be fun."

"Wes, this isn't playacting. It's my life."

"I know that, Will." He smiled. "And I also know some men who specialize in rough trade. Your blackmailer won't know what hit him."

I walked to the Peoples State Bank in the shadow of the Penobscot Building and got six one-hundred-dollar bills, leaving only a few dollars in my account. I considered trying again to see Elizabeth but didn't think I'd have enough time. Wesley was leaving Crowley Milner early to meet me back at my apartment at three thirty. Besides, the blackmailer was the only person I could think about now. I went home and paced, too keyed up to sit. In a matter of hours, I would be facing a man who may have been responsible for John Cooper's death.

It was almost four when a quiet knock sounded against my door. "Will?"

I looked through the peephole. Wesley, in a long gray coat, stood in front of three men in derbies and rumpled suits. I opened the door.

"Meet the Doyles," Wesley said. "They're going to be helping us out."

The oldest of them, a stout man with gray stubble on his sunburned chin, stepped forward and shook my hand, followed by the boys, who I now saw were twins. They were about the same age as Wesley and me, and were rawboned and rangy, with dark eyes and shocks of rust-colored hair poking out from under their derbies. None of the three spoke.

I was already a bundle of nerves, but Wesley appearing with characters such as these put a shiver up my spine. Mouth agape, I stared at the men for a moment before finally remembering my manners. "Please, come in." I opened the door all the way and led them into the parlor. The Doyles sat side by side on the sofa. I stopped in front of them. "Can I get you a drink?"

The younger men looked at their father. He nodded and grunted. "Whiskey. If you got it." He looked doubtful.

Wesley followed me into the kitchen. "Will, I'm so sorry you have to go through this."

I grabbed five glasses from the cupboard and set them on the counter. "Thanks for the help, Wes." I tipped my head toward the parlor and whispered, "Where did you come up with these guys?"

Wesley grinned. "From time to time I help Mr. Doyle with a few of his business concerns."

"Really?"

"Sure. You haven't seen all my talents." He nodded toward the parlor. "Doyle might not look it now, but he once went seventeen rounds with John L."

That made me feel better. "Are they armed?" I whispered.

He nodded. "In their business you always keep a gun handy. I've got one, too." Wesley pulled a little one-shot derringer from his pocket. He must have seen the skeptical look on my face, because he added, "It's perfect for close work in a crowd. The Doyles are carrying cannons."

"Would you have another I could use?"

He shook his head. "Not a good idea. The blackmailer said to come unarmed. If he searches you, you're done." He put his hand on my shoulder. I flinched. A question showed in his eyes for a second before he said, "With me and my friends watching you, you've got nothing to worry about."

I picked up three of the glasses and gestured for Wesley to take the other two. "Okay. So now what?" A shiver ran through me, and the two glasses in my right hand clunked dully against each other.

"We'll go over the plan," he said. "Such as it is." Wesley picked up the remaining glasses and headed back to the parlor. He seemed awfully at ease, as if dealing with a blackmailer was a daily occurrence for him. It was all I could do to hold on to the glasses.

We walked back into the parlor. I poured five shots of Jack Daniel's and passed four of them to my guests. Wesley and I sat on the upholstered chairs facing the other three men. The Doyles all slammed back their drinks in one swallow. I jumped up, grabbed the bottle, and handed it to Mr. Doyle. He nodded his thanks.

Wesley took a pull on his drink, crossed his legs, and settled back into the chair. "The plan is simple." He looked at me. "Will, you're going to give the envelope to the blackmailer—but *only* after you get the clothes. The rest of us will set up around you, watching. We'll follow the blackmailer, grab him when the time is right, and the Doyles will bring him back to their place. I'll meet you outside the Pontchartrain, and we'll go to their house for a little chat." He uncrossed his legs and tilted his head toward me. "And if anything, *anything,* goes wrong, we'll meet outside the main entrance of the Pontch. Got it?"

I nodded. I was way out of my depth here.

Wesley checked his watch. "All right, Will, you and Robert get out of here." One of the young men stood, and Wesley addressed him. "You keep an eye on Will until we get there. Wait for us at the ferry landing. In case anyone's watching Will, we're going to catch the next trolley."

I left first, trying to appear nonchalant while I peeked around me, looking for anyone paying too much attention. The only place I didn't look was behind me. I hoped Robert wasn't too far back. I also hoped he wasn't close enough to see the shivers passing through me every minute or so.

On the streetcar I caught his eye and quickly looked away, though I was reassured by his presence. After that, I stared at my feet until we got off at Jefferson and walked down to the ferry landing at the end of Woodward. The sun sparkled off the tops of the swells on the river. It was very warm for November, again near sixty degrees.

The *Ste. Claire*, a long white three-story ferry, sat at the dock. A small number of passengers trickled down the gangplank and past me, chatting gaily about their day on Bois Blanc Island. My vision had changed, dark around the outsides, like I was looking through a tunnel. I had a sudden overwhelming urge to urinate, but the train station was the nearest public facility. I couldn't go there yet.

I shuffled from foot to foot until I saw Wesley and the other two Doyles. Wesley nodded his head slowly. I hurried the last three blocks to the train station and stood under the redbrick clock tower. It was five minutes of five. Wesley stopped across the street and leaned against the wall with a newspaper. Mr. Doyle slouched about twenty feet away, studying his fingernails. The street was lined with horse wagons and automobiles, giving them some cover. One of the twins was stationed to my left, near the corner of the building. The other stood to my right, partially hidden between a red Oldsmobile Palace and a black Hupmobile coupé.

A man slammed into me from behind, nearly knocking me over. "Sorry," he called over his shoulder as he trotted down the sidewalk. I stuck my hand in my coat pocket and felt for the envelope. It was still there. Men rushed past me in a blur, hurrying into the station to catch a train or hurrying out, having disembarked. I was jostled repeatedly. Each time I checked for the envelope to be sure it hadn't been pickpocketed. Finally I just left my hand inside my coat, squeezing the envelope, and looked for the man who was blackmailing me.

Five o'clock passed with no contact. The depot grew even busier. Eventually I stopped paying attention, just stood there trying to ignore my bladder, feeling like I had a target painted on my forehead. I glanced up at the clock. It was 5:25, and still he hadn't shown himself.

Someone pulled on my coat sleeve. A boy of perhaps ten years old, with a recessed chin and heavy-lidded brown eyes, grinned up at me. "You're Will Anderson, ain't'cha?"

I looked around. Outside of my confederates, no one seemed to be paying attention to us. "Yes."

"Man says you got a envelope for him. Says I'm s'posed to get it."

I glanced around again. "Where is this man?"

"Says that's none a your business." He dug through his thick black hair and scratched the top of his head.

I squatted down, holding tightly to the envelope in my pocket. "You tell him I need my package before he gets this envelope."

The urchin was still grinning. "Says you'd say that. Money first or no clothes. Says the coppers wants 'em."

I didn't know what to do, but it didn't seem like I had a choice. I hoped the Doyles lived up to their billing. "All right. Where's the clothing?"

"Says it's in locker twenty-seven, but you can't get at it till I gets the envelope outta here."

The lockers were on the track side of the station. Even running, it would take me at least thirty seconds to get there, plenty of time for him to disappear. I exhaled heavily through my nose and took the envelope out of my pocket. The boy grabbed it, but I kept hold. "No funny business, right?"

His brow wrinkled, and he squinted at me. "You see me laughin'?"

I let go of the envelope, and the boy blended into the crowd. Though I thought it unlikely I'd find my clothes, I shoved my way to the back of the depot and looked inside locker twenty-seven. It was empty. I ran back out of the station, looking for the boy or Wesley and the Doyles. None of them were in sight, so I hurried up Woodward to the Pontchartrain Hotel and paced back and forth in front of it.

After ten minutes, a voice called out behind me. "Will!"

I whirled around, expecting to see Wesley. Instead, Edsel Ford, in a dark suit and homburg, climbed out of the blue Detroit Electric brougham his father had bought for him a few months earlier. He bounded up to me, hand extended. "Will, my chum! How are we today?"

I'd met Edsel a few years earlier at the Detroit Automobile Dealers Association auto show. We'd taken to each other but had never become good friends, mostly because he was five years younger than me—only seventeen now—but also because his father didn't hold much truck with the "High Society" crowd. I shook his hand, my eyes still searching for Wesley. "I'm kind of busy right now, Edsel. Could we talk some other time?"

"Oh." He looked confused. "All right." He fixed his dark eyes on mine and nodded toward the hotel. "I've got to rescue my father from a meeting with the Dodge brothers anyway."

I apologized, hoping I hadn't hurt his feelings. I needed all the friends I could get. He told me not to worry about it, clapped me on the back, and gestured toward his car. "Nice acceleration, but you've got to work on the speed. I'll give you the complete review the next time we speak." He walked backward toward the hotel's entrance. "I'll phone you."

I nodded absently, and he headed inside.

Another twenty minutes passed. My bladder about to burst, I ran inside and used the restroom, then ran back to Jefferson and headed east, looking down every cross street and alley. After ten minutes I doubled back and sprinted to the Pontchartrain. Wesley still wasn't there.

I again ran down to Jefferson and west past the train station, my head on a swivel, searching to no avail. Stopping in an alley, I bent over trying to catch my breath. The boy had disappeared. Wesley and the Doyles had disappeared. Panic gnawed at my insides. I ran through the alley shouting Wesley's name. The only reply was my voice echoing off the red-brick walls.

I walked back to the Pontchartrain and stood outside for a while, trying to decide what to do. Thinking Wesley might have gone back to the train station, I searched there—no luck. I hurried up Woodward and down every side street for a quarter mile. I was frantic, yelling his name as I pushed through the people on the sidewalks and streets. Back to the Pontchartrain. Nothing. It had been almost two hours.

I had been to the Pontch often for drinks and was friendly enough with the concierge to borrow his telephone to call Wesley's apartment, on the chance he had gone back there. No answer. I took another loop through the train station. A few people waited on benches, but the lobby had largely cleared out by now. I ran outside and scanned both sides of the road. The curbs, which had been full of automobiles, trucks, and wagons, were also virtually empty now, only two unhitched wagons in front of the station. I headed east again, running through neighbor-hoods of tenements, up and down every street and alley, past restaurants and stores, warehouses and offices. As I progressed, it got darker; few streetlights in this part of town. The stench from the street-side outhouses filled the air. Trash lay in the streets.

Between the buildings, I could see stars poking out of the black sky. I checked my watch. It was eight thirty. Three hours had passed since the boy took the envelope.

I kept shouting Wesley's name while I walked through the streets, now too tired to run. My voice was a hoarse croak. "Wes! Wes!"

A muffled groan filtered up from below me.

I was standing next to a stairway leading to a downstairs apartment. I leaned over the metal railing. A man in a torn gray coat lay facedown at the bottom of the concrete steps, his body sprawled across the stairs, his head on the landing. I recognized the coat.

"Wes! Oh shit, oh shit." I vaulted the rail and ran down the steps. Carefully, I pulled Wesley off the stairs, turned him over, and cradled his head in my lap.

His nose was bent to the right and swollen grotesquely. Blood cov-ered the lower half of his face, and his collar and shirt were stained red. His eyes were slits between bulging masses of flesh. His lower lip was swollen and split open. Blood oozed from a dozen cuts and scrapes on his face. Had I not known this was Wesley, I would never have sus-pected it.

"Will?" His voice was barely a whisper.

I leaned down close to his face. "Yeah, Wes, I'm here."

A tear squeezed out of his eye. "They're all dead."

# CHAPTER NINE

Over the protests of the nurses, I spent the night at Grace Hospital with Wesley. They drugged him before stitching his deeper cuts, setting his nose, and splinting his broken fingers. There was nothing they could do for the cracked ribs or the concussion. He was in the middle of a ward that smelled of iodine and soap. All twelve beds were occupied. The metal bed frames and the sheets were stark white, the walls a dingier tone. The night passed with one or another of the men groaning, crying out in pain, shouting for a nurse, or cursing God. It would have been a difficult place to sleep for anyone not on morphine, but for me, sleeping wasn't on the card anyway. Though I was tired, my guilt kept me awake to watch over Wesley from a chair pulled close to his bed.

Mr. Doyle and his sons had been in my apartment only a few hours ago. Now they were dead. It would be weeks until Wesley could sing, and it was unlikely he'd ever play the piano well enough to perform again. I had destroyed four men's lives by including them in this mess.

It was obvious now the blackmailer and killer were the same man. The thought that two men in Detroit were capable of such brutality was too much to believe.

Perhaps it was partially because of exhaustion, but I couldn't shake the feeling that this wasn't real. None of it. Not John's or the Doyles' murders, not the blackmailer, not Wesley beaten half to death. This was all some gruesome dream from which I needed to awake.

But the evidence was right in front of me. Gauze was wrapped around the top of Wesley's head. Most of his face was covered in bandages. Only his swollen mouth and the mottled purple bulges hiding his eyes were visible.

Around 6:00 A.M. he stirred and began to roll over. His body went rigid, and he cried out.

I put my hand on his arm. "Wes, stay still. You need to rest."

His eyes opened a crack. The irises slid across the red to look at me. "I couldn't do anything," he mumbled, his voice thick, words slurred.

"I'm so sorry, Wes. I didn't know . . ."

He nodded for me to come closer.

I leaned in.

"Did you get the clothes?"

I shook my head.

Wesley's tongue flicked out to wet his lips, and his eyes opened a little wider when he felt them. "We followed the boy to Adelaide Street. He went down an alley. Robert and Andrew followed him, and Mr. Doyle and I looped around the back." Tears began to spill down the sides of his face. "Doyle told me to stay behind him. We went into the alley. He grunted and just collapsed. The boys were piled up in front of him. I . . . couldn't move." His eyes, pooled with tears, searched out mine. "I just stood there, Will." His body shook as he sobbed. "I just stood there."

I touched his shoulder. "You couldn't have done anything, except maybe get killed with them."

His eyes closed. "The man said he was keeping me alive to give you a message."

"Do you have any idea who he was?"

"No." He winced from a pain deep inside him and looked at me again. "He was huge, but his face was covered and the alley was dark."

"Is there anything you remember about him?"

Wesley thought for a moment. "No."

"What was his message?"

He wet his lips again. "When he says come alone, he means it."

A Detroit policeman in a wool overcoat and bobby hat ambled up to us a few minutes later. He looked me over for a moment, twisting the ends of his waxed mustaches, before nudging the edge of the bed. "You awake?"

Wesley's eyes cracked open. "Eh?"

"What happened to you?"

Purely by instinct, I cut in. "He was jumped by a street gang. Young hoodlums."

The cop glared at me. "I didn't ask you." He turned back to Wesley. "What happened to you?"

Wesley groaned weakly and shut his eyes. He was going to let me take this.

After the policeman studied him for a moment, he shook his head and looked at me again. "All right. Where was he?"

"Over off of Second Street by Peterboro."

"What was he doing there?"

"He lives near there. On Peterboro."

"And who might you be?"

"I'm his neighbor."

"And does the neighbor have a name?"

"William. William Anderson."

"Were you with him when he was attacked?"

"No, I came by after."

"What were you doing there?"

"I was coming home—from work."

He eyed me carefully. "Don't suppose you could be mixed up on where you found him, do you?"

"No."

"You boys weren't looking for some fun down on Adelaide?"

"No."

"So you wouldn't know about three dead bodies down there?"

"No."

He kicked the bed. Wesley grimaced. "You weren't down on Adelaide?" the cop said.

"Nossir," Wesley slurred.

It was obvious the policeman wasn't satisfied, but a nurse came to give Wesley a shot and shooed the officer away. Wesley sank into a deep sleep.

I leaned back in the chair and considered whether I had done the right thing. It seemed important to distance ourselves from the Doyles, even though their murders were my best evidence there was another suspect. I needed to puzzle this out, but I was so tired.

I had to go to Riordan. I had to tell him I was at the factory that night. I had to tell him about my clothing, about the blackmailer. It didn't matter what happened to me now. The police had to catch the son of a bitch who had done this to John, to the Doyles, to Wesley.

But I couldn't go to Riordan. If I admitted I was at the factory, they would lock me up—forever. They wouldn't even try to find the real killer. Elizabeth needed my help, and I couldn't provide it to her from prison. I had to help her before I went to Riordan. Otherwise, it might be too late. But first, I had to get hold of Frank Van Dam.

At eight thirty I took the elevator down to the main-floor lobby and sat at the table of one of the polished mahogany telephone booths. I dropped a nickel in the coin slot and asked the operator for the Employers Association of Detroit.

After a few rings, a man came on the telephone and said in a flat voice, "Employers Association."

"Is Frank Van Dam available, please?"

"He doesn't work here anymore."

"Really?" That didn't make sense. "Did he quit or get fired?"

"I'm afraid I can't comment on that."

I tried my most commanding voice. "This is William C. Anderson, Jr., from the Anderson Carriage Company. I need a forwarding address or telephone number."

"I'm sorry, Mr. Anderson. I don't have any information about Frank," the man said. "I'll put you through to Mr. Whirl, if you'd like."

"Yes, please." J. J. Whirl was the secretary and spokesman for the EAD. I didn't know him well but thought he'd cooperate.

A few minutes later another man picked up the telephone. "I'm sorry, Mr. Whirl is unavailable. Should I leave a message for him?"

After asking him to have Whirl return my call, I rang off and leaned back against the wooden wall of the telephone booth. Frank loved his job. The only reason he would have quit—and likely the only reason he would have been fired—was if he was somehow involved in John's murder.

But he followed John around like a little puppy, hero worship in his eyes. Frank wouldn't have killed John or let anyone else do it. It just didn't make sense.

Frank had to be running from the killer. Whoever killed John was a threat to him as well. And he likely knew who that was.

I had to talk to Frank.

At nine, I stood in front of the Humes' door and took a deep breath before knocking. Alberts answered the door. Not hiding his irritation at seeing me, he looked me up and down, finally telling me to wait in the parlor.

A few minutes later, Mrs. Hume, who looked as if she could be Elizabeth's older sister, came down to speak with me. Sunlight beamed into her face, illuminating her delicate features and dark curls. "William." She spoke softly. "You know this is a difficult time for Lizzie. She really can't see you right now."

"Please, at least listen to me."

She squinted into the light, staring at my midsection, then raised her hand to block the sun. "What's . . . what's that on your coat?"

I looked down. My coat was blotched with Wesley's blood. I started, but tried to act calm. "Oh, nothing. Just dirty from working on cars."

She hesitated. "All right. What do you want?" She didn't ask me to sit.

"The night John was killed, he called me to say that Elizabeth was in trouble. He didn't say how, but he was panicked. She's in danger, I know it."

She gave me a sidelong glance. "Will." It sounded like an admonishment. "Why would *John* have called *you*?"

"I . . . I don't know. It didn't make sense to me, either."

"I'd suggest you go home. This is a difficult time for all of us." Her tone softened again. "Lizzie is hysterical."

I took a step closer to her. "Please. She's in trouble, and I want to help her."

"I'm sorry, Will." She put her hand on my arm. "I really am. I always liked you. But you need to understand that Elizabeth has no interest in seeing you."

Shaking my head in frustration, I said, "Look, I'm not trying to trick you. I think someone might want to kill her."

Mrs. Hume jumped back from me like I was charged with an electrical current. "Don't be stupid," she snapped. "The only trouble Elizabeth has is dyspepsia. Perhaps brought on by you abandoning her."

"Abandoning her? I didn't—"

"Go. We're really much too busy for your imagination."

"I'm not leaving until I speak with her."

She glared at me a moment longer, then spun and stomped out of the room. After ten minutes of pacing the parlor floor and still not seeing Elizabeth, I climbed the sweeping walnut staircase to the second floor and knocked on her door. There was no answer. "Elizabeth?" I knocked again. "Elizabeth?"

A door banged open on the first floor, and Judge Hume shouted, "Where is he? Where is that bastard?" A few seconds later his footsteps slapped against the stairway, and he roared, "Anderson, get the hell out of my house!" The judge ran up to me and stopped, quivering, a foot away, his fists clenching and unclenching. He was bearded and balding, perpetually red-faced, heavy in the fashion of prosperous men. Though he was about my height, he always stood ramrod straight, giving the impression he was taller. Now he spoke in a low, trembling voice, like the rumble of thunder. "Get out."

"Judge Hume, sir, I just want to help Elizabeth. You know—"

"Get out of here, you no-good son of a bitch."

"Please, sir, if I could just explain!"

He grabbed me by the collar and dragged me down the stairs to the front door, ignoring my protests. When he threw open the door, it re-bounded off the wall and hit him in the side, knocking him off balance, which made him angrier. With one hand on my collar and the other on the back of my coat, he threw me down the porch steps. I tumbled down the stairway, landing in a heap at the bottom. A sharp pain shot through my right knee.

The judge stood at the top, breathing like a steam locomotive. The thin strands of hair normally pasted over the top of his head were fanned out to the side. He pointed his forefinger at me. "Don't come back. Ever."

"Please, sir, I think someone wants to kill her. Let me explain."

He glowered at me. "No. I don't want to hear your explanations." He gathered himself and pointed to the front gate. "Out!"

I pulled myself to my feet. "All right, I'll leave." I turned and headed down the walk before looking back at him. He stood at the top of the steps, finger pointing over me toward the Detroit River. I pointed back at him. "You're making a mistake."

"I'm making a mistake? *I'm* making a mistake?" Spittle flew from his mouth in a fine mist. "You arrogant piece of dung. The only mistake I've made was not having you killed."

He knew what I'd done to Elizabeth.

I turned away, mumbling, "I'm sorry." I walked out the gate and headed downtown. Helping Elizabeth would be impossible. She hated me. Her father hated me. Besides, if I wanted to stay out of prison I had to find out who killed John Cooper.

As I walked down the sidewalk, eyes on the pavement, Cooper's tele-phoned warning went through my head. *She's in trouble, Will, big trouble.* He had paused for a second. When he resumed, anguish seemed to pour from his voice. *I can't fix it. I need your help.*

John had always believed he could fix anything. And he was nearly right. But now he was dead, killed by whatever malevolent force had taken the Doyles' lives with ease and without a second thought. Eliza-beth's trouble had to be intertwined with these deaths. I was sure she was in grave danger. Even so, I waffled on whether to stay or go back to the hospital, not certain how I could help either Elizabeth or Wesley.

Finally, I decided to wait Elizabeth out. Either her mother and father would leave and I'd try again to get into the house, or she would go somewhere and I'd follow her. There was nothing I could do for Wesley, and it was only a matter of time until I was arrested and my chance to help either of them evaporated.

I limped across the street to a grassy spot a block down from the Humes' and sat in the shadows under a maple tree still half covered with dulling yellow leaves. The street was lined with automobiles and wagons parked on both sides, but I could see the Humes' house clearly through the entrance to the boat ramp, empty this time of year. I picked up a maple leaf and began to idly pick it apart, tearing the brittle ochre skin alongside the veins.

The judge's glossy black opera coach, pulled by two jet-black horses, drove off a few minutes later, his personal chauffeur at the reins. The curtains were closed, but that was nothing unusual. Fearful of assassination, Judge Hume always had the curtains closed.

I watched the white wooden swing on the Humes' porch sway in the breeze, could imagine the creak of the chains as the swing moved back and forth. The porch had been our refuge from Judge Hume, the only spot he deigned public enough for us to be alone. Elizabeth and I would sit on the swing with glasses of iced tea or lemonade, feeling the heat from the other's body, perhaps allowing our fingers to intertwine in the shadows between us.

Five years had passed since we fell in love. Though we had been seventeen, impossibly young, our love was destined, it seemed. But it was gone in an instant, an instant that destroyed both of our lives.

I crumpled the remains of the leaf and threw it aside.

The morning passed with no sign of Elizabeth or her mother. I was beginning to think about abandoning my vigil and going to see Wesley when Mrs. Hume's coupé pulled up to the curb in front of their house. It was a black 1909 Baker Electric, purchased a few months after Elizabeth had made it clear she never wanted to see me again.

A young man in white coveralls climbed out, wiped down the door handle, and locked the car before walking west to catch a streetcar that would bring him back to the Rumsey Garage, the Baker dealer and servicer. I stood and stretched. A few minutes later Elizabeth walked out the front door with Alberts, who was dressed in a gray uniform with knee breeches. Elizabeth wore a periwinkle dress with white lace from her bosom to the dress's high collar, and a matching hat, its brim a yard wide, plumes of egret feathers falling down her back. Emaciated or not, she was breathtaking.

Alberts unlocked the passenger door, held it for Elizabeth, and climbed in the other side. They headed west toward downtown. I followed on foot. The speed limit and snarled intersections made it easy to keep the car's tall coach, not much different from the judge's horse-drawn version, in sight. They turned right on Woodward and right again on Gratiot before Alberts made a U-turn and pulled up to the curb opposite the J. L. Hudson building. Elizabeth got out and hurried into the B. Siegel clothing store. From across the street I saw her in the window watching the automobile as Alberts drove off. She turned away, and I ran across the street into the store.

From the entrance, I did a quick scan and didn't see her. I trotted through the store, looking around racks of colorful dresses and row after row of ladies' hats. Turning the corner into the men's department, I caught a glimpse of periwinkle as it disappeared out the back door. I ran through the store and burst out the back just in time to see Elizabeth, holding up the hem of her dress to keep it out of the alley's mud, turn the corner of the building, and head back toward Gratiot.

My first impulse was to chase her down and force her to tell me what was going on, but I decided that following her might be more enlightening. I peeked around the corner and waited until she turned east on Gratiot, then ran through the alley after her. I expected her to turn off on Broadway, Randolph, or Brush, but she kept going, walking a few steps and then running, seeming torn between speed and inconspicuousness. She looked back a few times, but I stayed a block behind her and out of sight.

Gratiot is lined with businesses and generally safe, but now she entered a dark territory of crumbling tenements and cramped wooden houses. When she turned down Hastings I almost broke into a run to catch her and drag her away. Gray buildings with laundry draped from broken windows slumped over a muddy dirt road filled with trash. The air was foul from the overflowing outhouses along the street. Filthy children played in the mud. Women talked and shouted to each other in Russian, Hungarian, Italian—a bouillabaisse of cultures crammed together.

Elizabeth slowed in front of a squat wooden building near the corner of Hastings and Clinton. The small sign in front simply read DRUGS. She stopped, and looked up and down the street. I ducked behind a horse cart buried to its axles in mud. When I looked out, she was gone. I took a few steps toward the store. The door of the drugstore banged open, and Elizabeth backed out, shouting curses at someone inside, then turned and ran to the equally decrepit wooden building on the corner. I hurried after her, but when I saw the sign over the door, I stopped short, frozen in place.

The sign, a weather-beaten board splashed with faded black paint, read THE BUCKET. I had never been here before, but I knew the name. The Bucket was the most notorious saloon in Detroit, its reputation for violence so great that the newspapers called it the Bucket of Blood.

# CHAPTER TEN

I swallowed hard walking through the mud toward the door Elizabeth had entered. Weathered boards showed through the gray paint flaking off the outside of the building. The sound of a piano playing a surprisingly good version of Joplin's "Elite Syncopations" filtered out under the thick wooden door hanging crooked over a battered sill. I hopped up on the boardwalk, grabbed the door's handle, and pulled it open.

The piano player, a young black man with a cigarette hanging from his lips, pounded on the ivories in the corner. The room reeked of stale beer, cigars, and sweat. A gray smoke cloud hung over a dozen men sitting hunched and lifeless at a chipped walnut bar. Three surly looking white men were playing cards with a grizzled Negro at one of the cracked wooden tables scattered about in no apparent configuration. Seeing the black man at the card table stopped me for a second. There were few Negroes in Detroit, and I had never been in a saloon that allowed them as patrons.

The only women I could see were a pair of prostitutes in heavy makeup and calf-length satin dresses who stood near the card players, rooting them on.

The energetic rag ended with a flourish, and the piano player started in on "Bethena," a mournful tune more in keeping with the environment.

The barkeep, unshaven and every bit as unkempt as the clientele, shouted at me, "He's not here."

I walked tentatively toward him over the stained plank floor, almost on tiptoes. "Who?"

"Whoever you're looking for."

I stopped behind a man on a stool, his head slumped atop the bar. "It's a she," I said. "The young lady who just came in here."

The barkeep spit tobacco juice toward an unseen spittoon and looked back at me with contempt. "She ain't here."

"No, she is." I tried to sound friendly, like I knew he had made a mistake. "I just saw her come in."

"She ain't here." He leaned over the bar and spit a brown wad on my right shoe.

I glanced at my shoe and struggled to maintain an even tone. "Look, I saw her come in here not two minutes ago. Just tell me where she is."

He hawked up a wad of mucus, and I was pretty certain I knew where it would be headed. "Please," I said. "I just want to get Elizabeth—"

"Big Boy!" the barkeep shouted. "Got us a tough guy!"

A man, well, more like a mountain, stood up at the other end of the bar and sauntered over to me with an amused smile on his face. He was tall, easily six-four, and huge, two hundred fifty-plus pounds of solid muscle. His head, the shape of an engine block and probably just as hard, had closely shorn dark hair exposing tiny ears. "I like playing with tough guys," he rumbled, "but you look like you might be a disappointment."

I held up my hands in front of me and backed away. "I don't want trouble. Really. I'm just looking for a girl."

"Ain't we all." He wore a sleeveless undershirt that exposed bulging biceps and triceps and a number of other muscles I was quite sure I didn't even have. I kept backing up until I reached the wall, and he stopped only when his chest touched my chin. Something cold and hard pushed against my ear. Without turning my head, I cut my eyes in that direction. A very large revolver was pointed at the side of my head. My guts roiled.

"We get a lot of hoodlums in here," the giant said. "But we don't get a lot of swells." The cold barrel of the gun caressed my cheek. "And when they get out alive, they never come back." He smiled. His big teeth stood out like pickets.

"Please," I said. "You don't understand. She's in trouble, and I need to help her."

He stepped back and used the revolver to turn me toward the door. The barrel jabbed me hard in the back, and I stumbled forward.

"If she wasn't in trouble before she came in here," the deep voice whispered in my ear, "then she sure is now."

He grabbed hold of my neck and slammed me against the door face-first. My nose crunched and exploded with pain. Bright lights flared in front of me. He tossed me out onto the street, and I collapsed in the mud, tears mixing with the blood streaming from my nose. It was quite a while before I could collect myself enough to stand. I gingerly touched my nose and almost fell back into the mud from the pain.

I didn't know what to do. To go back in would be suicide. Finally, reckoning a live coward had a better chance of rescuing Elizabeth than a dead hero, I crossed the street, hid at the side of an abandoned livery stable, and watched the door. I tilted my head back and pressed my handkerchief against my nostrils, trying to ignore the pounding in my head and the crimson blotches spreading on my shirt.

A few minutes later I heard a muffled scream. I ran toward the saloon, and the screams got louder. When I was halfway across the street, the door burst open, and the giant, holding Elizabeth by the hair, pushed her through it. Screaming hysterically, she flailed her arms at him to no effect.

"Hey!" I shouted, running up to them. "Let go of her!"

The bouncer pulled the big revolver again and stuck it in my face while continuing to hold Elizabeth at arm's length. She thrashed and shouted out vile curses.

A deep voice with an Italian accent purred, "No, Big Boy. Let him take Miss Hume away from here. She might need more motivation." A handsome man around thirty years old sauntered out the door, fitting a gray derby onto his head. He had an olive complexion, waxed mustaches framed by a sharp nose and a small mouth, and a thick shock of black hair.

Elizabeth reached around and slashed her fingernails across the giant's face. He backhanded her, and she flew onto the muddy street. I jumped toward him, but stopped when he thumbed back the hammer on the huge gun.

"I thought I told you to get out of here," he said, and threw a short left into my stomach that felt like it went all the way through me. I landed on the street near Elizabeth. My chest heaved as I struggled for air, a strange groaning noise coming from deep in my diaphragm.

The Italian man leaned over the edge of the boardwalk, careful not to get his shiny black shoes muddy, and looked into Elizabeth's face. "Think about my proposal, Miss Hume. I can make you happy again."

She screamed and leaped to her feet, swinging her fists, but the giant put a hand against her sternum and shoved her off the boardwalk, knocking her on her back again. This time she stayed there. The two men walked back inside the saloon.

Eventually I caught my breath and picked myself up from the mud. Elizabeth was still lying on the street, sobbing. I helped her up, pulled her hat out of the mud, and began walking her toward Gratiot, speaking in a soothing tone. "It's going to be okay. We'll get through this." My nasal voice sounded like someone else.

Elizabeth's body was shaking. I took my first good look at her face. Her eyes were wide, pupils huge. Her face glistened with perspiration, and a line of clear mucus ran from her nose.

"We need to get you to a doctor."

"No, Will," she murmured. "Just leave me alone."

"Elizabeth, you have to see someone."

She wiped her face with her hands, leaving dirty tracks, and tried to straighten her muddy dress. "I said leave me alone, Will. I'm taking care of it." Her voice quavered from the shivers racking her body.

I made up my mind. "No. You're going to a doctor." I bent down and picked her up by the legs, flipping her over my back. My nose started to bleed again. While I trudged along, she screamed and beat me with her fists. On Gratiot I flagged down a cab.

The driver, an old man with a long, wispy beard, said, "Extra buck on account of you're gonna mess up my cab." I nodded, and he jerked on the reins. His horse, which looked every bit as ancient as his owner, clopped to a halt and began to nuzzle at the weeds beside the road.

I climbed up on the step and dropped Elizabeth onto the seat. She curled up against the opposite side and cried. The cabbie turned around. After a long look at Elizabeth, he shot a conspiratorial grin in my direction that made me want to hit him. "Where to?" he said.

"Thirty-five hundred Mount Elliott. Dr. Miller's place."

I swallowed the aspirin and looked up at Dr. Miller. "Are you sure? She's a dope fiend? You didn't leave her in there by herself, did you?" Every time I spoke I was surprised by the nasal sound of my voice. I'd have thought the constant pain would have kept me clued in.

"Stay still." He held my head in both hands, turning it a little from side to side while he looked over his glasses at my nose. "If you're worried she'll disappear, she's locked in the other examination room. As far as the addiction is concerned, I can't say with absolute certainty, but she seems to be in the throes of withdrawal from an opiate. If I had to guess, I'd say heroin."

"How could that happen?"

"It's not as unusual as you might think. Most addicts are women, though they tend to be older than Elizabeth. Most often they become addicted to a patent medicine containing opium, and they try to cure that addiction with heroin."

I just looked at him, dumbfounded.

He shrugged. "That's what it's for. Though progressive doctors don't use it anymore."

His examination rooms were small but well appointed, with paintings of bucolic landscapes on the papered walls. Through the window I could see his garden, stark and lifeless under the gray November sky.

He opened a cabinet and grabbed a small white towel off the top shelf. Handing it to me, he said, "Hold this to your chin."

I took the towel. "I just can't see Elizabeth as an addict. Could it be something else?"

"I suppose so." He stroked his white beard. "She's certainly not volunteering any information."

"How long has it been since she's come in to see you?" I asked.

"Not since her . . . hospital stay last year. I believe she's changed doctors." He thought for a moment. "When was the last time you saw her?"

"Four, no, five days ago." I was losing track of time.

"Was she like this then?"

"No. She was thin, of course. She's lost a lot of weight since I last saw her before that. But she wasn't perspiring and shaking and acting like a lunatic. She was strange, but the opposite of today. When I told her her fiancé had been murdered, her reaction was muted, to say the least."

"Her fiancé was murdered?" Dr. Miller plopped down onto the chair facing me. "When?"

I'd never told him about Elizabeth and John. It was too late to withdraw the words. "Her fiancé was John Cooper, the man who was killed at the Anderson Carriage Company last Monday."

"Good Lord!" His eyes widened behind the little wire-rimmed glasses. "But you . . . Elizabeth . . ."

"I had nothing to do with it, Doctor. You've known me for fifteen years. You know I'm not a killer."

"No . . . no, I suppose not." He shook his head, clearing it. "No, of course you aren't." He was quiet for a moment. "But you say she had little reaction to receiving the news?"

I nodded.

"Then I'd hazard the opinion she is indeed a heroin addict and was under the influence when you saw her last. She should have twenty-four-hour-a-day medical supervision, starting immediately."

"Can she be cured?"

"Temporarily, at least. She needs a week at a hospital to have the drug purged from her system, along with a regulated belladonna delirium to ease the pain. Whether it's a permanent cure is entirely up to her."

I put my hands on my knees and levered myself to my feet. "Then let's get her to the hospital."

He pushed me back into the chair. "First, there's the matter of that nose. Towel to the chin."

I held the towel up, and he stepped around behind me. "Say, Will, I've had a strange noise coming from the undercarriage of my automobile. Perhaps you could—"

He jerked my nose to the right. Cartilage crunched. I shrieked. Blood poured down my face until he grabbed the towel, held it to my nose, and tipped my head back.

Dr. Miller went on with the conversation as though he had not practically ripped my nose from my face. "We can take my automobile to save time. I really would like your opinion on that noise."

I whimpered an okay. A few moments later, he gave me an ice bag for my nose and left the room. I sat with my head tipped back, ice bag held carefully, until he returned five minutes later with a clean pair of trousers and a white shirt for me to wear. He cleaned my nose, getting only a couple of yelps out of me, and plugged it with cotton. I put on the clothing and carefully held the ice bag to my nose. "Could we go now?"

"If you're ready." He put a finger to my chin and tilted my head back before opening the door and walking into the waiting room.

I followed him out. "Would you mind if I tell Elizabeth what we're doing? She's not going to be pleased."

He pulled a key from his pocket and handed it to me. "Here. I'll get the car ready." He took his duster from the coatrack and walked outside while I knocked softly on the door.

"Elizabeth? Lizzie?" There was no response, so I knocked a little louder and raised my voice. "Elizabeth? Can I come in?" Still nothing.

I unlocked the door and opened it slowly, peering into the room over the ice bag. "I'm coming in. Elizabeth?"

The curtains fluttered in front of an open window. The room was empty.

I hopped into Dr. Miller's coupé, and we scoured the streets around his office. When that produced no sight of Elizabeth, I asked him to drive me to her home. It was the only place I could think of. She wouldn't be going back to the Bucket.

Dr. Miller pulled to the curb and turned toward me, resting his left arm on the steering lever. "You know she can't be cured if she doesn't want to be."

I looked over the ice bag at him. "I can't give up on her." My voice was driving me crazy. *I cad gib up on her.*

"Will, you're not going to be able to help her."

I thought about Elizabeth. "Doctor, I owe her more than I could ever repay."

His lip twitched, a hint of a frown, but he started up again and drove to the Humes', parking just down the block in the only open space, wedged between a red Model T and a horse-drawn milk wagon. "I'll wait here for you. If she's home, and if she's willing to go, I'll drive you to the hospital. More likely, when she tells you where *you* can go, I'll drive you home."

I left the ice bag in the car and walked, head tipped back, down the sidewalk and through the gate to Elizabeth's house. I knocked, some-what tentatively, trying to frame an argument that would get Elizabeth to cooperate, if indeed she was here.

Alberts peered through the window in the door and gave a little start, I suspect at my condition. He eyed me for a moment before turn-ing away.

"Alberts!" I shouted. "Is Elizabeth here?" Blood dripped into my mouth.

He turned a corner and was gone. I pounded harder. "Alberts! Al-berts!"

Mrs. Hume's voice barked out from above me. "William! Be quiet this instant!" I leaned over the rail and looked up at the window. She was leaning out over the sill. Her eyes widened when she saw my face. "My God! What happened to you?"

"Has Elizabeth come home?"

Mrs. Hume huffed out a breath in exasperation. "Go away. Now."

I raised my arms, imploring her to listen. "I know what's wrong with her. She's a drug addict. She needs help."

Mrs. Hume slowly shook her head. "It's very sad, what's become of you, Will. Get some help."

"I followed her to the Bucket today! Would she go there if she didn't have a big problem?"

"My Elizabeth is a drug addict who frequents the Bucket." Sarcasm dripped off her words.

"But it's true! Dr. Miller just examined her and—"

"Don't lie to me. Now leave before I call the police." She slammed the window shut.

I stood on the porch for a few seconds and then shuffled down the walk. The driver of the red Model T bent down in front of his car and cranked the engine, which started with a *putt-putt-putt* that carried over the sound of the traffic. He jumped into the car, and without a look back, pulled out directly in front of a farmer in a hay wagon. The farmer jerked his reins to the left, into the path of a carriage coming from the other direction. That driver pulled his horses hard to the right, only just avoiding a collision with the wagon. I watched the Model T disappear into the heavy traffic down Jefferson, leaving the shouted oaths from the other drivers in its dust.

Something about the car nagged at me. Something I should remember. No matter how hard I thought, I couldn't find it, the memory like a fractured image from a forgotten dream.

Dr. Miller climbed out of the car and walked toward me. "Let me talk to her."

Alberts answered the door and stood aside for Dr. Miller. As soon as he'd gone in, Alberts closed the door. I stood on the sidewalk, waiting, hoping I would be invited in to explain.

Dr. Miller had been inside for only a few minutes when the door opened again and he hurried out. The door slammed behind him. He skipped down the steps and marched me to the car. "Mrs. Hume is not in a receptive mood. We'd better leave."

"She didn't listen to you?"

He pursed his lips and shook his head solemnly, then glanced back at me. "Home?"

I nodded. He drove down Jefferson. The road was packed with

bicycles and cars and trucks and wagons and carriages, each one on the tail of the vehicle in front if it, every driver in a hurry. Each cross street was a game of Chicken, the victor not the biggest vehicle, but the most courageous driver. The only consistent winners were the streetcars. They continued on regardless of traffic, the motormen confident their cow-catchers were sufficient to push other vehicles out of the way.

The rapid starts and stops only occasionally brought my awareness out of my head. Elizabeth was a drug addict, desperate enough to go to the Bucket. I had driven her to it with my selfishness and stupidity. I'd known her life would never be the same, never be what she wanted, but as I wallowed in my guilt I'd had no idea of the depth of her sadness. In a year, she'd changed from a vivacious, intelligent woman to an emaciated specter, barely alive.

I had to save her, yet I couldn't find her. And if by some miracle I found her again, I had no idea how I would save her. I was out of ideas. "Dr. Miller?"

He glanced at me for a second before returning his gaze to the road. "Yes?"

"What do I do?"

He was quiet for a moment. "Do you still love her?"

"Yes."

"Then you have to try. But you might get someone to help you." He reached over and gripped my shoulder. "These burdens are easier when shared."

He dropped me off in front of my building. I thanked him for his help and hurried inside. After I poured myself a drink, I chipped some ice off the block, wrapped it in a towel, and lay on the sofa, taking sips of bourbon while trying to keep the ice balanced on my nose.

I took a deep breath and let it out slowly. Elizabeth had disappeared. It was inconceivable she would have gone back to the Bucket after what had transpired there, and in her condition it was unlikely she would go see any of her friends. She didn't want my help; that much was clear. But I wouldn't abandon her. I'd go back to her house, camp out if necessary. When she came home I'd drag her to the hospital. I took a long swallow from my drink.

A door slammed below me and then footsteps pounded up the stairway and ran down the hall. A second later, my apartment door crashed open.

I jumped up and spun toward the door. Two policemen, one of them the rookie with the bottlebrush mustache, ran in from the foyer. Bottlebrush tackled me and flipped me over onto my stomach.

"What are you doing?" I yelled.

"Shuddup, asshole," was his reply. Blood dripped from my nose onto the carpet. He cuffed me, jerked me to my feet, and searched me, before pulling me down the stairs and out of the building to a horse-drawn paddy wagon on the street. The other cop, a powerful-looking man with a two-day beard, large, wide-set brown eyes, and a slack jaw, opened the barred door on the back, and Bottlebrush pushed me in.

The padded walls at one time had been white, but were now an amalgam of sweat and blood and shit and piss. Even through my injured nose, it stunk like a slaughterhouse, the smell of fear permeating everything inside the cage. I was dazed, but kept my head down, so I couldn't be seen through the barred windows on the back and sides, all the while imagining every one of my neighbors looking at the wagon.

My nose continued to drip blood as we made slow progress up Woodward. We were heading toward the Bethune Street police station—Detective Riordan's station.

Fear shot through me. Given the way the police had burst into my apartment, I didn't think I'd been arrested for harassing Mrs. Hume. It seemed more likely the killer, now that he'd gotten his money, had come forward with the clothing. Only slightly less chilling was the possibility the police had gone back to see Ben Carr.

If either of those had happened, my life was over.

When the wagon stopped, Bottlebrush pulled me out of the back.

"Why am I here?" I said, trying to sound indignant.

"I told you to shut up." He pushed me toward the station so hard that I nearly fell on my face. He and his partner marched me to the jail in the back and shoved me down the corridor of cells through a gauntlet of criminals, who described in intimate detail how they would enjoy buggering me, killing me, or both. Their taunts echoed off the brick walls of the jail. I kept my eyes on the floor and put one foot in front of the other, trying not to show my fear. I'd heard plenty of stories about what happens behind prison walls. I would be a target—for humiliation, beatings . . . rape. I struggled to tamp down the panic coursing through me, but it was impossible.

We stopped at an empty cell. Bottlebrush unlocked my cuffs and said, "Gimme your belt and shoelaces."

"What?"

He glared at me. "Now."

I unbuckled my belt and pulled it off, then unlaced my shoes. When I gave them to him, Bottlebrush pushed me into the cell, slammed the door shut, and locked it. The stench of body odor and shit filled the six-by-eight cell, the only contents a moldy cot and a crusted metal pail lying on its side in a corner.

I silently gave thanks that I had no cellmates.

I pushed the cot against the back wall and sat on the end, as far away from the door as I could get. As the hours passed, I got more and more afraid. Though it seemed obvious I'd been arrested for John Cooper's murder, I didn't know for certain.

The criminals in the other cells shouted and cursed, each time ripping all other thought from my head. The night lasted forever. I couldn't breathe, and the lack of alcohol made it virtually impossible to sleep. I caught short snatches, each time waking with a start to noises, real or imagined.

When I woke for the last time, it was still dark, other than a feeble yellow light from a gas lamp somewhere down the corridor. My breath puffed out in swirling white clouds. My hands were numb. My mouth was dry. One of my shoes lay on the floor. Shivering uncontrollably, I pulled my arms and legs in close to my body.

I needed a drink. Many drinks.

# CHAPTER ELEVEN

Footsteps echoed down the hallway, louder by the second. I sat up, trying to still the tremors in my hands. A pair of cops I hadn't seen before unlocked my door, clapped handcuffs and leg irons onto me, and pushed me down the hall to the back door of the station.

"Where are we going?" I said. My swollen nose made my voice unrecognizable.

One of the cops pushed me out the door. "We're gonna take a little ride."

"I want to talk to my lawyer."

He sneered at me. "Fuck your lawyer."

"Listen. This isn't right. I should be—"

He gave me a hard slap to the side of my head and together they threw me into the back of the wagon. The horses started off in a slow but steady gait.

A shiver ran up my spine. Where could they be taking me? It couldn't be anywhere good. Shivering, teeth chattering, I wrapped my arms tight around myself, trying to get control, having no success.

Half an hour later, the cops pulled me out of the wagon and brought me into the back entrance of another building. One step inside, I saw the cells—a jail. They handed me over to the jailer, who locked me in a filthy cell, much the same as my previous accommodations, again by myself.

As he turned the key in the lock, I grabbed hold of the bars and tried to stifle the sound of fear in my voice. "I demand to see my lawyer."

His hand dropped to the gun on his belt.

"You can't do this to me," I said. "Do you know who my father is?"

He grunted out a laugh. "I don't care if he's the czar of Russia. You're staying here today."

"At least tell my why."

"They don't share their plans with me, pal."

"Come on," I said. "You must know what's going on."

If he did, he wasn't talking. As the day progressed, the tremors in my hands increased in intensity, and I broke out in a sweat, soaking my clothes. The cell was cold, and my wet clothing stuck to me, making me colder still. My nose throbbed, and intense pains stabbed behind my eyes.

At some point in the evening, the jailer brought me a plate of food, sliding it under the barred door. "Dinner time," he said.

I jumped up from the cot and rushed to the front of the cell. "I need a drink. Could you bring me something? I've got plenty of money."

He stepped back and appraised me. At that moment I could see myself through his eyes—rich kid, good for nothing, shaking and sweating, desperate for a drink. Still, in a tone that wasn't unsympathetic, he said, "Sorry. No can do, pal." He moved on to the next cell.

"Please?" I called after him. "Please?"

He didn't come back. Again, I lay awake virtually all night. I couldn't remember the last time I'd really slept without at least half a bottle of bourbon in my system. That, and the noise from the other prisoners, kept me awake thinking about my predicament.

The next day was a repeat—up early, a ride to another jail, a day by myself wanting to die. It was excruciating. Not only did I feel terrible, no one would answer my questions. All I could do was sit on the cot or pace the floor. This couldn't be legal. My stomach felt like it had been ripped up. My head pounded. My clothing was soaked through, and my mouth felt like it had been stuffed with cotton.

The following morning another policeman delivered me to the back entrance of the Bethune Street station just in time for lunch—if you can call a plate of beans and a piece of stale bread a lunch.

I was back in Detective Riordan's house. I was in about as bad shape as I could be, on a day that could decide the course of my life.

Whether I liked it or not, it was pretty clear things were coming to a head.

Detective Riordan pulled a cigar from his coat pocket and swept it under his nose, inhaling the tobacco aroma. "You are a real hard case, aren't you?"

I was shaking so much there was no chance of keeping my voice steady. "What? No. What are you talking about?"

"That poor Ben Carr fella. Didn't hardly do anything, and yet he's an accessory to murder. With three little kiddies at home. That's going to be tough on them."

"He didn't do anything. And neither did I."

Riordan chuckled. "You took the Detroit Electric Victoria from the garage half an hour before our men found it in front of the factory. It would have taken you fifteen minutes to get there. You work fast, don't you? I'd have thought Cooper would have been a bigger task than that. Or did Ben help you kill him, too?"

"He didn't do anything. I changed the book."

Riordan just stared at me, a sour look on his face.

*God damn it.* "All right, I was there! Happy?"

He lit the cigar, puffing at it until his face was hazy behind the gray cloud. "Why'd you do it?"

"Why'd I . . . I didn't kill him, Riordan! It had to be the unions."

"Yeah, yeah, I've heard it before." He shook out the match. "Okay, I'll humor you. What were you doing there?"

"Cooper called me. At eleven. He said his fiancée was in trouble, and he needed to talk to me about it. I got the car and went. When I got there, he was already in the press."

"You told me before you always take the streetcar to work. Why'd you get the automobile?"

"Well . . . I thought I might have to leave quickly."

"You were afraid of your friend?" he said with a smirk.

"Yes," I muttered.

"Why?"

He clearly knew the answer, which startled me. I tried not to show it. "He wasn't my friend."

"And why is that?"

My head dropped. I stared at the table and mumbled, "His fiancée used to be my fiancée."

"What's that, Will? Could you speak up?"

I glared at him. "Elizabeth Hume and I were going to be married."

Riordan rolled the cigar around in his fingers, looking idly at the lit end. "I had me a talk with Judge Hume, Will. He says you threatened to kill Cooper."

I glared at Riordan. "If I did, I didn't mean it. It's just something you say when you're drunk."

"Oh, I don't say that, Will. You could say, 'It's something I say,' or 'It's something one says.' But not me. I don't say that."

"Look, Hume hates me. He'd do anything to get me life for this."

"You didn't tell me about this little love triangle before, Will. Why is that?"

"You know why, Detective. Because it makes me look guilty. But I swear I had nothing to do with John's murder."

He bit his lip, tightening the scar across his face. "Nothing to do with the murder." He chuckled. "The man who is going to marry your ex-fiancée is murdered at your father's factory, in your department, and you're the only one there when he dies, but you had nothing to do with it." He laughed again. "Old Mother Goose has nothing on you, Will Anderson."

"Do you really think I'd be stupid enough to kill John at the factory?" That sounded bad. I quickly added, "If I was going to kill him, which I wasn't. Someone is trying to frame me."

"Then why'd you run?"

"I panicked. I knew how it would look, and I just panicked. I'd been drinking."

"People say that's a problem for you, Will. The drinking, I mean."

I shrugged. "Look. You have to talk to Frank Van Dam. He doesn't work at the Employers Association anymore, and they won't say why. His mother says he's not at home but won't say where he is. I think he's running from whoever killed John."

Riordan blew a cloud of smoke in my face. "You're going to prison until you die. And there's not a single thing your daddy can do about it. For the first time in your silver-spoon life, you're on your own."

"Listen to me!" I was yelling now. "Find Frank! He's the key to this."

"That may be so," Riordan said with a smile, "but Mr. Van Dam moved somewhere out west before Cooper was murdered."

"He did?" I tried to regroup. "Well, you've still got to talk to him. He'll know why John was killed."

"I've already got that one figured out, Will."

I only had one arrow left in the quiver. "Well, then, whoever the real killer is, is trying to blackmail me."

"Blackmail now, is it?"

"Yes. He says he's got my clothes. When . . . when I got back from the factory I had blood on my shoes and trousers. I threw them away."

"Should have burned them."

"The next day I got a note saying someone had taken my clothes from the garbage and was holding them."

"Holding your trousers ransom, was he? And how much was he charging you for their safekeeping?"

"I gave him a thousand dollars. And I didn't get the clothes back."

"That wasn't very smart, was it?"

"No," I admitted. I wavered on telling him about the Doyles' murders and Wesley's beating. Wesley was the only one who could corroborate my story about the blackmailer, but I had to talk to him first. And I couldn't involve him in the Doyles' deaths. I wasn't sure it was in *my* best interest to tell Riordan about the Doyles. I had to think this through.

Riordan ground out his cigar in the filthy ashtray. He looked up at me and spoke, his voice lilting like a gentle stream. "Enough fairy tales, Will. Really. No matter what you say, and what strings your father tries to pull, you're going up the river. You need to think of your dear, sweet mother. What will it do to her if you drag this out? And what about your father's company? How long will this have to be out of the news before people forget? Would you buy an automobile from the father of a cold-blooded killer?" He sat back in his chair, pulled a *Detroit Herald* from his coat pocket, and looked at the front. "Hmm, the Electric Executioner." He rolled the words around in his mouth. "The Electric Executioner. Got a nice ring to it, doesn't it?" He turned the paper toward me. Stretched across the entire top of the page was ELECTRIC EXECUTIONER APPREHENDED.

I stared at the paper, not able to react. Riordan set it on the table and leaned forward. "We haven't released your name yet, but wait until we do. The newspapers haven't seen anything this juicy for years. Cooper was a big football star, and you picked such a nasty way to kill him. And it doesn't hurt that Elizabeth Hume is a real looker."

I stared into his eyes, getting angrier and angrier.

Riordan smiled. "The newspapers will practically put up tents outside the factory and your parents' and the Humes' houses. I guarantee you headlines like this every day. And not just in Detroit. This is national news. New York, Washington, Chicago." Laughing, he said, "Heck, this'll be big all the way around the world."

He got a faraway look in his eyes, and began to speak, his hand drawing out an imaginary headline in front of him. "'Wealthy Heir to Anderson Carriage Brutal Murderer.'" He thought for a moment and made the motion again. "'William C. Anderson, Jr., Convicted of Killing Cooper.' No, no." He laughed again before drawing his hand in front of him one more time. "'Electric Executioner Exterminates Romantic Rival.'" He grinned his jack-o'-lantern grin and winked at me. "Alliteration. They taught us the King's English quite well back in Ireland."

I stared at him, bleary-eyed. "I didn't kill him."

"Look, Will." He put a hand on my forearm and spoke quietly again, as if he were simply trying to get me to listen to reason. "If you confess, in a week or two this will all go away. But if you keep saying you didn't do it and take this to trial, well, you're going to be driving a nail into your mother's heart every day for months." He patted my arm. "You don't want that, now, do you?"

Anger flared in me. "Jesus Christ, Riordan. How many—"

He reached over the table and slapped me across the face, almost knocking me out of the chair. A stabbing pain shot through my nose. He sat back and smiled. "I don't like to hear the Lord's name taken in vain, Mr. Anderson."

I wiped the blood off my mouth and glared at him. "I want to see my lawyer."

"I don't care what you want. Tell you what. All you've got to do is confess, and I'll let you see your mommy and daddy."

"I'm done talking to you."

Looking disappointed, he sat back in his chair. "So that's the way it's going to be. All right. But I guess we've got some paperwork to do first. And I might as well get this out of the way." He stood, towering over me, and said, "William C. Anderson, Jr., you are under arrest for the murder of John Cooper." He walked out the door and slammed it behind him.

I sat there for another hour, hands trembling and legs twitching, before a cop opened the door. Without a word, he pulled me out of the chair and shoved me down the hallway to a wall-mounted telephone. I picked up the receiver and asked the operator for my father's office number. She connected me. The policeman slouched against the wall a few feet away.

Wilkinson answered. "Mr. Anderson's office."

I could barely summon the courage to speak. "Mr. Wilkinson," I muttered. "It's Will. I need to speak with my father."

"He's in a meeting right now, Will. I'll ask him to call you later."

"No! I need to speak with him now."

"Will, he can't just drop everything for you. He's got business to—"

"I'm in jail."

For at least three seconds the only sounds coming from the telephone were traces of ghostly voices, then Wilkinson said, "I'll get him."

A few minutes later, my father was on the phone. "You're in jail?" he demanded in a whisper.

I was so close to tears I didn't trust my voice. "Father, I need a lawyer."

"Where are you?"

I told him I was at the Bethune Street station.

"All right. We'll be there soon. And William?"

"Yes?"

"Don't tell them anything."


Mr. Sutton paced around the interrogation room like a tornado—in front of me, behind me, in front of me, behind me. "Christ, Will, we'd better start working on an insanity plea." His words shot from his mouth like bullets from a Gatling gun.

My father said Mr. Sutton was the best criminal attorney in Detroit, but he didn't look like anything special—average size, conservative gray suit, short brown hair parted in the center, thin lips, muttonchop whiskers. But if his mind operated as quickly as his mouth or his body, I might have a chance. He hadn't stopped moving since he entered the room.

I leaned forward and set my hands on the table. My handcuffs clanked against the wood. "I'm not insane, and I didn't kill him."

He stopped, leaned over, and spread his palms flat against the table. "But you're not going to tell the police about the Doyles or Wesley McRae?" The inactivity seemed too much for him, and he jumped away from the table and resumed his hurried circles around the room.

I hadn't planned to talk about Wesley or the Doyles, but I'd ended up telling him everything that had happened since I found John at the factory. "If I told the police about them, would it get me out of here?"

"It won't be enough to get them to drop charges, but McRae's testimony might be the difference between conviction and acquittal. You have to tell the police now." He stopped behind me, leaned in, and whispered, "And you have to tell them about everything, including the Doyles."

"I've got to talk to Wesley first. I'm not even sure he'll testify."

Sutton stopped pacing and shook his head in disbelief. "With his friend on trial for murder? He'll testify."

"We're not really friends," I said automatically, and regretted the words before they finished coming out of my mouth. I shook my head. "No, you're probably right. But I should talk with him first."

He sighed and looked up at the ceiling. "He's still at Grace Hospital?"

"I don't know. Probably."

"All right, I'll go see him when we're done here." I started to protest, but he waved me off. "I'll make it clear you're not saying anything about him until he gives his approval."

"Okay. But until then I don't want you to mention him. Or the Doyles. Look, you've got to find Frank Van Dam. He'll know who would have wanted to kill John." I explained to him who Frank was, and then said, "Oh, and I need a favor."

He looked at me, eyebrows arched.

"I need you to find out if Elizabeth Hume—Judge Hume's daughter— has returned home." He started to say something, but I cut him off. "It's personal." He nodded, and I finally asked the question that had been worrying me. "Can you get me out on bail?"

He jumped into the chair across the table. Lips pursed, he looked at me for a long moment while his hands tapped staccato rhythms on the wood. "Unfortunately, the arraignment and bail hearing won't be until Monday."

"It's . . . Friday today?"

He nodded.

"Shit."

"Exactly. But they are going to keep you in a cell by yourself, so you shouldn't have too much to worry about."

"Is this why they ran me around town for the past couple of days? So they could hold me without charging me?"

Sutton nodded. "It's called 'running the circuit.' Not legal, but it gives the police time to build a case without defense lawyers getting in- volved. I'm sure they were very busy investigating while they drove you around town. Your father and I have already lodged a protest with the mayor, for all the good it will do us. The police will just claim ad- ministrative mistakes were made." He shook his head. "But the good news is that, now that the story has broken, they're going to want the newspapermen out of here almost as much as we do. And you could be a political hot potato for the mayor, so I don't think they'll slow down the process any further."

"Will you be able to get me out of here Monday?"

He cupped his chin in his hand. "I think we've got a chance. You'll be formally charged, and the judge will either set bail or deny it altogether. The district attorney has made it clear he wants to keep you here, but with your family's reputation, bail's not outside the realm of possibility. If the judge does grant you bail, it's going to be a substantial sum."

"And if he doesn't?"

"Then you're here for however long it takes. Could be months."

A lead weight dropped in the pit of my stomach. Even with Wesley's testimony, I had no illusions about my chances of being acquitted. If I didn't get bail, I would likely be spending the rest of my life behind bars.

The catcalls began as soon as the guard and I walked back into the jail. Though I tried to hide it, inside I was quaking. If these criminals were set loose on me, I would have no chance. An idea began to take shape, and I weighed it carefully. Death would be immensely preferable to life in prison, especially life with no chance of helping Elizabeth.

By the time the guard locked me in my cell, I had decided: If I was granted bail, I would use the time to try to resurrect Elizabeth's life. When that was done, or if I wasn't let out, I'd find a way to kill myself. I wasn't going to spend the rest of my life in prison.

# CHAPTER TWELVE

The interrogation room was beginning to feel like my home away from home. Detective Riordan sat across the table from me while Mr. Sutton wore a hole in the floor behind me. His shoes creaked every time he spun around. When Sutton told me Elizabeth had returned home the evening I'd been arrested and that the police weren't pressing charges against Ben Carr, I had thought things were looking up. I had also thought Wesley's agreement to testify would make a difference. Now, looking at Riordan, I wasn't so sure.

He couldn't have looked any more incredulous if he'd tried. "So Will Anderson and his merry men traipse across Detroit to catch a blackmailer. Three of them are brutally murdered, and one is beaten within an inch of his life. By one man."

With a sinking feeling in my stomach, I nodded.

"That is precisely what happened, Detective," Mr. Sutton said. "The same man who killed John Cooper is also responsible for the murders of the Doyles and the attempted murder of Wesley McRae." He threw the blackmail notes down on the table in front of me. "Here are the letters Will received from the killer. All you have to do is read these to know he's innocent."

Riordan picked up the notes and glanced at each before tossing them aside. "I'll look at them." He sat back in his chair. "Where were we? Right. Will's compatriots were a convicted pervert and three common criminals." He turned to me. "The pervert I believe. But come on now. The Doyles? Thieves and cutthroats with an arrest sheet as long as my arm? What would they be doing with you and your fairy friend?"

I ignored his comments about Wesley and stared at him coldly. "I employed the Doyles to help with the blackmailer. I had never met them until that day." I certainly wasn't going to tell Riordan that they and Wesley had done "business" together. "Find the boy who took the money. He can lead you to the killer."

Riordan looked at a sheet of paper in front of him. "Find a boy who is 'approximately ten years old with brown hair and brown eyes, probably from the lower class, possibly Jewish.'"

"With a recessed chin," I added.

"Any needles in haystacks you'd like me to come up with while I'm at it? Anyway, you said you and McRae were near your apartment building, not down on Adelaide."

"I lied."

He looked up at Mr. Sutton. His eyes moved back and forth as they followed Sutton's pacing. "Mr. Sutton, I'm having a hard time keeping your client's story straight. He's not at the factory, then he is, he doesn't hate John Cooper and then he does. Now his buddy is beaten on one side of town and they know nothing of the three dead men, and then they're all best friends. Maybe we should have him write his testimony on a chalkboard so you can erase the parts you don't like. Then you wouldn't be tied down by little details like perjury."

Sutton stopped behind me and gripped the back of my chair. "Detective, there's no reason for sarcasm. Mr. Anderson was afraid, just like any boy in his position would be. He's telling the truth, and Mr. McRae will back him to the letter."

"No wonder, now that Will's got a crackerjack lawyer defending him." Riordan's eyes twinkled. "Next, he'll be on a spy mission for President Taft. And no doubt the president will back him as well."

———

The arraignment was short, but decidedly not sweet. I was charged with murder in the first degree, to which I pled not guilty, and the judge moved on to determine bail. He took his time, shuffling papers around in front of him, occasionally glaring over his reading glasses at me.

I'd finally gotten a shower and shave. It had been a shock seeing myself in the mirror. My nose was red and puffy, and bruises spread under both my eyes, deep maroon to blue and green. Still, I was generally clean and had even seen a little sunshine on my trip to the courthouse in the paddy wagon, though it was hard to enjoy with the sour reek absorbed into the padded walls.

The judge cleared his throat and looked at the prosecuting attorney, E. M. Higgins, a rotund man sweating his way through an ivory-colored summer suit. "What does the state recommend for bail?"

With a smug look at Sutton and me, Higgins said, "Your Honor, given the heinous nature of the act and the overwhelming evidence, the state would ask that you deny bail."

The judge turned to my attorney. "Well, Mr. Sutton?"

After arranging his notes on the table, Sutton leaped from his chair. "We would ask, Your Honor, that Mr. Anderson be released on his own recognizance—"

"That's outrageous!" The prosecutor jumped from his seat. "Your Honor!"

Sutton raised his voice over the top of the prosecutor. "—being that he is from one of the most respected families in Detroit and clearly not a flight risk."

"Mr. Sutton," the judge said, "your client is accused of murder in the first degree." He glanced at me, then looked back at Sutton. "But I don't believe Mr. Anderson is a flight risk, nor do I believe he is likely to perpetrate any violent crimes if he is released. I'm going to allow bail, but I'm setting it at two hundred and fifty thousand dollars."

The crowd behind me gasped and chattered among themselves. The judge pounded his gavel and spoke over the top of them. "Mr. Anderson, I am gambling on your character. Should you be able to raise two hundred and fifty thousand, you will be released until your trial. However, if you violate the terms of this bond, you will spend that time in the city jail. Do you understand?"

When I heard the amount of the bail, I slumped in my chair. Now I barely looked up to reply. "Yes, Your Honor."

The judge picked up the papers on his desk and straightened them. "I'll see you all back here for the preliminary hearing on Monday, November 28, at 9:00 A.M. Anything else?" He looked at Higgins and then Mr. Sutton.

"Yes, Your Honor," Sutton said. "Until the bond is posted, we would ask that Mr. Anderson is allowed to remain in solitary confinement for his own safety."

The judge looked amused. "Safety from what?"

"The other prisoners, Your Honor. Mr. Anderson, being, well, of a certain class—"

"Save your breath, Mr. Sutton. That's already been arranged by the mayor's office. Why do you think he hasn't been in the pound?" He banged his gavel. "Adjourned." He stood and walked out a door in the front of the courtroom.

Two hundred and fifty thousand dollars. I supposed there was some chance my father could raise that kind of money, but I couldn't imagine he would be willing to risk that much on me. I turned around and looked back at him. His face was ashen.

I spent the rest of the day and night in the same dank cell. Though it was freezing, I was covered in a film of sweat.

Life in prison. A death sentence seemed the more humane fate. At least then it would be over quickly.

A couple of years ago, my father had seen Thomas Edison kill an elephant with a 6,600-volt blast of electricity, powered by George Westinghouse's alternating current system. Edison's position was that AC power was too dangerous to be used in the home, unlike his own patented, and competing, direct current electricity. Edison continued trying to scare people off by publicizing the electric chair, a device lethal with AC power, but, of course, not with his DC system. Edison, however, lost "the War of the Currents" to Westinghouse. Though a few DC systems remained, AC had become the standard. A side effect of Edison's demonstrations was that a number of states, looking for a more humane method of execution, had switched from hanging to the electric chair.

Unfortunately, the Michigan legislature wasn't getting on board. With no death penalty, they had no need for "Old Smokey."

At first light I gave up trying to sleep. I was punchy. My nose still throbbed. I had a darkening heaviness about my head and couldn't remember when it had started. It felt like an integral part of me. I had spent the past year in the bottomless abyss of melancholy, but I'd never felt this bad. I would have finished myself right then had I been able to think of a way to do it.

In the late afternoon a surly looking guard opened my cell door and gestured for me to come out. "Time to go, Anderson."

"Where am I going?" Surely they couldn't be taking me to the state prison already.

He didn't say anything, just reached in, grabbed my arm, and shoved me down the corridor past the other cells. I held up my pants with one hand, shuffling along so my shoes wouldn't fall off. The criminals again taunted me, but I was too dazed to care.

I almost collapsed from relief when I saw my father and Mr. Sutton waiting just inside the large barred door leading from the jail into the rest of the police station. They were fidgeting, Sutton from habit, my father from nervousness. Without a word, my father handed me my black greatcoat, and both men turned and headed out of the jail. I pulled my arm away from the guard and hurried along behind them. We stopped at a window, where a smart-aleck cop returned my possessions, including my belt and shoelaces. I put them on, and we walked toward the exit.

Behind me the guard called out, "See you soon." I swallowed my response.

At the door stood two men who looked like policemen, but weren't in uniform. Sutton turned to me and said, "It's crazy out there. Just keep your head down and follow these gentlemen. And don't talk to anyone." He grabbed my elbow and turned me toward him. "Ever. Reporters are going to try everything to get you to talk. Everything you say will be twisted and rearranged to fit their story." He squeezed my arm and looked into my eyes. "If you can't do anything else, keep your mouth shut."

He gestured for the men to go outside. One of them opened the door, and they pushed through it into a mob of reporters. My senses were overwhelmed. The sun was bright, causing me to squint as though I had been in solitary for years. Men were shouting over the top of one another, clamoring for our attention. I was overwhelmed by questions, all some variation of a theme: Did I kill John Cooper?

My father and Mr. Sutton stood on either side of me. We were jostled continuously as we followed the two men who pushed and shouldered their way through the crowd. The noise was tremendous, voices shouting at me from all sides, cameras clicking all around me. I kept my head down and walked as close to the men in front as I could. We finally made it to the curb, where my father's roadster sat. He and I climbed into it while Sutton and the two other men shoved away the reporters.

The roadster pulled away from the curb with a squeal of the tires. My father got it up to fifth speed in a matter of seconds and took the first three corners at twenty-two miles per hour, looking back over his shoulder every few seconds to see if we were being followed. Satisfied, he dropped down to third and relaxed.

I could hardly believe I was back in the real world. Glancing at my father, I asked, "How did you get me out?"

He was quiet for a moment before looking over at me with a furrowed brow. "I put up the company against your bond."

I was stunned. "After I lied to you?"

He shrugged. "You're my son." He paused for a second and then said, "Would you like to come home?"

"Home? Your home?" It didn't seem possible he would still trust me. I had underestimated him. I hoped, for his sake, he wasn't overestimating me.

He shook his head firmly. "It's *our* home, Will."

"No. I won't do that to you and Mother. I should just go to my apartment." After the scene with the reporters at the police station, I could only imagine what the next few months would bring.

I really looked at my father for the first time and barely recognized him. He looked old and feeble. Lines cut deeply into his face. I was overwhelmed with guilt. "Father, I didn't do it. John called me, and I did go to the factory, but he was already dead. I'm sorry I didn't tell you everything before."

He remained quiet, his eyes on the road.

"Don't you believe me?"

He looked at me, surprised. "Of course I believe you. Even with the engagement, I don't think you would have killed John." He shrugged. "I don't think you *could* have killed him. But I don't know how you're going to get out of this. The evidence is overwhelming."

"I know." I glanced at him and said quietly, "Thank you for helping me."

Looking surprised again, he said, "You're my son, Will. Of course I'll help you."

He turned onto Peterboro and hit the brakes. A big man stood outside the door of my building, arms folded over his chest. In front of him were a dozen or so other men, some with cameras, some with notebooks. "He's one of Sutton's men," my father said. "Still, let's try the back. They say it's been quieter there." He threw the roadster in reverse and backed out onto Woodward, narrowly missing a coal wagon before he put the car into first and started down the road again.

He turned right on Charlotte and again onto Second Street. We approached the building slowly, the near-silence of the electric motor a real benefit. No reporters were in sight. "Stay inside if you can," he whispered, "and phone me if you need anything. Otherwise, I'll be back here Thursday at nine fifteen to pick you up. We're meeting with Sutton to discuss your defense."

I thanked him again and jumped out of the car. The bourbon bottle was calling me.

My father said, "Here, take this," and handed me a brown leather briefcase. "Thought you should know what you're up against."

I thanked him again, ran to the back door, and unlocked it. When I threw it open, a burly middle-aged man in a gray suit and derby stepped in front of me. "Hold up there, fella."

"What? I live here."

He looked at me carefully. "Oh, sorry, Mr. Anderson." He smiled and tipped his derby. "Carl Hatch. I'm helping to keep the pests out." He nodded toward the back stairs. "Go on ahead."

I took the stairs to the third floor two at a time. The corridor was empty, and I hurried to my apartment. I got inside as quickly as I could, threw the briefcase on the table by the door, and headed for the kitchen and the glistening row of Old Tub bottles. I used my teeth to pull the cork from one and took a long pull. The heat of the liquor filled my mouth and throat, then my midsection. Another long drink and the warmth spread throughout my body.

The apartment was still. A shaft of sunlight cut across the floor, dust motes cycling through it like tiny snowflakes. I took a deep breath and let it out slowly. The familiar scent of home: upholstery and carpeting, a slight mustiness, a hint of the kitchen—a dollop of coffee, a dash of grease. And, of course, the sweet caramel aroma of bourbon. My heart slowed. My breathing slowed. I was home.

I took a long bath, put on a fresh suit, and walked over to Wesley's apartment. He answered the door looking much better than he had the last time I'd seen him, though, to be fair, it would have been difficult to look worse. His face was bruised, his hands were bandaged, and he moved like an octogenarian, but the twinkle had returned to his eyes.

"Hey, convict," he said.

"I'm not a convict. Not yet anyway. Thanks for talking to the police."

He shrugged. "Don't expect them to believe me."

"No, I don't think they did. But thanks. Listen, Wes, I'm really, *really* sorry about getting you and the Doyles involved in this mess."

"That was my doing, not yours. I volunteered, remember? As did the Doyles. It wasn't your fault." He nodded toward the interior of his apartment and said, "Come on in." He didn't wait for me to accept, just walked back to the parlor.

I followed him, trying to ignore my hesitation. The man had almost given his life to help me, and I was still afraid someone would see me with him.

The parlor was immaculate. The wallpaper was ivory, vertically striped with fine blue swirls. A yellow floral-patterned settee and a matching pair of upholstered chairs, Louis XIV, I thought, surrounded a large mahogany coffee table. A small crystal chandelier hung in the center, and a pair of cut crystal lamps adorned the end tables. Against the wall, a small bar sat next to a sofa table topped by an oversized Victrola with dozens of records propped against it.

Wesley waved me to one of the chairs. "Sit, sit. How about a drink?"

"Sure, thanks."

"I don't have bourbon. Scotch okay?"

"That would be great. Nice place you've got here."

He ignored the compliment and gestured toward my face. "Looks like you took quite a shot. I'd like to see the other guy."

"No. You wouldn't. Trust me."

He bent over the bar, using his damaged hands to try to pour whiskey into a pair of glasses. I thought I should probably help him, but I didn't. He managed to pour a few fingers of Scotch into each glass, then brought me one, holding it between the palms of both hands. When he returned to the bar for his, he said, "I just got a record you should hear—Sophie Tucker. She's unbelievable." He fumbled with the disc record and Victrola, finally getting it to work. A dynamic female voice poured out from the horn. Wesley grabbed his drink and sat on the settee. Cocking his head to the side, he said, "So what are you going to do now?"

"Do? I . . . don't know."

"I'll tell you what I'm going to do. As soon as I'm capable, I'm going to find the son of a bitch who murdered the Doyles. And I'm going to kill him."

"Yeah?"

"Yeah." His face was red. "You don't understand, Will. I've been beaten more times than you could imagine. I don't do that anymore." He looked into my eyes. "He's a dead man."

"I believe you." We made small talk for a few minutes before I finished my drink and stood. "Well, I should probably be going. I've got a lot to catch up on."

With a grimace, he pushed himself off the settee. "Sure, I understand." He followed me to the door.

After I opened it, I turned back to him. "Thanks for the drink. And thanks for everything you've done for me. God knows I wouldn't have done it for you."

He grinned. "Friends, remember? And Will, my offer is still open. I want to help you. If it gets me closer to the killer, so much the better. Don't try to deal with this on your own."

I nodded. "Thanks." I stood at the door for a moment. "Wes?"

He waited.

"Sorry I've been such an ass."

He waved off the apology. "Don't worry about it. I knew we'd be friends." He smiled. "Eventually."

I laughed. Such an optimist had never lived. "What I said about not helping you out with something like this? Just give me the chance."

# CHAPTER THIRTEEN

Bottle in hand, I walked into my den and phoned the Detroit Electric garage. Elwood and Joe would never believe what had happened to me. When the phone was answered I asked for Elwood.

A minute or so later he picked up. "Hello?"

"Elwood, it's Will. How about I buy you and Joe a drink after work?"

"Will. Oh, uh, I can't tonight. I've got something."

"Since when do *you* have anything? Come on, one drink, ten minutes."

"No." He was firm. "I can't. Listen, Will, I've got to get back to work."

"How about tomorrow night then?"

"I'm busy tomorrow, too."

"All right, spoilsport. Let me talk to Joe."

"He's not here."

I glanced at the clock on the wall. "It's not even five yet."

"He had something, too. I've got to go." The line went dead.

I sat back in my chair and stared at the telephone. They both "had something" tonight? Neither of them had ever passed up at least a quick drink. It finally hit me. I was an accused murderer. In their eyes, my friends' eyes, the word "accused" meant nothing.

I sat in the den for a few minutes before walking across the hall and knocking on the door. When Wesley answered, I said, "Listen. I've caused you an awful lot of pain. I know it doesn't come close to returning the favor, but I'd like to have you over for dinner tonight." I hesitated, and added, "Just . . . friends sharing a meal."

He leaned against the doorjamb and crossed his arms. "You want me over for dinner?"

I nodded.

He appraised me for a moment. One side of his mouth turned up in a smile. "That'd be nice."

I asked him to come over in an hour or so for drinks, then turned to go back to my apartment.

"Will?"

I looked back to him.

A wry smile was set on his face. "I understand what the word 'dinner' means."

I felt my face go red. "Of course you—sorry." I retreated to my apartment. The briefcase my father had given me still lay on the table by the door. I opened the flap. Inside were about a dozen newspapers, from Sunday until this morning. Each had a front-page story about me, "the Electric Executioner."

I scanned through the articles. My heart began to pound as I looked at story after story of love, revenge, and cold-blooded murder, all prominently naming me, Anderson Carriage Company, and Detroit Electric. Judge Hume had been quoted several times, each time implicating me as the murderer. Enraged, I swept my hand across the table, scattering the papers over the floor, and then stomped into the parlor and fell onto the sofa.

I was no longer William C. Anderson, Jr., son of a successful businessman. Now I was the most infamous man in Detroit—the Electric Executioner.

I bit my lip as I waited for someone at the Humes' to pick up the telephone.

Alberts finally answered. "Hume residence." He spoke quickly, his voice rising in inflection at the end, almost a question.

I lowered my voice an octave. "May I speak with Elizabeth, please?"

He paused and then answered, sounding like Alberts again, words clipped, tone formal. "She's not in at the moment. May I take a message?"

"Uh, no. When do you expect her?"

"I'm not at liberty to discuss that."

Still in the deep voice, I said, "May I speak with Mrs. Hume?"

"I'll see if she's available. Who may I say is calling?"

For a second, my mind went blank. Then I said, "I'm with the Detroit police."

"What's your name and badge number?"

I had no idea what to say. A second later, a quiet click came from his end, and the line went dead.

"Shit!" I had to speak with Elizabeth or Mrs. Hume, but I couldn't go to their house. The judge would almost certainly be home by now. Tomorrow would have to be soon enough. I set down the receiver, and the phone immediately rang.

When I answered, words poured out in a rush. "Will? It's Edsel. I heard you were getting out today."

"I just got home."

"How are you holding up?"

"As you might suspect, I've been better."

"How about I take you out to dinner tonight?"

"Edsel, no. First of all, you don't want to be seen with me. Your father will kill you. Secondly, I'm not going out in public. And I've got plans—"

"Will, if you give in, the bad guys have won. You need to show them you're standing up straight, that you have nothing to hide."

"I really don't—"

"I'll be there in a few minutes." He hung up.

I set the receiver down. At least I had one friend—no, two. Neither Wesley nor Edsel had even asked if I was innocent. They just assumed it. Now I needed to convince everyone else.

The telephone rang again. I picked it up. "Hello?"

A reedy voice said, "Will? Will Anderson? This is Herbert Cole from the *Herald*. I just need a few minutes of—"

I slammed the receiver onto the hook and stalked to the parlor. The phone rang again. Another reporter. And again. Now I understood Alberts's suspicion. He'd been fielding lots of phone calls, too. I left the receiver on the table and shuffled back to the parlor, stopping at the window. A dozen reporters stood in front of the large man guarding the door. How in the world was I going to get to the market? I rummaged around in my cabinets and icebox, and came up with two cans of tomato soup, half a box of cornflakes, and a quart of slightly rancid milk.

There was only one thing I knew how to cook. I ran down the back stairs to the first floor and asked Mr. Hatch if he would be so kind as to pick up a roast, potatoes, and carrots from the market around the corner. He gave me a funny look but agreed.

When he returned, I asked him to let Edsel in if he came in the back, and asked him to pass along the information to his partner. On the way back to my apartment, I stopped at Wesley's to let him know Edsel would be joining us for dinner, then locked myself in my apartment again.

I lit a cigarette and wandered into the parlor. The sun was setting, and the light reflected off the top of my coffee table, showing a fine layer of dust. I stopped in front of the side window. The sky glowed around the houses on Second Street, starting red at the horizon and flowing into orange above. The few clouds drifting past glowed a delicate pink, like gigantic puffs of fairy floss from Electric Park. I stood at the window until the blue faded to steel and the final orange light extinguished.

I tried to enjoy it. I didn't know how many more sunsets would be in my future.

Edsel Ford, wearing a stylish dark gray suit and derby, rushed into my apartment, saying, "That nose doesn't look so good, Will. Are you all right?" His large dark eyes bored into mine.

Edsel was small and looked young for his age, but behind that facade was a thoughtful young man. Had I not known better, I would have said we were about the same age, which I attributed to his maturity and my lack of same. I had the impression he looked up to me. We could certainly appreciate each other's situation—wealthy, successful, driven fathers, and the expectation we would continue that tradition.

"I'm fine, Edsel, thanks." My voice was still dull and nasal. I told him about Wesley's injuries and asked if he'd mind eating in with us. Edsel agreed, gracious as ever. I brought him over to Wesley's apartment to introduce him.

Wesley was dressed in a blue pinstriped suit, an ivory cravat draped around his neck. Edsel held out his hand, but quickly dropped it when he saw the bandages covering Wesley's hands. "Wesley McRae. Hey, the Scottish Songster, right?"

Wesley began to give a theatrical bow, but quit, grimacing, after dipping half a foot. "At your service." He turned to me. "If you'll just give me a hand with this cravat, we can find a better address for dinner."

Edsel clapped his hands. "That's what I told him. No hiding."

"Wes, do you really feel up to it?" I said.

His eyes goggled. "Lawdy," he drawled, "if I don't get out of here, I'll go plumb crazy."

Edsel laughed. "We're going to get along just fine, I can tell already." He looked from Wesley to me. "Seriously, are you fellows all right? We *can* eat in, you know."

"If Wes wants to go," I said, "I'll go." The way I cooked, my roast could well be inedible anyway. "So long as we go somewhere dark where we won't run into anyone who knows me." I thought about how that might sound to Wesley. "I just don't want people bothering me about the murder, that's all." But that wasn't all.

"I know just the place." Edsel grinned and rubbed his hands together. "This is exciting. Feels like I'm doing something illegal."

I began tying Wesley's cravat, determined to treat him like any other friend. But it made me nervous. I certainly didn't want him to think I was interested.

A few minutes later, we snuck out the back door. Mr. Hatch kept the lone reporter out there away from us while we hurried to Edsel's car. I expected to see his Detroit Electric brougham, but instead a Model T roadster was parked at the corner. This was no ordinary Tin Lizzie. The car was bright red with black fenders and top. It sat lower than a standard flivver, had a longer hood, and seemed to be leaning forward, aching to speed. Again, it crossed my mind there was something I was forgetting, something about a car.

Wesley let out a low whistle. "She's a beauty."

Edsel's grin split his face. "It's a custom Torpedo model I put together with some of the men at the factory. We're going to produce a toned-down version next year." He laughed and waggled his eyebrows. "I've had her up over sixty."

Despite myself, I smiled, remembering a white-knuckled ride in a Model T on the ice of Lake Huron the winter before.

A rotund man stuck his head around the side of the apartment building and began running toward us. "Gentlemen," he called. "I just need a few minutes."

I helped Wesley into the right side of the car and squeezed in next to him, no time to worry about touching. Mr. Hatch grabbed the reporter and pushed him away, toward the front, but his rivals and the photographers, alerted by the commotion, streamed around the corner toward us.

Edsel set the spark and throttle, ran to the front of the car, and spun the crank handle. The engine burst out with explosions, first sporadic, then building to a roar, very unlike the normal *putt-putt-putt* of a Model T. Mr. Hatch and the other guard stiff-armed and tackled the reporters they could get hold of, but the rest of the men, all shouting for us to wait, dodged and weaved around them.

"Will!" one man yelled. "I'll give you fifty bucks for a five-minute interview." Mr. Hatch cut him off at the knees, and he hit the ground with a wicked thump.

Edsel pulled down his goggles, ran back around the car, and vaulted into the driving seat. He shoved the brake lever forward, mashed on the clutch, and jerked the throttle lever down. We squealed away from the curb, leaving a dozen disappointed reporters in the street behind us. A second later, Edsel pulled his foot up from the clutch, and we were in high gear, hurtling around the corner onto Temple Street.

I leaned across Wesley and tapped Edsel's arm. "So much for an inconspicuous escape."

He couldn't keep the grin off his face. "Yeah. Great, isn't it?"

I wondered how long it would take Mr. Ford to change him. Like me, Edsel took after his mother. He was an enthusiastic doe-eyed boy with the soul of an artist. His father's flintiness had yet to rub off on him, which gave me hope Edsel would be strong enough to hold his own with Henry Ford. Few people were.

He took Rowena Street into Corktown. After a few more turns, he stopped in the middle of a residential neighborhood in front of a little saloon called Abick's. I helped Wesley down, and we traipsed inside.

Edsel held the door for us. "Just what the doctor ordered. Dark and out of the way."

Gas lamps cast a sickly light on the interior, a mix of dark wood and plaster. A dozen tables, half of them occupied, took up most of the room. The bar that ran the length of the wall on the right filled the rest. The saloon echoed with laughter and shouts from men with Irish accents. No one paid any attention to us. Edsel led us across the sawdust-covered floor to a larger dining area in the back. A table was open in a dark rear corner. We sat in the shadows, Edsel and me against the walls, Wesley facing us. The aroma of roasting meat nearly overcame the background of beer and vomit.

A pretty brunette waitress sauntered over. "What'll you have?"

"Scotch," Wesley said and then gestured toward me. "Bourbon for him and—"

"No," I said. "Ginger ale." If I was going to do anything for Elizabeth, I had to be able to think.

Wesley cocked his head at me for a second before turning to Edsel, who hesitated, like he was trying to decide what he could get away with. He finally sighed and said, "Ginger ale here, too."

The waitress handed us menus and left to get our drinks. It was Irish fare, not my favorite, but for the anonymity the place offered, I was more than willing to put up with it. When she came back, Wesley and I ordered stew, and Edsel the corned beef and cabbage.

"I hope you don't mind me asking, Will," Edsel said, "but how bad was it? Jail, I mean."

I hunched over the table and spoke quietly. "I won't lie to you. It's frightening." I told them about the other prisoners, the taunts and threats, and the guards, menacing with their truncheons and guns. "But I was lucky. I got to stay in my own cell the whole time."

"But if you have to go to prison . . . ," Edsel began. He saw the look on my face and didn't finish the thought.

Wesley leaned over the table, jaw set, eyes narrowed. "If you do have to go back, you need to remember something—fur and feathers."

I just looked at him.

"Fur and feathers," he repeated. "In the wild, when there's fur or feathers on the ground, it means an animal has been either killed or injured. If it's injured, it's an easy target. And both the predators and carrion eaters like an easy dinner. Prison is the same. If you get hurt or show weakness, you'd better find somebody big to protect you. But if you do that, there'll be a cost."

"I don't think I'm going back." I wasn't going back.

"I hope you're right. But if you do, you've got to be tough. The men need to think you're dangerous. Here's something that might give you a fraction-of-a-second advantage." He tilted his head back a little, and there was just a hint of tension in his brow. But his eyes transformed. His lids had dropped a little, but it was more than that. Wesley the entertainer was no longer looking at me. This new man was scary.

"Dead eyes," he said. "You want to look at the man like you have a long history of putting away punks like him, and he'd just be another notch. But remember, it's not going to save you. Most guys in prison have that look. And theirs is real. So the second thing to remember is hit first, in the groin if possible."

I shook my head. "I'm not going back."

Edsel smoothed his dark hair and leaned forward. "How can I help?"

"Help?" I said. "You need to stay out of this, Edsel. It's too dangerous."

He sat back and folded his arms over his chest, a smile flitting across his face. "I'll find the killer."

"No!" Wesley and I said simultaneously.

"Our company has some pretty powerful resources. Let me have them do some digging. I won't get personally involved."

"No. It's too dangerous," I said.

"I'm getting to the bottom of this whether you want me to or not. Now cooperate."

I thought for a moment before agreeing. "So long as you stay out of it yourself." I nodded toward Wesley. "Wes tangled with the murderer, and he's lucky to be alive."

A grim expression settled onto Wesley's face, but he didn't say anything.

Edsel looked from me to Wesley and raised his ginger ale. "To finding the killer."

We clinked our glasses together and drank.

Wesley's head popped up. "What about the kid who took the money? The killer trusted him enough to let him do that. They must know each other."

"Yeah, I thought of that, too," I said, "but there are thousands of kids on the streets, and probably thousands more in the city who match the description. How in the world would we find him?"

After a moment, he nodded. "You're probably right. But let's keep our eyes open anyway."

Wesley had another Scotch, and we worked on our meals, which were surprisingly tasty. While we ate, Edsel grilled me about John Cooper's murder, looking for an angle he could use. "What was Cooper like?"

"Friendly, charming, but really tough. Not someone you'd want to make angry. He always seemed to be on the winning side. He was always on . . . the right side."

"What do you mean?"

"Well, of course he was human, but he didn't show that to many people. It was always important to him to do the right thing, the thing that was expected of a person like him—rescuing kittens from trees, pitching in on campus projects. You know, your prototypical hail-fellow-well-met."

Edsel was watching his glass as he swirled the ginger ale around. He glanced up and met my eyes. "But he did have a darker side?"

"Well, yeah, but doesn't everybody? Present company excepted, of course."

"So, what did he do?"

"It wasn't so much what he did as how much pleasure he took in certain parts of it. He loved the contact, the violence of football. After he took the EAD job, he'd tell me about the fights they'd had with union organizers. He always played down his part in them, but his eyes glowed just like they had during a big football game. I only saw him in action once. About twenty Teamsters were picketing our factory. John, Frank Van Dam, and about ten of their men came in and just laid waste to those poor guys."

Frank had taken out three or four of the union men with his fists, feet, and blackjack, but, as usual, John outshone everyone. He put down half a dozen of the organizers, swinging a four-foot-long axe handle like a baseball bat. One swing was all it took. After the fight, when I told him I had watched, he winked and said, "Ty Cobb ain't got nothing on me."

Edsel nodded. "What about this Frank Van Dam fellow? What was his relationship with Cooper?"

"They were best friends. Frank worked for John, and I think he may know who killed him. But Frank's disappeared."

"I'll have someone look into it," Edsel said.

"Frank quit his job before John's murder and moved out west." I took a sip of my drink. "Anyway, I think the most important thing is that the unions hated John. By killing him at our factory and framing me, they could get rid of Cooper and create a big problem for an open shop."

Edsel nodded. "That would seem the most likely scenario. So that leaves us with a pool of only ten thousand or so suspects. But I might be able to winnow it down a bit. My father's security men have been collecting information on the unions for the past couple of years. I'd guess

I can get my hands on a pretty complete file on the AFL unions and the Wobblies."

I reached across the table and held on to his forearm. "Don't you go and try anything crazy here. You stay out of it. And make sure your father's men know what they're up against. Whoever this is, he is not afraid to spill other people's blood."

# CHAPTER FOURTEEN

The noise in the saloon kept ratcheting up as more men and women streamed in, most packing into the front room. I pushed away the empty stew bowl, pulled my cigarette case from my waistcoat, and held it out to Wesley. He took one, and I grabbed one for myself. Edsel cleared his throat. He was looking at me with arched eyebrows and making a "hand it over" gesture.

"Edsel? You smoke?"

"Sure." He sat back, studying his fingernails, trying to look casual. "Usually it's Sweet Caporals for me." Raising his eyebrows again, he said with mock seriousness, "Sweet Caps. The purest form in which tobacco can be smoked."

Wesley laughed. "Maybe you ought to work in your dad's advertising department."

I held out the cigarette case for Edsel. After he chose one, I lit it for him and snapped the case shut. "Wouldn't your father skin you if he caught you smoking?"

"Oh, we've got an understanding."

I laughed. "You've got an understanding about smoking with Henry Ford. Sure thing."

He blew out a smoke ring and let his arm drape over the back of his chair. With a grin, he said, "Well, perhaps an understanding isn't quite the way to describe it."

I was taking a swig of ginger ale when Edsel said, "Oh, shit." He stubbed out his smoke and looked away.

A big man stumbled into the back room and looked around before going up front again.

"What's wrong?" Wesley said, turning to try to see what we were looking at.

I ducked my head. "Horace Dodge."

"And wherever goes Horace, so goes John," Edsel said. "You'd think they're Siamese twins. Could be entertaining, though."

"So long as they decide to pick a fight with someone else." I nudged Edsel. "They don't have a problem with you, do they?"

A lopsided smile appeared on his face. "Even drunk, I don't think they'd pick a fight with the son of the man who's making them rich."

"What the hell are they doing here?" I said.

Edsel shook his head. "I'd guess this is the only saloon in town they haven't been thrown out of yet." He shot his sleeve and looked at his wristwatch. "But the night is young."

The noise level in the front rose appreciably with the arrival of the Dodges. It was common knowledge in automobile circles that, sober, the Dodge brothers were obnoxious. It was better known, from the frequent newspaper articles detailing their brawls, that drunk they were dangerous. My father called the Dodges an enigma. They were sharp, if not brilliant businessmen, knew machining as well as anyone, were excellent negotiators, and were dogged and driven—perhaps as driven as Edsel's father. Like Henry Ford, they would work at a problem until it disappeared, a trait that unfortunately carried over to their personal lives, where they solved those problems with their fists and feet. Success hadn't changed them, though perhaps they were still adjusting to their newly won riches.

Regardless of Edsel's opinion, we needed to steer clear of these men. But there was at least one benefit to them being here. The Dodges were certain to become the center of attention, keeping the focus away from the alleged murderer hiding in the back.

Around ten, Edsel excused himself to answer the call of nature. At that moment, John Dodge walked out from the front of the saloon. "Hey, Edsel," he said. "Edsel Ford! How you doing, boy?" Dodge was in his mid-forties, a round-headed man leaning toward fat, with thinning red hair parted on the side and the swollen face of an alcoholic.

Edsel answered him in a voice too quiet for me to hear over the raucous sounds of the saloon. Dodge moved in close, his face only a few inches away from Edsel's. When Edsel excused himself and turned to walk into the restroom, he stumbled over Dodge's foot. The leather sole of his shoe slid forward on the sawdust. His feet slipped out from under him, and he fell, unceremoniously, onto his backside.

Dodge helped him up, apologizing all the way. Edsel was facing us and glanced at me with a smile. Dodge kept talking. Every time he'd look away, gesticulating toward the front room or staring up at the ceiling, Edsel mugged with wide eyes and exaggerated smiles or grimaces, stopping just as Dodge would look at him again. By the time Edsel was able to extract himself and retreat to the restroom, I was laughing so hard I was practically on the floor, and Wesley was holding his ribs while he whooped out laughs.

John Dodge turned and looked at us, head cocked, before strolling over. "Who you laughing at?" he said, speaking slowly, trying to enunciate—definitely drunk.

Wesley straightened up in his chair and smiled at him, no hint of alarm on his face. "No one. Just enjoying a joke."

Dodge turned to the front and called, "Hey, Horace! Horace!"

A few seconds later, his brother joined him, a quizzical expression on his face. He was also a chunky man, but thinner than John and better looking. He seemed every bit as drunk, however. "What?"

"These sonsabitches think Edsel Ford is a joke."

Horace narrowed his eyes and leaned over the table toward me. "You think Edsel is a joke?"

"No, no, you've got it all wrong," I said. "Edsel is our—"

"Whoa," John said. "I'm wrong?" He glanced at his brother before grabbing me by the front of my shirt and lifting me partway out of the chair. "I'm gonna . . ." He squinted, trying to focus on my face, and abruptly dropped me. "Well, hell. I was just about to pound a celebrity." He looked at his brother and gestured toward me. "This here's the Anderson kid, the killer!" He plopped into Edsel's chair and waved toward the waitress. "A round over here!" he shouted. "I'm buying one for my friend, the 'lectric esha-cutioner." He put his arm around me and pulled me close. "I owe you big." His whiskey breath poured into my face. "Finally, someone in the car business with a worse reputation than mine." He pounded on the table. Both he and his brother roared with laughter.

"We should probably be going," Wesley said, and began to stand.

Horace shoved Wesley back down in his seat and stood over him. "Didn't you hear John? He's buying."

Wesley winced, surely feeling it in his ribs. He held his hands up in front of him. "Fine, fine. We can have one more."

Still with his arm around me, John stared at Wesley, then turned back to me. "Looks like you guys been volunteering as punching bags!" He and Horace bellowed out another round of laughter, and John pounded the table with his free hand.

I lifted his arm from my shoulders and stood. "Come on, Wes. Let's go."

John Dodge grabbed my arm and tried to jerk me back into the chair. When I resisted, he stood and leaned in close to me. "You ain't going anywhere. I'm buying you a friendly drink."

Wesley threw an elbow into Horace's midsection, doubling him over, and stepped around the table, staring into John's eyes. "We're leaving."

With a grin on his face, John let go of my arm and began rolling up the sleeves of his shirt. Horace, a hand still over his solar plexus, straightened and took a step toward Wesley.

"Hey! Fellows!" Edsel called out, running up to us. "Let's just settle down, all right?"

John's attention wavered from Wesley to Edsel to Wesley again. Out of the side of his mouth, he said, "These friends of yours, Edsel?"

"Both of these gentlemen are my friends, John. I'm sure my father would appreciate you being more polite to them."

John Dodge glared at Wesley for a moment before stepping back. "All right. Okay." He forced a smile at Edsel. "Sorry about that. No harm done."

We got our coats and hats and walked toward the door, the Dodges fawning over Edsel the whole way. I was the last one out, and was turning to leave when I heard a quiet, "Anderson."

I looked back at the brothers. John squinted and grinned a bully's grin. "This ain't over."

When I got home I sat in my study and tried to read, but my mind kept going back to the row of bourbon bottles in the cupboard. It was infuriating and a little frightening. I had to quit drinking, but I couldn't concentrate. I read the same pages over and over, still having no idea what I'd read. Finally I went to the kitchen, for just one drink.

I fell asleep on the sofa, an empty bottle on the floor next to me.

At ten the next morning, not sure whether my guilt or the pain in my head made me feel worse, I wedged myself onto a streetcar and rode to the Humes', certain the judge would be at work.

He answered the door.

His eyes were wide, his face hopeful, until he saw me. He threw the door open and grabbed me by the lapels. "What have you done to her? If you've hurt her, I swear to God I'll kill you, you son of a bitch!"

A heavy weight dropped in my gut. "Elizabeth?"

"Don't play innocent with me, Anderson," he snarled. "Where is she?"

"But—she came home, didn't she?"

"As if you don't know. Tell me what you've done with her!"

I wrenched myself out of his grasp and shoved him away. "As you've probably seen in the papers, I've been in jail. How could I have done something with her?"

"When did you get out?" he demanded.

"I was arrested last week Tuesday and didn't get out until late yesterday afternoon."

He blinked. "I can check that, you know."

"Of course I know that, Judge. Now how long has she been missing this time?"

His brow furrowed, and a look of uncertainty appeared on his face. "She went out two days ago and hasn't come back." He turned to go inside but stopped. In a pitiful voice, he said, "She's been ill."

I returned home and spent the next hour pacing in my den. Elizabeth's disappearance had to be tied to her drug addiction, and I feared overdose. I thought to call the hospitals and the police, but the Humes would undoubtedly have done that already.

I needed to start at the beginning. She had gone to the pharmacy on Hastings and apparently not gotten what she asked for. That was odd. It didn't matter if she was addicted to heroin, morphine, or opium. They were all available for the asking at any pharmacy.

I phoned Dr. Miller. "With Elizabeth in the condition she was when you examined her, would a pharmacy sell her heroin?"

"No. Well, that is, not a reputable pharmacy. Before they sell an opiate, they're supposed to use their judgment as to whether the customer is abusing it."

"But there are pharmacies that would sell it to her?"

"Oh, certainly. Usually in the more sordid parts of town."

I thanked him and hung up. When I was walking out of the den, the telephone rang. I thought about ignoring it, given that it was almost certainly a reporter, but for some reason I answered.

It was Edsel. "I've got a report for you on the unions. Our security men have been working with the EAD to see if there's any chance they can pin Cooper's murder on the AFL or IWW. The Wobblies didn't even know who John Cooper was, and the AFL leadership has already turned over all their Employers Association files to the police. They swear they and their affiliates had nothing to do with it. Our men, though they'd never admit this publicly, believe them, and trust me, they'd love to stick the AFL with the murder."

This was not good news. "Okay, Edsel, thanks. I appreciate you checking."

"Oh, I'm not finished yet. I suppose finding Frank Van Dam is next." I could hear the smile in his voice.

"All right. But Edsel?"

"Yes?"

"Be careful."

"Not to worry, Will, my boy. I'll be very careful."

I hung up and called Sutton, asking him if he'd had any luck finding Frank Van Dam. He hadn't. I filled him in on what Edsel said about the unions, then hung up again and set the receiver on the table. If it wasn't one of the unions, I had no idea who could have wanted John dead. I hoped Frank knew. And I hoped Sutton or Edsel could find him.

I sat in the parlor, thinking about what Dr. Miller had said. Now I understood why Elizabeth went to the pharmacy on Hastings. But it didn't explain why she had gone to that horrid saloon. It appeared the handsome man with the Italian accent had something to do with the pharmacy or sold drugs illegally. Either way, he was involved.

*Son of a bitch.* I was going to have to make another trip to the Bucket.

I went straight to Wesley's apartment. He answered the door in black trousers, shiny black boots, and an undershirt. "Just getting dressed, chum. Come on in." He walked down the hall to a room at the end.

I stayed in the foyer. "Wes, I need your help again."

"You've got it. What can I do?"

"I need somebody to watch my back. At the Bucket."

His head popped out of the room. "The— Okay. When?"

"Tonight. And I think we should have guns."

Fumbling to button a sky blue shirt, he ambled down the hall toward me. "Tell me what we're doing."

I explained about Elizabeth's addiction, that she was missing, and that I was sure the Italian man could give us at least a clue to her whereabouts, but it would first involve getting past the giant. Wesley asked me questions about the layout of the saloon and listened carefully while I described it.

A thought hit me. "Wes, I think the bouncer could be the killer. He might be the only person I've ever met who could overpower John. You said the man who killed the Doyles was huge, and this guy certainly qualifies as that."

Wesley rubbed his chin, and a little smile turned up the corners of his mouth. "When I see him, I'll know. I hope his life insurance is paid up."

"You said you didn't see his face."

"I don't need to, I saw how he moves. I study that. I'm a trained actor, after all. To become someone else, I have to move like them, too."

"Good," I said. "Maybe we'll get lucky. But I can't figure out why they would kill John."

"Could Elizabeth's . . . situation have something to do with it?"

I considered the idea. "It's as good a theory as any. If John was buying her the drugs from these men, he could have run afoul of them somehow. And John wouldn't have backed off if they had a problem with him. John never backed off." I shook my head. "But if that's so, why would they frame me? I'd never even heard of these guys."

Wesley only shrugged. Neither of us could make sense of it.

"Now, about those guns," Wesley said.

"I'll go buy a couple this afternoon."

"Don't bother." Wesley returned to the room in back. A minute later, he reappeared with a pair of dark wooden boxes clutched to his chest. I followed him into the parlor. He set the boxes on the coffee table, opened them, and pulled out a pair of large pistols. "Colt Cavalry forty-fives. Got 'em from my pop." He held one out for me, and I took it. The revolver was huge, easily a foot long, the barrel more than half of it. The grip was dark wood, smooth to the touch.

"Single-action, so make sure you cock it before you try to shoot somebody." He tipped back an imaginary cowboy hat and drawled, "This here's the same gun Buffalo Bill's got. There's five bullets in there that'll stop anything, up to and including a bear."

"Good, because we may need to shoot someone about that size."

"Yup," he said. "Jes' pull back the hammer, point her, pull the trigger, and look down on the ground, 'cause that's where he'll be."

"I have fired a pistol before." I handed the gun back to him.

"Have you ever shot a man?" he asked, suddenly serious.

"Of course not."

"Me neither." With a bandaged hand, he spun the cylinder in one of the guns. "But if this is the guy who killed my friends, I'm going to tonight."

"Wes, if you're going to help me, this has got to be about finding Elizabeth, not getting revenge. If we can do both, okay. But Elizabeth has to be the priority."

Wesley sat on one of the yellow chairs, his forehead creased in concentration. "You're right. But if we find her and then I get a chance, he's a dead man." He tried to bend his forefinger far enough to fit it inside the trigger guard of the gun. After a moment, he gave up and awkwardly stuck his middle finger in far enough to reach the trigger. Sighting down the barrel at the wall, he made the sound of a gun shooting, and his hand jerked back from the imagined recoil. He looked at me again. "So, how are we going to do this?"

"I'd guess everybody in the place will be carrying guns, knives, or both. If we go in like wild Indians we'll be cut down before we get anywhere. We need to be careful. Maybe you go in first, get a feel for the place, and set up where you can see everything. Then I'll come in and, hopefully, find the Italian. I'll get him off someplace we can talk. You just watch my back."

He agreed, though he didn't seem satisfied with the role I'd given him. We decided to leave at ten o'clock. If the saloon was busy, it was less likely we'd be noticed.

The Italian man could fill in the blanks. I just had to get him to talk.

I ate a cold dinner and pottered around my apartment, nervously killing time. Around nine thirty, I started to dress, finally deciding on the outfit I wore when working on cars—stained brown trousers, a greasy blue shirt, and scuffed work boots. I pulled out an old black derby with a bent brim and grabbed my duster from the coatrack. Before leaving I took two long swallows of bourbon to clear my head. It helped still the tremors in my hands.

I collected Wesley, who was dressed in a similar fashion, though with a waist-length dark coat. We were just two recently-beaten-up poverty-stricken men out for a night on the town. I was fairly certain we looked as derelict as the average Bucket patron.

He handed me a gun. I tried to fit it in the pocket of my duster, but the weight of the thing made the whole coat sag to the right, and the wooden butt hung out to the side.

Wesley turned around and lifted the back of his coat. His revolver was tucked into his trousers. "With the long coat, you might want to try the front." He grinned. "But take care not to shoot off anything you're attached to."

Again, I felt a tug of trepidation. Though other men I knew would likely make the same wisecrack, it was different coming from him. But I smiled back at him just the same. I pulled out the waistband of my trousers and started to slide the gun inside, but stopped. I glanced up at Wesley with a grimace.

He chuckled. "Single-action, remember? Just don't cock it."

I stuffed the huge gun into my trousers and adjusted it, trying unsuccessfully to find a comfortable position. I finally gave up and left it in the middle, though with the barrel pointing toward my pocket. "Okay," I said. "Let's go."

At the bottom of the stairs, Carl Hatch gave us an all clear. We skulked out the back into a cold dark night, the glow of a half-moon just visible through the heavy clouds. After catching a Woodward Line streetcar to Gratiot, we walked down to Hastings. The street lamps were dim and widely spaced. Shadows moved through the street, shouting, cursing, laughing. The dark seemed to amplify the stench of the streetside privies.

Wesley and I shared a look, and he began to stumble toward the Bucket with the lurch of a drunkard. When he opened the saloon's door, a cacophony of music poured out, then quieted again when the door banged shut. I waited until a pair of men shoved past me and followed them inside, using their bodies to shield me from Big Boy. Through the haze of smoke, I saw him sitting in the same spot at the bar he had occupied last week. Over the normal saloon smells—stale beer, tobacco, and unwashed bodies—floated a sweeter component, some kind of smoke with which I wasn't familiar.

Wild music echoed through the saloon. The same man I'd seen before banged on the piano alongside other black men playing clarinet, trumpet, trombone, tuba, banjo, and drums. The music soared and swooped, similar to ragtime but untamed, improvisational.

One of the men in front of me spat a stream of tobacco juice onto the warped wooden boards at his feet before heading to the bar. As surreptitiously as I could, I scanned the room. There had to be a hundred men packed into the saloon, crowding the bar, playing cards, rolling dice, chatting up prostitutes. Wesley stood at the end of the bar nearest the door. I caught his eye, and he looked meaningfully at the giant and then back to me, shaking his head just enough to be sure I got the message.

Big Boy wasn't the man who killed the Doyles.

Wesley leaned on the bar with an elbow, turned toward the back of the saloon, and took a sip of his beer.

The Italian was nowhere in sight. I headed toward the back of the saloon looking for an office or storeroom, my face turned away from the giant. An unmarked wooden door in the rear wall seemed the only possibility.

I edged around the card tables, trying not to draw attention. Behind me, over the sound of the music, came a loud *crash*! I flinched and turned around. A man holding a pair of chair legs stood over another, who lay unconscious on the floor, the rest of the chair scattered around him. Big Boy jumped from his seat and began to stalk in their direction. The man holding the chair legs spun and ran from the saloon, holding the wooden posts in his hands like batons in a relay race. It appeared everyone was afraid of the giant, which in some odd way comforted me.

The wild music continued unabated. One little skull fracture wasn't enough to get the attention of the musicians. With everyone looking elsewhere, I hurried to the door in the back and turned the knob. It was unlocked. I pushed it open and slipped inside.

Wooden crates and beer kegs were stacked haphazardly against the side walls, leaving small crevices along a narrow walkway leading to a pair of doors in the back. One was ajar. The light was off, but I could see stairs leading down to a basement. The other door was closed, and a flickering yellow light leaked out underneath it. I pulled the gun, cocked it, and walked down the aisle. A murmur of conversation was just audible over the muffled music from the saloon. Then I heard the sound of chairs scraping against the wooden floor. I ducked into a shadowy opening between two stacks of boxes.

No sooner was I hidden than the storeroom brightened, and the voices became distinct.

"You swear you don't know?" a man said. He sounded familiar, but somehow out of context, and the music blaring in the saloon made the identification difficult.

"I do not," a man with an Italian accent said. "But I wonder . . ."

"Wonder what?" the other man said.

"If I were able to find her, I wonder if your gratitude would be such that you would allow me to run my business without interference." His voice hardened. "Or payoffs."

"You son of a bitch." Shoes scuffled. "Where is she?"

I peeked over the top of the boxes in astonishment. The handsome Italian was facing toward the door. The other man held him by the lapels, his back to me.

I didn't need to see his face to know it was Judge Hume.

# CHAPTER FIFTEEN

The Italian pried the judge's hands from his coat. "Judge Hume, you are trying my patience. If you want to find your daughter, I'd suggest you act more civilized. We are civilized men, are we not?"

I tightened my grip on the Colt.

Judge Hume spoke, his voice weak and broken. "What do you want?"

"As I said, I would be pleased to join in the search for your daughter. I want only for you to show your gratitude, should I be able to find her."

"All right, I will. Just give her back to me."

The Italian man said, "I'll do what I can, Your Honor. It will be a privilege to call a distinguished man such as you a friend. Now, please. I have other business to attend to." He turned the judge around and steered him toward the door.

I stepped out in front of them, leveling the gun at the Italian. "Where is she?"

Judge Hume's eyes widened. "Will?"

The Italian man straightened the jacket of his dark gray sack suit and tilted his head to the side. "Will? Ah, Mr. Anderson. I should have recognized you before. It is indeed a pleasure to meet such a celebrity. Do you intend to add me to your list of victims?"

"Where is she?" I repeated.

"As I told the judge, I do not know. And with all this rudeness, I'm not certain I will even look."

The judge stepped in front of me, anger flaring on his face. "Anderson, get out of here. You're just getting in the way."

"No," the Italian said. "Perhaps it is you who should leave, Judge Hume. I would like to speak with Mr. Anderson."

The judge spun back to the Italian. "But—"

"I'll contact you if I hear anything. Good-bye."

"But . . . I . . ." The judge again turned toward me. The anguish of a frightened father was etched into his face. It was unsettling. I'd never seen him like this. "Find her."

Narrowing my eyes at the Italian, I nodded. The judge staggered past me. Music poured in for a moment and then quieted as the door closed behind him.

"Come to my office, please." The Italian man stepped aside, sweeping his arm toward the back.

I motioned with the gun. "After you."

"If you insist." He strolled to the door, opened it, and walked around a small wooden desk to a chair set against the back wall. The office was small and cramped, lit by a pair of gas lamps mounted on either side of the room. The Italian unbuttoned his coat and sat at the desk, empty save for a telephone, and gestured toward one of the chairs facing him. "Please, sit."

I stepped to the side of the door, keeping the gun pointed at him. The barrel was trembling. "I'll stand, thanks. And keep your hands where I can see them."

He looked amused, but his hands stayed on top of the desk. "My name is Vito Adamo. I would like to speak with you about Miss Hume."

"What have you done to her?"

"Done? Nothing. I have not seen her since you took her away."

"Look, I'm fairly certain you killed John Cooper and the Doyles, or had one of your men do it. I know you blackmailed me. But I don't care about any of that. I just want to find Elizabeth."

He twisted the ends of his waxed mustaches and squinted at me for a moment, as if trying to understand a new language. Then he broke out in laughter. "The newspapers say you killed John Cooper. I did not. I do not know of the Doyles, and I know nothing of any blackmail."

He seemed sincere, but I had no idea how good an actor he was. I wouldn't give him the benefit of the doubt. "Where is Elizabeth?"

"What business is it of yours?"

I walked around the desk and stuck the barrel of the gun against his forehead. "Tell me."

"If you are going to kill me, please, do so. Otherwise, I would like to change the topic."

Pulling the trigger wouldn't help me find Elizabeth. I stepped back, keeping the gun trained on him. "So talk."

He pushed back his chair and crossed his legs, tugging at his trousers until the crease was straight. "As you are no doubt aware, the judge can be a most difficult man. I do not trust him. Even if I do find his daughter, I still need some, what is the word? *Lev-er-age?*" He spoke carefully, feeling the word in his mouth. "Is this it?"

"Yes. Something you can use against him."

He clapped his hands together one time. "*Esattamente.* Leverage."

"Like what?"

"Information that might cause him distress should it become public. I could use Miss Hume's situation, but I am trying to keep family out of this. It's not . . . *professionale.*"

"I don't know anything."

"I did not expect so. But Miss Hume does."

"How could you possibly know that?"

"I have an excellent source of information."

"I don't believe you."

Adamo sighed. "John Cooper told me."

"What? How do—did—you know John Cooper?"

"That is not important," he said. "Suffice it to say that Mr. Cooper and I were acquainted."

"Why would he tell you anything about Elizabeth?"

"He did not want Miss Hume's situation to become public. I helped him, he helped me."

The office door burst open and slammed against the wall. Big Boy stood in the doorway, his body stiff, eyes darting between Adamo and me. I swung the gun over to him.

Behind him, Wesley said, "Easy there, big fella." He pushed the giant into the room.

A blade pressed against my neck. Startled, I cut my eyes toward Adamo's chair. It was empty.

"Give me the gun, Mr. Anderson," he purred from behind me.

Wesley held his revolver up to the base of Big Boy's skull, his middle finger against the trigger. He was grimacing from the pain in his hand. "Let him go, or I'll blow your pet giant's brains all over this room."

"I do not think so," Adamo said. "You are a friend of Mr. Anderson?"

Wesley didn't respond.

"Well, no matter." The Italian's voice was cool and steady. "I will kill him unless you lay your gun on the floor."

"Let him go," Wesley said.

I felt a sharp sting as he pressed the blade into my neck. "Wes, get out of here. I'll handle this." I kept the gun pointed at Big Boy, but I couldn't hold it still. My guts were roiling.

"No, sorry," Wesley said.

Warm blood began to run down my neck. "I'm giving him the gun, Wes." I tried to steady the trembling in my voice. "Now get out of here."

He glanced around Big Boy. When he saw the blade cutting into my neck, he shoved the big man against the desk and aimed his gun over my shoulder.

"You'll be killing your friend," Adamo said.

"But I'll be killing you, too," Wesley said. "And muscle-boy."

Big Boy glared at Wesley, but stayed by the desk. The room was small enough that he could almost reach Wesley from where he was.

"I'm going to count to three," Adamo said, his voice coming from directly behind me, "and if you don't drop your gun I'm going to slit Mr. Anderson's throat. Of course, if you try to shoot me or Big Boy before that, I'll do it sooner."

I held both hands in front of me, palms out, the Colt dangling off my thumb. "Wes, leave." I couldn't put him in any more danger.

"One," Adamo said.

Wesley took a step toward us, trying to keep an eye on Big Boy at the same time. His eyes were wide, his confusion apparent.

The blade cut deeper into my neck. Blood ran down my chest. "Wes, get out of here."

"Two."

Wesley's mouth opened and closed. He finally shouted, "All right!" and set his Colt on the floor.

Adamo reached around and relieved me of my pistol. Big Boy picked up the other gun, turned to Wesley and, with a short chopping motion, hit him in the forehead with the pistol's grip. It made a sickening *thud*. Wesley staggered but didn't fall. Blood streamed down his face from a ragged cut above his left eyebrow. Big Boy raised the gun a second time.

"That's enough," Adamo said. "I have a need for these gentlemen."

The giant frowned at him but lowered the weapon.

"Now, to business." Adamo walked around the desk and sat. He opened a drawer and placed the gun in it. "Please, sit, both of you."

Big Boy shoved Wesley toward the desk. Wincing, he caught his balance and turned back to the giant.

"Wes," I said. "Sit. Please."

He glared at Big Boy a moment longer before sliding into the chair. I sat next to him, pulled out my handkerchief, and pressed it against the wound on my neck. Wesley did the same with the cut on his forehead.

Adamo clasped his hands on the desk in front of him. "Now, Mr. Anderson. The newspapers say you and Miss Hume were engaged. Is this correct?"

"Yes."

"And then she fell in love with John Cooper."

"Yes."

"What is she to you now?"

"She's my . . . friend."

Smiling, Adamo looked over our heads at the giant. "You would face Big Boy—twice—for a friend? No, I don't think so." He thought for a moment. "Does Miss Hume still love you?"

I grunted out a laugh. "Hardly."

"I have a proposition for you, Mr. Anderson. You have heard the phrase, 'One hand will wash the other'?"

I nodded.

"I will find Miss Hume for you, but I need something in return."

"What?"

"Of course I'm talking about her father's secret. She wasn't willing to tell me, even to get her drugs." Vito Adamo raised a finger to his chin, and his head inclined toward me. "Perhaps you would get it from her to save her life."

I wiggled around and blew into my hands. It was freezing. The cots in the Bucket's basement were hard and threadbare, and we had no blankets. The bleeding from my throat had stopped, but not before my shirt was glued to my chest. My teeth were chattering, from more than the cold.

Wesley and I lay, our hands and feet bound, on cots surrounded by dozens of others, all empty. Hundreds of cases of liquor and kegs of beer lined the walls. From time to time the newspapers alleged that Italian criminals brought in illegal liquor and immigrants without papers from Canada—this looked to be a way station, and the fact that Adamo was letting us see it made me very nervous.

A rumbling cacophony of music, shouts, and laughter poured down the steps, while playing cards splatted against a table near my cot. A swarthy young man with dark eyes glittering over sunken cheeks sat at the table with a deck of cards, practicing dealing off the bottom of the deck. It wasn't the first time he'd tried it.

I glanced over at Wesley. The blood on his forehead had dried in a crust on his skin, and his blond hair was matted and dark. "I'm sorry I got you into this," I whispered.

He frowned. "If you don't stop apologizing, I'm going to whack you a good one."

"Sorr—" I stopped myself. "Are you all right?"

He nodded. With a grim set to his mouth, he said, "But when I get out of here, these guys won't be."

"Remember," I whispered. "Elizabeth." In the back of my mind, I envied his confidence. I was too frightened to think about revenge.

"I know." He looked over the top of me at our guard and then met my eyes again. "When I saw Judge Hume walk out of that back room I just about went apoplectic. If he's involved in this, it can't be good."

"You know the judge?"

"I've been a guest in his courtroom. What was he doing here?"

"I think he was just trying to get Adamo to give him Elizabeth."

Wesley raised his bound hands to his forehead and tried to push a lock of hair out of his face. It didn't move, stuck in place by the blood. "How would he even know Adamo?"

The young Italian man shouted, "*Zitto!*"

I lowered my voice. "Adamo is p-paying him off." My teeth were chattering again. I clenched my jaw.

Wesley's eyes widened. "For what?"

"I don't know. But I think Adamo has Elizabeth stashed somewhere. I'm certain he's not going to hurt her, though. She's his bargaining chip."

A chair scraped. My cot flipped over on its side, and I tumbled onto the cold concrete floor.

The young Italian man stood over me, eyes blazing. "*Zitto!*"

"Settle down there, Michelangelo," Wesley said. "We were just chatting."

Without a word, the man walked around my cot and flipped Wesley's over. When he hit the floor, he groaned, followed by a sharp intake of breath. The Italian man kicked him in the side. Wesley cried out in pain.

"Hey!" I yelled. I rolled over, wedging myself between the two of them. "Leave him alone!" The Italian just walked back to the table and began dealing cards again. It wasn't likely that he even spoke English. The majority of Detroit residents were immigrants, and most lived in enclaves with their countrymen, so learning the language wasn't a necessity.

"I'm all right," Wesley said with a grimace. "Listen, Will, we'd better try to sleep. Who knows when we're getting out of here?"

I agreed. Wesley rolled over onto his side with his hands under his head and soon was snoring softly. I didn't expect sleep to overtake me tonight. Surrounded by a thousand bottles of liquor, I had nothing to drink.

Instead, I thought.

I was pathetic. The woman I loved and the man who'd helped me beyond all reason were both in the clutches of a ruthless criminal. I had to do something, but I couldn't concentrate. I couldn't even stop shivering. Fear had become my normal state. Since the moment I found John's body, I'd been afraid. Afraid of the police, the blackmailer, Judge Hume, the criminals in jail, John Dodge, Big Boy, and now Vito Adamo. And when I listed them off, I conceded I had very good reason to be afraid. But this wasn't anything new. It was simply a variation of the fear I had lived with since I could remember.

I had always been afraid of not living up to my parents' expectations, or Elizabeth's expectations, of letting down the people I loved. But as I considered the events of the past week, it occurred to me that the problem was something else entirely. It wasn't that I was afraid to look like an idiot to everyone else. The problem was that I wouldn't risk a serious effort toward a goal, for fear I would fail and prove to *myself* I wasn't good enough. Instead, I complained, threw blame elsewhere, and raised my eyebrows at the mistakes of others, all the while making it clear to everyone that I wasn't trying. If I didn't try, I couldn't fail. Everything I'd ever done had been motivated by the fear of failure.

If I was ever going to change that, I had to do it pretty soon. And in a way, my imminent death was liberating. Once my debt to Elizabeth was paid, I really didn't have a cause for fear.

But I couldn't stop shivering.

# CHAPTER SIXTEEN

A woman's piercing scream cut through the noise above us. The crowd quieted and the band faltered for a moment, but seconds later the volume level was back where it had been. I had no way of telling what time it was. At some point, the saloon quieted and, despite my shivering and thirst, I caught a few moments of sleep.

In the morning, the basement door opened, and Adamo shouted down the steps, "Angelo?" and something else in Italian.

The young Italian man grunted, pushed back his chair, and stood.

Adamo walked down the steps with a swarthy man who looked to be his younger brother. They stopped in front of me. "We were able to find Miss Hume and have moved her to a safer location," Vito Adamo said. "Are you ready to see her?"

I sat up. "Please. I can't take any more of your man's sparkling conversation."

"Oh, a funny man, very good." He turned to Angelo and barked out an order in Italian.

Angelo squatted down at my feet and worked the knots until the rope came free, then nodded toward the stairway.

I stood, shaking my legs to get some blood flowing, and turned to Vito Adamo. "I'm not leaving without him." I tilted my head toward Wesley.

"Angelo will safeguard your friend until such time as I am satisfied with your effort."

"He's got nothing to do with this, Adamo. Let him go."

"I am sorry, Mr. Anderson, but I also need some of this *lev-er-age* with you. Salvatore." He nodded to his brother. "Bring the boy." Vito Adamo began walking up the steps.

Adamo's brother shoved me toward the stairs. I glanced back at Wesley.

"Don't worry about me," he said. "I'll be fine. Take care of Elizabeth."

I called up the steps. "If Angelo hurts him, Adamo, you're going to pay."

He stopped and turned around. With a smile, he said, "Your friend will be fine. So long as you do your job."

"He better be." I followed Adamo up the stairs and out the front door to a green Hudson roadster. Salvatore and I sat in back, with Adamo in front next to the driver, a fireplug of a man barely five feet tall, with a heavy beard and what looked to be a permanent scowl.

Vito Adamo turned around. "I apologize for the delay. It took some time to find her."

"No apology necessary. It was a lovely night." I don't think terror normally activates my sarcasm, but for some reason I couldn't stop.

He frowned. "I hope you find the rest of your day as humorous, Mr. Anderson."

After a number of twists and turns, we stopped in front of a tenement in an Italian neighborhood. It was one of the old buildings—four stories of crumbling brick that was perhaps fifty years old but already falling apart. They were kind enough to allow me the use of a filthy street-side privy. As soon as I walked out the door, Salvatore pushed me inside the building to a battered wooden stairway that rose from the shadows. At the first landing, three young boys took one look at our party and bolted up the steps, leaving the pennies they'd been pitching on the floor. I tried to get a look at their faces, on the off chance one of them was the boy who took the blackmail money, but they were gone before I got a glimpse. Salvatore stopped long enough to steal their pennies before shoving me up the next flight. It was dim, almost too dim to see the gaping holes in the stairs. I tried to tread carefully, but it was difficult to do while getting a push in the back every few steps.

He pulled me out on the third floor, and we headed down a filthy corridor, stinking of fried fish and rot. Voices surrounded us, carrying through the walls—men, women, and children all speaking or shouting in Italian. We stopped at a small apartment with yellowed walls, darkened by a half century of smoke from the candle sconces around the room and the tiny stove in a soot-blackened corner. Though none of the plank floor was clean, most of the food remnants and trash had been thrown into a moldering two-foot-high pile. The only furniture in the room was a rickety oak table and a chair. Another young Italian man sat at the table, facing a closed door. A revolver lay in front of him.

"Where is she?" I said.

Vito Adamo motioned to the door. I turned the knob with my bound hands and hurried in. Elizabeth lay facing away from me atop a stained mattress, partially covered by a thin gray blanket. She wore a dark burgundy day dress and black button-top shoes. Behind her, some of the plaster had been torn from the wall, leaving gashes here and there of bare wooden planks, wet and rotting. Trash and moldy bits of food covered the floor. A sharp animal stench filled the room.

I knelt down next to her. "Elizabeth?" I nudged her shoulder. "Elizabeth?"

Her hand fluttered toward me and then settled back down at her side. She mumbled something, but I couldn't make it out. I leaned in closer. She stank of urine and a sour body odor. "Elizabeth. Talk to me."

"Go 'way," she muttered. "Leave me . . ."

I reached out and turned her onto her back. What I saw made my eyes close for a moment. A string of saliva stretched from her slack mouth to her shoulder. Dark half-moons painted her face underneath her eyes. Her cheekbones stood out in sharp relief from her skeletal face.

My heart ached. Slowly, she raised an arm and covered her eyes.

"Elizabeth? Lizzie?"

No response.

I looked up at the Adamos with venom in my eyes. "You sons of bitches. How can you do this to another human being?"

Vito spread his hands in front of him. "I do not make their decisions. And I would suggest you do not call us names. I will not tolerate it again."

I sat back on my heels. "She can't tell me anything when she's like this."

"Then I will give you twenty-four hours. And please understand. If you are not able to convince her to tell me what I want to know, I will kill you and your friend, and give Miss Hume to Big Boy. Be assured she *will* tell him. As I said, I do not wish to harm Judge Hume's family, but I must have this information."

He said something to Salvatore and nodded toward me before he turned and walked out of the room, followed by the other man. Without a word, Salvatore untied the knots on my wrists and left, closing the bedroom door behind him.

I sat on the floor next to Elizabeth and put a hand on her shoulder. She had been so beautiful, so full of life. Now death hung over her like a guillotine.

It wasn't much of a moral dilemma: Get information about Judge Hume's dishonesty or let Big Boy get it from her. I had to do it. If Judge Hume was extorting money from gangsters, he deserved nothing less. And if I couldn't get Elizabeth out of here, she would die. I had to get her off the drugs before my trial.

A door slammed. I walked over to the bedroom door and opened it a crack. Salvatore sat at the table with his arms crossed, squinty eyes glaring at me. The revolver still lay on the table. I closed the door and went back to Elizabeth.

Later that afternoon she rolled over on her side and looked at me with a sleepy grin. "Will, what are you doing here?" Her voice was husky, the words drawn out, lazy.

I stroked her head. "I'm here to help you, Lizzie."

"Help me? Help me get some more dope?" She laughed and broke into a coughing fit.

When she quieted, I said, "No. I'm going to help you get off it."

She laughed and was again racked by coughs. "Good old Will. Always wants to help."

I ignored her sarcasm. "That's right. I always want to help you."

"Then get me a drink."

There was nothing in the bedroom. I went to the door and asked Salvatore if he had anything.

One side of his mouth pulled back in a sneer. "Shut 'de goddamn door." His accent was heavier than his brother's. He seemed a lesser version of Vito—not as handsome, probably not as smart, certainly not as commanding. Vito was the boss.

I tried again. "She needs water. Oh, and we need a chamber pot. And another blanket."

He grinned. "Oh, sure. Maybe you like steak, baked potato?" He picked up the gun and aimed it at my head. "Shut 'de door, sonuvabitch."

I did. When I turned around, Elizabeth was tipping a small brown bottle into her mouth. I ran to her and snatched it from her hand. The label on the side read FRIEDR. BAYER & CO., and in large print HEROIN. It was empty.

She smacked her lips and laughed. A few seconds later she quieted and lay back again, her face serene. "Will." Her hand reached out for my arm. "You're my friend." Her eyes were halfway open.

"Yes, Lizzie, I'm your friend."

"Mmmm." She sighed and her eyes closed, a soft smile playing on her lips.


Yet another night passed slowly. I was cold and sweaty, exhausted, with a leaden ache in my head. The past week seemed more a nightmare than actual time passing, my memory a hazy recollection of horror.

It was still dark when Elizabeth shouted out in her sleep, startling me awake. I reached for her arm. She was ice cold, covered in goose bumps, and slick with sweat. I pulled her up against my chest and wrapped the blanket tightly around her.

She slept restlessly, muttering under her breath, shivering, her legs kicking out. Finally, a gray dawn began to appear through the window. Though Elizabeth's teeth chattered and her body was racked with shivers, another hour passed before she roused. Moving sluggishly, she pulled away from me and turned around. "Will?" She rolled over onto the mattress and covered her eyes with her hands. "Right. Will." Her hands shook. She made them into fists. "Leave," she said, her voice thick and dull. "I don't want your pity. Just go."

"First you need to tell Adamo what he wants to know about your father."

"I don't know what you mean."

"Elizabeth, I know he's been asking you. He's not going to let you leave until you tell him."

She was quiet.

"You must know your father's involved with Adamo," I said. "You can't protect him."

She looked back at me. Her face was drawn in the sharp lines of her skull, and her sunken green eyes showed more pain than I thought she could bear. "I don't know what he's doing," she said, sniffling. "He doesn't talk to me."

"Adamo says John told him you knew something."

She turned her head and looked out the window. "I don't know what John was talking about. I don't know anything." Her voice was flat, without inflection. I'd heard her use that tone before. She was lying.

I grabbed her arm. "He told me he'll have Big Boy get it out of you if I can't. Then he'll kill me. And he'll probably kill you." I turned her head toward me. "Do you want that? Do you?"

She looked at me, haunted eyes over meandering tracks where her tears had cut through the dirt. "Kill me?" Tilting her head, she looked up at the ceiling and wet her lips, seeming to taste the idea. "That might be nice."

Elizabeth lay on the mattress, coughing and shivering. I was cold, too. Even though the tiny stove in the other room was vented directly into this one, it had little effect, particularly with the frigid wind howling through the cracks in the ill-fitting window across from us. Only splinters remained of the windowsill, which had probably been used for firewood by a previous inhabitant during a moment of desperation.

How many dismal lives had passed through this room? No water, no heat, no gas, no electricity, holes in the filthy plaster revealing rot and mold. Dozens, perhaps hundreds of men, women, and children spent their lives in this dreary place in a constant struggle for survival, probably feeling every bit as hopeless as I did now. And this was a two-room apartment, the equivalent of a presidential suite in this building.

I'd never appreciated what I had—a loving family, friends, and, oh yes, money. As much as I loved the Detroit I knew, I hated this Detroit. And this was Detroit to many more people than the city in which I spent my life.

I sat next to Elizabeth, absently stroking her hair while I smoked my last cigarette. Our choices were limited. If she didn't tell Adamo what he wanted to know, he was going to kill us. If she did, I believed he would let us go. He seemed to have a strange sort of integrity. He didn't want to exploit Elizabeth's situation to resolve his problem with Judge Hume, which he could easily have done.

Our other option was to try to escape. I glanced at the crumbling wall next to me and pried off a chunk of rotting plaster. I could break through to the apartment behind, but if we escaped Adamo would almost certainly kill Wesley.

I had to convince Elizabeth to talk.

I realized I was going to miss my meeting with Mr. Sutton. It was odd to even consider something like that at this point, but it made me think of something else. "Lizzie?"

"What?"

"When John told me you were in trouble, was he talking about this? The heroin?"

"I told you," she said, coughing spastically. "I'm not in trouble." She wiped her nose on the sleeve of her dress.

There was no sense facing her problems when she wouldn't be around long enough to worry about them. Self-delusion is a wonderful thing.

I handed her my handkerchief. "Why don't you tell Adamo your father's secret and then tell your father Adamo knows about it? He'll be able to figure a way out of the situation. He's a smart man. Surely he can do that."

Elizabeth tucked her head down into her chest and curled up on the mattress. "He's my father. Let me keep a shred of dignity."

The last word made my blood boil. "Dignity? That's a good one. Look at you, lying there in your own filth. That's dignity?" I jumped up and towered over her. "If you want dignity, you'll get cleaned up. You owe it to yourself. Hell, you owe it to me. But that's not going to happen until you tell Adamo your father's damnable secret. You've got to."

She rolled over just far enough to look into my eyes. "I don't owe you anything," she spat. "I wouldn't even be here if it wasn't for you."

"My God, Elizabeth!" I shouted, slamming my fist into the wall. "I know that! But unless you let me help you . . ." I took a deep breath and gathered myself. "Unless you let me help you, unless you tell Adamo, he's going to kill you, Lizzie." I dropped to the floor next to her. "I can't let that happen. Please, Lizzie . . . What will it do to your mother and father if you never come home? They love you. You won't just be letting Adamo help you commit suicide. You'll be killing your parents at the same time."

She hesitated, then in a voice so quiet I barely heard her, she said, "He takes bribes."

# CHAPTER SEVENTEEN

I knelt on the dirty floor next to Elizabeth. "Who does your father take bribes from?"

"The DUR and—well, companies, mostly. But I know that every Friday a DUR man delivers lunch to my father at his office. Inside the lunch is a hundred-dollar bill."

It made sense. Since Mayor Pingree in the 1890s, the city had battled the streetcar companies for lower fares. When Detroit United Railway bought up all the lines to create a streetcar trust, the situation got worse. Many people couldn't afford the nickel fare, and the population explosion in Detroit made it virtually impossible to get a seat on any car. For the past ten years, the city had been trying to break up the DUR, take over the lines, or force them to lower fares. The DUR had recently sued to keep the case from leaving circuit court. So far, even though the public continued to suffer, that court had ruled on the side of Detroit United Railway.

Judge Hume presided over the circuit court.

"I think it's Friday today," I said. "Will you tell Adamo?"

She sniffled and wiped her nose on my handkerchief. "I don't know."

A dog started barking in the apartment behind us. I reached out for Elizabeth's shoulder. "Just do what I said. Tell your father about it. He can stop taking the money. Adamo won't be able to get any evidence, and I'll be able to get you the hell out of here."

After a moment she nodded her head.

The barking got louder. A man in the next apartment shouted in Italian. I heard a sharp *crack*. The dog yelped and began whimpering.

We waited for Vito Adamo. A woman shouted something at the man in the apartment behind us. He shouted back. They argued for a few minutes, a door slammed, and the man stomped down the hallway, his footsteps like rifle shots on the warped wooden floor. The apartment was quiet again. Elizabeth lay on the mattress, coughing and shivering, her legs shaking, kicking out.

Around ten, Vito Adamo's driver walked into the bedroom. Adamo followed him, twirling a black derby on his finger. "Do you have something to tell me?"

Elizabeth pushed herself upright and shoved the greasy hair out of her face. "If I do, you'll let us go?" Somehow, even under these circumstances, she sounded imperious.

"Of course. I am a man of my word."

She explained her father's secret to him. When she finished, Adamo consulted his pocket watch. "*Perfetto.* We will observe the judge today at lunch. If it is as you say, I will release you."

The Adamo brothers left, and the driver took Salvatore's spot at the table. I asked Elizabeth if she was sure this happened every Friday. She said she was, though she didn't look very certain to me. While we waited for them to return, Elizabeth lay down again. Her stomach began cramping, and she retched, over and over, nothing more than stomach acid coming up. She was becoming dehydrated.

"We need to get you to a hospital," I said.

"No." She wiped her mouth. "No hospitals."

"But you have to get off heroin. You have to get clean."

"I know." I thought I saw some resolve in her eyes. "I will."

"Then let me take you to a hospital. You need medical care."

"I won't do that to my family. I won't cause them any more misery."

I squatted down next to her. "What are you going to do?"

She rolled over and grasped my arm. "Stay here with me."

"You need a doctor. I don't know what to do."

"Just stay with me. Help me."

I tried again, and yet again, to talk her into going to a hospital, but she wouldn't be persuaded. I had to give her credit. Even now, Elizabeth was more concerned about her family than herself.

The Adamos finally came back around two o'clock. Vito folded his arms over his chest and looked at us with a thoughtful expression, as if he were trying to decide something. "I am satisfied. The young man who delivered the money was more interested in keeping his fingers than remaining quiet." He bent down in front of us with his hands on his knees. "I am going to trust you. You know things about me that could cause me harm. I do not normally allow that." An amused expression settled on his face. "For some reason, I like you. But please understand. If I even suspect you have gone to the police with this information, I will kill you. Both of you."

I nodded. "We'll be quiet."

"*Grazie.* We understand each other."

"What about my friend?" I said.

Adamo paused for a moment, considering. "I will have someone bring him here. You will need to persuade him that attempting revenge will only get him killed. And you. And Miss Hume." He straightened and turned to leave.

"Do you swear you and your men had nothing to do with John Cooper's death?" I said.

He turned back to me and shook his head. "I had nothing to do with it. I enjoyed doing business with Mr. Cooper. I had no problems with him."

I wasn't sure I heard him right. "You did business— What kind of business did you do with John?"

"His employers occasionally need men for work they don't want to do themselves. I help them." Again, he pantomimed one hand washing the other.

I nodded. The thugs who had beaten the IWW men at the factory now made sense to me. "How about Frank Van Dam? Did you do business with him, too?"

"To me they were one and the same."

"Do you know where Frank went?"

Adamo shrugged. "I do not."

"All right." Dr. Miller had said it would take a week to purge the drug from Elizabeth's system. If I was going to keep her away from her parents that long, we'd need to stay somewhere unexpected. Her father would have the police looking for her. "I'd like to ask a favor."

His smile grew larger, and he glanced at his brother, holding his hands in front of him like he was weighing a pair of melons. "The boy has *grande coglione*, eh?" Turning back to me, he said, "What would you like?"

"Can we keep this room until next Thursday?"

He agreed to rent us the room for fifty dollars, only five times the going rate for a decent hotel room. Since I didn't have the money with me, he told me to bring it to Big Boy at the Bucket before the end of the day. I thanked him and shook his hand, wondering as I did at the incongruity of thanking the man who had kidnapped and threatened to kill us. Salvatore handed me a key to the apartment, and they left.

I locked the door and sat with Elizabeth in the bedroom while I waited for Wesley to arrive. An hour or so later, I heard the apartment door slam. The bedroom door opened, and Wesley was shoved into the room, his hands still bound in front of him.

"Thank God," I said. "Wes, are you okay?"

He shot me a grim smile. The expression clashed with the crusty blood covering one side of his face and the bruises around his eyes. "It would take someone more capable than that lot to hurt me." He glanced at Elizabeth lying on the floor and took in a sharp breath. "Is that Elizabeth?"

I nodded.

"My Lord." His eyes didn't leave her, but he held his hands out in front of me.

I began working the knots loose, trying to keep from touching his broken fingers. "Can you stay with her while I get some supplies?"

"Supplies? We need to get her out of here."

"No. She wants to get off the drugs, but she won't go to a hospital."

"Let's just take her."

I untied the final knot and unwrapped the rope from around his wrists. "Wes, I don't know a hell of a lot about drugs, but one thing I do know is that nobody quits unless they want to. She's saying now she wants to quit. If we force her to go to a hospital, she might change her mind. And if the newspapers got wind of it, it would kill her."

Wesley shook his head vehemently. "There are private hospitals for this sort of thing, Will. This is stupid."

"I promised her."

He blew out a breath in frustration. "You are one stubborn SOB."

I smiled at him. "Thanks. So can you stay?"

"Yes, of course."

I knelt down next to Elizabeth. "Lizzie?"

Her eyes opened halfway.

"I've got to leave for a little while. Wesley will be here if you need anything."

Her eyes, pupils dilated, darted toward me and then away. She rolled over on her side, groaning.


After a trip to the nearby general store, I returned to the filthy apartment with a fifty-pound bag of coal, another bag filled with supplies, and a pail of water. My head was finally clear, and I felt like I had at least a modicum of energy. Before I went into the bedroom, I set the bags and water on the floor, and hung my duster on the back of the chair in the main room, careful to keep the bottles in its pockets from clanking together.

Wesley opened the bedroom door. When he saw me, he stepped out and pushed the door shut. "She's sleeping." He had cleaned his face. A one-inch gash had scabbed up on his forehead, surrounded by a bruise that blended into the others around his eyes.

I stopped and stared. "I'm so sorry, Wes. I should never have gotten you involved in this."

He stared back at me. "How many times do I have to say this? We're friends. Friends help each other."

"Not like this . . . Thanks, really." I carried the bag of coal to the little stove in the corner. It was a cast-iron box stove from early in the last century, now more rust than iron. The wall around it was pitch-black from soot. "Before you go, you and I need to talk."

Wesley cocked his head.

"I know I said we needed to forget about revenge until we found Elizabeth. But as far as Adamo is concerned, I need you to forget about it—period." While I talked, I emptied the ash box into the pan underneath and started feeding pieces of coal into the stove.

"What? That son of a bitch almost cut your throat, and you want to let him off? You can't be serious."

I turned to look at him head on. "Wes, Adamo said he'd kill all three of us if we gave him any trouble or went to the police. No matter what we do, he'll kill Elizabeth. We need to file this one away and forget about it."

He glared at me with his hands on his hips for a moment before looking away. "Yeah, all right. None of those guys was the killer, anyway."

I walked back to the table and began emptying the bag of supplies—food, clothing, blankets, candles, soap, washcloths, a pair of drinking glasses, tobacco and cigarette papers, and a chamber pot. "How did you figure out so quickly it wasn't Big Boy?"

"The killer didn't move anything like him." Wesley lumbered around the room in a parody of the muscle-bound Big Boy.

I slid over into the chair, careful not to shake my coat, and began rolling a cigarette.

"The killer was probably as big," he said, "but he was smooth, graceful."

"None of those other guys could be the killer?"

Wesley shook his head. "But if Adamo was behind the murders, he's smart enough to hide the killer away somewhere. He's probably on his way to Palermo, or wherever he came from."

I bit my lip and thought. "I don't think it was Adamo. Maybe he's a better actor than I'd give him credit for, but he seemed genuinely surprised when I accused him."

"Keep an open mind. Hey, did Edsel ever get back to you?"

"Oh, God." I dropped the cigarette. I'd forgotten Edsel was on a mission that would send him into a world of hardened criminals and murderers—no place for any sane person, much less a seventeen-year-old boy. "Wes, I need you to call him, warn him off. Tell him to stop everything and stay out of this."

"He said he wasn't going to do the digging himself. He's a smart kid, Will. He'll be fine."

"No. Tell him to stop."

Wesley shrugged. "All right. But keep in mind that with no information from him, Adamo's still our only suspect."

"You're right. But I'm not risking Edsel's life on this." I finished rolling the cigarette and held it up to Wesley. He shook his head.

"Oh, speaking of phoning," I said, "I've got a doctor coming over here. He was going into surgery but said he'd come tonight. I don't suppose you could escort him, could you? He sounded awfully nervous about coming to this neighborhood after dark."

"Of course I can."

After I told him where Dr. Miller lived, I stood and walked around the table to Wesley. "If you ever need help with anything—anything—let me know. Until the day I die, I'll do anything I can for you." I put my hand on his shoulder. "You're the best friend I've ever had."

He scuffed a shoe on the floorboards in mock embarrassment. "Aw, shoot. I likes you, too." His smile changed to a puzzled look, and he sniffed the air in front of me. "Did you have a drink?"

I took another step back and lit the cigarette. "Oh, yeah, just one. Clear the mind and all, you know?"

He nodded and smiled, but his eyes were wary.

"I think we're all— Oh, wait," I said.

"What?"

"Have you got fifty bucks?"

"Not on me, but yeah, 'course."

"Could you bring it to Big Boy? I told Adamo I'd get him the money today. Rent."

Wesley's mouth dropped open. "Rent? My God, Will, what the . . .

Yeah, I'll do it. Should I bring him anything else? Perhaps a dozen roses and a box of chocolates?"

I grimaced. I knew it was crazy. "No, the rent will suffice. And I'll pay you back."

After he went to the door and opened it, he paused and looked back at me. "Boy, are you lucky I like you."

I forced a grin and hooked my thumb toward the door. "I know. Now get on home."

As soon as Wesley left, I locked the door behind him and hurried over to my duster. I was salivating. A bottle of cheap whiskey filled each of the four inside pockets. I set the cigarette on the edge of the table and slipped out the bottle I'd already started. I used my teeth to pull out the cork, raised the bottle to my mouth, and tipped my head back. The first long swallow burned my throat. The second spread that familiar warmth through my midsection. On the third I felt the first touch of the slow eclipse that would darken my mind and get me from this day to the next.

It would keep me from thinking.

# CHAPTER EIGHTEEN

While Elizabeth slept, I stayed out at the table sipping whiskey. Not enough to get drunk, just enough to keep that smooth feeling from leaving my head. Wind whistled in through cracks in the wall. This room was even colder than the bedroom.

A baby started crying in the apartment behind me. I took a drink. A minute later, two men walked past in the hallway speaking Italian, their footsteps like the fall of a hammer on the wooden floor. I took another drink. The baby kept crying. I wished someone would do something about it, but it just got louder and louder. I pulled the salt pork from the bag of supplies I'd bought and looked at it for a moment before setting it on the table. More people thudded past in the hallway. I drank some more. I didn't realize I'd been sitting so long until I noticed that the orange glow inside the stove was much brighter than I remembered. Sunset wasn't far away.

I heard a scuffling of feet on the floor of the bedroom. Elizabeth started gagging. I put away the bottle, went to the bedroom door, and knocked softly.

"Go away!" Elizabeth screamed.

I opened the door.

She was squatting in the back corner of the room facing the wall, hunched over with both arms cradling her stomach.

"Elizabeth!" I rushed into the room and knelt beside her.

Her hair hung in sweaty lanks over her face. Vomit stained her dress, filling the room with its stench. "Oh, God, Will, go!" She wailed and cried, her voice thick and wet. "Go!"

How could I have stayed in the other room so long? I turned her head toward me and combed back her hair with my fingers. "No, Lizzie. I'm staying. Help will be here in a couple of hours. We're going to do this together."

She sobbed, and her mouth stretched open in a ghastly rictus. "I'm afraid. It hurts." In a sudden movement, she reached out with both hands and grasped the front of my shirt. "You've got to get me more," she said, eyes wide, unfocused.

"Lizzie, I can't."

"I can taper off." Tears and mucus streamed down her face. "Just let me do that."

My heart was breaking. But I couldn't. "No, honey. You've already started." I caressed her cheek with the back of my hand. "It'll get better soon, I promise."

She threw my hand off her and jerked me forward, my shirt held in an iron grip. "You bastard!" she screamed. "You bastard! I should have killed you!" Her screams soon melted into sobs, and she let go of my shirt and curled up on the floor in the fetal position, crying and moaning. Finally, she fell asleep.

The room was becoming rose-tinted by the sunset. The delicate glow through the window softened her form until I saw her as an Impressionist portrait, beautiful but diffuse, each measured brushstroke incomplete yet creating something approaching perfection. I loved this woman. I had hurt her like no one else ever could. But at least I was suffering, too.

I went out to the table, picked up the bottle, and carried it into the bedroom, leaving the door open so I would be sure to hear Wesley. Leaning my back against the wall, I slid down to the floor and had another drink or two in the deepening gloom. Some time later, a soft knock sounded against the apartment door. I hurried out to the table and felt inside my duster for the empty pocket. After I slid the whiskey bottle inside, I called out, "Who's there?"

"Will, it's me," Wesley said.

To cover the whiskey on my breath, I bit a chunk off the salt pork and chewed it while opening the door.

Wesley guided Dr. Miller into the apartment with a gentle push in the back. "Have you noticed it's a little dark in here?" Wesley said. He flicked his lighter with his bandaged hands.

"Sorry." I swallowed the pork and grabbed a candle off the table. Wesley lit it, and I slipped it into the wax-caked sconce on the wall. The yellow light threw long, flickering shadows across the room.

The doctor's eyes flitted about nervously. Wesley looked worried, but I knew his concern was for Elizabeth and me, not his surroundings. Dr. Miller tightened his grip on his black medical bag. Glancing at the bedroom door, he said, "How's she doing?"

"Not well."

"You know she needs a hospital."

"She won't go," I said. "This is the only way. There's no reason I can't do this, is there? I mean, with your help?"

"It's not a good idea. Elizabeth's life is at stake here."

"You said it yourself, Doctor. The only way she'll achieve a permanent cure is if she wants it. She wants this. Maybe that will be enough."

Dr. Miller set his medical bag on the edge of the table, shaking his head slowly. "All right. But I must insist that I examine her first."

"That's fine with me," I said. "Elizabeth may not be quite so enthusiastic."

He adjusted his spectacles and gave me a sidelong glance. "She is here of her own volition?"

"Yes, but I'm not sure she'll admit that right at this moment."

He cleared his throat and looked away. "You understand . . . I can't be a party to any . . . criminal activities."

"Criminal? Doctor, she asked me to do this. She wants to get off heroin, but she's afraid to go to a hospital." I grabbed hold of his arm. "Right now she's in serious pain and isn't rational. I need your help."

The bedroom door cracked open, and Elizabeth peeked out. "Dr. Miller," she said, her voice trembling. "Come in here. Just you."

The doctor poured a glass of water from the pail, took a deep breath, and entered the bedroom, closing the door behind him. For perhaps a minute, he spoke to her in low, soothing tones, but her voice became louder and more strident by the second.

Then Elizabeth shouted, "But you don't know what *he* did!"

Dr. Miller said something quietly.

Her tone turned to pleading. "If I just had a little more . . . I can taper off, Doctor. Please, please . . ." Her words dissolved into sobs.

The doctor's voice was a murmur through the thin apartment walls. After a few minutes they both were quiet.

The doctor finally came out of the room with his medical bag under one arm, wiping his hands with a handkerchief. "She'll sleep now." He tucked the handkerchief into his breast pocket and smiled. "It took a few minutes for Elizabeth to admit she was here with you willingly, but her basic decency came through. That's a good sign. You may be able to pull this off."

He set his bag on the table and rooted around in it for a minute before pulling out a pair of brown medicine bottles, a small spoon, and a large bottle of pills. He held out the small bottles. "This is belladonna extract. It counteracts some of the effects of the heroin and causes a delirium that helps mask the pain of withdrawal." He put a hand on my shoulder. "But in too large a dosage it will kill her. Do you understand?"

I nodded.

He pointed to the other bottle. "These will help to purge the drug from her system. I gave her a single teaspoon of belladonna and three of the pills with a full glass of water. I'm going to observe her for a while to make sure the dosage is correct. Would you mind if I use that chair?" He pointed to the chair that held my duster.

"No, not at all," I said, rushing over to it and carefully removing my coat. When I laid it on the floor, the bottles made a muffled clunk. I stiffened for a moment before I recovered and brought the chair to him. Neither he nor Wesley appeared to notice the sound.

Dr. Miller took the chair and opened the bedroom door again. "You two may take a break if you'd like. I suspect I'll be watching her for at least two hours. Will, do you have something I can wash her with, and anything else for her to wear?"

I took a washcloth, a bar of soap, a towel, and a flannel nightgown from the table, and carried them into the bedroom along with the pail of water. Dr. Miller shut the door when I left. I sat next to Wesley on the floor near the stove with my back propped against the wall.

He reached into his right coat pocket with his thumb and forefinger, and awkwardly pulled out his little derringer. "Sorry, it's all I've got left," he whispered. "One shot, and it's not a man-stopper by any means, but it'll slow somebody down if you need to use it." He dug half a dozen bullets out of his waistcoat pocket.

I slipped the gun and ammunition into the inside pocket of my jacket. "Thanks, Wes. I don't know what I'd do without you."

He grinned. "Well, you'd certainly have a lot less sunshine in your day."

"Wes, if you don't mind me asking, what the hell are you doing in Detroit?"

"As opposed to, let me guess, New York?"

"Well, yeah. You've got the talent."

He was quiet for a moment. The hum of Elizabeth's voice carried through the wall.

"You never know." He picked up a scrap of newspaper from the floor, crumpled it up, and began tossing it in the air and catching it. "Perhaps I'll make it to the Great White Way someday. But I kind of like being a big fish in a small pond. In New York, I'd be a minnow in an ocean."

"Could you explain something to me?" I said. "I was cruel to you. And not just once. Over and over. Yet you still tried to be my friend. Why?"

He glanced at me with a tentative smile. "You reminded me of my-self. I haven't always been the *bon vivant* man about town you see be-fore you. For most of my life, I've been hurt and angry, but most of all filled with self-loathing. Because of what I am."

It was my turn to be quiet. After a moment, I said, "What turned you around?"

"A . . . friend." His eyes cut to the floor. "He made me realize I wasn't a freak. He helped me believe I was a good person."

"I'd like to meet him." I meant it.

His face clouded. He threw the ball of paper onto the pile of trash in the corner. "We're not friends anymore. The truth is he's why I stayed in Detroit. But he left last summer."

"What happened?"

"What ever happens? One person changes and the other doesn't, or changes in a different way. One grows weary of the other. What was once joyful becomes painful. The bloom withers and dies."

We sat quietly for a few minutes. I watched the coals flare in the stove. Elizabeth's voice rose in the bedroom.

"So, what was she like?" Wesley said. "Before."

I wrapped my arms around my knees and brought them up to my chest. "She loved me. It sounds so simple, I know, but that's what I remember. Whenever she saw me her eyes would light up, like her love was a spark burning so brightly it couldn't be contained." I shook my head. "I never realized how much I should cherish that look. Until it was gone."

The coals popped and hissed. I pulled out my wallet and handed him Elizabeth's note. "She used to send me letters at the office. I finally asked her to stop because the other managers were needling me. It was too embarrassing." I could feel tears begin to well up in my eyes. "She loved me, Wes. She loved me, and I made her stop."

Wesley handed the note back to me. "We all have regrets, William. It's part of being human." We sat for a while in a companionable silence. He cleared his throat. "So you seem to have gotten past it."

"Past what?"

"Past who I am." He smiled. "You know, an entertainer."

I nodded, surprised at myself. "I have. I don't care if you're an 'entertainer' or a Mexican spy or a Martian. You're an amazing fellow."

"Thanks. You know, I don't want to bugger every man or boy who comes along any more than you want to have sex with every female you see. I may be wired a little differently, but we're more alike than you'd know."

"No. I'm not like you." I sighed and then turned my head so he could see my eyes. "But I wish I was."

Hours passed before Dr. Miller opened the door and asked me to come in.

Elizabeth lay on her back tucked into a pair of warm blankets. Her eyes were closed, and she was having an animated yet unintelligible conversation with some unseen person.

Dr. Miller gestured toward her and said, "I'm happy with the dosage. One teaspoon and three pills every six hours until next Tuesday unless her behavior changes significantly."

"But that's . . . five days. I thought you said it takes seven."

He nodded and pulled out another small bottle. "Five days of belladonna, two more under sedation, to be sure the drugs have been fully flushed from her system. Hallucinations are perfectly normal in a belladonna delirium. Under no circumstance is she to be left alone at any time. Force her to drink as much water as you can. It will hydrate her and help flush out the heroin." He cleared his throat, looking uncomfortable. "Her vomiting should clear up in a day or so, but, for the most part, she won't have control over her bodily functions. You really should have a woman here, a nurse, to keep her clean. I know many who I'm sure would be discreet—"

"No. I'll do it." I took his arm and led him to the door. "And Doctor, could you call my father and let him know I'm not up to any trouble? Please don't tell him what I'm doing or where I am. Just assure him I'll be in contact as soon as I can."

"Certainly." He smiled at me. "It's a noble thing you're doing, Will. I just hope you know what you've gotten yourself into." Before he left, Dr. Miller made me promise to have Wesley phone him at least once a day to apprise him of Elizabeth's condition.

As he and Wesley were leaving, I said, "Be careful out there. This isn't the best of neighborhoods."

Wesley grinned and gave me a thumbs-up. It seemed an ironic gesture, given that his thumbs were the only digits protruding fully from the bandages.

They left. I walked into the bedroom and sat on the floor next to Elizabeth. She was quiet now. The light from the candle on the wall danced, shadowing the hollows on her face and washing out what little color she had left. She could have been a corpse. I checked her pulse to make sure she wasn't.

Occasionally she murmured in her sleep but seemed to be resting comfortably. I brought the bottle of whiskey into the bedroom and resumed my watch. As the night wore on, she became more agitated, but settled down again with her next dose of medicine. Exhausted, I blew out the candles and walked to the only window in the room. Elizabeth couldn't escape through the locked apartment door. I was going to make sure she didn't leave via a third-story window. I laid down underneath it and fell asleep the second my head hit the floor.

Sometime in the night it became cold enough that I woke shivering. I lit a candle, and was in the other room loading coal into the stove when Elizabeth began babbling, her words slurred by the belladonna.

"John?" She sounded alarmed. "I can't believe you would . . . Who is she?"

I walked into the bedroom. Elizabeth was standing facing the doorway. The candle was guttering in the sconce, throwing exaggerated shadows that danced behind her. She buried her face in her hands and wept.

I took hold of her arm and tried to coax her to the mattress. "Come with me, Elizabeth."

She resisted and turned to me. "No. I can't go with you, Frank. It's wrong." Her eyes looked right through me. "I don't love you."

"Frank? Van Dam?"

She was quiet for a moment. "That's sweet, Frank," she slurred. "But I can't. I'm so sorry."

I improvised. "Come away with me, Elizabeth," I said, trying to impersonate Frank.

"No, I can't. You have to understand."

"Where am I, Elizabeth?"

She began to babble nonsense words. After another minute she allowed me to lay her down on the mattress.

I didn't think she knew any Franks other than Frank Van Dam. She said she couldn't go with Frank because she didn't love him. Interesting, as Detective Riordan was so fond of saying. Was this a random hallucination, or was there some basis in fact for this conversation? I was going to have to talk with Dr. Miller about the effects of belladonna.

# CHAPTER NINETEEN

Wesley returned in the morning. "You've got a problem, Will," he said, hurrying inside. He set a pile of clean clothing and blankets on the table. "The papers are full of hysterical ravings from Judge Hume about Elizabeth being kidnapped."

I cursed. "Of course they are. I need to phone him. Can you watch her for a while?"

"Sure. Oh, that reminds me. I tried phoning Edsel, but he wasn't in. I left a message for him to cease and desist."

"Thanks. Keep trying, will you? I want to be absolutely certain he stops."

Wesley nodded.

I checked my pockets and found almost three dollars. A phone call, some food, another bag of coal, and two more bottles of cheap whiskey would cost about half that, and I'd still have some emergency money. "Thanks, Wes. Okay, well, I should leave now. You ought to get into the bedroom in case Elizabeth's awake."

"Sure."

As soon as the bedroom door closed behind him, I took the three remaining whiskey bottles from my duster and, as quietly as I could, hid them under the pile of trash in the corner of the room.

I ran down to the general store around the corner. It was a small shop, and shabby, with half-empty shelves, but the Italian shopkeeper kept it swept and clean. The telephone sat on the counter toward the back, offering little privacy, but I wasn't going out on a search for another one. I dropped a nickel into the coin box, and when the receiver unlocked, I raised it to my ear and asked the operator for the Hume residence.

Alberts answered and nearly hung up before I could tell him I was calling about Elizabeth. I asked for the judge. Only a few seconds later, he was on the phone. I told him Elizabeth was with me now and was safe. He demanded I bring her home immediately. I told him she was a heroin addict. He didn't sound as surprised as I thought he would, but he was no less insistent that I bring her home. I explained why I couldn't, that she had to beat the addiction on her own terms. He continued to argue with me. I had to hang up on him.

Instead of solving the problem, I had made it worse. Now the police would know for certain she was with me.

Next, I phoned Dr. Miller and asked him whether the experiences in Elizabeth's hallucinations could actually have happened. He waffled. It was possible, but there was no way to know. That wasn't helpful. Elizabeth's conversation with Frank may have been provoked by a real-life experience. Then again, it may not have. I needed to find out.

I decided to buy three bottles of whiskey. We had enough food to last the week. Neither of us was eating much.


When I got back to the apartment, I threw the coal next to the stove before hanging my duster on the chair and cracking open the bedroom door. Wesley was leaning against the wall, looking out the window. Elizabeth lay curled up on the mattress with the blankets tucked around her. Wesley saw me and came out to the main room.

I told him about my conversation with Judge Hume. We decided I needed to stay inside the apartment for the duration, though Wesley volunteered to come back at night and watch Elizabeth while I got some rest. I thanked him but told him no. I was responsible for her.

After a moment, he nodded. "Do you need anything else?"

I bit the inside of my cheek. "Well, yeah. A couple bottles of Old Tub would help pass the time."

He appraised me for a moment. "Sure. Tomorrow soon enough?"

I scratched a fleabite on my forearm, looking down at it like I'd just been bitten. "Yeah, sure. That would be fine."

Before he left with our stinking clothing and blankets, Wesley checked our supplies and refilled our water pail from the well down the street. He even emptied the chamber pot. He was a *good* friend.

When I gave Elizabeth her next dose of medicine, I decided to wash her. I worked around the nightgown, keeping her covered as well as I could, and didn't look at any more of her body than I absolutely had to. Still, it was impossible not to notice her condition—hipbones and ribs standing out in sharp detail, breasts flattened against her chest as if punctured, arms and legs like sticks. It made me want to cry.

Keeping my eyes averted, I dressed her in a clean nightgown, then changed the sheet and tucked her into two of the new blankets. For the rest of the day I kept spooning out the medicine. At times, Elizabeth had vivid hallucinations—talking to unseen people, fleeing from demons, drifting around the room with her arms outstretched as though flying. Other times she lay sleeping, as still as the dead. During her few lucid moments, I fed her and forced her to drink as much water as I could.

And, of course, I spent much of the day and night fortifying myself with the whiskey. Even with the bourbon Wesley was bringing, the liquor wasn't going to last the week.

I dozed when possible, always sitting or lying under the window to be sure Elizabeth didn't try to jump. Wesley came back Sunday morning with more clean clothing, another stack of blankets, and most important, two glistening bottles of Old Tub. I asked him to get another bottle of belladonna from Dr. Miller. He did me one better. A few hours later he returned with the doctor.

After he examined Elizabeth, Dr. Miller came back into the main room and said, "You're doing a fine job, Will." He set his medical bag on the table and brought out another bottle of the drug. "This is more than enough to last until Tuesday night. Her withdrawal symptoms are decreasing, though she will continue to cramp for another day or two."

He set his hand on my shoulder. "Make sure she gets plenty of water. Discontinue the belladonna Wednesday morning, but continue to give her the pills and start her up on the sedative. Same dosage. Bring her to my office Thursday afternoon."

I thanked him again for his help. Wesley led the doctor to the door, and they padded down the hall—the only quiet walking I'd heard since I'd been here. I spent the day staying just sober enough to keep an eye on Elizabeth. The first bottle of Old Tub emptied quickly. I blended the second one with the rotgut, making it a little more palatable, before refilling the first bottle halfway. I left both bourbon bottles on the tabletop.

I kept myself sedated during the day and slept the sleep of the dead under the bedroom window, though I woke hours before the sun rose. Elizabeth was sleeping Monday morning when a fist pounded on the apartment door. I was groggy and still a little drunk.

Wesley called, "Will? Will?" He sounded excited or afraid, I couldn't tell which.

I jumped up and hurried to the door. When I opened it, Wesley thrust a *Detroit Journal* into my hand and pointed at the headline—front-page center. My mouth fell open.

Plastered across the top of the page was this:

*JUDGE HUME ARRESTED IN EAD BRIBERY SCANDAL*

I read the beginning of the article.

> *Circuit Court Judge Reginald Hume was arrested today by the Michigan State Police on multiple felony charges of receiving rewards for official misconduct. It is alleged that the judge accepted large sums of money in exchange for decisions favorable to the Employers Association of Detroit. Also implicated were a number of EAD officials, although police are not releasing any names at this time.*

I looked up at Wesley. "This is the connection to John. This is why someone killed him. He had to have been involved."

"Do you think Elizabeth knew about this?"

I frowned. "With her father and fiancé both involved? She must have."

Wesley reached back into the hallway and pulled in a small bag of coal. "So what are you going to do?"

I thought for a moment. "I'm going to get her to tell me about it." I threw the newspaper onto the table. "Say, have you spoken with Edsel yet?"

He shook his head. "I've left several messages."

"I'm sure there's a good reason he hasn't called back. But keep trying, okay? I don't want him to get hurt."

Wesley nodded. He kept me company for another hour, then left for Crowley Milner to sing. Even though he still couldn't play piano, he was a hot commodity. When he left I settled in for the day.

The more I thought about Elizabeth, the angrier I got. Her father and John were involved in an ongoing criminal activity. She had to know about it, but didn't tell anyone even though John was murdered. She could have added two and two—John and her father were committing a high-profile crime, John was murdered, therefore that crime was the basis for John's murder.

Could she have been complicit in his death? It didn't seem possible. Elizabeth was no killer. But she had to know something.

The rest of that day and the next, I asked her questions each time the belladonna started to wear off. There seemed to be a brief window during which I could direct her thoughts, and I quizzed her repeatedly about John and Frank and her father, but I got no answers, coherent ones anyway. I thought my luck would change on Wednesday when the belladonna wore off, but the sedative kept her sleeping twenty-two hours a day, and dazed and unfocused the rest of the time. By Thursday morning, my frustration had reached a boiling point.

One way or another, today she would tell me about her father and John.

Eight hours had passed since Elizabeth's last dose of sedative. She had been stirring for the past hour, but with normal movements, not the jerks and twitches that accompanied her withdrawals. Her face even showed a touch of color.

It was time she found out what had happened to her father. I woke her and propped her against the wall.

"More medicine?" Her voice was still lazy, but she looked alert.

"No, we're done with that." I knelt down on the floor next to her and had her drink a glass of water, then I fed her some bread with slivers of meat. After she ate, I gave her the newspaper with the article about her father's arrest. "Read this."

She blinked a few times, trying to focus on the print. "Arrested?"

"You knew your father was taking bribes from the Employers Association, didn't you?"

"What?" She rubbed her face, stalling.

"John was paying off your father, wasn't he?"

"They didn't talk to me about things like that."

"But you knew it, didn't you?"

She was quiet for a moment. "Yes."

"Did it ever occur to you John might have been killed because of this?"

"I don't know." She lay down on the mattress and curled into a ball, tucking her arms and legs in close to her.

"Your fiancé is murdered, and you know he's participating in an illegal activity. And you don't know if you thought he might have been killed because of it."

"I've been sick, and it's your fault. Leave me alone."

"All right then, tell me this. Was John an informant? Was he talking to the state police?"

"I don't know."

I took a deep breath and let it out slowly. "Do you think your father could have been involved in John's death?"

"No." The word seemed to come out automatically.

"Why not?"

"He loved John."

"Loved John enough to go to prison for him?"

She didn't answer.

We left the apartment at 2:00 P.M. With the lapels of my suit coat raised and Elizabeth enveloped in her coat, I hailed a cab to take us to Dr. Miller's. We were lucky enough to get a Yellow Bonnet to stop for us, one of the Chalmers 30 limousines, black with a bright yellow top. We sat on opposite sides. Elizabeth huddled down in her seat, glum and brooding. I looked out the window, not feeling much different.

I tried to sort out my feelings for her. I had loved her with every fiber of my being. I had grieved her loss for more than a year. And now I had thrown my life away trying to save her. Back when we were together she was intelligent and warm and fun. Now she was a drug-addicted liar. I still loved her, yet she disgusted me.

Once we emerged from the slums, I saw that the city had transformed. Christmas decorations had sprung up out of nowhere. Evergreen boughs wound around the street lamps, wreaths hung on doors of homes and businesses, tinsel adorned trees alongside the roads. But stranger yet was the stillness. The streets, normally crammed with vehicles on a Thursday afternoon, were empty. I leaned forward and asked the cabdriver why that was.

"It's Thanksgiving," he said. "Where ya been? China?"

Thanksgiving. I had never missed a Thanksgiving dinner at my parents' house and suspected Elizabeth hadn't, either. My family—mother and father, sisters and their husbands and children—was sitting down to turkey, sweet potatoes, and pumpkin pie. Amid all this insanity, life went on.

Just not for us.

It was a quick drive to Dr. Miller's house. His butler answered the door and let us in the side entrance to the office. A few minutes later the doctor greeted us, and he and Elizabeth went into an examination room for fifteen minutes or so. When they came out he was forcing a smile. She looked miserable.

"She's going to be fine." Dr. Miller patted Elizabeth's shoulder like a kindly grandfather. "Bed rest, food, water." He turned her toward him.

"But it's up to you. You've done the hard part. Now you have to stay strong."

Sighing, she nodded and looked at her feet.

The cabbie was still waiting at the curb when we left the office. I guided Elizabeth inside first and climbed in behind her. After I gave the cabbie the Humes' address, he pulled away from the curb.

I tapped the armrest with a finger and spoke casually. "Why didn't you go with Frank?"

Elizabeth's eyes darted toward me. "What?"

"He loved you. Why didn't you go with him?"

"I don't know what you mean."

"Elizabeth." I shook my head. "Don't even try. It was practically all you talked about while you were on the belladonna."

"But I don't . . . He didn't . . ."

"It was because you didn't love him, wasn't it?"

She looked away and answered quietly. "Yes."

"Tell me about it."

After a brief hesitation, she said, "All right. But give me a cigarette first."

"When did you start smoking?"

She shrugged, staring straight in front of her.

I pulled a cigarette from my case and handed it to her. Lighting it, I said, "So?"

She took a long drag. "Okay. I got a letter from him."

I tried not to show my surprise. "When was that?"

"A few days after John was . . . you know."

"What did he want, besides for you to come with him?"

"He said he was sorry he left without saying good-bye. He wanted me to know that he went to Denver to get away from the Employers Association, that it was turning him into a bad person."

"Right. And how were you supposed to get hold of him?"

"He said he'd contact me." She glanced at me and then dropped her eyes to the floor of the cab. "Frank always liked me." She was talking so quietly I could barely hear her over the road noise and the taxi's gasoline engine. "He tried to help me out after I got addicted. He told me John had a mistress. Frank said he'd never do that to the woman he loved." She took another drag on the cigarette and let the smoke drift out from the corner of her mouth.

"Could I see the letter?"

"I threw it out. I like Frank. I don't love him." She looked out the window and gave a quiet laugh. "He said he would come back for me in his merry Oldsmobile. His words."

When she said "his merry Oldsmobile," alarms sounded in my head. That niggling thought that had been bothering me for so long finally coalesced, hitting me like a lightning bolt. At the train station, one of the twins had been standing next to a red Oldsmobile touring car—a red Oldsmobile Palace touring car. I cursed.

"What?"

"Frank's red Oldsmobile! It was at the train station when the Doyles got killed and it was gone when I went back. Frank was involved in the bribery. He's on the run. Son of a bitch. It's Frank. Frank's the killer."

# CHAPTER TWENTY

Elizabeth looked bewildered. "Train station? Doyles? What are you talking about?"

"Never mind that." I grabbed hold of her arm. "It was Frank who killed John. I'm certain of it."

Her mouth tightened. "That's crazy. Frank wouldn't have killed John."

"He was involved in the bribery, too, wasn't he?"

"I don't know."

"Elizabeth!"

"I don't know." She shook my hand off her and looked out the window. "No one ever said."

"I'm betting he was. And that's why he killed John. Frank is a violent man. You have to stay away from him."

"That's ridiculous."

"If he loves you, wouldn't he do anything to be with you?"

The cab jerked to a stop. A trolley was crossing the road in front of us. "Well . . . No. Not Frank. They were friends. He looked up to John."

"But John had you. And maybe John was going to testify against him. Frank couldn't be with you if he was spending five to ten in the penitentiary. Elizabeth, you need to wake up. Frank's a killer."

Her brow furrowed. The cab started up again. After the clacking of the trolley's metal wheels had faded into the distance, she said, "I don't know. Perhaps you're right." She looked uncertain and young, too young to have to deal with this nightmare.

"I am right. If you hear from him again, you've got to tell me."

"Well . . ."

"Promise me."

She tapped her ash into the ashtray and took another pull on the cigarette. The ember was almost touching her fingers.

"Elizabeth, you've got to promise me. I just want what's best for you."

She opened her window a crack and flicked her cigarette butt onto the street. "All right. If I hear from him again, I'll let you know."

"But why would Frank frame . . ." Then it hit me. "Elizabeth, did you tell Frank about . . . your situation?"

She looked back at me, her eyes dull, blank, dead. "Whatever are you talking about, Will?"

"You know."

She stared at me for at least ten seconds before turning away and looking out the window. "Not that I remember. But there's a lot I don't remember." She was quiet for a moment. "And a lot more I wish I didn't."

We rode the rest of the way in silence.


After leaving Elizabeth outside her home, I directed the cabdriver to my apartment, fantasizing about a hot bath and a change of clothes. When he turned onto Peterboro Street, I was happy to see an empty lawn in front of my building. Whether it was because of Thanksgiving or not, the reporters had given up, at least for now.

The fare came to $2.20. The cabbie waited at the curb while I ran inside to grab some more money.

Two steps in, my throat collided with a solid object. My feet flew out from under me, and I landed hard on my back. That same fat policeman leaned over me, a stupid grin underneath his bottlebrush mustache. My throat was on fire.

"That's called a clothesline, chorus boy. Remember that the next time you want to run." He cuffed me, and he and his muscular, slack-jawed partner dragged me to a horse-drawn paddy wagon parked off Second Street. I only now realized that I hadn't seen one of Sutton's men at the door of my building.

The cabdriver followed us, protesting all the way that I owed him money. At the back of the wagon, Bottlebrush pulled out his truncheon and tapped it against his palm while staring at the cabbie, who wisely decided to retreat. When I climbed in the back of the wagon, Slack Jaw shoved me, and I fell to the floor of the stench-ridden cage.

"Asshole," I muttered, and pushed myself up into a seated position. The wagon rocked as the cops climbed on. The reins snapped, and the horses clopped along, moving the wagon in a hypnotic rhythm—forward, pause, forward, pause.

The rhythm didn't calm me. The longer I sat in the back of the wagon, the more enraged I became. I was innocent, yet I was headed back to jail, almost certainly because of Judge Hume. It seemed unlikely I'd be leaving again before I was sent to prison for the rest of my life. And I just kept taking it, a lamb to slaughter.

Why? Why did I accept this treatment? I wasn't afraid to die, but I continued to let Wesley, the Doyles, Mr. Sutton, fight my battle for me. Wesley had been shit on all his life and still had more fight in his pinkie than I had in my entire body. He didn't even have a stake in this game, other than his friendship with me, yet he was a samurai while I cowered in the dark, afraid of getting hurt.

I screamed out an animal roar, and another, and shook the bars at the back of the cage with all my might. I was through being everyone's patsy.

At the Bethune Street station, the policemen handed me over to a guard, who shoved me back into the jail and down a darkened redbrick corridor. I tried to shake his hand off me and was rewarded with a smack to the side of my head.

Unlike the last time I was here, the criminals in the cells we passed didn't harass me. To all appearances, I belonged here, not a swell, an easy mark. That was a start.

The guard stopped at a large cell near the beginning of the hallway, uncuffed me, and unlocked the door. Three men lay on a matching number of benches, four others on the filthy concrete floor. Two toughs stood by the door, arms crossed over their chests, menace in their eyes.

The guard pushed me into the cell and slammed the door shut.

I ignored the men and walked toward an unclaimed section of brick wall, trying to look mean.

"Hey," a voice called from behind me. "Mary Ann."

I turned slowly and gave the man Wesley's dead-eyes look.

He had a week's growth of beard over a narrow face, eyes close together. His small mouth turned up in a grin, exposing a number of dark spaces where teeth should have been. He glanced at his partner, eyes wide. "Eww, he's a scary one, ain't he?" Neither of the men were particularly big, but they had the look of predators—grim sets to their mouths, tendons taut in the forearms, an unmistakable animal gleam in their eyes.

The first man looked down at my feet. "Them's some nice boots you got there. I could use some nice boots."

I said nothing, just kept giving him the dead eyes, as I got angrier and angrier.

The man sauntered over to me, his face now inches from mine. "I bet you'd like to give me them boots for a Thanksgiving present, wouldn't you?" His breath reeked of rotting teeth.

A white-hot ball of rage rose from my gut. I kneed the man in the groin as hard as I could. His body jackknifed toward me. I grabbed hold of his greasy hair with both hands and jerked his head down as my knee thrust up again, catching him squarely in the face. He fell to the floor, groaning and cupping his genitals in his hands. I kicked him in the stomach, twice, before I was able to get control of myself.

Barely breathing hard, I stared at the other tough, eyes dead again. He looked away. I kept staring at him. "You want my boots?" I really wanted him to want them.

He didn't look at me. "Uh, no, no, my shoes is fine."

I turned and walked over to the bench, adrenaline pumping through my veins, and sat next to a man who had managed to stay asleep through the ruckus. I looked around the cell, blank face topped by dead eyes. No one returned my gaze. I wasn't happy or exultant over my victory, but I felt a satisfaction I never had before—pleasure derived from hurting someone.

Maybe I had a chance for survival in a place like this after all.

The rest of the prisoners left me alone. I sat on the bench and thought. I had to have been arrested because of Elizabeth. As soon as she talked to the police, they would let me go. Between now and then I had to keep myself in one piece.

My hands began to tremble. This time it wasn't from fear, I was sure. Even though the cell was cold, I was sweating profusely, and my stomach had an ache that could only be assuaged by one thing. I *needed* a drink.

Sometime past dawn a guard walked down the corridor toward us, carrying chains that clanked louder and louder with each step. He unlocked the cell door and pulled me out into the dim hallway. After cuffing my hands in front of me and locking metal bands with a short chain between them onto my ankles, he pushed me down the corridor. I shuffled along, trying not to fall.

Detective Riordan awaited me in an interrogation room, another featureless ivory box with a heavy oak table and two matching chairs in the center. He was sitting facing the door. With a snide smile, he said, "Nice to see you again, Will."

"I wish I could say the same."

"That nose looks pretty bad. What happened?"

"I fell down the stairs."

"Must have been a long fall."

I didn't say anything.

He sat back. "Judge Hume has made some serious allegations against you, Will. Kidnapping and drugs, among other things. What do you have to say for yourself?"

"Wow, I've been busy, huh?"

This time it was Riordan who didn't respond.

"Look, Elizabeth was with me of her own free will. She's home now and fine. Besides, you know Judge Hume's a crook. Why would you believe him?"

"Yeah, I'll have to concede that one. But still, Miss Hume was missing for more than a week, you were missing almost as long, and now you're both back and everyone's fine and dandy?"

"Talk to Elizabeth."

"I'll do that, Will. But she's in isolation right now." He leaned forward and stared at me. "She's too traumatized to speak with anyone."

I shook my head. "That's bunk. Is her father out?"

Riordan probed the inside of his cheek with his tongue. "Yup. Never set foot in jail. The wheels turn fast when you're a circuit court judge."

"The judge is the one who's traumatized. She's fine. Look, do you have any interest in catching the real killer?"

"The way I see it, he's already caught."

This was crazy. I was innocent. Anyone ought to be able to see that. I leaned toward him and spoke slowly, enunciating each word. "Frank Van Dam killed John Cooper."

I thought I saw a flicker of uncertainty in Riordan's eyes before he frowned at me and said, "Haven't we talked about this?"

"His car was at the train station the night the Doyles were killed, and it was gone a few hours later. Frank was one of the few men who could have gotten close enough to John to surprise him. He moved west, you were right about that—to Denver, by the way. But not until he killed John." I didn't know for sure about Frank's involvement in Judge Hume's bribery, but I put it out there anyway. "John and Frank were paying off Judge Hume. I'll bet John was talking to the state police, and Frank had to keep him quiet."

While I was talking, Riordan pulled a cigar from his coat pocket and studied it, rolling it in his fingers, a picture of boredom. When I was done, he glanced up and said, "Finished?"

I was furious. "Riordan, even *you* can't be this stupid. You know I didn't—"

His right hand shot out and caught me in the mouth, knocking me straight over backward. I tried to jump to my feet, but I got caught up in the manacles and went down again. I took my time getting up, glaring at him as I did. He just sat back in his chair and smiled at me. "You will treat me with respect, Mr. Anderson."

My mouth tasted of blood, and one of my front teeth was loose, but I wasn't going to give him the satisfaction of knowing how badly it hurt. I spat on the floor, picked up the chair, and sat again.

He gestured for me to continue, but the punch had knocked the conversation out of my head. I stared at him until he said in a monotone, "Riordan, even you can't be this stupid. You know I didn't . . ."

Right. "You know I didn't kill John," I finished. "If I was going to do that, I'd have cozied up to him for quite a while before luring him away to somewhere quiet. You'd never have found the body."

He tilted his head to the side, smiling. "So you thought about it, did you?"

"No, and it doesn't matter anyway. I didn't do it."

"Oh, by the way," Riordan said. "I got your clothing. Thanks."

"What?" I was totally blank.

"Your clothing. Thanks for sending it over."

*Oh, shit.* "You . . . got my clothing?"

Riordan shook his head and sighed. "Do we really need to play charades anymore? Just give it up, Will."

"You think I sent you the clothes? It was Frank. He's the blackmailer and the killer!"

"I'd agree with you on part of that. I think the man who sent me those clothes killed John Cooper."

"You can't possibly believe that's me. I gave you the blackmail notes. He threatened to send you the clothes if I didn't follow his instructions."

"Yeah, funny thing about those notes."

"What about them?"

He made a big production out of pulling them from his coat pocket and tossing them on the table, then gestured for me to pick them up. "Go on," he said when I hesitated. "They're yours."

I picked up the notes and, with both hands, began sliding them into my coat pocket.

"No, leave them out. Look at them carefully."

I glanced at the notes. "I've seen them before."

He stood and came around to my side of the table. "See there?" He pointed to a word on the first note, then pointed to another one on the second. "And there?"

"Yeah. So?"

Riordan bent down and squinted at me. "The *s*'s are lighter on the top than the bottom."

I looked more carefully. It was true. I shrugged but was beginning to get a sinking feeling in my stomach.

"Now look closely at the *m*'s. The bottom of the middle line is darker than the other ones."

While I looked, he strolled over to his chair, flipped it around, and straddled it, his arms resting on the back, a Cheshire grin plastered on his face. "We found a typewriter that has the same problems. In fact, it was an exact match."

"It wasn't mine."

"Well, you're right about that. The letters didn't come from the Underwood in your apartment. But they did come from an Underwood. At the Anderson Carriage Company."

"What?"

"Detroit Electric division." He was taking pleasure in dragging this out. "Managers' office."

"That can't be."

"Oh, but it could. A typewriter in that office matched." Riordan shook his head, another one of his damned sardonic smiles on his face. "You'll never guess whose desk it was on."

# CHAPTER TWENTY-ONE

I still had my boots the next morning when Mr. Sutton arranged to have me moved to solitary for the weekend. I spent most of Saturday sweating, with tiny tremors in my hands, but that night I was able to buy a quart of homemade whiskey from a guard for ten dollars. I was to pay him Monday after I saw Sutton, or I'd be back in the holding pen where he'd make sure I got the complete treatment. It was worth the risk. I nursed the bottle, saving almost half of it for Sunday. It got me by.

Much of my time was spent thinking of Frank Van Dam sitting in my office at the factory, at my typewriter, writing letters to me. Was he pensive, sorry to be killing his best friend and framing me for it? Or had he smirked at his cleverness, congratulating himself for planning a perfect crime? If so, the anticipation must have been delicious—framing me, taking my money, toying with me—a cat playing with a mouse before it bites off the head. What fun.

No matter what it took, he was going to pay.

Elizabeth filled my thoughts the rest of the time. I had risked my life for her and spent a week in a filthy hovel nursing her back to humanity, yet three days after I brought her home I was still locked away—three more days of deprivation and degradation. Her father almost certainly was keeping her from getting hold of Riordan, but he couldn't watch her twenty-four hours a day. They had a telephone, a car, neighbors. Surely—if she cared at all—she could have gotten me out of here.

Whether I'd repaid my debt or not, I was through with her.

The next morning my father and Mr. Sutton met me at the courthouse in a small musty room that smelled of delousing powder. Cobwebs obscured the tops of the two tall windows that looked out from our slightly elevated position onto the street. Like the interrogation rooms with which I'd become all too familiar, a sturdy oak table and a pair of matching chairs were the only furnishings.

The guard waited to unlock my chains until we were all in the room. While he did, my father looked at the floor instead of me, his face craggy, full of worry lines. A dark suit and a white shirt dangled over one of his arms. In the other he held a pair of black dress shoes.

Sutton folded his arms across his chest. "It was nice of you to show up for the preliminary hearing, Will."

I had totally forgotten about it. I shrugged. "I was busy."

My father handed me the clothes. "Here. Put these on."

I tried to decipher the look on his face. "Did Dr. Miller call you?"

He nodded, biting the inside of his lip. "He didn't say what you were doing, but said it was important." He set his hand on my shoulder. It was an intimate gesture, meant to be reassuring, a father telling his son he would be all right, but it made me more nervous. He was scared to death. "I called him back on Tuesday, after the newspapers began running their speculation on Elizabeth's whereabouts. He said she was with you and was fine. And that I'd be proud of you." He hugged me tightly. I couldn't remember the last time that had happened.

As I dressed, Sutton explained what I should expect. The state would present evidence and witnesses to establish probable cause. He would cross-examine the witnesses to look for weaknesses in their testimony, and if possible, raise questions about the evidence.

"But don't be angry," Sutton said, "if you think I'm not being aggressive enough or presenting enough of our defense. This is a hearing of probable cause. Regardless of what I do, the state has more than enough evidence to bring this to trial. I'm not going to show them our hand."

I knew how bad the evidence looked. For now, I was more interested in getting out of jail. "Am I going to be let out of here when we're done?"

"No." Sutton dropped his briefcase on the table. "Your bond has been revoked pending charges for the abduction of Elizabeth Hume."

"But I— Has anyone spoken with Elizabeth yet?"

"No. According to the police, her parents insist she's too traumatized from her experiences over the past week."

"Still?" This was about as bad as the news could get. If the judge had any psychological control over Elizabeth, she might never speak with the police. "You've got to talk to her," I said. "She'll confirm she was with me willingly." At least I hoped she would.

Sutton nodded. "We'll get to her one way or another. I know how badly you want out of here." He sat at the table and slid a sheaf of papers out of his briefcase. "Once that's cleared up, you should be set free again."

I fell into the battered wooden chair across from him. "Did anyone tell you about my clothing or the typewriter?"

Sutton's eyes darted to me. "What?"

I sighed. "The killer sent my bloody clothing to Riordan. And the police claim the blackmail notes came from the typewriter on my desk at work."

Just for a second, Sutton's face clenched, like he was absorbing a blow. "Your bloody clothing." He glanced up at my father and then turned to me again. "Fortunately, you've already admitted you were there. We may be able to mitigate the damage from the clothing." He shook his head slowly. "But the typewriter on your desk. You're not giving me much to work with here." He glared at me. "Any other revelations?"

"Yes, Frank Van Dam killed John and fled to Denver." I explained my reasoning, and told him about the letter Elizabeth had received from Frank.

As I spoke, Sutton began nodding. When I finished, he said, "When did Elizabeth receive this letter?"

"She said it was a couple of days after John was killed. She didn't remember exactly when."

Sutton tapped out a rhythm on the edge of the tabletop with his forefingers. "What sort of relationship did *you* have with Van Dam?"

"I don't think he liked me."

"Do you believe he disliked you enough to frame you for murder?"

I shrugged. "Maybe."

"So you think John was an informant?"

"Probably. I just don't think he would have gone along with a scheme like this. And if they had enough evidence to arrest Judge Hume, someone had to be talking."

My father cleared his throat. "Why couldn't Judge Hume and Van Dam be working together? The judge could have helped Frank kill John."

I hadn't thought about this possibility, but it made sense.

"No." Sutton shook his head so hard his muttonchops swayed. "Judge Hume is an idiot, to be sure. But a murderer? Definitely not."

I leaned in toward him. "What better reason could he have for keeping Elizabeth from coming forward about this supposed kidnapping? He wants me to look guilty. Look, Judge Hume is a criminal. Do you know of a man named Vito Adamo?"

Sutton thought for a moment and shook his head. "No."

"I'm pretty sure he's a Black Hand boss, and he's paying off the judge. I saw them together at the Bucket."

"The Bucket?" my father exclaimed. "What in the world were you doing there?"

"It's a long story. My point is there's a lot you don't know about Judge Hume. And he hates me. I don't believe he would have been enthusiastic about killing John, but if it was going to save his bacon, I think he'd do it. And I know he would have loved to hang this thing on me. By killing John in my department at the factory, he could get rid of me and his legal problem at the same time."

Sutton hesitated before he nodded. "I suppose it's possible."

My father was looking at me, a puzzled expression on his face.

"What?" I said.

"I didn't realize the judge . . . Why would he hate you?"

"Another long story." One I would never tell him. "Suffice it to say he does."

Sutton turned to my father. "You're sure no one but your managers and security people have access to your buildings after hours?"

"Yes."

Sutton's fingers played a rapid rhythm on the table. "How about the Employers Association?"

"No," my father said. "No one else has our keys."

I jumped in. "But John must have. When he called, he said for me to meet him in the machining room."

Sutton looked at my father again. "Is it feasible Cooper could have gotten a copy of the door key?"

My father's shoulders lifted a fraction of an inch. "Possibly. If our security guards got sloppy. EAD people have been in the factory almost constantly since the unions started sniffing around."

"Frank and John spent a lot of time in the security office," I said.

Sutton jumped up from his chair. "I think Will may be right. It seems a reasonable assumption." He turned toward me. "We'll look into Judge Hume and the Denver lead right away. I had a few men digging into the unions, just to be sure, but they haven't found anything. It looks like your friend Edsel was right. And contrary to your father's opinion, I still believe it's worthwhile to look into your competitors. Why couldn't this be a scheme to defame Detroit Electric?"

My father rounded on him. "Look here, Sutton. This 'scheme,' as you call it, has nothing to do with our competitors. We're just not significant enough to warrant something like this."

"You said you were passing Baker as the number-one electric brand in the country."

"Walt Baker is a gentleman. What you're proposing is outrageous."

"Then what about the luxury gasoline car companies?"

My father frowned. "Forgive my language, but we're nothing more than a pimple on their backsides. This year we're going to ship fewer than fifteen hundred automobiles and a thousand trucks. So, yes, that's more

than our electric competitors, but it's a drop in the bucket of total automobile sales." He shook his head vehemently. "You may not understand
the dynamics of this business. Electrics are women's automobiles—easy
to start, easy to operate, but not manly, not for the adventurer. We're trying to change that, but at this point our gasoline competitors don't give
a tinker's damn about Detroit Electric."

Sutton shrugged and began to gather up the papers on the table.
"Just trying to consider all the possibilities."

"I want you to be clear on this," my father said. "This is not one of
those possibilities. Whoever is behind this scheme is trying to frame
Will, not defame my company."

Sutton gave him a grudging nod.

"Mr. Sutton," I said, "are the clothing and the typewriter business
going to keep me in jail if Elizabeth comes forward?"

"That all depends on the judge adjudicating your case." He turned to
my father. "*And* how much pressure you can level on the mayor." Looking at me again, he said, "The clothing is another building block in the
state's case, but assuming Elizabeth does come forward, you may get out
again. The fact that the notes were traced to your typewriter doesn't add
substantively to the state's evidence regarding the murder of John Cooper." Sutton looked at me sourly. "It just destroys whatever was left of
your credibility." He thought for a moment. "I'm going to make Denver
the priority. If we can't find Frank Van Dam, I don't like our chances."

My heart sank. If an optimist like Sutton thought I would be convicted, what hope could I have?

It was almost time for the hearing. My father left to be seated in
court while Sutton and I waited in the little room.

I still had some business to attend to. "Oh, Mr. Sutton," I said, trying to be casual. "Can I borrow twenty dollars? I owe a guard." And I
was going to need another bottle.

"You don't want to owe anybody in there, Will. The guards aren't
much better than the prisoners." He pulled his wallet from his coat
pocket, and took out a ten and a pair of fives. "Stick them inside your
boot. You're going to get searched again when you go back to jail."

I thanked him. We waited another half an hour before a guard led us to the defense table. My father was sitting behind us in the front row. He greeted people with a firm grip, looking them in the eye, daring anyone to make a comment. Even under these circumstances, he was a strong man. I knew I was lucky to have him for a father, but for the first time I understood that money had little to do with it.

Knowing that a trial was a foregone conclusion, I didn't pay much attention during the hearing, although I heard enough to make *me* vote for my conviction. Sutton said little while District Attorney Higgins presented his evidence, and almost nothing when asked to present my defense. One thing was crystal clear—unless we found Frank Van Dam, I would be convicted and sentenced to life in prison.

Three days later, Detective Riordan stood outside the cell door with a smirk on his face that made his scar pucker. "So, Will. Looks like you fell down some more stairs."

I didn't say anything. The body search on my return to jail had turned up the money. Those guards kept it. My guard didn't get paid. Actually, I'd been lucky. The other occupants of the holding cell hated the police so much that, even though I was a member of the also-hated upper class, they were more interested in defying authority than taking out their frustrations on me. Still, I had a number of additional cuts and bruises, though to be honest, I think the criminals were only going through the motions.

He glanced down at my feet, now partially covered by a ripped-up pair of two-tone spectator shoes.

"What happened to your boots?"

I crossed my arms and tried to look bored.

"Suit yourself." Riordan gestured to the jailer to open the door. "The lucky boy gets to go home for the holidays." Taking hold of my elbow, he pulled me down the corridor. "Seems the Humes aren't going to press charges on the kidnapping. I guess someone got to Miss Hume, huh? McRae, maybe?" He stopped and turned me toward him.

I kept my mouth shut and fixed my eyes on a rust-colored oval staining the dirty plaster just to the right of his head.

"It's too bad I can't give you a ride on Old Smokey," Riordan said.

I shrugged. I still thought it a better alternative to life in prison.

He smiled, and again my eyes slipped to his jagged purple scar. "Unfortunately, we live in the wrong state. But I don't care who your father is. You're not getting out of this. You're going to the big house for the rest of your miserable life."

I cocked my head at him. "How'd you get that scar, Riordan?"

He leaned down in my face and growled, "That's none of your business."

I met his eyes. "Are we finished here?"

He looked at me for a long moment before jerking my arm forward and pushing me out of the jail.

Mr. Sutton and his two thugs waited at the entrance. One of them handed me my greatcoat, and we ducked out into a howling wind. This time, there was no mob scene. A few reporters tried halfheartedly to get a quote, but it was clear the newspapers were now concentrating on bigger game—probably Judge Hume.

Sutton and I sat in the back of his Pierce-Arrow touring car. I shoved my hands into my pockets and huddled down, trying to block some of the cold wind stinging my face. Once we were away from the police station, Sutton said, "All right, some housekeeping. The trial is set to begin on Monday, January 30. That gives us two months to get our defense together. Between now and then, we'll meet as needed to go over our progress. If you need anything or think of anything else in the meantime, phone me."

I nodded. "Did you find Frank yet?"

"No, but the Pinkertons are on the job. Their western office is in Denver, and they know the town like the backs of their hands. They've already talked to the police, and now they're canvassing all the hotels, apartments, and flophouses in the area. It's just a matter of time." He patted my leg with an ungloved hand. "We'll find him. Oh, and in case you weren't paying attention during your bail hearing, if you leave Michigan, you'll be violating the terms of your bond. You'll be back in jail for the duration. Don't even think about going out there yourself."

"I'm supposed to just sit and do nothing?"

Sutton patted me on the leg again, but quickly and hard like he was playing the drums. "Listen, Will, I know this is difficult. But you can't seriously think you'll have better luck at finding Van Dam than the Pinkertons will. It's what they do." He pulled absently at his mutton-chop whiskers. "Besides, he's not the killer."

My head jerked involuntarily. I stared at him. "No, I'm certain Frank murdered John. It had to be him."

"You need to listen to me carefully." Sutton took a deep breath. "I'll get this out of the way first, since I'm sure you'll hear it eventually. When Frank was thirteen years old, he was arrested for attempted murder."

"What?"

He nodded. "Apparently a neighbor—a thirty-four-year-old man, by the way—accused Van Dam of beating him nearly to death. The neighbor claimed it was a misunderstanding regarding his intentions toward Frank's mother. He was in the hospital for a month. Frank denied the charges out of hand. The man had been arrested a few times for his involvement in confidence schemes, so the police questioned his veracity. The case was dropped for lack of evidence. That was Frank's only trouble with the law."

I tipped to the side as the big automobile swayed. In front of us, a group of city workers in white coveralls were loading a horse carcass into a wagon.

Sutton continued. "Frank's a born and bred Detroiter, went to Cass Union High School, no college. Started at the Employers Association in '06. Sharp, articulate, ambitious. Since the attempted murder, he's never been arrested, though there have been plenty of accusations of violent crimes, all related to his job. Sounds like a potential murderer, right?"

I nodded, waiting for the "but."

"But . . ." With a grim smile, he began ticking off points on his fingers, which were turning red from the cold. "His mother claims he left for Denver, Colorado, to find his fortune on Monday, October thirty-first—Halloween. He resigned from the EAD that same day, with the same story he told his mother. He sent her a letter from Denver on November third, saying he'd write again when he settled. She hasn't heard from him since. John Cooper was killed at midnight on the second. It would have been impossible for Frank to make it from Detroit to Denver to mail a letter in less than a day."

I frowned. "Well, what's she going to say? Of course she'd say Frank wasn't around when John was killed."

Sutton shrugged. "I saw the letter and the postmark. It was his handwriting."

"Someone else could have mailed it for him."

"True, but I'm not finished. Point two—my men polled Van Dam's neighbors and scoured all his regular haunts. Nobody's seen him since the day he quit his job—two days before Cooper's death."

"But his car was at the train station."

"Are you certain? There's more than one red Oldsmobile Palace in this city."

"No, I'm not one hundred percent certain. But nobody seeing him doesn't mean he was gone. He could have been hiding to build his alibi."

Sutton held up a hand. "Listen to me. Most troublesome, he took a sleeper to Denver on October thirty-first and stayed at the Oxford Hotel from November second through the ninth."

I was deflating. "He took a train to Denver two days before John was killed?"

"He bought two tickets, and the conductor confirmed the berth was filled. A Mr. and Mrs. Frank Van Dam spent eight nights at the Oxford."

"He's not married."

"If you were checking in to a hotel with a girlfriend, how would you register?"

I conceded the point.

"There's no evidence whatsoever that Van Dam returned to Detroit. It's difficult to get any information out of the Employers Association with this Judge Hume mess, but a connection we have there says you were right about the bribery. Frank was involved. I'd say he hightailed it to avoid prosecution. That would explain why he's so hard to find."

"And you're still so sure Judge Hume wouldn't have done this?"

Sutton thought for a moment. "I can't see the judge as a killer. Besides, everyone we've talked to said he loved Cooper."

I wasn't giving up on Frank. "Even if Frank didn't kill John himself, either he or the judge could have hired someone to do it. If they were both complicit in the bribery, they both had a motive."

Sutton held his hands out in front of him. "I don't disagree with you. Either of them could have hired someone. But if we can't find the killer and get him to confess, we have to place Frank in Detroit on November second or the judge at the factory that night. If we can't do that, it's going to take Svengali to convince a jury you didn't kill John Cooper." He grimaced. "And I'm not Svengali."

I shook my head, frustration boiling out of me. "Are you looking at the EAD, too?"

"Of course. But no one there is going to be implicated unless Frank turns up again and testifies. If they keep their mouths shut, they're all home free."

"What if the judge or the Employers Association had someone follow Frank to Denver and kill him there? That would explain his disappearance."

He shrugged. "It's possible. But that wouldn't help us a bit. It would just prove Frank didn't kill Cooper." He patted my shoulder. "I've got half a dozen detectives digging into everything. Leave it to me."

When he dropped me off in front of my building, the lawn and sidewalk were empty. It looked like the reporters were going to leave me alone—at least for now. Still, I was dispirited. I had been certain Frank had murdered John and the Doyles. If he hired someone to do it, we would have to sift through thousands of people to find the killer. If Frank was eliminated as a suspect, it seemed certain that either Judge Hume or the Employers Association was behind the murder.

Frank was probably the only person who could put all the pieces together. And he had disappeared, no more tangible now than the half of John Cooper pulverized in the roof press.

Frank had been in Denver. I was back to square one.

But still, the car nagged at me.

# CHAPTER TWENTY-TWO

One of Sutton's men was sitting in a wooden chair at the base of the stairway. Before heading up to my apartment, I shook his hand and thanked him for his help. I didn't even want to think about how the last couple of weeks would have gone without these men.

I locked my apartment door behind me and grabbed a bottle of bourbon before heading into the bathroom. I wasn't sure I could handle seeing my reflection, so I kept my eyes averted from the mirror while I took off my clothes and climbed into the tub. After a long bath and about half the bottle, I fell into my bed and slept.

The next morning I braved a look in the mirror. The swelling on my nose had gone down a little, but now both my eyes were blackened and a cut on my lip had scabbed over. I looked like a deranged raccoon.

I sat at my desk and flipped through my accumulated mail. My father had sent me a check for one hundred dollars. God knows I needed it, but it was humiliating to have to rely on his charity. I threw it onto the desk and sat back. This had to end.

Even though I couldn't leave the state to look for Frank, I could still try to run down a lead or two. I phoned the Employers Association. J. J. Whirl, the EAD's secretary, had never returned my call; though, to be fair, between the tenement apartment and the Bethune Street jail I hadn't been home enough in the last two weeks to receive phone calls from anyone. Again, a secretary told me he was unavailable and took a message for him to call me back.

By lunchtime I still hadn't heard from him, so I shrugged on my coat and hurried through driving sleet to the trolley stop. Not only was I a manager at Anderson Carriage, I was the son of the owner. If I showed up on Whirl's doorstep he would have no choice but to talk to me. It was a short wait for a streetcar, and even better, I was able to get inside it, out of the weather. All the way downtown, wet snow splatted against the car's wooden top and splashed to the pavement around it.

At the EAD office I asked for Whirl and was promptly "escorted" from the premises by a pair of rough-looking men. They didn't even listen when I told them who I was. I tried to get in again. They had locked the door. I stood outside in the soaking sleet for an hour, accosting everyone who left the office, but the closest I came to getting any of them to speak with me was a few threats. I hadn't been expecting much, but I certainly hadn't expected this.

There didn't seem to be any point in continuing to freeze, so I headed over to the Detroit University School to speak with Edsel. I didn't know what time it let out, and had to wait almost an hour. My clothes were soaked through, but fortunately, I was able to spend that time inside the stately gray granite building. I stood next to the radiator and had nearly dried out by three fifteen, when young men began to hurry past, out of the building. A few minutes later I saw Edsel walking toward me, deep in conversation with another boy.

"Edsel!" I called.

He looked startled. "Will." He said something to his friend and patted him on the back before trotting over to me. His black oilskin duster billowed out behind him like a cape. "I've been trying to get hold of you for a week," he said.

"Didn't you get Wesley's messages?"

"Wesley phoned me?"

"Numerous times."

He shook his head and sighed. "My father. I knew I shouldn't have told him I'd met Wes. He doesn't approve of show folk. Please give Mr. McRae my apologies." He hesitated, his face tight with anxiety. "Say,

Will, I wanted to ask you about him." He leaned in and whispered, "Is he, you know, a homosexual?"

"Edsel, Wes is a good man. Isn't that enough?"

He thought for a moment. Nodding, he said, "Yes. I suppose it is." Seeming satisfied, he pointed to my face. "How is it that you look worse now?"

"It's a long story." I took him by the elbow and walked him toward the doors. "I need you to stop looking into the murder. It's too dangerous."

Edsel grinned and arched his eyebrows. "Don't you at least want to know what I've discovered?" He opened one of the doors and nodded toward a restaurant across the street. "Let me buy you a cup of coffee."

We waited for a coal wagon and a pair of men on horses to pass, then walked carefully over the slippery cobbles to the little coffee shop, and more carefully still on the slick white tiles covering its floor. A dozen or so wet customers sat at the small walnut tables, most with both hands around a steaming coffee cup. The air was filled with the comforting scents of coffee and fresh-baked bread.

After stripping off our wet coats, we sat at a table in the back corner, away from the other customers. A matronly woman in a stained white apron took our order for two coffees. I had a chill in my bones coffee wouldn't warm, but unfortunately, coffee shops didn't serve my preferred beverage.

While we were waiting, Edsel leaned in and said, "You knew John Cooper killed someone in a football game?"

I nodded.

"He was accused of a variety of crimes by union organizers over the past couple of years—assault and battery mostly—but since the police and the Employers Association have the same agenda, he was never arrested. Our source with the state police said Cooper was involved in the EAD's bribery of Judge Hume, though he didn't know to what extent."

"Did you hear anything about John talking to the cops?"

Our coffee arrived. Edsel tipped some cream into his cup and idly stirred the coffee, waiting for the waitress to leave. "No, we had a hard time just confirming he was involved. Now, Judge Hume. Of course, he's never previously been arrested or even accused of a crime as far as I can tell. Most people who know him aren't exactly complimentary, but no one thought he would kill John Cooper."

"That's what Mr. Sutton said." I frowned. "It seems to me a man like the judge would do anything to stay out of jail."

Edsel shrugged. "I'm just telling you what I heard."

"How about whoever was behind the bribery at the Employers Association?"

He blew over the top of his coffee and took a sip. "That trail seems to end at Cooper and Van Dam. No one at the EAD is saying anything, and the state police say they have no evidence that anyone other than the two of them was involved. And that brings us to Frank Van Dam." He leaned forward again with both elbows on the table, looked up at me with narrowed eyes, and whispered, "He's the killer."

I thought I'd hear him out before disabusing him of the notion. "Why do you say that?"

"First of all, he'd already tried to kill a man." Edsel sat back, waiting for my reaction.

I disappointed him. "I know. When he was thirteen." I quickly recounted to him Mr. Sutton's findings.

"Oh. He told everyone he was moving west, but I didn't know he'd gone to Denver. And he was there when Cooper was murdered?"

I nodded, grimacing.

"So much for that." He threw up his hands and fell against the back of his seat.

I pulled a pair of cigarettes from my case, handed one to Edsel, and tapped mine on the tabletop a few times. Sticking it in my mouth, I said, "I know. It's frustrating. He seems like the only one besides the judge with a motive."

Edsel took a drink of coffee. "Frank told everyone he'd had enough of the big city and was thinking of ranching. Funny thing, though . . ."

I leaned forward, lit his cigarette, and then mine. "What's that?"

"Another man at the labor bureau, apparently a friend of Frank's, said Frank told him Cooper was moving out west with him."

"Why would he . . . Maybe they both were going to run."

Edsel pushed his coffee aside. "Perhaps. Or he was setting it up so that when John disappeared no one would be the wiser." He wasn't giving up easily.

I took a drag off my cigarette and shook my head. "That *might* have made sense. But John would have had to disappear for anyone to believe that story."

"Frank must have had a change of plans. There's no reason he would have killed Cooper so publicly other than to frame you." His head tilted a little to the side. "Did something happen between the two of you recently?"

I looked away, thinking of Elizabeth. "Not that I remember."

"I could have someone at our Denver dealership look into Frank's whereabouts. Perhaps they could find something."

"No. It's too dangerous. And Sutton's hired the Pinkertons to find him."

"I'll keep digging."

"No. Listen to me, Edsel. Since we last talked I found out that Frank and Judge Hume were both involved with violent criminals. And you already know Frank's an attempted murderer. This is way too dangerous."

Edsel picked a spot of lint off the crease of his trousers before fixing me with his dark eyes. "I'll be careful."

"No. You're done. I appreciate what you've gotten for me, Edsel. It's a real help. But I'm not going to have you risk your life."

He looked into my eyes and then glanced away with a shrug. "All right. I'm not a dunce. I get it."

"You're telling me the truth?"

"Sure thing, Will. I'm too busy anyway. My father said I'm to stay home this weekend with my schoolwork, and I'm going camping with him and Mr. Edison next weekend. It'll be all I can do to stay caught up on homework next week."

"Good. I don't want you getting in over your head." Even though Edsel's maturity outpaced his years, I had to remind myself he was seventeen years old. At his age I was invincible. Now I knew how fleeting that feeling could be. I didn't want Edsel learning the hard way.

On the way home, I stopped and bought a pair of Browning M1900 semiautomatic handguns, one for Wesley and one for myself, along with two boxes of ammunition. The pistols would fit in a coat pocket or belt, and would fire seven .32 caliber bullets in the time it took to squeeze off two shots with a .45. I'd never owned a handgun before. Now felt like the right time.

Before I left the store, I loaded one, switched on the safety, and stuck it in the small of my back. The gun went in the drawer of my nightstand, where it would be handy. I planned on carrying it everywhere until the murderer was caught.

The next morning I gave one of the guns and a box of bullets to Wesley and then stayed inside my apartment most of the next two days, leaving only for newspapers and bourbon. Exhausted and beat up, I needed a little time to recharge my batteries, so to speak. I didn't see a single reporter on my lawn either day. It looked like they had given up for good, or at least until the trial. I thought I'd call Mr. Sutton and have him pull the guards—no sense wasting any more of my father's money. But I didn't. The security blanket was much too comforting for now.

When I flipped through my mail on Monday, a letter in an Anderson Carriage Company envelope caught my attention. Inside was a pair of tickets to the Miles Theater for Saturday night, along with a note from Mr. Wilkinson saying my father had gotten me the tickets so I could relax a little. My father, never a fan of vaudeville, apparently knew how badly I needed to be distracted.

The headliners were Blatz the Human Fish and Millie DeLeon, "the Girl in Blue." All I really knew about either was that they were immensely popular. The show had sold out in hours.

I sat at my desk with a glass of bourbon, trying to decide whom I should ask. After almost four years courting Elizabeth and the last year spent in a daze, I had no woman friends. I decided to invite Wesley. He needed some fun as much as I did.

I walked across the hall and asked him. He couldn't go because he was going to be making his return to the Wayne Williams Orchestra on Saturday, though only as the featured vocalist. The bandages had finally come off his hands, but he was still far from able to play the piano. I congratulated him, and we had a drink to celebrate.

When I got back to my apartment, I sat in the parlor, again puzzling over whom to ask. Edsel was going out of town. I wouldn't ask Elwood or Joe. Perhaps I could ask Ben Carr as a peace offering, though Ben didn't seem the kind of man who approved of vaudeville. But I kept coming back to Elizabeth. She was the only person I really wanted to ask. This was ridiculous. I needed to move on. I vowed I would do it, but it didn't seem to take right away since the rest of the day was fogged by a bottle and a half of bourbon.

I was startled awake the next morning by a telephone ringing next to my ear, piercing my brain like an ice pick. My head bounced off my desk, and I sat bolt upright. When I recovered from the jolt of pain, I picked up the receiver, more to end the ringing than to find out who was calling.

Mr. Sutton's voice shot out, fast and excited. "Will, I have it on good authority that Judge Hume is cooperating with the state police."

I pulled the receiver an inch away from my ear and fumbled to pick up the base of the telephone. "Really?" It came out as a croak. I cleared my throat. "He's admitting he's guilty?"

"Looks that way. This could be the break we need. Even if he doesn't tell them he knew anything about Cooper's murder, if he admits he and Cooper were involved in this mess it's going to throw a great deal of doubt on you being the killer."

I grunted out a laugh. "I never thought I'd be thankful for anything Judge Hume did."

Sutton chuckled. "You just might spend the rest of your life outside looking in, instead of the other way around."

"When is this supposed to happen?"

"They're still negotiating the details. If I know Judge Hume," he paused, "and I do, that's going to take a while—a week, perhaps. But he'll do it. They've got him dead to rights."

I thought for a moment, looking for the dark cloud surrounding this silver lining, but I couldn't see one. "Maybe you're right. This might save me."

"I know a man down at the *Herald* who would love this," Sutton said, his voice jubilant. "If you don't mind, I'm going to run the story past him, see if we can get some good publicity for a change."

"Absolutely. Let 'er rip. Oh, Mr. Sutton?" I peeked through the window blinds at the front lawn—still no reporters. It was stupid to keep wasting my father's money. "You can pull your men off my building. There's no reason to keep them here anymore."

"Are you sure? Your father said he'd be happy to pay for them until the trial's over."

"I'm sure. Nobody's bothered me since I got out of jail this last time. What's it been? Five days? I'll be fine."

He agreed, and we chatted for a few minutes before ringing off. A little later I caught myself whistling while I tidied up my bedroom. I hadn't been this happy for a year.

What am I saying? I hadn't been anything approaching happy—not for a single moment—since Elizabeth almost killed herself aborting our child.

In truth, it was three months before that. The day I wouldn't think about—now or ever.

I poured myself a very large drink.

# CHAPTER TWENTY-THREE

First thing Wednesday morning, I ran out and picked up a copy of the *Herald* from the newsboy on the corner. Plastered across the top of the page were six words that made me light up like a department store window—JUDGE HUME THE REAL ELECTRIC EXECUTIONER? The reporter didn't come right out and say I was innocent, but the story was slanted in that direction. He believed it was too much of a coincidence that John Cooper, Frank Van Dam, and Judge Hume were all involved in the bribery scandal just before Frank disappeared and John was killed. The police were trying to locate Frank now; although, as Mr. Sutton had said, only as a possible witness.

It looked like Sutton might be right. Judge Hume's testimony would deflect a lot of the interest from me and create a reasonable doubt. If I was lucky, he'd confess to the murder or implicate Frank. I had a chance.

I woke Wesley and showed him the article. We split a pot of coffee and a coffee cake he'd baked, and chatted until he had to get ready for work.

When I returned to my apartment, I telephoned my father at his office.

He sounded happy. "The sun's shining a little brighter today, isn't it?"

I looked out the window. The sky was as gray and heavy as pig iron. "Um . . ."

"Figuratively, son. The article in the *Herald*."

"Right. Yes. That's why I'm calling. Now that suspicion is shifting away from me, could I come back to work? It's embarrassing to take your money to do absolutely nothing, and I'm bored to tears."

He didn't say anything for a moment. "Let me think about that, Will. Tell you what. Come by for Sunday dinner, and we'll talk about it."

After we rang off, I cleaned for half an hour or so before deciding I had to get outside. Since my pantry was bare, I grabbed my grocery basket from under the sink and headed out to the market on Woodward—though only after I tucked the pistol in my belt at the small of my back. The air was wet and cold, a soggy blanket covering the city. But I didn't care. I strolled down the sidewalk like it was a sunny spring day.

I turned into the little corner market, a shop perhaps fifteen feet wide by fifty feet deep. Rough wood shelves lined the walls. Another tall row of shelving ran down the middle of the store. There was just enough room in the aisles for two people to pass without being intimate. I waved to Peter, the shop owner, a hearty man in a crisp white apron, who was arranging cans behind the counter. My first stop was the produce section, where I picked up a few apples.

I turned to continue down the aisle and ran headlong into a woman who had just begun to lean in next to me. My momentum pushed her back into a stack of pumpkins. I dropped my basket and grabbed her arm, only just catching her before she fell.

"I'm sorry," I said, still holding her forearm, frozen like an idiot. Something about her caught my eye. She wasn't beautiful in the conventional sense, but she was exotic—tall, with black hair and the darkest eyes I'd ever seen. Her mouth was too big and her heart-shaped face seemed vaguely asymmetrical. When she smiled at me, I saw what caused it. Her expression came more from the right side, the left lagging behind a little. Somehow it made her more attractive.

"Thanks for catching me." Her voice was quiet and melodious, with a European accent. She laughed. "That was close."

"Gosh, I wasn't paying attention. Again, I apologize."

She glanced down at her dress and began to straighten it. Trying not to be obvious, I looked her over. I guessed she was in her midtwenties.

Under a long blue overcoat, she wore a blue cotton day dress that revealed a slim but curvy body. I checked her finger. She wasn't wearing a wedding or engagement ring. The more I looked, the more I liked. The attraction was more than visual, but I couldn't put my finger on it. I looked into her eyes, and I wanted her.

I held out my hand and said, "Will Anderson." She didn't recognize me—no look of shock or fear.

She took my hand in her feather-light grasp. "Sapphira. Sapphira Xanakis." With a smile, she said, "It was nice running into you, Will Anderson." She turned back to the produce.

"Likewise." I began to walk around her but stopped. "Say, Miss Xanakis? It is 'Miss,' isn't it?"

She turned back far enough that I could see her smile. "Yes it is, Mr. Anderson."

"Could I perhaps buy you a cup of coffee sometime?"

She blushed. "Well, Mr. Anderson, we haven't been formally introduced, but . . ."

"But . . . You'll see me?"

After she looked down at the wooden floor for a second, she returned my gaze. "You're not a cad?" She bit her lip. I wanted to nibble at it.

"Not at all. I'm a perfect gentleman."

"You would need my father's permission."

"I'd be happy to speak with him."

"Well . . . Perhaps you could call this weekend."

"That would be perfect. I just happen to have a pair of tickets for the show at the Miles Theater on Saturday night. I'd be honored if you would accompany me."

"That sounds lovely."

"Perhaps dinner first?"

She nodded, just a hint of a smile playing on her lips. "If my father allows it."

I told her I'd come by at six, and she gave me her address. I recognized the street. It was downtown, only a few blocks east of Woodward, right on the edge of Greektown.

When she walked away I pinched myself. I'd never had this kind of luck.

The next night Wesley came to my apartment for drinks and dinner. I cooked a pot roast with carrots and skinned potatoes, and even baked a loaf of bread. While the meat and potatoes bubbled away, we sat in the parlor with glasses of Old Tub. He'd decided to drink bourbon when he was at my place.

Wesley took a sip and leaned forward. "I saw the articles about Judge Hume possibly being the killer. What a break." He raised his glass, and we both took a drink. "But one thing's certain—he's not the man who killed the Doyles."

"No, and I don't suspect he killed John, either—at least not with his own hands. But I'm sure there's a wide selection of cutthroats who would have been happy to do it for the right price."

He nodded. "Have you been able to find out anything else?"

I told him I had suspected Frank Van Dam was the killer and why, but had since found out he'd been in Denver when John was killed, and he'd mailed Elizabeth a letter from there around the date of the murder. "Now he seems to have fallen off the face of the earth. But . . ."

"But what?"

"It's probably nothing. Elizabeth jogged my memory. I could have sworn I saw his car at the train station that night. And when I went back later, it was gone."

Wesley's face darkened. "Really. But you're not certain?"

I shook my head. "He's not the only one in town with a red 1909 Olds Palace touring car, but there aren't many. It just makes too much sense it would be his."

Wesley looked up and to the right, his eyes darting back and forth. "Red Oldsmobile Palace. All right. Just down the street from the station. I saw it." He shifted his attention back to me. "What does Van Dam look like?"

"He wasn't there, Wes. He was in Denver."

"Humor me."

"He's a very large man—six three or so, probably two hundred and forty pounds. Not quite a John Cooper, but he's big and strong."

Wesley sipped his drink, eyes on the floor. After a moment, he said, "How does Van Dam move? Is he graceful or clumsy? Lithe or muscle-bound?"

I thought about it. "I don't know if I'd call him graceful or lithe, but he's closer to those than clumsy or muscle-bound. I've seen him fight. He's a buzz saw."

Wesley bit the inside of his cheek, his head nodding slightly. "Could have been him. The man certainly knew how to fight. When it comes to a scrape, I'm no Mary Ann, but I never even saw it coming." He set his drink on the end table and shook his head. "But he was in Denver?"

"So the Pinkertons say."

We sat quietly for a moment before he said, "What did Van Dam want from Elizabeth, anyway?"

I grunted out a laugh. "He said he was going to come back for her. Like every other man, it seems, he had fallen in love with Elizabeth." I smiled at Wesley. "Well, nearly every man."

Grinning back at me, he shrugged. "She seemed nice."

"Which reminds me," I said. "I met a woman yesterday."

"You did? Well, good for you."

"You could say I ran into her. I was at Peter's, and as usual, not paying attention. I almost flattened this beautiful Greek woman standing next to me." I wagged my eyebrows. "But my natural charm must have shown through. I asked her to the show at the Miles, and she accepted."

"You just about knocked her ass over applecart and still had the wherewithal to ask her out?" He raised his glass. "Here's to the new Will Anderson."

"I couldn't believe it, either." I took a gulp of my drink. "And her name is as exotic as she is. Get a load of this . . ." I trailed off. Wesley was frowning at me. I couldn't tell if he was serious. "What?"

"What about Elizabeth?"

"What about her?"

Wesley was pulling a cigarette from his case. He stopped in mid-motion and laughed. "What about her?" He stuck the cigarette in his mouth and talked around it while he patted his pockets, fumbling for his lighter. "Far be it from me to judge you, but you spend a year and a half practically in seclusion, mooning over your lost love, and now it's 'What about her?'" He stopped searching and held the cigarette in front of him, eyebrows raised.

I pulled a lighter from my jacket pocket, leaned forward, and lit his cigarette. "No, you're right, but . . . it's just not going to work. I shouldn't have to give up any chance of happiness because of her, should I?"

"Hey, I agree with you completely. I'm just glad you're finally getting on with it."

I lit a cigarette for myself, took a drag, and blew the smoke toward the ceiling, feeling a twinge of guilt, like I'd betrayed Elizabeth.

On Saturday I made an early morning trip to the liquor store. For the walk home, I automatically slipped the bottles of Old Tub into the inside pockets of my duster. It was juvenile, and it wasn't anyone's business whether or what I drank, but I couldn't escape the years of propriety drummed into me. I felt like a kid sneaking liquor past his parents.

I read and sipped a few drinks, but just a few. I wanted to be in good shape when I picked up the lovely Sapphira Xanakis. Just after five o'clock, I dressed in black tie, tails, and top hat, then filled a flask and secreted it away in my jacket pocket. I peeked out the front window and still didn't see anyone on the sidewalk in front of the building. We had hit the bleak early winter days of a mere nine hours of daylight. It was already dark, but not pitch-black as so often in the winter. The sky had cleared, and a scatter of stars and a full moon made the sidewalks glow as if illuminated.

I considered bringing my gun, but decided it was worth the risk to go to the show unarmed. If Sapphira saw the pistol, I'd never be able to explain without telling her about my situation. I put on my black overcoat, locked my apartment door, and hurried over to Woodward, stopping first at the flower shop for a bouquet of roses. The air was crisp, though the lack of wind was letting oily coal smoke settle over the city. It was still early enough in the season that I noticed it. By the end of December the smell of burning coal would be so pervasive as to seem a natural component of the air.

I stood at the corner waiting for the trolley, wondering what Detective Riordan was doing tonight. Maybe spending some time with his "kiddies." I felt a sharp pang of regret. Had I not been such an idiot, that could have been me.

A streetcar came in. I shoved my way on and hopped off downtown, walking the last four blocks to Sapphira's house on the modest neighborhood's wooden boardwalk. The outside of her two-story home was well kept though nondescript, red brick and white wood, part of a long row of similar houses. Almost every parlor window in the neighborhood except Sapphira's showed off Christmas trees festooned with popcorn strings, tinsel, and ornaments. Before going up the walk, I took a drink from the flask.

Sapphira answered the door almost immediately. "Hi, Will," she said with a big smile, like I'd made her day by showing up. She wore an emerald silk dress with a rounded décolleté neckline and a simple strand of pearls. A matching wide-brimmed hat with a green silk ribbon sat atop her upswept dark hair.

She was even more attractive than I remembered. "Good evening, Sapphira. You look beautiful tonight." I brought out the roses from behind my back. "In fact, you put this bouquet to shame."

"Why, thank you," she said, taking the flowers from me. "Won't you come in?"

I expected the house to smell of moussaka or shish kebabs or something, but instead it was infused with a gentle scent of jasmine. She excused herself and went into the kitchen to put the flowers in a vase. I peeked into the parlor. Walnut end tables topped by Tiffany lamps flanked a green silk sofa and matching chairs—everything atop a richly patterned Oriental rug. I was impressed. These were very expensive furnishings for an immigrant family. Mr. Xanakis was likely a formidable man. I glanced down the hallway, wondering why he was waiting so long to grill me.

Sapphira soon returned wearing a stylish black overcoat and black kid gloves. "I'm sorry that you will not be able to meet my parents this evening. My father was called away, and my mother's not well."

"Oh, I'm sorry to hear that. Should we do this another time?" I couldn't believe the words came out of my mouth.

"That is so gallant. But no. My parents trust me." A warm smile lit up her face. "And I believe I can trust you, Will Anderson."

My dreams had never been this wonderful.

We had dinner at Flanagan's Chop House. It was dark, and we sat at a booth with red satin upholstery and a single candle. I couldn't take my eyes off Sapphira. In the flicker of the candle, her eyes were dark stars, her smile the light from the sun. No one but Elizabeth had ever affected me this way. Sapphira told me of her life in Greece, the journey to America with her parents, and her job as a cigar roller at the San Telmo factory. Her father owned a restaurant, and her family had worked its way up to become part of the emerging middle class. She was very proud of that.

I had a couple of bourbons before we ate, and Sapphira joined me in drinking a bottle of wine with dinner. She sipped the wine and picked at her food, spending more time talking than eating or drinking. I told her I was in the automobile business, but little else, constantly turning the conversation back to her. While she talked I could stare at her, and anyway, I didn't want her to know anything about me until I had her hooked.

We took a streetcar to the theater. After we checked our coats in the cloakroom, I steered her downstairs to the saloon for a drink before the show. It was a dark room, with green wallpaper and a long, polished walnut bar. A cloud of cigar smoke obscured the ceiling. I elbowed my way through the crowd, predominantly men, all getting good and soused for the evening's entertainment. I was nervous leaving Sapphira unaccompanied and kept looking back at her while I waited to be served. She gave me reassuring looks whenever she wasn't being chatted up by other men.

I ordered an Old Tub and a glass of red wine, and was waiting for them when a pair of familiar laughs boomed out from down the bar. I put a hand up to the side of my face and turned just enough toward the sound to see them.

John and Horace Dodge stood against the bar ten feet away from me.

# CHAPTER TWENTY-FOUR

I turned back quickly, keeping my face averted from the Dodges. When the bartender returned with the drinks, I set a dollar on the bar and hurried back to Sapphira. "Maybe we should find our seats," I said, and took a step toward the door.

"But . . ." She pointed to the glasses in my hands.

"Oh, right." I stopped and gave her a sheepish grin. "Sorry."

I led her to a table in a dark corner of the saloon. We made small talk while we finished our drinks, but I couldn't concentrate. I expected one of the Dodge brothers to see me and make a scene. At best, Sapphira would learn I had been accused of murder. At worst, well, I didn't want to think about it. When we finished our drinks and walked past the bar, I kept my face turned toward the doorway.

Our seats were in the front row on the left side of the stage. On the way down the far left aisle, I scanned the theater for exits. Alarmed fire doors were placed near the stage on both sides. Other than them, it appeared the only exit was through the lobby. I was going to have to be extremely careful. We would be exiting through the same doors as the Dodges.

As we sat, I looked around us. The theater was good-sized, with perhaps a thousand plush burgundy seats, almost every one already filled. Though I saw a number of women, most of the people here were men, florid-faced and bleary-eyed from drink. Vaudeville crowds tended to lean toward men, though much less significantly than this one. I felt a tug of apprehension, wondering what kind of performance this Mademoiselle de Leon put on. This could be embarrassing, but there was nothing to do for it now. On the positive side, the Dodge brothers were nowhere in sight.

I pulled my cigarette case from my pocket and offered one to Sapphira before taking one myself. To my surprise, she accepted and leaned in for me to light it. I saw just a hint of cleavage as her jasmine scent wafted over me.

The lights dimmed, and the band began to play. The first act was a singer, followed by a contortionist and a comedian. I paid little attention. Sapphira sat close to me, really enjoying herself, belly laughing at the contortionist and grimacing at the comedian's dismal jokes. She was refreshing, less inhibited than any woman I'd ever dated, though still just within the bounds of propriety.

When the lights came up, I suggested we stay in our seats during the intermission. Not only did I want to avoid the Dodges, I realized I was already quite drunk. She agreed without hesitation.

After another singer and a gymnastics act, the burgundy velvet curtain raised on Blatz the Human Fish. A huge water tank, filled to the brim, had been placed in the middle of the stage. Sitting at a table inside was a fleshy man with thinning hair, a newspaper in his hands. He wore a dark suit with a red tie patterned with yellow fleur-de-lis. When he finished a page he dropped it, and the paper undulated like seaweed to the floor of the tank. It was an odd act, to say the least, but the longer he sat there the more interesting it became. I couldn't see an air tube, and he certainly appeared to be submerged. I had no idea how he did it.

A few minutes later, he set down the paper and began eating a steak and a baked potato. He sawed off huge chunks of meat and shoveled them into his mouth in a manner reminiscent of President Taft, whose eating habits were regularly displayed at the motion picture houses. The baked potato looked soggy, but that didn't deter Blatz in his eating enjoyment. After each bite, he daintily wiped his face with a napkin and took a sip of wine. Finished with his dinner, he belched (clearly audible from the audience) and picked up a trombone from the bottom of the tank. He'd been underwater for a good ten minutes by now.

He lifted the trombone to his mouth, took a deep breath, and began to blow. A muted Sousa march filtered out of the tank and washed over our heads toward the mezzanine. The capacity crowd hooted and cheered. Sapphira and I hollered right along with them. It wasn't that he was a good trombonist. He had probably taken the name Blatz from the wretched sounds coming from his instrument. But, after all, the man was playing trombone underwater.

When he finished, the lights came up again. Even though I was having a wonderful time, I couldn't help but think about the Dodges. They were certain to be at the bar at every intermission, if, indeed, they left it at all.

I leaned toward Sapphira, again taking in her delicate fragrance. "Would you like to get a drink somewhere we could talk?" I was moving too fast, but this might be a good time to escape without a confrontation with the Dodges.

She playfully hit me on the arm. "No, silly. We haven't seen Mademoiselle DeLeon yet. But a drink might be nice."

I had no choice. We walked up the aisle together, her arm in mine. I kept my head down until we were on the stairway. As soon as I entered the saloon I spotted the Dodge brothers. They stood where they had earlier, toward the end of the bar. I brought Sapphira to the same dark corner, hurried to the other side of the bar, and squeezed up to the front. Keeping my face out of the Dodges' sight, I raised my hand to get the bartender's attention. I was playing with fire but decided I'd rather risk a beating than look like a fool in front of this woman. With a bourbon and a glass of wine in hand, I rejoined Sapphira. My luck held. We managed to finish our drinks and get back to our seats without incident.

We sat through a family of acrobats and a horse that solved mathematical equations before the band began playing an oriental tune, serpentine and undulating. A shout came from the crowd. A bare leg emerged from behind the curtain, a rounded knee leading to a supple milky-white calf that tapered to the most delicate ankle I had ever seen. A shiny blue high-heeled shoe dangled at the end of that beautiful leg, and, with a swell from the orchestra, the toe arched upward.

I was just sober enough to realize this might get awkward. I shot a glance toward Sapphira. She smiled at me, no jealousy or anger on her face.

The leg drew back, and Millie DeLeon peeked around the curtain, her lustrous brunette hair in ringlets around her face. She was beautiful. Her high cheekbones and full, pouting lips gave her a mysterious Asian look. Now she stepped out, her filmy blue dress rippling in her wake. She moved slowly, sinuously, across the stage, her body moving in time to the alluring music. A diaphanous garment slipped to the floor. And another. And yet another. I stared in raptured silence while the rest of the men's shouts drowned out the orchestra.

Now she wore only her shoes, garters, and stockings, and a tight piece of blue nothing that revealed every curve of her body. Mouth open in wonder, I gawped at her long legs and rounded hips, wasp waist and generous breasts. Her stomach began to roll, up and down, up and down, in a hypnotic motion.

The audience silenced.

She shivered and shook, breathing faster and heavier. Moans, deep and throaty, poured from her lips, and then yelps, her eyes rolling, body contorting in an orgasmic frenzy.

I was entranced. Thought of anything other than the woman on the stage had long ago left my mind. I shifted in my seat, not too drunk to be physically aroused.

When her shuddering finally abated, Mademoiselle DeLeon stood still for a long moment with her eyes closed, seeming to gather herself, before reaching down and unsnapping the inside garter on her right leg. The stocking sagged against the smooth surface of her thigh. She walked to the front of the stage, stretching the garter, aiming at this man and that one, teasing us all. Finally she let it go. The garter flew over my head and landed in the fifth row, where a scrum broke out. Millie stepped out of her shoes and unsnapped the other garter on her right leg. The stocking slipped down to the floor. She repeated the tease, finally shooting the garter to the right side of the audience. The next garter went to the center. The band appeared to be playing, but was entirely inaudible beneath the primal roar of the crowd.

She unsnapped the final garter, and her left leg was bare. She sashayed in our direction, hips rocking side to side, and beckoned me forward with a curl of her index finger.

I stared at her, surprised beyond action. She repeated the gesture. I raised a finger to my chest and mouthed, "Me?"

Millie nodded.

I glanced at Sapphira. She smiled. "Go. It's fine."

Elizabeth would not have been so understanding—had she still cared in the least what I did.

I stood, egged on by the roars from the other men in the audience, all of them, no doubt, wishing they could trade places with me. Millie took a step back, her finger still summoning me, and another step, and I was onstage, mesmerized. She held the garter up to the audience and then slid it across my lips, back and forth, back and forth, gazing into my eyes. I could barely stand. She took my hand and placed the garter in it, and leaned in to kiss me. Her perfume, a blend of ginger and cinnamon and a thousand other spices, settled over me like a fine mist.

The roar of the crowd enveloped us in a cocoon. As she kissed me, she ran her hands up and down my back in a pantomime of passion. After a moment, Millie put her hands on either side of my face and pulled back. Turning to the audience, she gave a delicate curtsy while holding my hand. When the applause died down, Millie kissed me on the cheek and gently pushed me forward. I looked back and blew her a kiss as the curtain dropped, and then turned and hopped off the stage, ready to apologize to Sapphira, however insincerely, for my crude display.

Sapphira, however, was laughing so hard her whole body was shaking. After she stopped convulsing she took my arm, and we began walking down the row of seats to the aisle. It was only then the realization that I'd made myself a target for the Dodge brothers cut through my drunken haze. Unless they had stayed in the saloon for Millie's performance, which I doubted, they had surely seen me onstage.

I tried to march Sapphira up the aisle, but we were stopped again and again by men pounding me on the back, offering their congratulations, and making lewd remarks. I tried to push through them and move forward, a salmon swimming upstream. Sapphira was staring at me with narrowed eyes and a question on her face. I ignored it and practically dragged her to the coat check and out of the theater.

We were walking out the door when a man said, "There he is," and then yelled, "Anderson!"

I cursed quietly. It was Horace Dodge. He stood next to his brother on the sidewalk outside the theater. The sharp glare of the electric lights on the marquee washed out his skin, turning him a ghostly white. John Dodge was facing the building, hidden in the shadows. He turned toward us. An arc of piss splashing off the wall turned with him.

I froze. Her voice tight, Sapphira said, "Will?"

John Dodge shook off the last few drops and tucked his penis back into his trousers. "I told you before I wasn't done with you, Anderson, you goddamn sodomite." Both of the brothers advanced on me.

I gave John the dead eyes. He didn't slow down.

Sapphira pulled on my arm, tugging me in the other direction. "Come on, Will, let's go."

John sneered. "Brought your whore along tonight. You got a lot of class."

I couldn't let him get away with that. "Apologize, Dodge, or so help me . . ."

"So help you what, Margery?"

Sapphira tugged at my arm again. "Will, please, leave it."

Just as I looked at her, John Dodge shoved me to the ground. I landed hard on my backside. Dodge crossed his arms over his chest and, his voice full of scorn, said, "Listen to your whore, Anderson. Run away, you little pussy."

I had to defend Sapphira's honor. I jumped to my feet and took a wild swing at his face. My arm connected with his jaw, and it sent a shock down my arm. He staggered. Before I could regain my balance, his brother grabbed me by the lapels, pulled me into the alley, and knocked me over a pile of rubbish. He began kicking me in the ribs, and John dove on top of me, throwing lefts and rights at my face. Though I tried to shove and buck him off, it was useless. He outweighed me by a good seventy-five pounds. I threw punches at him, but with no leverage my fists did nothing more than glance off him while he drove fist after fist into my face, bouncing my head off the dirt. Jumping forward, he sat on me with his knees pinning my shoulders to the ground. I couldn't move my arms.

He slapped me in the face. "Oh, the poor little Electric Executioner." He slapped me again. "Not so scary after all, are you, killer?" He slapped me again. "Millie DeLeon ought to see the little fairy now." He slapped me again. "Does the witty-bitty Executioner need a hanky?"

I struggled, writhing back and forth under him while he kept taunting and slapping me. I might as well have been in primary school being beaten by the school bully.

From the corner of my eye I could see that Horace now had hold of Sapphira. She was struggling with him and shouting. When John finally tired of slapping me, he stood, chest heaving, and spit a wad of mucus onto my face. "Goddamn pussy." The brothers walked out of the alley.

Sapphira knelt down next to me. "Will? Will, are you all right? Do you need a doctor?"

I propped myself up on my elbows. My head was boiling hot and hurt everywhere. Sharp pains came from a dozen spots up and down my body from Horace's kicks. But my pride was in the worst shape.

"No," I said through puffy lips, not quite meeting her eyes. "I'm fine. He didn't hurt you, did he?"

She shook her head.

I pushed myself to my feet, and the alley spun for a moment before it locked into place. I wiped my face and brushed off my jacket, looking out toward the street at the crowd that had gathered there. The burn of humiliation was settling in. "I've got to go."

"No." She took hold of my arm. "Come back to my house. I'll get you fixed up."

"I can't. I've got to go."

"But, Will . . ."

I turned and hurried out of the alley, pushing through the onlookers. Sapphira followed closely behind. The crowd seemed to be in good spirits. Now I heard my name murmured by people around me.

I looked back at Sapphira. "I'm sorry. You can find your own way home, can't you?" I didn't think I'd ever be able to look at her again.

"Well, yes, but . . . Let me at least get you fixed up first."

I shook my head and turned away, fumbling for my wallet. My lips kept swelling. I thrust a five-dollar bill at her. "This should get you home. I'm sorry, Sapphira."

She didn't even seem to notice I'd given her the money. "Let me come with you then, Will," she pleaded.

"I'm sorry. But I just . . . can't." I spun on my heel and hurried off into the dark.

All the way home I kept to streets with few or no street lamps, staying in the shadows. It took me more than half an hour to make it home, and by the time I reached the back of my building I had gotten control of myself. I fished the key out of my pocket, unlocked the door, and crept inside, praying no one saw me. I didn't want to have to explain my condition, even to Wesley.

I tiptoed to my apartment door, turned the key quietly, and slipped inside. After I switched on the lights, I headed for the bathroom, stripping off my jacket, tie, and shirt as I did. My top hat was already gone, probably on a hobo's head by now. I washed my face and risked a glance in the mirror. I didn't look as bad as I'd feared, though my lips had swollen to near twice their normal size, and my head looked like someone had filled it full of air with a bicycle pump. Leaving my clothing on the floor, I walked to the bedroom.

The first thing I noticed was that my bed was unkempt. The sheets were rumpled and piled up in a heap. I was sure I'd made my bed that morning. The next thing I saw was a black jacket and trousers, and a gray and white striped ascot, folded neatly over a chair. At the side of the bed lay a pair of black oxfords, with stockings, garters, and undershorts piled up next to them.

The room stank of shit.

I walked closer. It wasn't that the sheets were piled up. Someone was underneath. I pulled back the covers and froze in place. A stout man lay sprawled on his back across my bed. He wasn't breathing. His skin was tinged blue. His head was turned away from me at an impossible angle.

I leaned over the bed to look at his face. It was Judge Hume.

# CHAPTER TWENTY-FIVE

I'm not sure how long I stood over my bed staring at Judge Hume. His eyes bulged. His swollen tongue protruded from his mouth. A purple line encircled his neck, the skin inflamed. In death, the judge didn't look like a powerful man. He just looked sad and pathetic, with lonely strands of hair pasted over the top of his head, rolls of fat bulging through his midsection, shriveled penis curled into a nest of graying pubic hair.

I was much more lucid than I had any right to be. Perhaps the alcohol and the events of the evening had inured me to the shock, but I found myself thinking rather clearly. My mind went to Elizabeth. First her fiancé, now her father. Maybe she was the one the killer was trying to hurt. But even if that were true, he was every bit as interested in destroying me.

For half a second, I considered calling the police. I had an alibi and credible witnesses. But my alibi would hold up only for portions of the last four hours. If the judge had been killed earlier, or in the past hour, I'd be sunk—and that was assuming, with me wrapped up so neatly, Riordan would even concern himself with the time of death. No. If the judge were found here, I would never see daylight again. I had to move the body—two hundred pounds of inert flesh.

I wondered how the killer had gotten in. The door was locked. No one but my parents had a key. If I was going to begin suspecting them, I might as well give up right now. Besides, how he got in wasn't the problem. It was how I was going to get the body out that worried me.

I threw on a shirt, ran to Wesley's, and knocked quietly on the door. No answer. I knocked again, a little louder this time. He wasn't home. I ran back into my apartment. Dragging the body down the stairs was out. The commotion would most likely draw attention from other residents.

It would have to be the fire escape. I rolled him over onto the center of the sheet. His flesh was rubbery, cool to the touch. The stench was sharper now. A shudder of revulsion rose from my gut. I pushed down my disgust and got back to work. Underneath him I found a short length of rope tied in a noose. I threw the rope and his clothing over the top of him, wrapped him in the sheet as tightly as I could, and tied it in a knot over his head and below his feet. When I tugged on the end of the sheet, the body moved more easily than I'd expected. It slid off the bed and clunked onto the floor in a heap. One of Judge Hume's legs and all the clothing spilled out.

With another shudder, I tucked the leg back inside the sheet and ran to the kitchen for a canvas shopping bag. After dumping the rope and clothing into it, I pulled my gun from the nightstand and stuck it in my belt, then dragged the body out of the bedroom to the parlor. I reached for the window latch and found it already unlocked.

All those nights drinking on the fire escape. Would I have remembered to latch the window after a bottle of bourbon? Wesley had been able to swing himself up from the ground. Why not someone else? Especially a tall, muscular man like Frank Van Dam.

I opened the window and leaned out, looking through the metal grid of the fire escape's landing. The lights in the apartments below mine were off, and no one was in the street. I grabbed the body from under the arms and pulled it up to a sitting position. When I did, the head clunked against my chest like a bowling ball. I dropped him.

Tears came to my eyes, and I slumped to the floor, pushing the body away. I couldn't do this. But a few moments later, I stood and took a deep breath, then lifted the body and maneuvered it to the windowsill, where I propped it up and then climbed out onto the landing. I reached in through the window, grabbed the body from under the arms, and dragged it out onto the fire escape.

Tires squealed in the distance.

I rushed back inside, threw on my duster, and slung the bag over my shoulder before sprinting back to the parlor and climbing out the window again. I grabbed hold of the knot at the top of the sheet and pulled the body around the corner to the steps. Somehow I managed to get him onto my shoulders in a fireman's carry.

The engines of gasoline motorcars revved as they got close, tires squealing around corners. I had no doubt as to their destination.

Bent under the weight of the judge, I climbed down the steps to the second-floor landing, feeling the strain in my back and knees. I released the last set of stairs, and they crashed to the lawn with an incredible racket. I got to the ground as quickly as I could, one hand on the back of the judge's neck, the other over his knees, then turned and awkwardly pushed the lower section of the stairs back up. I hobbled across Second Street into the alley between the houses, and had just reached Third Street when cars screeched to a stop behind me. Men shouted. A car door slammed. And another. Yellow light from lanterns careened wildly across the walls.

Detective Riordan's voice called out, "Malone, around back! Don't let him get past you."

Manic energy surged through me. I staggered to the next street and the next, barely able to support the weight of the judge's body. My breath shot out in clouds of steam, visible in the pale white glow of the full moon.

I couldn't stop and rest. If I dropped Judge Hume now, I would never get him back onto my shoulders. I stumbled along, reeling from the weight, until finally I came to what I'd been looking for—the cornfield. Stubbly cornstalks jutted up in rows, the space between them just wide enough for Judge Hume's body lengthwise. I dropped him about fifty feet from the street and fell to the ground panting, feeling pain in every muscle in my body. Exhaustion washed over me.

When I felt I could, I rose to my knees, laid the bag and my coat beside me, and plunged my hands into the cold ground. On top the dirt came out in clumps, and I was able to push it to the side, but once I'd gotten down a few inches, the soil was harder, nearly frozen.

I sat back and tried to think. A huge oak tree near the street was silhouetted against the lights of the city, its bare limbs reaching up to the sky. I pushed myself to my feet and ran to the tree. Branches and leaves littered the ground around it. I picked up a sturdy limb and returned to the body.

Stabbing my makeshift pick into the earth again and again, I dug mechanically, prying up the soil and using my hands to push it out of the hole. I was making progress now. Another foot and I could bury him.

A low hum became audible underneath the sound of the limb thudding into the dirt. I stopped and listened. The noise clarified to the *putt-putt-putt* of a gasoline engine. I dropped to the ground and looked out toward the street. The lawn in front of the redbrick three-story on the corner began to brighten. A motorcycle turned the corner toward me, its headlamp augmented by a lantern propped onto the handlebars. The rider was bundled against the cold in the dark blue overcoat of the Detroit Police's Flying Squadron. I rolled Judge Hume into the hole and lay on top of him, pressing myself as flat as I could, though much of my body was still exposed. Panic was an eyelash away.

The engine quieted. I couldn't see the motorcycle, but it had stopped almost directly across from us, no more than two or three rows down and perhaps seventy feet away. The kickstand clicked, and boots hit the cobbles. Springs creaked as the rider pushed his weight off the seat. His boots scraped against the pavement and then hit gravel. He was walking into the field.

Run? Stay? I didn't know. I was so scared I wasn't sure I could run. The light bobbed away and continued around the perimeter of the field. I realized I wasn't breathing. I reached behind me and pulled the gun from my belt. The policeman's mutterings were carried by the breeze—mostly curses, with Riordan's name mentioned more than once. He reached the corner farthest away from me, and I tensed, ready to run.

But he spun around, the lantern whirling with him, and let out a loud curse.

I was sure he'd seen me. I pressed myself farther into Judge Hume's soft stomach and loins, intertwined our legs, and pushed my head down to the side of his. The policeman was cutting across the field. I held my breath again. The soft thud of boots into the dirt got louder. The light from his lantern illuminated the sheet next to my face. I laid the gun next to Judge Hume's midsection. No matter what happened to me, I wasn't going to shoot a policeman.

He passed within thirty feet of us. The light dimmed and the sound of footsteps got quieter. He crossed the gravel shoulder and started the motorcycle again. With a loud curse directed at Riordan, he hacked up a wad of phlegm and spit it out before slowly driving away.

My muscles unclenched. I reclaimed my pistol and pulled the judge out of the hole. In another ten minutes, I'd dug deep enough that I could bury him. I rolled him in, threw the bag in after, and used my hands to shovel dirt over the top of his body. Once I'd gotten the ground fairly level, I stood and stomped down on it, getting it packed, trying to forget what was underneath.

I knelt down again and smoothed more dirt over the top, hoping what seemed right in the dark of night would look normal in the morning. After I spread the extra dirt in the field around me, I went back to the oak tree, felt around on the ground for a branch with leaves still on it, and carried one back, dragging it behind me to cover my footprints. When I was as certain as I could be that my path was hidden, I dropped both branches by the tree and lay back, panting, on the ground.

Judge Hume—obviously—wasn't the killer. Regardless of whether he had been involved in the murders of Cooper and the Doyles, someone else was doing the dirty work.

Frank Van Dam *had* to be the killer. Someone else took that train to Denver. The Mr. and Mrs. Van Dam at the hotel were different people. Frank was big and strong and tough, and not afraid of anything, other than perhaps going to prison with the socialists and anarchists he'd helped lock up over the years. Frank's car was at the train station. He'd been implicated in the bribery. No one else could have had as much motive. John Cooper was probably talking to the police and, if so, would have sent Frank to jail. The Doyles had merely gotten in the way, but the judge was definitely talking to the police. After going so far already, Frank wouldn't have risked that, either.

I may have been just a convenient scapegoat, the easiest person to blame for the murders. Was Frank that cold, to destroy an innocent man?

Not likely. He had found out about Elizabeth. I was certain now. He loved her. Therefore he hated me.

Pushing myself to my feet, I stumbled away from the field back toward my apartment, again cutting through alleyways, staying in the dark. Two streets over, I found a water pump at the back of a house. I stripped down to my undershorts and drenched myself with water, scrubbing at my hands, arms, and face, trying to rid myself of all traces of Judge Hume and the field in which he lay.

I was shivering uncontrollably. I told myself it was only from the freezing water and the cold night, until I felt tears again begin to well up in my eyes. Trying to compose myself, I dried off with my duster and dressed, then hid my gun in a flower bed on the side of the house.

I had to go back to my apartment. The police had obviously been tipped that a body would be found there, and they'd be waiting for me. My alibi expired almost two hours ago. The longer I waited, the guiltier I'd look. Judge Hume's disappearance coinciding with too much unaccounted-for time could equal life in the pen.

That result was too likely already.


A uniformed policeman shoved me into my apartment. Detective Riordan was in the parlor, sitting sideways on my sofa, his dirty brown brogans up on the cushion. A cold wind blew into the room through the open window. Four bottles of Old Tub sat on the coffee table.

They'd searched my apartment.

"Hello, Will." He took his time getting up. "See," he said, nodding toward the bottles. "Somehow I just knew you were a bourbon man."

"What are you doing in my apartment, Riordan?" I tried to sound indignant, but I was sure the detective could hear the fear in my voice.

"Oh, I think you know that." He reached out and smoothed the lapel of my duster. "Looks like somebody beat the hell out of you again."

"Yeah." I turned away from him and headed for the bathroom.

Riordan grabbed my shoulder and spun me around. "Tell me about it."

"It's none of your business." If I cooperated too easily, he'd know I was lying.

He pushed me against the wall, the front of my shirt bunched in his fist. Leaning down into my face, he growled, "Everything you do is my business."

"All right, give me a minute."

He let go of me and stepped back.

I took off my duster and draped it over a chair. "It was John Dodge." I explained what had happened outside the theater. "There were plenty of witnesses." This time, if they didn't find the body, I was safe so long as I kept my mouth shut.

"You're just getting home?"

I nodded.

"Then why are your jacket, shirt, and tie on the floor?"

"I . . . wore those yesterday."

His eyes gave me nothing. "Where are the rest of the clothes you were wearing tonight?"

"Outside the Miles Theater, I guess. If someone hasn't already stolen them."

Riordan didn't say anything.

I shrugged and tried to sound casual. "Can't fight with all that stuff on, can you?"

He gave me a grudging nod before gesturing toward the window. "Why's the window open?"

"Oh, airing out the place."

"I'd say it needs it." He nodded toward the bedroom. "What happened back there?"

"What do you mean?"

"I think you know what I mean. What were you doing in the bedroom?"

I felt an icy jab in the pit of my stomach. "Nothing." I tried to think of what I could have left in the room.

Riordan glanced at the policeman who'd brought me in. "Do you suppose this milksop has ever told the truth?"

The cop shrugged.

Riordan shoved me toward the bedroom. When I saw the room I began to search my mind for an explanation, but I was frightened and tired and drunk. I just stared.

The bed looked like it had been torn apart, the blankets and lone sheet scattered across and off it. The rocking chair sat crooked, facing the wall. The wardrobe stood open, doors askew. The reek of shit had diminished, but it was still there.

"What?" I said, looking back to Riordan. I couldn't think of anything else to say.

"'What?' he says." Riordan grinned. "Looking at this, what would you say happened here?"

I tried to look innocent. "I don't know. I guess I'd say nobody's cleaned my bedroom for a while."

"I'd say it looks like you had a lover's quarrel with one of your fairy friends. I'd say it got out of control and you killed him."

"I don't know what you're talking about. My room's messy. So what?"

His lip curled, and he glared at me from under his fedora. "How about the smell?"

"What about it?"

"You know, Will, when a man struggles for his life, it's normal for his bowels to release. Unless you crap in your bed, I'd bet somebody got killed in here. You wouldn't know anything about that, would you?"

I shook my head.

"Where's the other sheet?"

"What other sheet?"

He blew out a breath in frustration. "The other sheet from your bed, you simpleton."

"I just use one. Less to wash that way."

Riordan ripped the sheet off my bed. "You won't mind if I take this one, then? In case we happen to find another that matches?"

I shrugged. He didn't need my permission. "Is there anything else I can help you with?"

"Yes, there is. What would we have found here this evening if the idiot who answers the telephone at the station had phoned me when he got the call?" He poked me in the chest with a big finger. I stumbled back half a step. "This time tell me the truth." He advanced on me, jabbing me in the chest again.

I got my balance, braced my legs, and glared back at him. In a tight voice, I said, "Nothing. You would have found nothing."

He leaned over, his face inches from mine. "What did you do tonight?"

"I went to the show. I got beat up. I walked home. I was humiliated." I nodded toward his scar. "Surely you can understand being humiliated."

A smile began to spread across his face. "You seem to have grown a pair over the last week or so." He half turned, like he was going to leave, and then spun and kicked me in the groin with one of his big boots.

I collapsed onto the floor, doubled over, retching.

Riordan stood over me and waited until I'd brought up my dinner and about a quart of bourbon. "I liked you better before."

# CHAPTER TWENTY-SIX

The next morning I shuffled to the bathroom from the couch, where I'd spent the night. Even though I'd changed the bedding—and thrown out everything from the night before—I couldn't imagine sleeping in my bed.

Pain coursed through my body. Every muscle fiber, organ, and bone hurt, though the stabs in my gut and groin courtesy of Riordan's boot were the worst. After swallowing a handful of aspirin, I stood over the toilet bowl and tried to urinate. I'd go a little and stop from the pain, then go a little more. The thin stream was tinged pink.

I hobbled to the kitchen, reached up behind the flour, and brought down one of the bourbon bottles. I'd already pulled out the cork and raised the bottle to my mouth when I hesitated.

I was destroying myself. That realization was nothing new. But today, for some reason, it mattered.

I stared at the red and white label on the bottle of Old Tub. Somewhere in the back of my mind a soothing voice told me to take a drink. It would feel so good going down. The anticipatory burn in my throat, the warmth spreading through my body, the darkening around my mind that would dull the pain, help blur the memories. My mouth began to turn up in a smile. I could already taste the bourbon, feel the burn, the warmth. It would be so good.

Another minute passed. I was still staring at the bottle.

The voice was the dead man inside me. He'd been trying to escape for more than a year. Had I been in this shape a week ago I would have let him out, let him stick my head in the oven and turn on the gas. After getting so drunk I'd believe him when he told me it was the only thing to do.

But not today.

I turned the bottle of Old Tub upside down over the sink, my head turned away, trying not to smell the sweet caramel odor while the bourbon splashed into the sink and down the drain. I followed that with the other three bottles of bourbon in the cupboard, and then all the bottles from the liquor cabinet in the parlor.

This wasn't the first time I'd sworn off alcohol, but I was determined it would be the last. Elizabeth had been able to escape the clutches of heroin. Surely I could stop drinking. Sober, I might have a chance to save myself from Frank Van Dam and Detective Riordan. If I kept on like I was, I would only be digging another grave, this one for myself.

Every motion brought a new round of pain, but I suffered through it long enough to break off a sturdy piece of wood from the pile next to the fireplace. I wedged it into the frame of the window overlooking the fire escape. Frank would have to find another way in.

The gun was a loose end that would have to wait until tonight. It was hidden well enough, and I couldn't very well stroll over to someone else's house in broad daylight and pluck a gun from their garden. I went back to the parlor and lay on the couch all morning, moving as little as possible while I tried to sort through the jumble of ideas bouncing around my mind. Judge Hume had been murdered, and I'd been framed for it. I was killing myself with liquor. I'd been made a fool in front of a woman I thought I might care for and only made the humiliation worse by running away. Every time I thought of Sapphira my cheeks began to redden, and I felt the humiliation anew. I'd never be able to see her without thinking of last night.

I'd never be able to see her.

Around one, my telephone rang. I steeled myself and rolled slowly to the edge of the couch, then lowered my legs to the floor and unfolded myself an inch or two at a time. That was tolerable. I hobbled to the den and answered the phone. It was my father, asking why I wasn't there for dinner.

"Dinner? Oh, right," I said, grunting out a laugh. "I was going to phone you. I'm not feeling too well."

"Not feeling well enough for your mother's prime rib?"

"No, I should just stay in bed today."

"We'll bring it to you then."

"No!" I said, much more forcefully than I intended. I didn't want them seeing my condition, much less the condition of my apartment.

"I've got something to discuss with you, Will. We should talk today." His manner was casual, but given the state of the rest of my life, I was certain it would be something bad.

"Gosh, well . . . all right. I'll come to your house. I suppose I could use some home cooking."

"Excellent," my father said. "I'll have Mother hold dinner for a bit."

"I'll be there as soon as I can." I cleaned myself up and dressed, every movement a painful reminder of the night before. My hands were shaking when I tried to tie my cravat. The shaking hadn't stopped by the time I walked up the sidewalk to my parents' house. It was a two-story shingle-style Victorian with an inviting shade porch and rough-hewn wood shingles on the siding and steeply pitched roof. My father always said it was "spacious but not ostentatious." I used to agree. Now it seemed more a monument to excess, along with the rest of the neighborhood. I knocked. Somehow just walking in didn't feel appropriate anymore.

My father opened the door and gaped at me.

I remembered my swollen face. "Ah, just a little scrape with the Dodge brothers."

"Those sons of— Have you reported it to the police?"

"No. Not necessary. It's over." I stepped inside and took off my boots.

My father's face was turning red. "Were there witnesses?"

I nodded.

"Then get those boors thrown in jail. God knows they deserve it."

"No, Father, no. Please, let me deal with it."

He finally relented. Underlying the smell of beef and potatoes cooking in the kitchen was a peculiar odor, which I realized was the normal aroma of my parents' house. It didn't smell like home anymore. We walked to the kitchen, where I had a conversation with my mother that was nearly identical to the one I'd just had with my father, except with a little more hand-wringing on her part. During dinner my father seemed distracted.

When we finished eating, he asked me to join him in his den. I followed him into the walnut-paneled room with its rich scents of leather and polished wood. Bookcases covered every wall, a huge globe on a floor stand filled one corner, and a telescope by the window pointed up at the sky.

My father walked straight to the bar. "Brandy?" he said, looking over his shoulder at me.

"No. Thanks."

He turned around and appraised me. "I don't think I've ever heard you refuse a drink."

"Just don't want one right now." I didn't feel like going into it with him.

He gave me a sour look. "I think you're going to want one."

"Why? What's happened now?" My mind filled with a vision of Judge Hume's body lying on my bed. I tried to blink it away.

He finished pouring himself a drink and walked to his desk, where he pulled out a magazine and handed it to me. "Look at that."

I lowered myself into a red leather club chair across from him. The magazine trembled in my hands. A Baker Electric advertisement took up the entire front cover of the December 8 issue of *The Automobile* magazine. The headline read BAKER ELECTRIC GOES 244.5 MILES ON ONE CHARGE OF EDISON BATTERIES.

A new world record. My only accomplishment—gone.

My father took a sip of brandy. I could smell it from across the desk—oak and grapes and alcohol. The scent itself was intoxicating. I threw the magazine on his desk and stared out the window at the barren trees.

"I'd like to discuss a few other things with you," he said.

I could feel my mouth tighten. More logs for the already-blazing fire. I looked back to him.

He squirmed in his chair and finally said, "Mr. Sutton mentioned your relationship with Wesley McRae. It's simply not right."

"Father, Wesley is a friend. A good friend. He's probably the best person I know."

My father harrumphed. "Yes, well, you know how people talk. And if two unmarried men live across the hall from each other and spend time together—"

"Father. He's my friend. That's the end of it."

"You're right, you're right. I'm sorry." He took a quick drink of brandy and cleared his throat. "On a brighter note, I've thought about what you asked."

I stared at him blankly.

"About coming back to work."

"Oh." It didn't seem so important now.

"I'd like you to be in charge of the DADA show."

"Really?" I sat up straight. Now that Detroit was becoming the center of the American automotive industry, the Detroit Automobile Dealers Association was spending a fortune to prove it to the rest of the world. The only show that could compete was the original, the New York Auto Show, held at Madison Square Garden. Since Detroit had the equivalent of "short-man's syndrome" when the subject was New York, the automobile men of Detroit would work twice as hard and spend twice as much to prove they were better. The result was the finest auto show in the country, probably the world.

It was also the biggest sales week of the year for Detroit auto manufacturers, and the competition would be strong. My father was putting a lot on my shoulders. This show could make or break the year for Detroit Electric. He really did believe in me—though it probably didn't hurt that the show ran from January 16 through 21. It would be finished nine days before my trial began.

I'd still be free—assuming Judge Hume's body wasn't found.

My father looked at his brandy while he swirled it around in the snifter. The rich brown liquid sparkled in the electric lights of the room. "You'll have to coordinate with sales, choose which models to show, work with advertising, everything."

I thanked him.

His head tilted back a little. "Once we get this trial behind us I'd like to get you back on track—learning the business, the whole business."

"Thanks. You won't regret this. Oh, and I forgot to thank you for the tickets." It wasn't his fault I'd been beaten and framed for yet another murder.

"Tickets?"

"For the show at the Miles."

"I didn't give you any tickets." He was quiet for a moment. "Will, are you all right?"

"I'm . . . fine." I waved my hand in the air. "I was thinking of something else." Of course he didn't send me the tickets. If Frank could type out blackmail letters in my office, he could certainly get hold of a piece of Anderson stationery and an envelope. What better way to get me out of my apartment?

My father set his glass on the blotter. "Did you hear about Byron Carter?"

Byron Carter was the man behind the Carter-Car Company, which he had sold to General Motors a few years before. "No. What happened?"

"He died yesterday. A few weeks ago he stopped to help a woman whose car had stalled. He didn't check the spark first."

"Oh, no. What happened?"

"When the engine backfired and the crank spun back, it broke his arm and smashed his face and jaw. Gangrene set in. He never recovered."

"Gosh, I'm sorry. I know you were friends."

"Henry Leland is beside himself. He and Byron were very close. Leland's saying he'll come up with a fix for the self-starter if it's the last thing he does. He swears he won't have his Cadillacs hurting people that way."

"Good for him. I'm sure Mr. Carter's death was a real blow."

"It's high time someone did something about that hand crank. It's a menace." He shifted in his chair and let out a sigh. He looked miserable.

"What?" I said.

"Well . . . I feel terrible saying this, but I'm worried about what might happen if Leland actually produces a self-starter that works."

"Why? People don't buy electrics just because they're easy to start. Gasoline automobiles are always going to have all that noise and smoke. Society women would never drive one."

"Perhaps. But the cards are already stacked against us." He began to tick off points on his fingers. "Gasoline automobiles are cheap. Electric automobiles are expensive. Gasoline is practically free. Electricity is expensive. A gasoline automobile can be driven anywhere the fuel can be delivered, whereas electrics are almost exclusively city cars." He dabbed at his forehead with a handkerchief.

"For now. But rural areas are getting electrical service. And don't forget the Edison battery. Electric cars' average mileage going from fifty to more than a hundred?" I leaned forward and got a stab in the gut. "Father, trust me on this. Electrics will always be the choice for people who can afford them. Who wants an automobile farting noxious fumes on them if they can avoid it?"

He looked thoughtful and nodded slowly. "You may be right. So long as we stay at the top of the range we should be fine. It's Baker who's got the problem, now that they're going for the mid market."

By the time I left, my mind was swirling with ideas for the auto show. But I had an ominous feeling. My thoughts kept coming back to Judge Hume. His body lay under a few inches of soil in the cornfield. Assuming dogs didn't dig him up sooner, he would certainly be found when the field was plowed in the spring. And given that he was buried in my sheet only a few hundred yards from my apartment, it wouldn't take a genius to figure out I was involved.

I needed to get rid of the body—permanently.

I spent the rest of the day on two tasks—trying to determine what to do with Judge Hume's body and keeping myself from drinking.

I nearly decided to leave the body where it was. Yes, it would be found, and yes, the evidence would point to me as the killer, but the thought of touching it again filled me with dread. Practicality finally won out. If I wanted to regain my life I had to put Judge Hume's corpse somewhere it would never be found. I considered asking Wesley to help me, but quickly decided against it. If I were caught I would pay the price. I wouldn't risk his life and freedom again.

My first idea was to bury the body deeper in the cornfield, but the field was too close to my apartment and was surrounded by houses. With the hard ground, the digging would be a noisy business, and I might be heard. It was a miracle no one had phoned the police when I buried him. The body had to go somewhere else.

I would need a large motorized vehicle, but I couldn't turn any of my friends or family into accomplices. An electric would be ideal because of its silent motor, but the only car to which I had access was the company's Victoria. It had a tiny trunk and a single bench seat, only large enough for two people to sit upright. I could just picture the face of the policeman who stopped us. No. I needed a truck and had no way of securing one until tomorrow. It would have to wait a day.

For a brief moment I considered bringing the body to the factory or the garage and dumping it into the acid tank. No body, no murder. But not only was it too horrifying to seriously contemplate, with the garage manned twenty-four hours a day and guards now posted at the factory, it was also too dangerous.

My next thought was to weigh him down and dump him in the river.

I didn't have a boat and couldn't rent one without potentially messy paperwork. To have any chance of him not being found, I would have to get him out near the middle, which meant I'd have to swim his body far out into the river along with enough weights to sink it. Even in warm weather I'd be joining him at the bottom.

I had to bury him somewhere else, and it had to be close.

Then it hit me—Zug Island. It was just outside the city, and most of

248 | D. E. Johnson

the ground was piled with garbage. Nobody would find him there. Detroit Iron Works owned the island but used only a small portion of it near the river for their huge foundry. The four-lane bridge over Short Cut Canal was fenced off and guarded to limit access to the property, but a railroad bridge crossed it on both sides, which were still heaped with garbage from the island's earlier days as a dump.

When I was sixteen I'd gone to Zug on a dare with some prep school friends. We'd taken the tracks across the canal and sneaked through the piles of garbage to the ruins of Samuel Zug's mansion. It was rumored to be haunted, and we were all frightened, though our teenage bravado carried us through. We continued on to the foundry, where a stink like burning rubber mixed with coal smoke overcame the powerful stench of rot soaked into the ground. We squinted against the brilliant light pouring through the massive open doors into the hellish environs of the blast furnace. We'd spent more than two hours on the island and never saw or heard a train. It should be safe to cross the bridge—but I'd do some reconnaissance before I started driving around with Judge Hume's body.

The task of staying sober was even more difficult.

The little voice in the back of my head kept reasoning with me. *I don't have a problem. Who wouldn't drink with all this going on? One drink won't hurt. I'll think more clearly.* I nearly left my apartment a dozen times—*Just for one, that's all I need.* But I didn't.

I retrieved my gun around midnight and went straight to bed. I went back to bed at two, and again at four, and again at five. Each time I was sober. Finally, overcome by exhaustion, I dropped off into a restless sleep.

When I woke at nine o'clock, I thought, *I made it one day. Now I'll make it another.* Tiny snowflakes drifted past my window, a reminder that winter was upon us. I threw the blankets to the side and made to swing my legs off the bed, but was halted by a sharp stab in my groin. Then the pain began to register from my sides, face, and stomach. After a minute, I tried again—very slowly. I slipped on my robe and forced myself to look in the mirror. My lips had returned to somewhere near their normal size, and the bruising on my face was beginning to fade. I still looked like I had tried to take on a grizzly single-handed, but I was encouraged nonetheless.

After dressing, I went outside in the snow just long enough to buy a *Herald* from a newsboy on the corner. I peeked around to see if anyone was paying attention to me. It seemed a reasonable bet the police would be watching, but I saw nothing out of the ordinary. When I got home I sat at my desk and looked through the paper. Since I wasn't in jail, I knew Judge Hume's body hadn't been discovered. But his disappearance was big news. The speculation was that he was running to avoid prosecution. Police were searching every boat they could find on the Detroit River to try to keep him from escaping to Canada. They'd already arrested a boatload of illegal Italian immigrants crossing from Windsor in the dead of night.

Despite the grim circumstances, I laughed. Even dead, the judge was a problem for Vito Adamo.

For some reason that laugh forced the weight of the circumstances onto me. The remains of Elizabeth's father lay in a field. What was she to think? Her fiancé murdered, her father vanished. Now I would defile his body again.

I couldn't falter. I didn't kill Judge Hume. All I was trying to do was to survive, same as he would have. Pushing the horror from my mind, I concentrated on the task ahead. I needed to rid myself of the body and for that I would need a Detroit Electric truck. I phoned my father at his office. Wilkinson connected me.

"Hello, Will. I thought we might see you this morning."

"I'm just tying up a few personal details before I begin my work on the show." That was certainly true. "But I want to get started tonight. Have we got a 601 I could run through its paces?"

"I would imagine. But what for?"

"I've never driven one. I need to be familiar with it if I'm going to promote it." Once, I had been proud of my honesty, but now lying seemed as natural as breathing.

"Makes sense. I'll have Wilkinson look into it and phone you with the details."

We rang off. I lay on the parlor floor stretching my sore muscles for the better part of an hour until Wilkinson called me back, saying I could pick up a 601 panel truck at the garage that evening.

I sat at the kitchen table, gazing out the window. Pebbly snowflakes scattered before a stiff wind that shook the bare gray branches of the trees in the backyard. One limb in particular caught my eye—a skeletal arm with bony fingers reaching out to the heavens.

An image of Sapphira's dark eyes, high cheekbones, and lustrous black hair filled my mind. At the same time, my stomach lurched. The association of Sapphira with the night at the theater would be too strong to ever overcome. I would forget her. Anyway, people I knew had begun turning up dead much more frequently than I cared for. Since I hadn't told her where I lived, it was unlikely she would find me. And after the exhibition I put on, it was even less likely she would try.

I had an odd thought. Had the Dodge brothers not beaten me outside the theater, I would have spent a good portion of the night with Sapphira, and Judge Hume's body would have been found in my apartment. I would be in jail now, never to leave.

John and Horace Dodge had done me a favor.

# CHAPTER TWENTY-SEVEN

Half an hour later, gun tucked into the small of my back, I took a trolley downtown and then another to the corner of Jefferson and West End. From there I headed toward the river, trying to ignore the saloons lining the street and the trembling in my hands. Snowflakes plummeted down, now larger and wetter, melting to slush on the cobbles but adding to the thin graying layer on the ground. The road ended abruptly at a series of warehouses and factories, redbrick buildings darkened with soot. The factories billowed clouds of oily black smoke from chimney after chimney, the plumes drifting over the river to darken the Windsor sky.

The building closest to the island was a warehouse with tiny windows set high on the walls. As casually as I could muster, I cut around it and hurried to the train tracks. To the north, this track divided into dozens of branches, but only one headed south to Zug Island. Even though the wind was strong at my back, I smelled the island before I saw it. I could have found the way with my eyes closed. Past the bridge was nothing but hills of heaped trash skinned with snow, blocking the view of the foundry. Judge Hume's body could lie there forever, and no one would be the wiser.

The tracks were in good shape and the bridge, though still a hundred yards away, was obviously intact. I don't know why I was worried, what with the constant flow of pig iron from the foundry to all points east and west.

My biggest concern now was how far I'd have to carry the body. I'd come in on the closest street, and I wasn't sure about driving onto private property with the body in the back of the truck, particularly since night watchmen were sure to be on duty here on the riverfront. I'd have to improvise, something that—clearly—was not my strong suit.

By the time I returned to the warehouse, all that was left of my footprints were slight depressions from my weight in the grassier areas. If the snow continued, I'd leave tracks, but they would disappear quickly.

I went back out to Jefferson and walked east. When I was about a quarter mile down the road, a train roared out from the island, dozens of gray boxcars clacking along the track. In front of me, a security guard in a wrinkled gray uniform slouched against a redbrick building underneath a sign that read SIMPKINS IMPORTS. I ambled up to him and smiled. "Good afternoon." I shouted to be heard over the train.

He looked at me, eyes wary. He was an older man, thin, with a deeply lined face.

"Say, I pass by here all the time," I said, "and I've always wondered what you import." I pulled my cigarette case from my coat pocket and held it out to him.

He took a cigarette, and I lit it for him. The sound of the train was fading into the distance. "Much obliged," he said, and shrugged. "They import paper. Nothing worth stealing, if that's what you're thinking."

"No." I laughed. "I'm not a thief. I was just curious."

He shrugged again and looked away.

I gestured with my head toward the back of the building. "All these trains must drive you crazy."

"You get used to it."

"It's got to be the worst at night. Just when you think you're going to get some peace and quiet, another train comes by."

"Nah. Unless they're really busy, the trains stop around six."

"Hmm." I pulled out my watch and glanced at it. "Well, I'd better be going. Thanks for the conversation."

"Don't mention it." He took a drag on the cigarette, and I headed for the streetcar stop.

I went home and spent a couple of hours reading in my office. My chair sat next to the radiator, and I moved closer, feeling the warmth cut through the winter chill. Finally, too nervous to wait around my apartment, I began to wander the streets.

The snow continued. An inch of wet slush covered the cobblestones and sidewalks, and began to freeze as the temperature dropped. I picked my way carefully through the dark, certain a fall on the pavement would break me in two. As I moved along, my sore muscles began to loosen.

I walked through the Detroit in which I'd grown up—stone Beaux Arts palaces, Victorian mansions, columned Greek Revivals, and brick and stone skyscrapers rising from the glow of the street lamps into the dark as if they continued on to Heaven itself. For dinner, I stopped downtown at a little French café, refusing wine though the waiter pressed me on the subject. I was determined to maintain my sobriety but understood for the first time how difficult it was going to be. Social situations—lunches, dinners, after-dinner chats with friends, parties, the theater, everything—involved drinking. It was normal and expected. To refuse was to be rude. I was in for a lifetime of awkward moments.

After dinner, I wandered north through the falling snow past "Sauerkraut Row," the German part of town, filled with breweries, cigar factories, marble works, and homes. Wreaths adorned most doors, and parlors shone with the Christmas trees' sparkling glass ornaments.

I checked the load of my pistol and headed toward the other Detroit, the city with which I'd only just become acquainted. First I looped around to Hastings Street, perhaps a quarter mile north of the Bucket, where I saw the first cracks in the facade. Street followed street with unintelligible store signs in Hebrew and Cyrillic script, and dozens of buildings of dark, cramped apartments. Their stoops were occupied by bands of young toughs, like armies holding territories. Near as I could tell, none of them was the boy who had taken the blackmail money.

I continued toward the river, walking through a section of Greektown, though I skirted the area in which Sapphira lived. From there I plunged into an unfamiliar area east of downtown. The buildings were crumbling, the streets reeking of shit and piss and rotting garbage, and crammed with humanity. Children huddled together over garbage can fires. Couples hurried past the entrances to alleyways with fearful glances over their shoulders. Rough-looking men with derbies pulled down over their brows leaned against walls and in doorways, appraising passersby. I looked them in the eye. The confidence given me by the gun must have shown on my face, because they let me pass.

My hands and feet were numb, but I continued toward the river, into Black Bottom, the city's small enclave of Negroes. The buildings here were mostly rickety wood, starting with two-story houses only a few feet apart, many with lean-tos attached haphazardly to their fronts and backs. Next came one-story shotgun shacks jammed together in a line, which led finally to the thrown-together wood and tin shanties abutting the coal yards next to the river.

Blinded by the magnificence and grandeur of the city I knew, I had thought Detroit was different than this. But to these people—Russians, Greeks, and Blacks, as well as the Italians, Irish, Poles, Flemings, Hungarians, Turks, Chinese, and all the rest—this was the reality. Nothing more or less than the nightmare result of a dream smashed against the shores of the Promised Land. Detroit hadn't yet gained the opulence or sunk to the depths of New York, but only because it hadn't had time.

I wanted to sink into an ocean of bourbon.

Around ten I walked up to the front door of the Detroit Electric garage and rapped on the window, my movements spastic from nervousness. I took a deep breath and blew it out, trying to build some enthusiasm.

Ben Carr looked through the window. He hesitated before opening the door, probably remembering what had happened the last time I showed up here at night. "We've got the 601 ready to go," he said, not quite meeting my eyes. He gestured vaguely over his shoulder at the boxy black truck, which stood in front of the closed garage door. The electric lights in the room were bright, sparkling off the shiny finishes of the automobiles arrayed around the outside walls. I was taken, as I always was, by the fresh-air ozone scent of the building.

I extended my hand to him, and he took it. "I'm so sorry, Ben," I said. "No matter what happens to me, it was wrong to get you involved in this mess."

His face relaxed a little. "Thank you, sir. I'm sorry I couldn't help you, but I . . . I just couldn't."

"I understand. I can't tell you how relieved I was when Detective Riordan said he wasn't pressing charges against you."

Ben looked at his feet. "You know I got to testify."

"Of course you do. But don't worry. I'm going to get out of this," I said, with a great deal more confidence than I felt.

His eyes darted to mine and then away again. "I left the logbook on the front seat of the truck. Don't forget to fill it out."

"Sure, thanks."

He began to turn around, hesitated, then spun and marched toward the back of the garage. "Just leave it on that stool by the tool crib," he called over his shoulder. "I'll get it later."

I watched him until he turned the corner into the office. He wanted my handwriting in the logbook. I couldn't blame him. I walked over to the truck, wrote the details in the book, and set it atop the stool.

The truck was nothing fancy, just a twelve-foot-long box with a cutout in the front for a bench seat over the white Motz cushion tires. The only thing in front of the driver other than the steering wheel—which I thought awkward in comparison to the steering lever on our automobiles—was a one-inch wood panel that held the headlights.

I walked around to the back and swung the doors open. A tool kit and spare tire were inside, but nothing else. There was plenty of room for a body—for a number of bodies. With its one-ton capacity, I reckoned I could get eight or nine more Judge Hume–sized corpses inside without taxing the suspension or motor. And the way my life was going, that could come in handy.

After I opened the garage door, I climbed in the truck and checked the voltmeter. The batteries were fully charged. That gave me a range of at least fifty miles—much more than I needed. I pulled onto the street and parked just long enough to close the door and get cursed by the driver of a black Locomobile roadster. Turning left onto Woodward, I headed north, back to my apartment for some supplies. The street had begun to quiet, tomorrow a workday.

I pulled up to the curb opposite my building and climbed the stairs. I was unlocking my door when Wesley popped out of his apartment.

"Hi, Will," he said. "Thought that sounded like you." He did a double take. "What happened to you now?"

"Nothing. Just a little misunderstanding with the Dodge brothers."

He shook his head slowly. "Why don't you come in for a drink and tell me about it?"

"No, thanks. I've quit, actually."

"Drinking?"

I nodded.

"Good for you." He smiled. "Well, you want to come in for a ginger ale?"

"I'm going to have to take a rain check. I've got to take care of something tonight, just some work I'm catching up on. My father's put me in charge of our booth for the Detroit Auto Show."

His smile widened. "Congratulations. I'm really happy for you."

"Thanks." I looked to the inside of my apartment. "I should get to it. See you."

"Okay. But let's have that ginger ale soon."

I turned back to him. "Absolutely. Thanks, Wes."

He nodded and slipped back inside his apartment. There were a few things I wasn't going to do any longer. One was drink. Another was involve Wesley in my problems.

I changed into a black shirt, trousers, and boots, and fit a black fedora on my head. Then I gathered my supplies—a shovel, a lantern with a black cowl, a clothesline, and a huge plaid blanket I never used, similar to dozens I'd seen at picnics or warming spectators at spring and autumn sporting events. I shrugged on my black greatcoat and tried to decide what to do with the next few hours.

I considered taking a drive but realized I couldn't risk using any more of the batteries' charge than necessary. Nor did I want to leave the truck parked in front of my building. I drove to the end of a dark street, parked, and began steeling myself for the gruesome task ahead.

It was after midnight when I drove to the cornfield.


Snow crunched under the tires as I eased my foot onto the brake in front of the field. The truck rolled to a stop with a shudder and a squeak of the springs. I sat still, listening. In the distance, a gasoline engine revved. Other than that, it was unnaturally quiet. Snow fell on snow in a silent ballet.

I looked out at the field, and my heart sank. Streetlights lit the area just enough to illuminate a smooth white sea, only occasional stalks rising far enough to break the surface and give any indication of rows. Having only a vague memory of the body's location before the snow, I thought this might well be an impossible task.

But I had to move the body. I stepped down from the cab and crept around to the back of the truck. Taking care to be quiet, I opened the doors, climbed inside, and lit the lantern with my lighter before closing the cowl far enough to allow only a sliver of light to escape. I opened the door and climbed back out onto the snow.

The huge oak tree stood to my left. I tried to triangulate the position of the grave, using the tree and the road, but without the rows to guide me it was impossible. When I walked onto the field, my boots sank through the snow, and I could feel the U-shaped depressions between the rows. Still, everything looked the same.

I took my best guess and pushed the shovel down through the snow. Given that the judge was covered by only a bit of dirt, it was a tentative attempt, but even so, the shovel stopped after a few inches. I was certain the ground around the grave would be softer, so I moved ahead a few feet and tried again. That spot was just as hard. I stepped over to the next row and pushed the blade of the shovel into the earth again with the same result.

Half an hour later, I was frantic, slashing the shovel into the hard ground. The falling snow had hidden my earlier footprints, and I couldn't remember where I'd dug and where I hadn't. I started over, working methodically down one row and then another, until finally the shovel chunked into a softer piece of ground. Digging carefully now, I found the handle of the bag containing Judge Hume's clothing and the rope used to kill him. I shut off my brain and dug out the body.

When I'd removed most of the dirt, I could see Judge Hume's form inside the sheet—body rigid, knees slightly bent, hips twisted a little to the right. I pushed my hands into the dirt underneath his shoulders, took hold of him under the arms, and tugged him out. His body didn't change position, either frozen or in rigor mortis. After I stripped off the sheet and tucked it inside the bag, I hesitated. Seeing the corpse in the sliver of light from the lantern filled me with pity. Now simply a pale blue figure with bulging eyes, open mouth, and swollen tongue, the judge had been just a man, a father, not some loathsome devil bent on ruining my life. Everyone deserved to die with dignity, not be violated like this.

I dropped to my knees next to him. "Judge Hume?" I whispered. "Your Honor? I know you only wanted the best for Elizabeth. I'm sorry I wasn't the man you thought I should be. You were right. I wasn't good enough for her. And I'm sorry beyond measure for this." I wrapped him in the blanket and secured it with the clothesline.

Even though the temperature was in the twenties, sweat dripped from my face. I threw the strap of the bag over my shoulder, dragged the body to the truck, and hoisted it into the back along with the bag. Then I returned to the field, filled in the hole, and stomped down the earth. By the time I finished, snow was beginning to erase my footprints. I took one last look around, climbed behind the wheel, and eased the truck back onto the road.

Heading southwest, I cut through neighborhoods as I worked my way down to Jefferson, keeping my speed at a safe eight miles per hour. Had I been driving a gasoline motorcar, I don't think I'd have been able to regulate my speed at all, but I was fortunate electrics stayed consistent.

I had a plan. When I reached the island, I would hide Judge Hume's body and bury the sheet, the rope, and the clothing in different places. Then I'd return and bury the body. It was risky carrying everything together, but the longer I had the body or any of the bag's contents in my possession, the more likely it was I'd be caught.

When I turned off Jefferson onto West End, I stopped and watched the buildings to the sides and in front of me. A deep dark sound, like the mumbling of a lunatic, carried on the air from Zug's gigantic blast furnace.

An open door in the warehouse brightened. A night watchman carrying a lantern hurried out, took a quick look around, and hurried back inside. I waited another five minutes. Seeing no movement, I put the truck into first and rolled forward, leaving the headlights off. The floodlights on the buildings and the faint white glow from the foundry provided all the light I needed.

I pulled the truck into the shadows at the side of the road and stood next to it for a moment, looking around and listening, before I opened the back doors, grabbed the bag, and pulled the body partway out. It didn't seem likely I'd be able to balance both the judge and the shovel, so I decided to get the judge to the island first.

I threw the bag over my shoulder, squatted down, and slid the blanket-wrapped corpse out over the other shoulder, thinking I'd carry him like a wood plank. When the balance felt about right, I tightened my grip over his waist and stood. The body tipped over my back and hit the ground with a *thud*. I fell backward over the top of it, making just as much noise.

Cursing inwardly, I squatted in the shadows for a moment. It didn't seem anyone had heard. I struggled to lift the body onto my shoulder, but it was impossible. When I carried Judge Hume the night he'd been murdered, his body had formed to the contours of my neck and shoulders.

Now he was a two-hundred-pound rock lying on the ground.

I started dragging him toward the tracks. Pain sprung anew from a dozen spots on my body. I was wringing with sweat before I'd even reached the back of the warehouse. There, I stopped, leaned against the wall, and slid down to a seated position next to the body. My breath shot out in great plumes of steam. I wouldn't be able to stop again until I reached the bridge, four times as far as I'd already come. And I couldn't sit here any longer, either.

I stripped off my greatcoat and left it next to the building before I again slung the bag over my shoulder and dragged Judge Hume's body to the tracks and then alongside them. The body dug up and pushed aside odd bits of trash and the few chunks of coal not already scavenged by the poor, and left a rut in the snow as if I'd run a toboggan over it. Though I could still smell the island, the falling snow tamped down the stench to a tolerable level. The foundry's roar was loud, insistent, and its white light flared and ebbed like a gigantic welder's torch, casting an unearthly glow on the riverfront.

My fingers were cramping, and I ached everywhere, but I kept pulling. The light from the foundry was brighter here, but I was cloaked in the elongated shadows reaching out from the island.

I finally reached the bridge and collapsed on the ground next to the judge's body. This was going to be a trickier business. The bridge was perhaps a hundred feet long and no wider than a train. Even though the canal was only forty feet across, the ground fell away quickly underneath the bridge, which was elevated thirty feet above the water. All but ten feet on either end had the potential for a dangerous fall. A four-inch gap lay between the slats under the tracks, and there were no side rails to keep a person from pitching over into the canal.

Apparently the bridge hadn't been designed for dragging bodies to the island.

I looked both ways down the track and felt the rails, checking for trains. Though it seemed likely the security guard was right and no trains were running, I couldn't take chances. Satisfied, I pulled the judge's corpse up over the metal rails and began dragging it across the bridge. The snow made the wooden slats slippery, and I stepped carefully from one to the next, keeping my eyes on my feet. This was taking much longer than I had expected. My pace was of step, tug, step, tug, and the judge's feet bumped over every slat with a pattern of rhythmic thumps I felt more than heard, what with the low thunder of the foundry behind me.

When I was about halfway across, the bridge began to vibrate. I glanced up in front of me and saw nothing, then dropped the body and turned around.

A headlight, only a few hundred feet away, raced toward me, getting larger by the second.

I froze. There was no time to run back across. The train was nearly on the bridge now. I stepped to the side of the body and rolled it over the edge. The train's horn blared a deafening blast. I leaped from the bridge a split second before the train would have hit me, and the wind from its passing spun me in the air. The pitch of the horn changed from high to low as the train rocketed by and I plummeted toward the canal.

When I hit the frigid water, the shock ripped the air from my lungs. Reflexively, I tried to take a breath and began choking, coughing, and sucking in even more water. I flailed my arms and legs, reaching for the surface. The bag's handle slipped off my shoulder. I grabbed for it and found only water. The strong current swirled away from River Rouge, pulling me toward the Detroit River. I fought it and thrashed with numbing limbs, barely able to breathe through racking coughs. Somehow I made it far enough that my hands hit bottom, and I pulled myself up to the shore. I vomited onto the snow, the spasms continuing long after the water had been purged from my lungs.

The feeling wasn't returning to my body. Still coughing like a consumptive, I sat up and rubbed my legs, shivering uncontrollably, trying to get enough friction to regain some feeling, some warmth, before hypothermia claimed me.

The bag was gone. I looked through the falling snow to the water, expecting to see Judge Hume's blanket-clad corpse bobbing out from the mouth of the canal into the river. Nothing was visible other than the tops of the swells, sparking with the flares of the foundry's blast furnace.

I stumbled back toward the warehouse, hugging myself in a vain attempt to stave off the cold. When I was almost there, light from a lantern bobbed around the front corner of the building. I dropped to the ground, trying to stifle my coughs, shivering so hard my teeth felt like they were being jarred loose. The lantern didn't move for a moment, then disappeared around the corner again. As quickly as caution would allow, I hurried to the building, stripped off my clothing, and wrapped my greatcoat around me. When I dropped my pants, the pistol fell with them. I'd forgotten I had it. I scooped it up and tottered on numb legs to the truck. After a quick look around, I climbed in and drove to my apartment. I soaked in a hot bath for a long while, then drove back to the Detroit Electric garage, still wheezing.

I had compounded my problem. Judge Hume's body would surface, ensuring he would be found. But worse, I had lost the bag containing his clothing, the murder weapon, and my sheet—in one neat little package. If someone found that bag and turned it over to the police, Riordan would have all the evidence he needed to put me away forever.

# CHAPTER TWENTY-EIGHT

I spent most of the next day on the couch with a cup of hot tea. My head was stuffy, I had a low fever, and I was still coughing, though with less force and frequency. To distract myself, I went out to the corner and bought a stack of newspapers.

Every one had a feature story about Judge Hume's disappearance on the eve of his meeting with the state police. Now joining the speculation that he was on the run was the theory he himself had been murdered by someone he was going to implicate—conjecture I had no interest in confirming. Because of the Hume/Cooper connection from the bribery scandal, I was mentioned in every article, but not as Judge Hume's murderer. Any speculation in that direction went to Frank Van Dam, who they all agreed was involved, either as Judge Hume's coconspirator or his enemy.

I started to call Elizabeth but hung up before the operator answered. What would I say? I couldn't very well tell her not to worry, he's fine, he'll be home soon. I went back to the couch.

The next morning, feeling much better, I took a streetcar to the library and searched for information on the buoyancy of bodies. I found an article in the *British Medical Journal* that said in cold water a corpse would stay submerged for at least a week, and sometimes as long as a month, before bodily gases accumulated to the extent that it would float. I probably had a little time before the body surfaced. The bag I was less certain about.

With barely a month until the auto show opened, I threw myself into the work, stopping only long enough to pore through newspapers looking for any mention of the judge's body or my bag. So far, my luck had held.

I created layout after layout of the floor space, worked with sales to get commitments from our dealers to provide salesmen for the show, and collaborated with our advertising department on signage. Mr. Edison was paying us to promote his battery, so I devoted a large space to extolling the virtues of a battery that would allow for long touring trips through the country. Advertising had already put together a display recounting the trouble-free thousand-mile trip Joe and I had made through the countryside in September. Edison batteries powered us all the way. The trip was well publicized and highly successful, although we'd had to abort the ascent of Mount Washington in New Hampshire due to inclement weather.

The rest of the signage emphasized our reputation and service, bragged a little (*Behind the car stands the largest electric vehicle factory in the world*), and finished with the standard hyperbole (*A Detroit Electric is a health-giving, invigorating, care-forgetting necessity*).

Christmas came and went, a more somber affair than usual. My family tried their best to cheer me up, knowing only that the recent developments in the bribery scandal made it less likely I'd be convicted of Cooper's murder. They didn't know I was free only because Judge Hume's body and my bag were still in the river. On Christmas morning, my sisters' children opened their gifts with squeals of delight. Somehow I knew with absolute certainty I'd never watch my own children do the same. I went to bed at eight o'clock with a pillow covering my head.

Two days later, in the early afternoon, I was on the second floor of the Detroit Electric garage inspecting the vehicles we planned to bring to the show. Half a dozen mechanics were at work on cars spread across the rest of the floor. It was noisy, the men talking over the grind of the air compressor and the sounds of metal banging on metal.

I tried to tune them out and concentrate. The most important car we would be showing was the Model 17 underslung roadster ($2,000 with standard lead batteries). It was a rakish beauty half a foot closer to the ground than anything we'd previously made, with a long "engine compartment" (actually a trunk) in front. It sat gleaming, deep blue body over straw-colored chassis, in the front of the garage.

The market was evolving at a glacial pace. More cars at the show this year would be enclosed coupés and broughams, but the majority were still roadsters—open-topped touring cars poorly suited for cold-weather driving, but well suited for the average man's image of himself as a rough-and-tumble sportsman. The Model 17 was our attempt to break into that market. If Detroit Electric was to succeed in the long term, we had to make automobiles that were considered "manly."

Since the 601 panel truck was going to be in the show, I had only two more choices, and they both needed to appeal to our current demographic—rich women.

I eyed the brewster-green Model L extension brougham ($3,400 with Edison batteries) that I'd chosen for the prime position in front. It was gorgeous—a picture-book Cinderella opera coach in a rich green tone. The metal fittings and headlamps were polished brass, and the white cushion tires gave the impression the car was floating on air. I poked my head inside. The interior was as luxurious as the exterior. Rich, green Waterloo broadcloth, folded diagonally and buttoned in place, covered the well-padded seats, and a crystal flower vase hung on the passenger side over the leather toilet-and-card case with its built-in watch.

I moved to the next car, a maroon Model 22 coupé—our bestseller ($2,500 with standard lead batteries, $3,100 with Edisons). It was a shorter version of the Model 10, less the new ultraquiet shaft drive we were featuring on our top-of-the-range models.

Until now, Baker had been the only electric with shaft drive.

The final vehicle was the black 601 panel truck. I was familiar enough with it.

I was getting ready to go to the factory when I heard a commotion in the stairway. Edsel and then Wesley raced around the corner and stopped, panting, in front of me.

"We've got it," Edsel said. His face was flushed. He threw his great-coat over the side of the roadster, and the words tumbled from his mouth. "He was in town."

"Who?"

"Frank Van Dam."

"What are you talking about?"

Edsel took a deep breath. "I'd better slow down before I pass out."

"Hold on." I looked around at the mechanics staring at us and nod-ded toward the battery room. "Let's go in there." After ignoring me for more than an hour, Elwood had left thirty minutes earlier for the fac-tory, so I knew the room was empty. I herded them through the door and closed it behind us. We were enveloped in the rotten-egg stink of sulfuric acid. "Okay now. *What* did you find out?"

Edsel glanced at Wesley, who grinned and leaned against a test bench, gesturing for him to take it. "It was your idea, kiddo. You tell him."

Edsel's big brown eyes were wide, and his breath came in short bursts. "I'd better start from the beginning. One of our security men told my father what I was up to, and he made them quit. So I was on my own." He began pacing in front of the tanks on the back wall, march-ing one way and wheeling around in the other direction.

I took a quick look to be sure the chains securing the tops of each tank were locked in place.

"About the only things I really knew about Frank Van Dam," Edsel said, "were that he worked security for the labor bureau at the EAD, and he drove a red 1909 Oldsmobile Palace touring car. Nobody at the Employers Association would talk to me, so I decided to track down the car." He looked up at me, a smile growing on his face. "Wesley helped."

"Okay," I said, gesturing for him to speed up. "What'd you do?"

He could hardly speak around his grin. "After Wesley cleared his schedule for me, I phoned all the Oldsmobile garages in the area on 'official business' for the Employers Association. We were doing an audit of our employees' automobile expenses and needed their coop-eration. I set up appointments with all of them. I'm too recognizable, and too young, to pass for an EAD auditor, so I drove Wes around and he went in, complete with an EAD badge I swiped from my father's office."

"And?"

"We hit the jackpot." Edsel looked at Wesley again. "You tell him. You did it."

Wesley nodded. "Frank may have told his mother he was leaving town, but he was here until at least November second. He dropped off his car at the Olds shop down in Wyandotte on Friday, October twenty-eighth, and picked it up November second—the day John Cooper was murdered."

"So he wasn't on the train," I said. "He didn't mail the letter to his mother—or Elizabeth."

Wesley shook his head. "He wasn't in Denver. The man was certain. Frank had all his service done at that garage. He dropped off the car, and he picked up the car. I've got the proof right here." He pulled a folded piece of paper from his pocket. "Complete service order. Shows the time and date in, and the time and date out. He picked up the car at three o'clock on Wednesday, November second." Wesley pointed to the bottom of the page. "See there? His signature. It matches the others they had on file."

"Nine hours before John was murdered." I met the gleam in Wesley's eyes with my own. "We've got him. It *was* Frank."

Edsel cleared his throat. "Another tidbit that might be helpful. We checked out the telephone number Frank left with the garage. It's not registered in his name."

"Really? Whose number is it?"

"I think it's a woman. Get a load of this name." He pulled a notepad from his jacket and glanced at it. "Sapphira Xanakis."

I sat stunned for a moment before saying, "Sapphira?"

They both looked at me, wide-eyed with surprise. Wesley recovered first. "Do you know her?"

"Frank knows Sapphira?" I was incredulous. Then the pieces all came together. "Son of a bitch. She was trying to keep me out of my apartment until the cops found—" I stopped. "Never mind. Did you find out anything else?"

"We rushed over here as soon as we got this," Edsel said, "but I can get her address for you, too."

"Don't bother," I said. "I've got it."


I seethed. Sapphira had set me up. I wanted to hit her, hurt her, punish her like I'd been punished. But first I needed to find out where Frank was.

When I saw the look in Wesley's eyes I knew it would be difficult to shake him, but Edsel was another matter. Under no circumstances would I involve him any further. Wesley and I tried to talk him into going home.

He finally agreed. "All right. But let me at least give you a lift. No, one better. Use my car."

"What are you driving today?" I asked.

"The Detroit Electric."

"A blue brougham with the initials *HF* on the door? I don't think you want us taking that." He started to say something, but I cut him off. "And not the Torpedo, either. It's almost as recognizable." I turned to Wesley. "Do you have your gun?"

He shook his head. "No, it's at home."

I looked back to Edsel. "How about giving us a ride? I can't let you do anything else."

With a minimum of grumbling, Edsel drove us to our building. I thanked him again, and he dropped us off before turning back onto Woodward and continuing farther up toward his neighborhood.

Wesley and I jumped over the soot-covered piles of snow along the side of the street and hurried up the walk. He opened the door for me, and we ran up the stairs.

"How do you know this Xanakis woman?" he said.

I gestured toward his apartment. "Let's talk in there." Once inside, I told him Sapphira was the woman I met at the market and took to the show at the Miles Theater.

"You said something about her keeping you out of your apartment. What's that about?"

"I'll tell you on the way."

Wesley grinned, but his eyes were deadly. "So you're not going to fight me on going with you?"

I shook my head. As much as I wanted to leave him out of this, without Wesley I stood little chance of killing or capturing Frank. We ran to the streetcar stop, pushed our way onto the first trolley, and rode to an intersection near Sapphira's house. While we walked the last three blocks, clomping over the snowy boardwalk, I told him about Judge Hume's murder and my subsequent loss of his body.

"You idiot," he said. "I could have helped you."

"I know." I put a hand on his arm and stopped him. "But I didn't want to risk it. I have a hard enough time living with myself as it is. I can't get you killed or thrown in jail."

He slapped me on the back of the head, knocking my derby into the snow. "I knew you were a goop, but you outdid yourself this time."

I brushed off the hat and fit it back onto my head. "Don't we have more pressing matters than insulting me?"

He gave me a sidelong glance. "For now."

We began walking again. When we turned onto Sapphira's block, I pointed out the white two-story to Wesley. We stood next to a big elm tree on the corner and studied the house for a few minutes. It was a standard Michigan winter day, gray and dusky. Many of the nearby houses had lights on, but none showed through the windows of Sapphira's house.

"They don't know me," Wesley said. "I'll go up there selling something—life insurance. As soon as someone answers the door, I'll pull the gun. Then we'll all go inside."

I couldn't think of anything better, so I nodded. We switched off the safeties on our pistols. Wesley crossed the street, marched up to Sapphira's front door, and knocked. No one answered. He tried again. And again. Then he vaulted over the porch rail into the front yard and peered in one of the windows, his hands cupped around his face. A second later, he waved me over. With the gun in my hand, I ran across the street and joined him.

"Interesting interior design," Wesley said. "A masterpiece of understatement."

I stepped up and looked through the window into the parlor. There was no green sofa with matching chairs, no walnut end tables, no Tiffany lamps, no Oriental rug—just pale green walls and a scuffed walnut floor.

She was gone.

We checked the other windows, but the view was the same—more empty rooms. Our next stop was the Hammond Building, where we took the elevator to Mr. Sutton's offices on the tenth floor. A man escorted us into a boardroom with thick burgundy carpeting, a twenty-foot-long polished mahogany table, and a dozen black leather chairs.

A few minutes later, Sutton bustled in. "I've just gotten off the telephone with the Pinkertons," he said, slipping into the chair next to me. "They had some interesting news."

"So do we." I nodded to Wesley.

He explained what he and Edsel had done. Sutton's head began nodding after a few seconds, and a smile crept onto his face. When Wesley showed him the service order, Sutton exploded from his chair. "That's it, Will," he said. "That's our reasonable doubt."

I grinned. "What's your news?"

His eyes narrowed. "First describe this Sapphira."

"Tall, Greek, pretty." I shrugged. "Exotic looking, I guess you'd say."

He patted my arm and gave me a sly grin. "The Pinkertons discovered a little more information about Van Dam's stay at the Oxford Hotel in Denver. It was 'Mrs. Frank Van Dam' who checked in on the evening of November second. Who do you suppose her description matches?"

I nodded. "Makes sense."

"She said she and her husband had just gotten in from Detroit, and he would be joining her momentarily." The sitting was too much for him. He jumped up from the chair and began pacing. "Our men showed a picture of Frank around the hotel. A few of the employees thought he looked familiar, but no one was certain they saw him. Apparently she was seen in the company of a number of men, though a particularly big man was with her when she checked out."

Wesley slapped the table. "So *she* mailed the letter to Frank's mother. And to Elizabeth."

It finally made sense. "Frank was staying at her place while she set up his alibi." Another thought struck me. "Wait. John Dodge said something about me bringing a 'whore' to the theater. I thought he was just being an ass. But maybe Dodge knew her. If Sapphira's a prostitute, Frank could have used her to set up John."

Sutton nodded.

"But no one at the hotel could identify Frank?" I asked.

"It's a very busy place with hundreds of guests at any time, and it had been six weeks . . . The clerk who checked out the Van Dams could only recall that he was large—very large."

"It had to be him."

Sutton stopped pacing and stood in front of me. "First, I'm going to bring this evidence to Detective Riordan. Then I'm going to gather as many reporters as I can and lay out these facts for the public. You weren't the only one to have motive and opportunity to commit murder." He talked like he was trying to convince me. Habit, I suppose, from spending so much time in front of a jury. "Frank Van Dam killed Cooper to avoid prosecution in the EAD bribery scandal. As a trusted associate, Frank would have had the opportunity to surprise him. On top of that, Frank had been previously arrested for attempted murder, and we have proof he was in the Detroit area at the time." He gestured toward me. "You, on the other hand, are a University of Michigan graduate, the son of a man with an impeccable reputation who is a pillar of the Detroit business community, and you have no criminal record."

That all sounded good to me.

Wesley and I stopped for dinner on the way home. In deference to my situation, he didn't drink, but I'm sure the other patrons thought we were soused. We joked and hooted and laughed like a pair of drunks, finally going home around midnight.

The next day, the newspapers ran with Sutton's information, along with confirmation from the Oldsmobile garage manager that Frank had, in fact, been in the Detroit area on November 2. Both Frank and John's fingerprints had been found in Sapphira's house. There wasn't much doubt that she and Frank had conspired to kill John. An editorial in the *Herald* went so far as to say the district attorney should drop his case against me, under the headline: VAN DAM ELECTRIC EXECUTIONER!

My jubilation began to fade later that day as the specter of my bag and Judge Hume's body rose again in my mind. The next week and a half crawled past. I tried to stay focused on the auto show, but every day was one day closer to the inevitable discovery of the evidence that could put me in prison for the rest of my life. At the time, it seemed it would almost be a blessing when they finally found him, and I could get this over with.

I felt much differently on the afternoon of January 6 when someone pounded on my door, and I looked through the peephole.

My favorite policemen, Bottlebrush and Slack Jaw, stood in the hallway fondling their nightsticks.

# CHAPTER TWENTY-NINE

I backed away from the door on tiptoes, my stomach grinding. They'd found Judge Hume. They'd found my bag. I was going to jail. My eyes darted to the fire escape.

One of them pounded again, this time with his nightstick. The door shuddered with the force. I'd never get away before they broke it down. Taking a deep breath, I opened the door. The cops grabbed me and shoved me downstairs to a Chalmers police car waiting at the curb, not even letting me get my coat. They were silent all the way to the Bethune Street station, ignoring my questions and protests. I couldn't stop my legs from shaking. This was my last view of the world.

At the station, they dragged me to a darkened room with five other men, who stood in a line facing a window. Three were older toughs who looked like cops. The other two were younger, disheveled and unshaven, obviously just brought out of jail.

Slack Jaw put his hand on my chest and shoved me against the wall between two of the older men. The lights came on, bright electric lights. I faced the window, trying my best to look innocent. Behind the window was nothing but darkness.

"Turn to your right," another policeman said.

Both the younger men and one of the cops turned left. Eventually everyone faced right.

"Turn to your left."

This time everyone got it.

"Face the window."

A minute later, the other policeman shut off the light and Slack Jaw shoved me down the corridor. I clasped my hands in front of me to hide their trembling. At the end of the hall, he pushed me into another small, musty room.

Detective Riordan waited at the table, puffing on a cigar, rubbing his hands together like he was watching his favorite meal being brought to the table. With a grin, he said, "Got you now, Anderson."

Icy fingers ran down my back. Riordan's whole person radiated glee. "Dumping Judge Hume's body off the Zug Island train bridge in the middle of the night. Might not have been a bad idea if that train hadn't come along."

They'd found the body. I'd been seen. My knees started to buckle, but I caught myself. I kept my face expressionless. If I had learned anything, it was to keep my mouth shut, no matter what. "I don't know what you're talking about."

Riordan sneered. "Please. The engineer saw you. He just picked you out of the lineup."

My throat was so tight air could hardly pass through it, but I tried to keep my voice steady. "I don't know what you're talking about."

He sat back and folded his arms across his chest. The smoldering end of his cigar glowed orange under his elbow. "Sit down, Will."

I slid into the chair across from him.

"Why do we have this same conversation over and over? I know you did it. An eyewitness identified you. Face it, Will. You've got to give it up."

I stared at the tabletop. "I want to see my lawyer."

"Not this time," Riordan said. He stood and strode to the door. Before he walked out, he looked back over his shoulder at me. "Don't say I didn't give you a chance."

My hands trembled. I made them into fists.

Two hours passed before the door opened again. Bottlebrush and Slack Jaw sauntered in.

"Hello, Will," Bottlebrush said. "Nice to see ya again." He took off his bobby hat and carefully set it on the table, then hung his coat over the back of Riordan's chair. Slack Jaw did likewise. They began rolling up their sleeves.

Bottlebrush nudged his partner. "Oughta see the joint his ma and pa live in. Anderson here's a regular prince."

Slack Jaw just stared at me, smiling. His large brown eyes were so far apart as to be almost on the sides of his head. Bottlebrush walked around to the back of my chair and jerked my hands behind me. A cold metal ring snapped around my right wrist and then my left, the short chain between them looped through the wooden slats of the chair back. He pulled out my chair and spun it around on one of the back legs, then leaned down in my face. "Last chance, Nancy-boy. 'Fess up. Course, I'd rather you didn't. Yet."

Without really thinking about it I gave him the dead eyes.

Bottlebrush laughed. "He's a regular tough guy, ain't he, Steve?" He rocked his head from side to side and rolled his shoulders, loosening up.

I clamped my jaw shut and tensed my muscles for the beating. A shiver went up my spine.

Behind me, the door opened. Riordan said, "Hold it."

Bottlebrush did his best impression of Slack Jaw. "What?"

"Just thought I'd run something past ol' Will here," Riordan said. "I'll let you have him in a minute. Unless he wises up."

He walked around in front of me and leaned against the wall, his ever-present cigar clamped in his teeth. The other cops left.

"I want to see my lawyer," I said.

Riordan puffed on his cigar. "Would you like a smoke? Calm your nerves a little?"

My legs were bouncing up and down. I stopped them. "No, I wouldn't."

He reached over and put a meaty hand on my shoulder. "Listen, Will, I don't want to make this any harder on you than I have to. I've been talking to the DA. I convinced him to give you a deal if you confess.

And you're going to confess, either to me or," he gestured toward the door, "to those two. Higgins said he'll take life in prison off the table. Of course, it doesn't matter to me either way. I've got you wrapped up now. Just thought I'd offer." He winked at me. "Wouldn't want you to think I'm a bad guy."

I stared at Riordan, trying to figure his angle. He had an eyewitness but wanted to give me a deal? I guess he thought I was stupid, a reasonable assumption given my decisions since Cooper was murdered. For once my foolishness had gained me an advantage. "Gosh, Detective Riordan, that's awful nice of you."

He didn't seem quite sure what to make of that. "You can tell me, Will. Let's end this like gentlemen."

"Why haven't you arrested me?"

"Just a technicality, boy—"

"If your witness identified me, you'd have charged me and trotted me out in front of a herd of reporters." I stared up into Riordan's ice blue eyes. "So like I said before, I don't know what you're talking about."

He twisted his fists into the front of my shirt and lifted me from the floor, chair and all. "Why'd you kill him, Will? Frank Van Dam's nothing but a ruse and you know it. You killed him, too, didn't you?" He threw me back. The chair tipped over, and my head smacked against the floor.

Colored lights exploded in front of me and then everything went black.

That evening, my father and Mr. Sutton picked me up from the jail. I still hadn't been charged. Once we were in the back of Sutton's Pierce-Arrow, my father asked if I was all right. I lied. I told him I was. The back of my head felt like I'd been hit with a sledgehammer. The driver pulled away from the curb, and I nestled down in my coat to block out the frigid wind. Why couldn't Sutton buy a coupé?

"Did they tell you?" Sutton said. "Judge Hume's body was found this morning."

"I thought it might have been."

"A fisherman on Fighting Island found it frozen to the crook of a birch tree overhanging the river."

"Did he find anything else?" I wanted to swallow those words as soon as they came out of my mouth.

"Like what?"

"You know, clues, evidence, that sort of thing?"

"Not that I know of. But there is some good news. The state police just took over the investigation of Judge Hume's murder, and they want to question Frank Van Dam. Both he and John Cooper have been implicated in the Employers Association scandal."

"Really."

"Yes. And they're suspected of fostering a relationship between the Employers Association and certain criminals, who supplied the EAD with men for their union-breaking activities."

"Vito Adamo."

"They haven't said, but it stands to reason."

I talked with my father about family matters the rest of the way home, waiting until they dropped me off to allow myself a sigh of relief. They might have found the judge, but my bag hadn't surfaced.

My luck was still holding.


The train was already in front of the Humes' house when I arrived an hour early for the funeral. A plain black car with no name or number, black bunting overhanging every window, sat in front of three regular DUR trolley cars, similarly decked out. The motorman sat in his seat in the front car, and two somber men in black suits and top hats stood motionless at the side of the funeral car, ignoring the snow drifting down from the sky.

The windows of the Humes' yellow and white Queen Anne were also draped in black. The huge oak trees in the yard were bare, stripped of their greenery by the season. A coating of gray snow covered the ground.

I felt more than a little trepidation climbing the steps to the house.

Mrs. Hume's reaction upon seeing me could range from fury to dismay, if she was even in condition to acknowledge I was there. But I had to speak with Elizabeth, to offer my condolences and my help.

Alberts answered the door, dressed in his usual dark gray suit with waistcoat, a black armband his only sign of mourning. His eyes widened a bit when he saw me. He hesitated but allowed me in, having apparently had no specific instructions on what to do if I arrived. On the way to the parlor, I passed a gilded wall mirror, covered, as all their mirrors would be, in black crepe.

A closed coffin—satin-finished dark walnut with burnished brass fixtures—sat at the head of the room, opposite the blazing fireplace. Elizabeth and Mrs. Hume were perched side by side, backs ramrod straight, on austere wooden chairs. Both women wore black from head to toe, with heavy crepe veils covering their faces. A lavish spread of food and drink—meats, cheeses, fruit, desserts, and dozens of bottles of wine—sat on a large table in the middle of the room. A smaller table stood next to it, piled with gifts for the guests—black kid gloves for the men and gold mourning brooches for the women. Four men stood in a corner, talking quietly. A heavy flowery odor hung over the room.

I approached the ladies. "I'm so very sorry, Mrs. Hume, Elizabeth. I know how much you loved him."

Mrs. Hume's head jerked up when she heard my voice but sank again when she saw me. "Thank you, William," she murmured.

Elizabeth forced a smile onto her face. "Thank you, Will. Thanks for coming. I know it must have been hard."

I just nodded, knowing this was not the time to discuss my differences with her father.

"Could . . . Could I talk to you?" Elizabeth said, dabbing her eyes with a handkerchief.

I nodded again.

She turned to her mother. "Would it be all right if I spoke with Will for a moment?"

Mrs. Hume nodded, her head moving just a fraction of an inch.

Elizabeth patted her knee. "I'll be right back." She was trying to be reassuring, but her voice trembled like she was on the brink of tears.

She got her coat before leading me out through the kitchen to the back porch. The wind had died, and it was very quiet. Large white snowflakes floated down in front of us into the gray backyard, covering the arbor's dead vines in the empty garden.

Elizabeth glanced toward the door and raised the veil from her face. "Have you got a smoke?" Her eyes were red-rimmed and hollow with dark rings underneath.

"Of course." I took one from my case and lit it for her, then another for me.

She took a deep drag and leaned against the painted white post, staring out at the gray snow. "I need to apologize to you. I tried to get to the police when you were arrested for kidnapping me, but my father practically had me under house arrest. I got word out as soon as I could. And I should have told you right away that John was paying off my father. But I knew my father couldn't have been involved in the murder, and it was all so hazy." She turned and looked at me. "Everything was hazy."

I touched her arm. "Don't apologize. Your instincts were right. But are *you* all right?"

After a moment she said, "I still want it." Her voice was thick. "I salivate just thinking of it." She glanced at me and turned back toward the garden, shaking her head ever so slightly.

"It started with Dr. Kilmer's Female Remedy," she whispered. "I'd been having some pains, woman pains, and John said his mother swore by it. After I used it for a week or so, my stomach began to bother me, so he bought me some dyspepsia syrup. In a month I couldn't go more than a few hours without them." She shoved her hands into the pockets of her coat and turned around, leaning with her back against the rail. "I found out they both contained opium. Rather than go to a doctor and risk the scandal, we decided to try heroin to cure me. I liked it." She looked at me again. "It let me forget. John bought the heroin for me from the pharmacy on Hastings. With my family's reputation at stake, I couldn't buy it."

A tear slipped down her cheek. "When John died—was killed—I didn't know what to do. I bought a bottle from a pharmacy downtown, but the pharmacist grilled me like I was a derelict. I was sure the pharmacy on Hastings would sell it to me, but the man refused. He said I had to go see Vito Adamo. You know the rest." She looked away and hugged herself.

"Elizabeth, I don't know what to say. None of this would have happened without me."

"How do you mean?"

"Well, you know. What I did."

She took a long pull on the cigarette and swallowed the smoke before blowing it up toward the heavy clouds. "What did you do?"

"You know."

Her head tilted a little to the side, and her glittering green eyes met mine, a challenge behind them.

I turned and stared out at the skeletal trees in the Humes' backyard. "I knew you didn't want to . . ." I trailed off, knowing that was wrong. I started again. "I forced you to . . ." That still wasn't right.

When the words appeared in my mind, I swallowed hard. For nearly a year and a half I'd been able to keep them at bay, keep them hidden away in some deep recess of my mind, while they sat there moldering, rotting, gnawing chunks from my sanity.

I took a deep breath and said the words for the first time. "I raped you."

# CHAPTER THIRTY

Elizabeth didn't react. She just leaned against the porch rail looking out at the gray world beyond. I turned her toward me. "I know being drunk is no excuse. And being a goddamn man isn't, either. There is no excuse. I'm so sorry. I was stupid, selfish. I'd give my life to make it right. But there's no making it right."

Her eyes searched mine for a moment before she turned away. "It wasn't all you. I may not have been as drunk as you were, but, well . . . I was caught up in the moment, same as you."

"No. None of this is your fault."

"Yes it is, Will. Give me some credit. If I'd tried hard enough I could have stopped you, but I didn't want to. It's only over the last few weeks that I've realized what really happened. I couldn't live with the idea that I wanted to do that with you. I blamed it all on you. But it wasn't all your fault." She wiped her eyes and took a quick drag on the cigarette.

"Elizabeth, you told me to stop. I didn't. It's as simple as that. You shouldn't feel guilt over something *I* did."

She shrugged, a forlorn little shake of her shoulders. "I've got plenty to feel guilty about. What's a little more?"

Our baby would have been almost eight months old now.

I put my hands on the porch railing and leaned against it. "I wish . . . you had kept it, still married me."

"Marry you? After that?"

"I know." I wanted to be dead.

"Pregnant on the first try. Beginner's luck, huh?" Elizabeth spat out a laugh that sounded like a sob. For a long while she stared out at the gray nothingness of the backyard. A pair of crows began cawing at each other atop one of the old oak trees.

"Why didn't you go off somewhere?" I whispered. "Have the baby adopted? I'm not judging," I added quickly. "Far be it from me. It just . . . it just seems like that would have been easier."

She turned toward me, her eyes glassy, pooling with tears. "Yes. It seems that way to me now. But then . . . I don't know." Her lower lip trembled. "After you . . . we . . . did that, I couldn't live with the shame. How would I tell my mother? What would it have done to my family?" Now her voice turned colder. "The Humes don't conduct themselves that way." I could hear her father in the last sentence.

She looked up toward the trees, her face tight with the effort of keeping herself from crying. "It was a boy. A son. Our son." She burst out in tears and buried her face in her hands. "I'm going to Hell. And I deserve to. I killed him. I killed our son."

The anguish in her voice nearly brought me to my knees. I took her in my arms, and our tears mixed on the front of my suit. "You did what you thought you had to, Lizzie. You did the best you could. You always do. It's me. It was always me."

Her body shook against mine. "I'm not able to have another baby, Will," she sobbed. "I can't live with that."

Her words hit me like a runaway truck. "My God, Elizabeth. I didn't know. I'm so sorry."

We cried a while longer and then stood holding each other, joined in guilt. Our life together had always been so perfect that I thought it was destiny. But destiny can only bring people together. We were destined to meet, to fall in love, to be given a chance. I had cast aside that chance in one drunken moment, a moment that would always connect us. Our lives would be intertwined until the day we died, but rather than in joy or hope, we would be joined in sorrow and pain, sure as if we were shackled together with barbed wire.

Elizabeth stepped back and wiped her face. "In case you've wondered," she said, "I haven't heard from Frank again."

I nodded and lit another cigarette for each of us. We stood looking out at the backyard but not really seeing it, lost in our thoughts.

After a few minutes, she rested her elbow in the palm of her other hand, holding the cigarette up near the side of her face. "I think it's odd," she said.

"What is?"

"Oh, nothing. That people are starting to call their parlors 'living rooms.' What does that even mean?"

That was not what I expected. "I don't know. It is a stupid name, though."

"I'll tell you why." She was still looking out at the garden. "These 'funeral parlors' springing up everywhere? Death rooms. A parlor is a death room, whether it belongs to you or a professional mourner." She turned to me. "I'm so very tired of all this, Will. All this death. I just want it done."

"I know, honey." I hesitated but finally asked her a question I'd wanted to ask ever since John was murdered. "Elizabeth, you believe I'm innocent, don't you?"

"I wouldn't be talking to you if I didn't."

"Thank you. I couldn't kill anyone. And I've caused you too much pain already. I'd rather you spend your life with another man than have you endure that. We'll never be together. I've accepted that. I just want you to know I wouldn't hurt you again. Ever."

"I know." She flicked her cigarette butt into the backyard and pulled the veil down over her face. "I should get back to my mother."

I nodded.

When she reached the door, she turned back to me. "I hear you're working again."

"Yes. I'm setting up the booth for the car show next week."

"Good." I saw a tentative smile behind the veil. "I'm glad."

For four years Elizabeth had dazzled the crowds at the auto show on Society Night. Surrounded by millionaires and their wives, she turned every head in the building. I smiled to think of it. I'd never been more proud. Of course, I hadn't understood just how lucky I was, believing it was only my due to have the most beautiful woman in the world on my arm. "Thanks, Lizzie."

"Perhaps I'll see you there," she said. "At the show. I was thinking of going on Society Night."

"Really?"

"For better or worse, you got me interested in automobiles. And God knows I need something to take my mind off all of this."

"I'll look for you."

"Around eight?"

"That would be fantastic."

I hadn't thought Elizabeth could ever stop hating me, and I had no illusions about the prospect of a second chance. But perhaps we could be friends. Perhaps I could help her forgive herself, repair her life, move on.

But there was no guarantee I'd still be free next week. The bag with Judge Hume's clothing, the rope, and my sheet was still out there.

Somewhere.

I read at least one newspaper every day and kept my eyes open for the police. I was spending fourteen hours a day on the auto show, not because there was so much work to do, but because it kept me from thinking. Disaster seemed only a moment away. It was unlikely my bag would forever remain at the river's bottom. Frank and Sapphira had disappeared off the face of the earth. My trial was looming larger every day. And I was finding it increasingly difficult to refrain from drinking. That little voice in the back of my mind kept up the pressure.

*Just one. One drink won't hurt. Everybody drinks. I can control it.*

*Just one.*

But I stood resolute. And I realized that somewhere along the line I had decided not to kill myself if I were convicted. I'd fight, and my family and friends would fight alongside me. By remaining sober, I had even regained a little self-respect. I felt better than I had in a long time.

The puffiness had disappeared from my face (from both the alcohol and the beatings), and I felt energetic and alert.

But the dead man kept tugging.

The Employers Association continued to insist the bribery was a private matter between Judge Hume and two misguided ex-employees. Mr. Sutton's men tried to bribe and threaten information out of an EAD manager with a questionable personal life. Even then he wouldn't talk.

Meanwhile, District Attorney Higgins crowed to the newspapers that his case against me was sound, and that he would "lock up the heinous murderer, William C. Anderson, Jr., for the rest of his natural-born life."

Should I be convicted, I was hoping for the opportunity of an un-natural-born life to follow, though I didn't have a great deal of confidence in that, either.


Because of another show at Wayne Gardens, we had only two days for setup. We were scheduled to bring in our cars at 10:00 A.M. on Saturday. At 8:30, I bundled up and walked to Woodward to catch a trolley to the Detroit Electric garage. The oily stench of burning coal was strong, the northerly wind driving in heavy smoke from the factories. Snowflakes seemed to turn gray before my eyes, darkening as they swirled to the ground, not quite covering the sooty clumps already there.

I glanced around as I walked. Looking for the police and Frank Van Dam had become an unconscious habit. While I waited for the trolley, I reached behind me with both hands in the small of my back and stretched, though I really just wanted the reassurance of touching the gun tucked into my belt.

Since it was a workday, the crowds had thinned out an hour ago. Only a handful of people stood with me on the curb, hands in pockets, shuffling from foot to foot. A streetcar stopped, and I wedged myself on board. When I arrived at the garage, Elwood and Joe, the men I'd considered my best friends only a few weeks before, mumbled their greetings and then ignored me. I suppose being arrested for murder is as good a test of friendship as any.

I ferried the roadster alongside the river, splashing through the slush down Jefferson to Wayne Gardens, Detroit's biggest and swankiest convention center. Three of the chasers from the garage followed me in the other vehicles. Once we were inside and the cars had been cleaned and polished to a high sheen, we pulled them into our booth, between the KRIT Motor Car Company and Overland Motor Sales. I directed the layout.

The blue roadster went behind and to the side of the green extension brougham, with the maroon coupé in back. The truck had to go behind the booth, in a small annex that had been added to the building. Space at Wayne Gardens for this show was like gold. So many companies had been turned away from the Detroit Automobile Dealers Association show that a second one, under the banner of the United Automobile Dealers Association, was setting up at the Regal Motor Company's new factory, tripling the space available. It had been filled as well.

But the real show was at Wayne Gardens. The who's who of the auto world would be displaying here, with the up-and-comers (at least in their minds) relegated to the Regal factory.

When our cars were set up, I wandered the pavilion. Ladders and scaffolding were everywhere, with hundreds of workmen swarming the walls and ceilings. Huge panels of white rose bowers adorned with artificial red roses already covered the walls of the first floor, but the second floor and ceiling had a long way to go.

I went back on Sunday and helped hang our banners and signs. All but a few of the bowers were installed. The effect was extraordinary. I felt as if I had walked into a huge rose garden, filled with the most wonderful toys on earth. Scents of leather, oil, grease, wood, and brass polish wafted through the building, comforting odors I'd always associated with my father. The rest of the booths were being completed, and I strolled through the building, taking in all the new automobiles. Shiny new cars and trucks filled both floors. I paid special attention to the other electrics: Hupp-Yeats, Waverley, Phipps-Grinnell, and Raush & Lang. Even though it was a short trip from Cleveland, Baker was nowhere to be found. That was a good sign.

We were ready when the show opened on Monday, and by Wednesday we'd already taken more orders than we had during the entire 1910 show. It looked like my father had his work cut out with the roadster, though. We'd only sold one. Thankfully, sales of broughams and coupés more than made up for it.

I spent most of my time by the truck in the annex, keeping a low profile. The focus had to be on the vehicles, not me. I wanted to phone Elizabeth, firm up our meeting for Thursday night, but the show kept me running from before dawn until the early hours of the morning. By the time I got home I was exhausted, and it was too late to call anyway.

On Wednesday I got my father's permission to take the next morning off so I could tour the show at the Regal factory. First thing Thursday, I headed out to the trolley stop. The week had been cold, with highs in the teens, but this morning it was already near fifty. Mist rose from the ubiquitous piles of sooty snow to mottled gray clouds hanging low and heavy over the city, and trickles of snowmelt wended their way through cracks between the cobbles to storm sewers at the corners. I stopped at Wayne Gardens and dropped off my tuxedo for Society Night before taking a streetcar to the Regal factory.

The UADA show was impressive, particularly considering they'd had only ten days to put it together. Red, white, and blue bunting hung from the support pillars and between booths, which packed the cavernous building, giving the factory the ambiance of a county fair. I wandered through the show for three hours, though I could have easily spent the entire day drooling over the displays of cars and accessories—horns, odometers, wheels, taillights, tops—that went on and on.

The automobile business had certainly arrived.

The trip back to Wayne Gardens took considerably longer than I expected. Fog was beginning to settle in, adding an ethereal quality to the city. The temperature was at least in the midfifties now, and water from all the melting snow was backing up the storm sewers, with brackish ponds deepening at street corners. Traffic was nearly at a standstill, and the streetcars weren't faring much better. I had to change cars four times. When I finally arrived at our booth, my father and Mr. Wilkinson were waiting for me. I apologized for being late.

My father waved it off and clapped me on the back. "The way this show is turning out I wouldn't mind if you took the rest of it off. That said, I have one more thing for you to do. Henry Leland is going to be speaking with newspapermen in Conference Room A at three o'clock. It's about the self-starter. I'd like you to take a look at it."

"Me? Why?"

"We've got dealer meetings all day. I'd like your opinion."

I reached the conference room at two forty-five and could barely squeeze inside. Reporters, photographers, and automobile men packed the smoke-filled room. Henry Leland was bent over the stripped chassis of a Cadillac with another man, who was checking the wiring that connected the car to an electrical contraption about the size of a shoebox. Another wire ran from the other end of the device to a battery.

Over the sound of a hundred loud voices, I heard, "Will! Hey!"

Edsel stood about ten feet away from me. I shouldered through the crowd to his side. He smiled and shouted in my ear. "Come to see how the other half lives, eh?"

"Sort of. My father wants to know what I think of Leland's baby."

Edsel grimaced. "My father doesn't want anything to do with it. He said he won't touch it until it's the same price as a hand crank. It's all about price to him."

"Seems to be working." Unlike Henry Ford's two previous efforts, Ford Motor Company's sales growth was astronomical.

Henry Leland, a grandfatherly man with wavy silver hair and a long Vandyke beard, cleared his throat a few times, politely asked for everyone's attention, and finally blew out an ear-splitting whistle. Everyone quieted and turned their attention to him.

"Like many other men," he said, "I've been working on a self-starter for years. Until now, I've never had any better results than anyone else. But," he held up a finger, "I am intelligent enough to look outside our company when the need presents itself.

"Gentlemen, I'd like to introduce Charles Kettering, the man who not only invented the electric cash register, but also the electricity generator you know as the Delco. He's got something to show you."

Kettering was a thin, hatchet-faced man in his midthirties, with thick black hair, a long chin, and a hooked nose. "The only self-starters that have worked up until now, at least with any regularity," he said, "are half the size of an automobile. So I started with the size. It was really a short step from the work I've done previously. It's near completion, and it will add less than a hundred dollars to the retail price of an automobile." After he gave a brief summary of how the starter worked, he turned to Leland. "Should we show them?"

Leland smiled and looked out at the crowd. "Would you like to see it?"

A weak chorus of affirmation answered him. One man called out, "Show it already."

"Can't argue with that enthusiasm," Kettering said. He held up a key before sticking it into a slot and flipping a switch. The engine turned over, and again.

Then it roared to life.

# CHAPTER THIRTY-ONE

When I returned to the booth, my father, Mr. Wilkinson, and Mr. McFarlane were in the annex with a dealer, huddled at the front of the 601 truck. The room was filled with the background rumble of many hundreds, perhaps thousands, of voices. A few minutes later, the other man left, and my father greeted me effusively. His demeanor was jovial, but I could see the concern in the intensity of his eyes and the tightness of his jaw.

"Well?" he said. "Did it work?"

I shrugged. "The demos always do. That doesn't mean anything."

Mr. Wilkinson pulled on his beard. "It was Kettering, correct?"

"Yes. Charles Kettering."

Mr. McFarlane grunted. "How big was it?"

I showed them with my hands. "Shoebox, give or take."

They all exchanged looks, but McFarlane waved a hand in front of him. "Ach, an automobile's not a store, and a self-starter's no cash register. It'll shake to pieces, freeze, or short, just like all the rest."

"I don't know," my father said. "Kettering has impressive credentials. If it works . . ." He glanced at McFarlane with a shrug.

"Do you really think it's going to be such a problem?" I asked.

"Well . . ." My father grimaced. "It's no secret that our greatest competitive advantage is easy starting. But we've got lots more going for us." He forced a smile onto his face. "We'll be fine."

"Either way," I said, "we own the high end, right?"

"Right." My father clapped me on the back, and I went up front to help the salespeople.

At five, the general public was herded out of Wayne Gardens so preparations could be made for Society Night. I snuck outside for a break and some fresh air. The river wasn't fifty feet from me, yet when I opened the door all I could see was a misty white cloud. A heavy blanket of fog had dropped over the city.

After a smoke, I helped our men straighten up the booth and then changed into black tie for the evening. I checked myself in the mirror half a dozen times, making sure I looked my best for Elizabeth. At seven the orchestra began to play Mozart's "Eine Kleine Nachtmusik," and the society crowd started to trickle in.

I leaned against a trellis, watching the crowd. This was my first real reintroduction into automotive society since the murder, and I was nervous about what sort of welcome I would receive. Red and green lights peeked through the rose-covered trellises in a soft mimicry of the night sky. Every car shone—brilliant reds, burgundies, greens, blues, and blacks—reflecting the spotlights into the eyes of the spectators, who were now crowding the hall. The men all wore black top hats and tuxedoes with tails, and many of them carried jeweled or gilt canes. The women sported dazzling evening dresses in a rainbow of colors, sparkling with rhinestones. Elaborate chapeaus bedecked with ribbons, jewels, and feathers topped their heads. Though the price of admission had been doubled to a dollar for Society Night, price wasn't the real barrier to entry. It was clothing that kept out the less fortunate.

The royalty of automobiledom strolled past me, unaware of my presence. In scarcely five minutes, I saw Commodore A. L. McLeod of the United States Motor Company, W. V. Macy of Locomobile, Clarence Smith of Stevens-Duryea, and A. W. Shafer of Alco.

I was thinking about going back to the booth when, behind me, a man said, "Hey, Anderson."

I knew that voice. I spun around, fists clenched.

John Dodge stood next to his brother, both in ill-fitting monkey suits. He smiled at me. "Listen, I'm really sorry about what happened before." He reached out toward me.

I almost punched him but held back when all he did was tuck something into the chest pocket of my tuxedo.

"Sometimes, me and Horace, well . . ." He looked at his brother, then down at the floor, bashful. "Sometimes we get a little carried away, you know?"

I reached into my pocket to see what he had given me. It was a hundred-dollar bill. I held it out to him. "I don't want your money."

He held up his hands in front of him, a gesture of surrender. A vague smell of grease wafted up to my nose. "Nope. That's yours. I'm a big enough man to admit when I'm wrong."

I slipped the bill into the pocket of his bulging waistcoat. "If you want to make it up to me, give this to charity."

His eyes narrowed, and his head tilted a bit to the side while he appraised me. Finally he grinned. "Fair enough." He held out his hand. "Friends?"

I smiled back, but left my hand at my side. "Let's not get carried away."

He broke eye contact first.

I returned to the Detroit Electric booth. An older man with a monocle was leaning forward in the driving seat of the roadster, gripping the steering lever like an oar. Next to him, his wife sat back with her arms crossed. Couples were seated in our other automobiles, these with the wives in the driving seats. The husbands assumed the air of experts, and our salesmen explained the intricacies of driving an electric, such as they were, given that turning a key and pushing a lever forward were all that was needed to make the cars work.

I helped the salesmen, though I'm sure I checked my watch a dozen times before it was finally eight, and at least twenty more times by nine thirty, when I decided to phone Elizabeth. Although it hadn't been a rock-solid commitment, she said she was coming. It wasn't like her to just not show up without an explanation. I excused myself and hurried to a pay phone at the front of the pavilion.

Alberts answered. I asked to speak with Elizabeth.

"Mr. Anderson?"

I assumed this was the signal to hang up, but I tried anyway. "Yes, it's me. Will."

"But . . . Miss Hume said she was meeting you at the car show. She took out the automobile at seven o'clock."

I hurried back through the crowd to our booth, hoping I'd find Elizabeth laughing about some traffic hitch or car problem that had delayed her. She wasn't there. Panic began to tickle at my mind.

I pushed through the crowd and out the front door. Visibility was perhaps twenty feet, the fog even thicker now. I ran along the streets, looking for the Humes' black Baker Electric coupé. The curbs were lined with automobiles, more than I'd ever seen in one place, but none of them was the Humes'.

I ran back to Wayne Gardens and through the pavilion to our booth. My father and Mr. Wilkinson were chatting with a distinguished gentleman who was leaning his bulk on a cane.

"Father! Have you seen Elizabeth?"

He looked annoyed at the interruption until he saw my face. He asked the man to excuse him and pulled me aside. "No, I haven't seen her. Why?"

"She was supposed to meet me here. I'm afraid something's gone wrong."

He put a hand on my shoulder. "Calm yourself. Perhaps she just got delayed."

"No. She left the house three hours ago to meet me here. Something's happened."

"Mm." He turned to Wilkinson. "Why don't you make some telephone calls—police, hospitals, et cetera. I'll take a lap around the show with Will and see if we can find her."

He waved over a salesman to speak with the gentleman, and we hurried through the pavilion, looking into every booth, even shouting into the ladies' rooms. She simply wasn't here. Not sure what to do, we returned to the booth to wait for Wilkinson.

My father tried to reassure me. So many things could have delayed her, he said, though he ran out of ideas once he'd offered car trouble and traffic tie-ups, neither of which would have kept her from both her home and the show for three hours.

Wilkinson soon returned. He hadn't gotten any information. He'd left the telephone number of the Wayne Gardens office with the police and hospitals in case she did turn up.

I wandered the area around the convention center and phoned the Humes' house twice more before finally leaving Wayne Gardens near midnight. Alberts had the police out looking for her, though he hadn't said anything yet to Mrs. Hume. He was afraid that, after all that had already happened to their family, it might be too much for her. I promised to phone him if I found Elizabeth, and he said he'd try to get word to both my father and me if she came home.

I trotted perhaps a mile along Jefferson from Wayne Gardens to the Humes' house, the path she would have taken to get to the auto show. The fog made it difficult to see, but I could discern no trace of Elizabeth or her car. Finally I caught a streetcar back to my apartment and phoned every hospital and police station in Detroit. She wasn't at any of the hospitals. The police had no information. I phoned Alberts again, and then my father. Neither had heard anything.

Though I said nothing to either of them, there seemed to be only two possibilities as to why Elizabeth had disappeared for this long. The first was heroin. The second was Frank.

I wasn't sure which would be worse.

Wesley got home from the Palace Gardens Ballroom around two, saw my lights on, and stopped by. When the telephone rang, we were arguing about which of us would stay by the phone while the other searched for Elizabeth.

I ran from the parlor into the den, grabbed the phone, and shouted, "Hello!"

Music played in the background—brassy, wild music—but no one said anything.

"Elizabeth! Is that you?"

"Will?" The woman's voice was muffled, the sound throaty and lazy.

"Elizabeth?"

I heard breathing.

"Are you at the Bucket?"

No reply.

"Elizabeth, where are you?"

The receiver clunked onto the hook.

I hung up and again raised the phone. Wesley had followed me into the den. I glanced up at him. "Get your gun." He ran from the room. When the operator came on, I shouted, "Police headquarters! It's an emergency!" Wesley was back standing in the doorway before the call was answered. I told him what I'd heard.

Finally, a man grumbled into the phone, "Detroit Police."

"There's been a murder at the Bucket!" I shouted. "The killer's still there!" I doubted the police would go to the Bucket for anything less.

I threw down the phone and grabbed my pistol. We ran out of the building and began sprinting toward the Bucket, cutting through yards and vacant lots, splashing through slushy piles of snow, taking as direct a path to the saloon as we could. Our sense of direction was hopelessly muddled in the thick fog. We made several wrong turns, only realizing our mistakes when we came upon a street sign vaguely lit by the dim white orb of a nearby street lamp. I found Brush Street and ran down the sidewalk, pausing only once to check a sign, to be sure we were going in the right direction.

"Like last time," Wesley panted, leaping over a puddle. "I go in . . . see what's what . . . you follow me."

"No," I wheezed. I couldn't catch my breath, but sped ahead of him. "I'm first . . . I'm going to kill . . . that son of a bitch."

"I'll be right . . . behind you," Wesley said. "Save some for me."

At Adams, we left the road again and ran between the apartment buildings and businesses. Though it felt like hours, it may have taken only twenty minutes to get to the saloon. As we ran down Hastings, slipping over the thawing mud, I began to hear music—the brassy, wild music I'd heard on the telephone. The Bucket's sign finally appeared through the fog. I slowed, only for a second, looking for police cars, motorcycles, or wagons, but there were none to be seen.

I burst through the door, gun in my hand. After the disorientation of the fog, it was a shock to be able to see. The saloon was packed with drunken men and a handful of prostitutes. The music was louder now. Big Boy's stool was empty.

I shoved my way through the crowd, toward the only telephone I'd seen when I was here. In the back of the saloon, I yanked open the storeroom door, ran to the office, and kicked in the door, holding the gun in front of me.

Vito Adamo was sitting behind the desk, his face expressionless. He held a double-barreled shotgun aimed at my chest. A dark-haired woman in a green satin dress sat facing him in one of the office chairs.

Someone grabbed me from behind and jerked my gun hand behind my back. A big arm wrapped around my neck and squeezed. My gun was pointed at the floor. I tried to twist it back toward him, but he was too strong. I pulled the trigger anyway. The shot was loud in the small room but did nothing except splinter a floorboard. He ripped the gun from my hand, released my arm, and clamped a handkerchief over my face. I smelled science class—chloroform. I struggled against him, tried to hold my breath. It was only now I realized Wesley hadn't followed me into the office.

The woman turned her head and looked at me from the corner of one dark eye. A smile dimpled her cheek. It was Sapphira.

In my peripheral vision, I saw Big Boy toss Wesley's limp body onto the floor next to me. My eyes cut to Adamo.

"I am sorry, Mr. Anderson," he said with a shrug, "but my business associates have to take priority."

My mind fogged, darkened. My motions slowed. Finally I just slumped. The man set me on the floor. Shapes and colors metamorphosed together in wavy lines, blurring, bending.

Even so, just before I passed out, I would have sworn I saw a ghost.

# CHAPTER THIRTY-TWO

A cold floor hummed under my cheek with a deep vibration. I had a tremendous headache. I smelled rotten eggs, oil, metal.

My eyes cracked open. Metal tanks loomed over me. Pairs of red and black cables dangled from a board filled with levers and switches. Through a window I saw machines—saws, drills, welders, presses—all skyscrapers from my perspective on the floor. I was in the old battery room at the factory.

The vibration increased, the hum getting louder. A muffled woman's voice at the edge of hysteria rose over the sound.

I tried to get to my knees but couldn't seem to push myself up. My hands didn't work. Slowly it dawned on me that they were tied behind my back. My legs were bound together as well.

A woman screamed, soft and dull like she was far away.

Something was in my mouth. I tried to spit it out but couldn't. A gag. A handkerchief separated my jaws and cut into my cheeks. I raised my knees to my chest, rolled over, got my legs under me. Leaning back against a tank, I pushed myself to my feet. The room spun. I steadied myself until the sensation passed.

The vibration deepened, got stronger. The hum kept getting louder.

I began to remember Adamo's office and Sapphira. The voice seemed closer now, familiar-sounding. Motion through the doorway caught my attention. A large man set a woman on the floor perhaps thirty feet from me, her legs bound, hands tied behind her back. Her head jerked from side to side, long dark hair twisting. I couldn't see her face, but I knew it was Elizabeth.

The man—Big Boy—straightened and lumbered to a machine. My mind was fogged, but I was sure Wesley had eliminated him as a suspect. He said Big Boy moved differently than the murderer, but he was here, right in front of me.

He bent down next to the machine and tugged on some ropes. Now I saw a pair of legs—a man's legs—hanging down from the top, no, the middle, of the machine, a press.

The roof press.

A rope around the man's ankles bound them to the base of the machine. His arms hung off the sides, wrists tied, elbows bent back from the pressure. As I watched, his hands became fists and strained against the ropes, jerking and pulling to no effect. Big Boy checked each rope. Seeming satisfied, he leaned against the side of a welding machine, waiting.

I hopped toward the press. A chain rattled behind me. The man on the press lifted his head a couple of inches—Wesley.

A chill ran through me. A rope around his neck pulled his head back against the bottom plate of the press. He saw me looking at him and cut his eyes toward Elizabeth. He was trying to talk to me, his voice urgent, but the gag in his mouth made it impossible to understand him. Still, I knew he was saying to forget about him, save Elizabeth.

I had to save both of them. I took another hop toward Wesley. My hands jerked back, and I lost my balance. I slammed sideways into the base of one of the tanks and crashed to the floor. Twisting around, I tried to see behind me. My wrists were bound together with rope. A metal chain with a padlock was looped between them and around a leg of one of the tanks—the acid tank. The chain that locked the top of the tank in place was missing. My eyes darted to the nail by the door that normally held the padlock keys. They were gone.

I kicked my legs out, trying to free them from the bonds. It was useless. I had no more success with the rope around my wrists. I leaned back against the tank and pushed against it, hoping to raise it enough to slide out the chain. The tank didn't budge. My heart pounded in my ears. There had to be some other way. I eyed the bin of iron rods outside the battery room door, each one longer and heavier than a baseball bat. If I could get free, I might have a chance. I worked myself to my feet again and began to scrape the rope against the metal edge at the top of the acid tank. The chain clanged against the side. I pushed back against it to muffle the sound and kept scraping. My right wrist grated against the metal, the edge cutting into my skin.

Elizabeth jerked her head around and looked at me. Her eyes widened. She thrashed against the ropes and shouted into the gag cutting across her mouth. A long rope was coiled up next to her, one end tied in a noose.

The hum kept getting louder. The press was warming up.

I caught just a hint of the echoes of leather soles slapping against the concrete floor outside the machining room. I dared to hope it was help—the police or my father's security guards coming to our rescue.

Big Boy's eyes fixed on the wide doorway leading in from the rest of the factory.

A huge man in a dark suit walked in, movements sure, calm. He passed in and out of the shadows from the pillars and pulleys, striding down the aisle. I couldn't believe my eyes.

"That was too bad," he said to Big Boy, and stepped out into the light, exposing his handsome face and muscular frame. "I didn't want to kill the guard."

I could only stare.

It was John Cooper.


Cooper strolled over to Big Boy and pressed a wad of cash into his hand. Big Boy stuffed the money in his pocket and said, "Are we finished?"

Cooper nodded, and Big Boy walked out of the machining room without a look back. Once he was gone, Cooper moved around to the side of the press and bent down to look at the pressure gauge. "We're getting there," he said. "Only a few more minutes." He tilted his head toward me. "Of course, I could use a second opinion. I've only used this thing once."

John Cooper—alive? Then everything clicked into place. Other than Frank's car, every piece of evidence that had convinced me Frank was the killer—the need to escape prosecution in the bribery scandal, the other large man's fingerprints, the conspiracy with Sapphira—pointed to John as much as they did Frank. It just depended on which of them was still alive. A telephone call, a class ring, and a monogram had been enough to make me believe it was John in the press.

He walked over to the battery room's door. I stood still. John crossed his arms and leaned against the frame. I pulled against the rope, but it didn't give at all. Blood flowed down my hands.

"You know, Will, I'm really sorry you had to be the fall guy. You were a good friend, at least until you ruined Elizabeth. Since then, well, you really haven't been anybody's friend, least of all your own. I was shocked when she finally told me. Will Anderson? A rapist?" He shrugged. "You had to pay for that."

I scraped the rope against the edge, moving my body as little as possible. The roof press stood only twenty feet away, directly across from me through the open doors. Wesley's arms and legs strained against the ropes. Elizabeth tossed from side to side on the floor nearby, trying to free herself.

"I've missed you, Will," John said, tucking a long brown curl behind his ear. "But I don't mind telling you that you've created a lot of difficulty for me. The Pinkertons and the law are right on my tail. I can't hide anymore." He raised a big forefinger. "Now, if you'll keep quiet I'll take off the gag. But I'm not going to listen to screaming and begging." He hooked a thumb over his shoulder toward Elizabeth. "I've had my fill."

I nodded. He reached over my head, untied the gag, and pulled it away from my mouth.

"John, why are you doing this?" I said.

He walked back to the press and bent down, looking again at the gauge. I scraped harder and faster. The press sounded like it was nearly ready. John lifted a welder's mask from the chair next to the machine and fit it onto his head, the mask tilted back so I could see his face.

Wesley's arms and legs twisted and pulled. He arched his back, trying to free his head, but the loop around his neck cut into his throat as he did. I kept scraping, but had to slow again so John wouldn't notice. My wrist burned with pain.

With a rueful smile, John said, "One thing leads to another. You know? I didn't really have a choice. Frank told me the Staties were talking to him about Judge Hume. I didn't want to bribe the old fool in the first place, but I had to follow orders. It's not a team if everyone doesn't do their part. It was obvious I'd be going to jail. I wasn't going to do that. Anyway, everybody would think John Cooper was a crook. That couldn't happen. I've always been the good guy."

He looked off and chewed on the inside of his cheek. Elizabeth hadn't stopped shouting into the gag since I'd awoken, but now she was quiet. The hum of the huge press was the only sound I could hear.

I had to keep him talking. "You don't have to do this, John. We won't say anything. You can still get away."

The chain clanged against the side of the tank again. John's eyes cut back to me. I stood still.

"I wish it were that simple, Will, I really do. Unfortunately, I *do* have to do this. Unless it's crystal clear to the police that you killed Judge Hume and me, they're going to keep looking for Frank. Sooner or later they're going to find me."

"The police will figure this out. They'll catch you."

"No," he said. "The pieces fit together too well. The story will be that killing me and Elizabeth's father wasn't enough. You couldn't live without her. In a fit of jealousy, you return to the scene and kill the woman who jilted you, along with her lover." Nodding at the length of rope on the floor, he said, "Then you commit suicide." He pulled a piece of paper from his coat pocket. "And you even typed out a letter to that effect. A tragic story, but only too believable after you killed me the same way. Elizabeth would have been enough. It's unfortunate you brought someone with you." He nodded toward Wesley. "Obviously, I can't let him live, either. That's your fault, not mine." He bent down and looked at the pressure gauge again.

I pressed the rope against the tank as hard as I could and worked my hands back and forth, everything slippery from the blood. I couldn't let Wesley die.

John straightened abruptly and turned back to me. I slowed the scraping but pressed back hard against the tank. "By the way, how did you ever get rid of Judge Hume's body? I thought that one would nail down your conviction for sure."

"One thing leads to another," I said, deadpan. "I didn't really have a choice."

He nodded. "Point taken."

I was scraping into bone, but I kept working my wrists against the tank. "How could you have thought you'd get away with killing Frank?"

"The plan was perfect," John said. "I talked him into leaving town with me, running west, getting new identities."

"But he was your friend. Why would you kill him?"

"I didn't want to kill him any more than I want to kill you, but I needed a body to take my place, and I couldn't let him talk."

"You killed your friend, John. Now you're killing your fiancée. This isn't you. You need help."

John just shrugged and continued his thought. "And I guess what was left of Frank passed as me. It's funny, in a way. He always wanted to be like me. I suppose that's why he went after Elizabeth, even though the drugs had already made her perfectly pathetic."

"Why take the clothes and blackmail me?" Blood dripped from my hands to the floor.

He frowned. "I needed the money. I think I did pretty well with only two days to plan. But I couldn't make a large withdrawal from my bank account without raising suspicion." He glanced at the gauge again.

I scraped the rope, scraped my wrist, against the tank. The rope felt like it had loosened a bit.

"But you." He grunted out a laugh. "The one guy I knew who would take a kick in the ass and turn the other cheek. You have to understand. It would have been easier to just kill you and plant enough evidence to ensure there'd be no investigation. I didn't want to do that. We were friends, after all. So I set you up perfectly, and now it looks like you're going to get off." He glanced down at Elizabeth. "Well, you were, anyway." He shook his head sadly and looked back to me. "But it's too late now. I can't leave anything to chance. Sorry." He bent down again and looked at the gauge.

"John! Don't do it," I begged. "He didn't do anything. Neither did Elizabeth. Kill me!"

He straightened and looked at me, expressionless. "Turn around, Will."

Wesley's body contorted as he bucked and pulled against the ropes. Elizabeth was quiet.

I scraped the rope harder and harder. "John, I swear he won't say anything. Let him go!"

He sighed. "Turn around, Will."

"No, John. You don't have to do this. Please!"

"Suit yourself." He flipped the mask down over his face and walked around the press to the operator's position, standing behind the metal barricade.

"John!" I screamed. "No!"

A switch clicked. Almost faster than the eye could see, the massive top plate of the press crashed down toward Wesley's body.

# CHAPTER THIRTY-THREE

Elizabeth screamed. I squeezed my eyes shut, but not quickly enough to miss the huge steel plate slamming into Wesley. Only my tears kept me from seeing the impact clearly.

I shouted, screamed, swore. "John, I'm going to kill you!" I scraped harder against the tank, ignoring the pain. "I'm going to fucking kill you!"

The top plate lifted off Wesley. His arms and legs hung limply against the sides of the roof press. The rest of him was gone, puddles on the floor, debris on the other machines.

"I swear, John. I'm going to kill you." I screamed again, an animal scream, as I twisted my wrists, pulling against the rope. "You son of a bitch!"

He walked back around the machine, the mask pulled up from his face. I could just see him through the hair and sweat and tears in my eyes. "Will, I told you to turn around. And if you keep up that racket, I'm going to gag you again."

"You fucker. You fucker. You're a dead man, Cooper." I jerked my head to the side, flipping the hair out of my face. Now I spoke slowly, staring into his eyes. "You are a dead man." I kept scraping my wrists back and forth. The rope was definitely looser. I had to be close.

He chuckled. "I suppose you're right about that. I could probably come up with a death certificate to prove it." He walked around the press, careful to keep his feet out of the blood, freeing the ropes, now loose, that had bound Wesley's neck, wrists, and ankles to the machine.

I was scraping against raw nerves, cutting into bone, but I kept working the rope against the tank.

Cooper cleared Wesley's remains from the press with the sweep of one huge arm before effortlessly picking up Elizabeth and placing her on top of it. She squirmed and twisted and screamed while he secured her neck and ankles, then untied the knots on her wrists and bound them to the side of the machine.

I was drenched with sweat, crying from the pain, straining as hard as I could to pull my hands apart.

John finished with the ropes and took a step to the end of the press, looking down into Elizabeth's face. With a hand caressing her cheek, he said, "Elizabeth, I'm truly sorry. If it helps any, this won't hurt a bit. I touch a button, and you go to sleep."

I twisted my wrists again. The rope snapped, and the chain clanked to the floor. John didn't react. He was leaning over Elizabeth, murmuring softly and stroking her cheek.

I bent down and began to untie my legs. Both my hands were covered in blood. The white of bone showed through the back of my right wrist. I tried to blink away the tears so I could see the knot.

"You shouldn't have betrayed me, honey," John said. "And certainly not with Frank."

She cursed him, shouting strangled epithets into the gag.

The knot fell away. I bolted from the battery room, grabbed an iron rod, and ran at John. When I pulled the rod from the bin, it pinged off another. He looked up, surprised, just in time to see me swinging it at his head.

He got a hand up and tried to duck. The rod glanced off his hand, barely slowing. It caught him above the ear. His head snapped down, and he staggered back a few steps, but somehow kept his feet. Blood poured from a gash on the side of his head. He stood blinking, dazed. I drew the rod back, took a step toward him, and swung again, as hard as I could.

He ducked. The rod whistled over his head. My momentum spun me around, and I slipped on the wet floor. The rod slid out of my bloody hands and clanged away, skittering down the aisle. I caught my balance and ran back to the bin of iron rods. Before I could pull one out, a big fist crashed against my skull.

I fell into the battery room and slid across the floor. John walked through the doorway, an automaton, one slow step after another. I scrabbled to my feet, picked up the chain, and swung it in a circle over my head, faster and faster. John kept coming. When he was close enough, I swung the chain at him with all my strength. He caught it in one massive fist and jerked it away from me.

My eyes darted around the room. A weapon. I needed a weapon.

John advanced on me, backing me into the corner. I feinted one way and went the other, trying to escape from the room, but his hand caught my shirt. He pulled me toward him. I grabbed the edge of the acid tank and held on, kicking at him. He lost his grip and stumbled back a step.

I only had one chance. I shoved back the top of the acid tank, cupped my right hand and dipped it into the acid, then flung it toward John's head.

The acid splattered against his face, and he bellowed like a wounded bear. My hand felt like it was on fire. John rubbed his face, already becoming red, blistering. I tried to duck around him, but he caught my arm and threw me into the back corner. My head bounced off the wall, and I collapsed. Before I could get up, John grabbed the front of my shirt and lifted me from the floor.

He wrapped both hands around my throat and squeezed while he pushed me back against the wall. I punched him, kicked him in the groin, and ground the acid on my right hand into his eyes. He shook his head and bellowed again, but his grip didn't slacken. I couldn't breathe. I tried to pry his fingers off. He squeezed harder. I reached out behind me, hoping to find enough leverage to push him away. My right hand glanced off a charging cable. I began seeing points of light.

Raw blisters were bubbling up on John's cheeks and forehead, but his face showed no pain. His mouth was tight but only from the effort of choking the life out of me.

I felt around behind me for the charging board—above me, to the right. My hand searched the board and found the power lever. I switched it on, then reached up with both hands, groping for the cables. I found one and then the other. With my last bit of consciousness, I pulled the cables forward and jammed them against his temples.

Liquid fire poured into my neck. A split second later, a thunderclap hit the room. I flew away from the wall and bounced across the floor. Lines of sparks arced through the air. Smoke poured from the charging board.

I lay on the floor, every muscle in my body snapped taut from the electric shock. Finally they relaxed enough that I could push myself up on an elbow. John lay sprawled on his back against the legs of the acid tank, one arm bent underneath him. He was drenched in blood. I hobbled out of the room to the bin of iron rods, grabbed one, and turned back to John. He hadn't moved. Smoke drifted up from his hair.

I ran to the roof press and began untying Elizabeth, her eyes wide, tears rolling down the sides of her face. Her dress was dark in spots, wet. I tried to concentrate on the knots. I could barely touch them, blisters popping from the pressure. My hand burned as if inside a blast furnace. Once I'd managed to free her neck and hands, she untied the knots binding her ankles, and we hurried away from the press. When we reached the machining room's doorway, I dunked my hand in a bucket of water and glanced back, looking for John. The wall blocked my view of most of his body. All that was visible through the door of the old battery room was half of one of his arms, elbow to hand, lying on the floor, fingers splayed out. If he was alive, I saw no evidence of it.

Elizabeth helped me through the factory and out into the cold night.

It was my third day at Grace Hospital when Detective Riordan finally came to see me. I'd tried phoning him several times, desperate to learn the fate of Cooper's accomplices, but I couldn't get him on the telephone.

The other policemen gave me no information. Of course the newspapers were packed with the Electric Executioner story, but there was no mention of any criminals other than John Cooper. Every article contained the word "irony." I finally killed the man I'd been accused of murdering.

Elizabeth had been in to see me the day before, to wish me well before she and her mother took an extended recuperative trip to Europe. She didn't know when they would be back, and I got the impression she didn't look forward to the return. Her eyes never met mine. In fact she was barely able to look away from my hand, or what was left of it, encased in a thick coating of white paraffin wax.

Shortly after the factory disappeared in the veil of fog, I'd plunged my hand into a wet snowbank until it was numb, though I couldn't get up the courage to scrub off the acid. That was done an hour later by a doctor who filled me with morphine before cleaning my wounds with a wire brush, amputating what was left of the last knuckle of my fourth and fifth fingers, and finally, to prevent infection, pouring melted wax over the raw, red chancres and exposed bone of my hand and wrist. I had been in and out of a morphine haze ever since, my hand still burning as if on fire.

The raw nerves reminded me of my sins, a reminder Dr. Miller said would be with me twenty-four hours a day for the rest of my life. There was a chance, if I worked hard enough, that I could regain partial use of my hand. Otherwise, it would be little more than a claw.

Detective Riordan stuck his head through the door of my room, an antiseptic white box barely big enough for him to fit. "Good," he said, "you're awake." In the dim light, his scar was almost black.

I shifted in the bed so I could see him more clearly. "Did you catch Sapphira?"

He folded his long winter coat, draped it over the chair back, and leaned against the wall. "No."

"Did you at least get Vito Adamo and Big Boy?"

He shook his head.

My stomach roiled. "You must be joking." I could feel my face turning red with anger.

Grimacing, Riordan shrugged. "They went to ground. I doubt Adamo's even in the country now. But he'll be back. I'll find him. And I'll get that big ape, too."

"Why didn't the cops show up at the Bucket?"

"The uniforms don't go to the Bucket. Adamo pays too much. And they could get hurt."

I took a deep breath and blew it out, trying to calm myself. "That's quite an organization you work for, Riordan."

He spread his hands in front of him. "I'm just telling you how it is."

"What about the Employers Association? John said he was ordered to bribe Judge Hume."

"That may be. But I doubt they were involved with the killing. Murder isn't good for business." He crossed his arms over his chest. "Speaking of murder, someone turned in a bag yesterday. Found it frozen into the ice on the river. I'd say you are one lucky guy."

I hadn't been thinking of myself in those terms. I cocked my head at Riordan. "Yeah?"

"Sheet, rope, clothes—nice sheet. Looked familiar. I don't know about thread counts and such, but it's an expensive one. The kind you might find in the apartment of a swell."

I just looked at him.

He smiled with the right side of his mouth. The scar side stayed where it was. "But I lost it. Well, actually, somehow it got burned—like you should have done with those clothes of yours. Too bad, huh?"

"That is too bad."

"No sense confusing things now, right?"

I squinted at him for a second. "No. No sense confusing things."

Now he smiled with his whole mouth. "I've been wrong before."

"Is that an apology?"

"No," he said, "just a statement of fact. I've got a job to do. I do it as best I can." He picked up his coat and turned for the door, then hesitated and looked back at me. "You asked me a question before." He pointed at his scar. "I got this from a Knights of Labor thug when I was a rookie. Just about cut off my head."

"A union man."

He nodded. "I was doing my job. Helping out the EAD, you know. But I don't have any love for them. Or what they do." He walked to the door, put a calloused hand against the jamb, and said, "We've all got secrets, Will. Remember what I said—everyone's guilty of something."

I turned over his words in my mind as I watched him walk out the door. Riordan was right. Everyone *was* guilty of something.

But not everyone had been punished.

# ACKNOWLEDGMENTS

While there are many genuine historical characters in this book, it is a work of fiction. I have done my best to make the actions and personalities of the characters consistent with the historical record, but have taken liberties with the particular events that occur in this book. (Note: Detroit Electric was a real and thriving electric car company in 1910, and the mileage records are real, which makes one wonder about the advancements, or lack thereof, in battery technology over the past hundred years.)

Many people are responsible for the good things in *The Detroit Electric Scheme*. First and foremost, I'd like to thank my early readers—the people who gave me good suggestions and much needed support throughout the writing of this book—Shelly, Nicole, Grace, and Hannah Johnson, and Yvonne Cooper. I can't thank you enough for the help you've given me.

Thanks to the UICA Writers Workshop, the crucible that molded the book to its current form—with particular thanks to Steve Beckwith, who has no qualms about beating my ideas into submission, Albert Bell, whose support and guidance over the past four years has been crucial to whatever success I can claim, and also to Christine Ansorge, Patrick Cook, Greg Dunn, Vic Foerster, Jane Griffioen, Fred Johnson, Norma Lewis, Karen Lubbers, Roger Meyer, Paul Robinson, Dawn

Schout, and Nathan TerMolen, as well as the others who orbit the strange planet that is our writers group.

Thanks to Marc Schupan, who gave me a nudge in the right direction at a crucial time in my life, Galen Handy, the last vestige of Detroit Electric, who so unselfishly shared his time and a wealth of information about the company (and gave me the idea that led to the opening scene), Greg Rapp, for vetting the legal aspects of the story, Emilie Savas and Yvonne Cooper, for medical advice, the Benson Ford Research Center at the Henry Ford Museum, the Detroit Public Library and their National Automotive History Collection, the Michigan State Library, the Detroit Historical Museum, and the Gilmore Car Museum. The information given to me by these people and organizations was priceless. All mistakes are mine.

Thanks to Cherry Weiner for believing the book had potential, and to Daniela Rapp—first of all for liking the book, but also for making the editing process so painless.

Finally, I'd like to thank Loren Estleman, without whose help this book may not have been noticed.